Other Avon Eos Books by
Jane Routley

MAGE HEART

Fire
Angels

JANE ROUTLEY

AVON · EOS

AVON BOOKS, INC.
1350 Avenue of the Americas
New York, New York 10019

Copyright © 1998 by B.J. Routley
Library of Congress Catalog Card Number: 97-94883
ISBN: 0-380-79427-6
www.avonbooks.com/eos

First Avon Eos Mass Market Printing: April 1999
First Avon Eos Trade Printing: June 1998

AVON EOS TRADEMARK REG. U.S. PAT. OFF. AND IN OTHER COUNTRIES,
MARCA REGISTRADA, HECHO EN U.S.A.

Printed in the U.S.A.

WCD   10 9 8 7 6 5 4 3 2 1

◆Cast of Characters◆

THE HOLYHANDS FAMILY

    Marnie Holyhands—Dion's mother
    Her seven children (in order of age)
    Tomas
    Silva
    Byrda (killed at 10)
    Tasha
    Karac
    Hamel
    Dion

OTHER FAMILY MEMBERS

    Mouse Hallie—Dion's cousin and owner of the inn
    Uncle Louis Greve—Mouse's maternal uncle
    Martin—Tomas' son
    Needra—Silva's daughter
    Derrum—Silva's son
    Dally—Tasha's daughter
    Radiance—Hamel's wife
    Jeanne—Hamel's mother-in-law
    Shine—Hamel's son.

Shad Forest—a woodcarver

Parrus Lavelle—a Gallian Mage

THE KLEMENTARI

Symon the Raven

Causa the High Dreamer

Beg the High Mage

Tarwon the Youth

PLAYERS IN THE STRUGGLE FOR MORIA'S THRONE

Leon Sahr—Duke of Gallia and Ishtak

Lady Julia Madraga—Last survivor of the Madraga family

Lord Gerard Hawksmoor—Lady Julia's cousin

Patriarch Sylvestus—Leader of the Orthodox Aumazite Church

Lord Sandor Sercel—Lord-Elector of Middle Moria

Lord Lucien Sercel—his son

Lord Alceste Rouget—Lord-Elector of Northern Moria

Lord Anton Rouget—his son

Lady Blanche Shomnee—Lady-Elector of Southern Moria

Hierarch Jarraz—Last surviving leader of the Church of the Burning Light and Lady Blanche's maternal uncle.

Darmen Stalker—Hierarch Jarraz's secretary and negotiator

Ren Daniel Devoirs—Head of the White College of Moria

Ren Garthan Redon—Gallian Mage. Friend of the Duke

Lord Matteo Utrello—Head of the Council of State

Lord Quercy—Leader of the Southern troops

Lady Anne Estez—Lady Julia's companion

THE OESTERADD PENINSULA

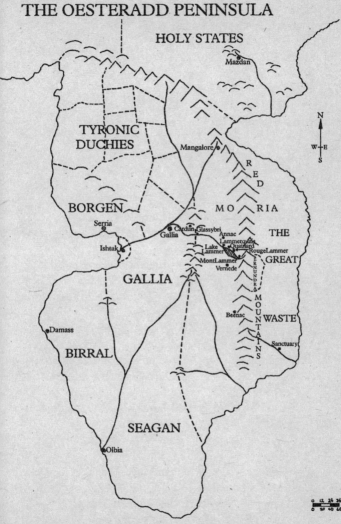

HOLY STATES

Mazdan

TYRONIC
DUCHIES

Mangalore

R
E
D

BORGEN   M O   R I A

Serria   THE

Cardun Glassybri
Gallia   Annac
Lake   Lammergrab
Lammer   Quaillard   RougeLammer   GREAT
MontLammer   Lammer
Vernede

GALLIA   WASTE

Beenac

Damass   Sanctuary

BIRRAL

Ishtak

N
W—E
S

GALLIA

SEAGAN

Olbia

E
R
U
N
D
R
A

M
O
U
N
T
A
I
N
S

0 12 24 36 miles
0 20 40 60 Km

◆ Prologue ◆

Moria.

By midmorning they had crossed over the pass. Looking west, the great flat green plain of Southern Moria was spread out before them. Alain, Master Kintore's Morian servant, sat patiently as the Klementari mage turned and took one last longing look back east where his beloved country of Ernundra lay. Ernundra the beautiful—the country within a country, surrounded as it was on all sides by Moria. Although it was two days' ride away and they could see nothing of it through the morning's haze, Alain understood something of what Master Kintore felt for his homeland.

"It is like a pulse," Master Kintore had said once, "or a distant beacon glowing warmly inside your mind. Even when you are far away, even when you are on the other side of the Red Mountains, you can still sense its shining prescence. Even when we cannot see her, Ernundra lets us know that she loves us, that we belong to her, that we are not alone."

It was a beautiful place. Sometimes Alain could not imagine how Master Kintore had found the strength to leave it, especially for the dubious privilege of living in Northern Moria as Klementari Envoy to Duke Henri at the court of Mangalore. There were few Klementari living in the north,

1

which was not suprising; at best Northerners regarded the Klementari with nervous respect, which could change quite readily to bitter hatred. Alain had had insults, and once or twice even blows, from other servants for serving one of the "moonies" or "witchpeople." Master Kintore only laughed ruefully and said, "They shall be better when Duke Henri lets our mages come here and the people become used to us." There was something in what he said. To know the Klementari was to love them. Alain was devoted to Master Kintore and regarded him more as a beloved uncle than a master. Personally, though, if he'd been Master Kintore, he would have let those sour northern bastards rot and stayed at home in beautiful Ernundra.

Perhaps Master Kintore was thinking the same at that moment, for he sighed and moved his shoulders as one taking on a burden, before he turned and nodded at Alain to take the road down the western side of the Red Mountains

For all their love of home there were many Klementari who lived outside Ernundra. They could be found all over Eastern and Southern Moria, sometimes even married to Morians. Here they were greatly famed for their magecraft, and loved for their strange unearthly beauty, their gentle kindness, and the generous way they dispensed healing and other small magics even to those who could not pay.

At midday the two men stopped for a meal at an inn at the foot of the Red Mountains. When Alain came in from seeing to the horses he found Master Kintore in intense conversation with a woman whose fair hair, high cheekbones and dark eyes proclaimed her one of the Klementari. From the affectionate glances and greetings of the other customers, Alain guessed she must be their local healer or Dreamer.

"The ban on foretelling still stands," said Master Kintore to the woman, whom he had introduced to Alain as Enna Thurre. "The madness of the Dreamers continues. While I was in Ernundra, three died while struck by foretelling. Two more have been driven from their wits and can only babble of darkness." He sighed. "Such a terrible thing."

"What killed them?" asked Thurre. She was a big handsome woman with a face more suited to laughter than the deep fear it showed now. Though who could blame her for being afraid? Visions of the future appeared to certain of the Klementari without their even seeking them. Lately such foretellers, or Dreamers as they were called, had been dying, seemingly without cause—a matter which troubled even the King of Moria.

"We cannot say. Shock and fear we think. The Istari are strangely silent on this matter." Master Kintore's face was bleak.

Usually a trip to Ernundra and a night spent in the Spirit Chamber communing with the Istari, the spirits who guided and protected the Klementari, revitalized Master Kintore, but this time he had come away full of anxiety.

"The Istari are blind," he had said to Alain. "For once, they cannot see what comes." He had been absent-minded and worried since then.

Now Thurre caught his sleeve intently. "I have wondered. . . . Could it be that some terrible fate awaits the Klementari? Could these Dreamers have seen it?"

Master Kintore shrugged.

"It has long been in my mind to do a foretelling," continued Thurre. "No, no, not by visions," she went on at Master Kintore's horrified glance. "With the cards. I have some gift with Prophecy Cards. This morning, it seemed to me they had something to say, but I was afraid to look. Can you not feel it too?"

She took a cloth-wrapped bundle from her bag and placed it on the table between them, and with these words she unwrapped the bundle. The cards inside were white with a pattern of leaves painted on their backs. Alain saw a look of temptation come onto Master Kintore's face.

"Do you have visions when you use them?" he asked.

"Never," said Thurre. "Only a clear sense of their meaning. I am not a strong foreteller. Come, I shall do it, yes? I feel it is time."

"Yes, yes. Why not?" Master Kintore leaned forward eagerly as the woman shuffled and reshuffled the cards.

The inn was full of normal midday noise and bustle. People ate and drank and laughed. The serving wench was arguing with some nearby customers over the quality of the stew. The landlord, a huge beefy fellow, held three tankards under the taps to fill them. Thurre reached for her first card. People nearby glanced at the two mages with mild curiosity. It was an ordinary moment in an ordinary day.

And yet in that moment the world ended for thousands of people.

Thurre gasped. The card slipped from her fingers and fell upon the table. It was The Famished Land, the death card. In that moment she must have seen Ernundra die.

Suddenly all hell broke loose. Both mages were standing, both of them choking, hands on faces, eyes staring at some terrible sight.

"Master!" cried Alain as Master Kintore screamed like a man in his death agonies, pitched over on his side, and fell to the floor choking out screams—screaming and screaming, blood-flecked froth coming from his mouth. Alain leapt at him, trying to help or hold him.

Then suddenly a blast of hot red light burst open the doors and windows and a wave, a great whirlwind of mindless terror, swept over everyone. The beefy landlord's fingers dug into his horrified face. People flung themselves on the ground screaming, tears running down their cheeks like frightened children, thrashing about on the ground. Alain was so unmanned by fear he wet himself as he fell to the ground clutching Master Kintore.

How long did he lie there, abjectly trembling and crying at nothing? The next thing he knew people began shouting. He looked up and saw Thurre struggling in a group of them, white-faced, rolling her eyes madly.

"Don't leave me. Don't leave me," she was bellowing. There was a knife in her hand and blood at her throat.

"Help us, help us," those struggling with her cried.

But Alain was too afraid to stay. The room stank of abject terror—the stink of sweat, shit, and piss. Folk still thrashed about on the floor, screaming and wailing. Yet Alain could see nothing to be afraid of.

Master Kintore was silent. His eyes were open, but there was no life in them, though his heart still beat. Alain lifted him up and carried him from the room. He ran as a rabbit runs from a hawk, hunched over to be as small as possible.

Outside the Red Mountains loomed over the village as they always had, but the sky above them was no longer blue. Huge billows of grey ash rose from behind them, turning the sun to a sick red ball. A faint wailing howl could be heard in the distance.

The air was hot and heavy, and the distant howling pushed Alain to the edge of panic. He felt a horror at the idea of the ash falling on him. With shivering hands, he tied Master Kintore to his saddle. All the time, he did not know, indeed could not even think about, what he feared so abjectly. He had always thought himself a brave man, but now he leapt onto the saddle and took off, whipping the horses hard in a frenzy to be away, though there was no need to do so. They were as terrified as he.

It was a nightmare journey home to Mangalore even after the fear had gone. For nine days Master Kintore did not speak. He simply stared into space. This was the man whom Alain had seen knock thieves from their horses simply by looking at them and change himself into a mighty eagle at will. Now he was as helpless as a little child—worse, like a little child who has no will to live. Fortunately nobody interfered with them. Everywhere people were dazed with shock and grief and the countryside was covered in a sticky, sickly grey ash.

As they got further north and came upon people who had not felt the terror that had come over the Red Mountains, there were those few whose love of drama and self-importance had overcome their horror, who wanted to talk and talk of the disaster. It was from them that Alain learned the meaning of it all—how Luisange, Dean of the White College of Magic in Moria, had joined with the White Colleges of several other lands to destroy two necromancers who had been troubling the coast of Moria; how unbeknownst to the mages, one of the necromancers, Jubilato, had recently brought a bound demon through into our plane; how the demon, Smazor, freed by his master's death, burst forth in a frenzy of hunger that in a few hours had laid waste to all of Moria between the Red Mountains and the sea, before the United White Colleges had managed to send him back to his own plane. In years to come the event would become known as "Smazor's Run."

Had the terror at the inn been an echo of the cry of horror from so many throats as the demon bore hungrily down upon them, or was it the terror all life naturally feels when close to such a destroyer? The question haunted Alain all though that journey.

Somewhere on the way home, Alain sat briefly outside a tavern with a priest who had looked at the destruction through a Bowl of Seeing. He described the blackened, ashy land, the skeletons of trees, the endless piles of bones with flesh still rotting on them like the leavings of a gigantic slaughterhouse. Somehow Alain knew that this was what Master Kintore still saw before his staring eyes. He wanted to weep unmanfully for the green and peaceful land he re-membered from their journeyings beyond the Red Moun-tains. Over half of Moria had lived on that fertile plain between the Red Mountains and the sea. The capital, Ruinac, had been there. The king had perished and all the court. All suddenly gone. And Ernundra, the beautiful land. . . . Most of the Klementari had lived there. He wanted to weep for himself and his poor orphaned master, one of the few sur-vivors of his race.

The priest continued contemptuously, "And Luisange has killed himself now, they say. Serves him right. Stuck up mages. Now look what their meddling has done." Alain left him quickly before he gave in to his feelings and smashed a fist into the priest's smug face.

Once he knew of the disaster, Alain watched his master closely lest he, like Thurre, try to kill himself. He wondered if Kintore would recover from the terrible shock and if, when he came to himself, he would still have his magely powers.

There was worse to come.

Though he had sent messages ahead, when they reached Master Kintore's house in Mangalore, the courtyard gates were locked against them and there were no lights in the windows. Alain knocked and knocked, but no one answered. But as he stood not knowing what to do, a woman stepped out of the shadows. It was Master Kintore's cousin, Mathinna, a plump jolly woman who had kept house for him. At least she had been plump and jolly. If he had thought of Mathinna at all it was with hope that she had not suffered from this thing as his master had, for though she was a full blood Klementari she had no magical powers.

But she had obviously suffered greatly. She had lost much weight and moved like one in pain, and her voice was hoarse as if her mouth was full of ash. Yet Alain was so glad to see her that he threw his arms around her, a familiarity he would not have dared earlier.

"Duke Henri has confiscated Master Kintore's house," she told him. "He says since there is no longer a Klementari nation, there is no need for a Klementari embassy. He has been confiscating much property these last few days and dismissing my people from their positions. It has been foretold that soon he will drive us from the city."

"He cannot do that," cried Alain.

"He has pronounced himself King," she said, "and the Electors, those who are left, have agreed that it must be so."

This was terrible news. Not only did Duke Henri hate the Klementari, but he disliked independent mages as well. He thought the only place for them was in the church as priests.

Mathinna had taken refuge in the house of a healer, and this was where she now took Alain and Kintore.

The healer, Nesta, was a short dark woman, but she had the high cheekbones and dark eyes of the Klementari nonetheless. She showed Alain a bed for Master Kintore and where to get water to wash him.

"I will make something to ease his grief," she said.

When Alain returned with the water, he saw that Master

Kintore had come back to life at last. He and Mathinna were weeping in each other's arms.

"I was left behind," he was crying. "Oh Sweet Mother Earth I was left behind. I want to die, Mathinna. I want to die."

They were the first words he had spoken these nine days. Alain was relieved to see his tears, and yet at the same time it was painful beyond measure for him to see a man he had always looked up to reduced to such a state.

In the other room, Nesta was pounding seeds with a pestle. Her face was tired and wounded-looking, but determined. Alain stood and watched her for some time before she noticed him.

"Where is Mathinna?" she asked and then said, "You left them alone together? You stupid man!"

She rushed into the inner room to find Mathinna standing over the bed uncorking a poison bottle. With a magical blow Nesta dashed it from the woman's hands and it smashed on the floor, the liquid sinking instantly into the stones. Mathinna began to scream hysterically.

"You babies," Nesta shouted at them. "How can you even think of it? How can you leave me alone?"

"I want to die," cried Mathinna, crouching on the floor dabbing her hands at the poison. And Master Kintore lifted up his face with his swollen red eyes leaking tears and said quietly, "There is no place in the world for us now. The Istari are dead. We are alone."

Alain would have let them take the poison, but Nesta slapped both their faces.

"Hear this," she said. "The end of the Klementari is not here. We have another destiny now without the Istari, and it will be revealed in time. We must live and grow and help each other till that time so that our ways are not lost. I speak with the voice of foretelling. I saw the vision this very morning and so have others."

Later, when they were both safely in drugged sleep and Alain was helping Nesta clean up, he remembered how Nesta had struck his master and he turned to her with a small-minded anger in his heart.

"You lied in there, didn't you?" he said. "I don't believe you saw any such vision."

She gave him a hard determined look, a look that made him feel petty for speaking so.

"It doesn't matter if you believe it, as long as they do," she said.

◆

Family

◆

◆1◆

Gallia. Over 100 years later

$\mathfrak{S}$itting dozing against the dark shed wall, I had another dream of the hungry woman and her glowing red eyes. Only a waking dream, thank Tanza! The fright woke me easily. In a jump I found myself back in Woolly the Mead's rickety cowshed sitting cross-legged on the smelly straw with a crick in my neck. Grey light was seeping in through the cracks in the walls, and from outside came the sound of raucous birdsong greeting the fresh dawn. Woolly was leaning over the stall chirruping at something, and when I staggered stiff-legged to his side, I saw that the calf was up taking its first drink.

"A fine young lassie calf," beamed Woolly. "You've brung us luck again, Madame Dion. Here."

Sleepily I took a gulp from the flask Woolly offered me and discovered too late that it was the fiery honey spirit which had given him his nickname. Drinking mead at dawn—it was definitely time to go home, and after I had stopped coughing and he, torn between amusement and apologies, had stopped thumping my back, we went outside and he helped me saddle up Pony. Or rather he saddled Pony and I watched, bleary-eyed with tiredness, while his wife came

13

out of the hut and stood patting my arm and offering me a bed in their hut.

There was no chance of my staying with the Meads. A one-room hut housing a family of seven is no place to catch up on sleep. I refused as politely as I could, tied the cheese and the flagon of mead that constituted my healer's fee to the back of the saddle, hauled myself up, and rode off into the misty morning.

To the east the sky was still pale and faintly pink. A heavy dew had silvered the grass and hedgerows. Still, a country district like Cardun rises early. As I passed down the muddy track that wound through the village, I could hear babies crying or early morning coughing coming though the walls of the little thatched huts along the way. I met Big Petro and Jacko the Leg walking out to their fields with hoes over their backs, and Maria Prima was already pulling weeds from among her vegetables.

"You be careful, Madame Dion," called Maria as I passed. "I saw them Wanderers passing through last night. The forest will be crawling with 'em."

Possibly she was looking for an argument, for she looked a bit disappointed when I simply nodded and went on. But I was too tired to be bothered with our usual wrangle, in which I tried to convince her that Wanderers were entirely harmless, and even worthwhile people, and she maintained that they were thieving drunkards and whores.

A little way beyond the village the forest began. Under the towering trees the air was redolent with the delicious smells of damp earth and sweet oil. It was the most delightful time of the day. Though the dawn chorus had ended, flocks of honey parrots were still squawking among the sweet oil blossoms and the silvery calls of kurrajongs filled the air. It was so peaceful here with nobody else about. Pony ambled along steadily.

I must have nodded off in the saddle, because suddenly I was in the great cathedral again. It was roofless, its arches straining up at the sky like broken ribs, and up above the stars peered in at me watching, watching like hungry cats.

Before me was a white statue of Mother Karana. So beautiful, Mother Karana, but as I stood marvelling up at her, her eyes suddenly flickered to red. Glowing hungry red. She smiled a wet red smile. Cold shock went though me. I must run! I couldn't move! I must . . . Her claws bit into my arms. Her eyes. Oh God her hot red eyes. It felt like my heart was being pulled forth in a thin red line. The pain. The pain. Sucking out my soul, killing me. The agony, oh God! No!

"Cark!" came a loud cry in my ear. I started awake and almost fell off the back of the now stationary Pony.

We were standing at the back of my hut beside Pony's little stable. Pony was calmly eating hay out of the hay stack. There was another carking noise. It came from a big black raven that was sitting on the nearby woodpile watching me with beady black eyes. Ravens were regarded as lamb-killers and birds of ill fortune in Cardun. I did not tell my parishioners that I fed them as I fed all animals that came near my hut.

I'd certainly fed this raven before. He was a regular visitor who even had a name. I called him Symon. It was not my habit to call animals with the names of people, but this raven just seemed to be a Symon. He distinguished himself by being inordinately fond of cheese, which he much preferred to raw meat.

"I bet you'd like some of this cheese Woolly gave me, wouldn't you, you handsome devil," I said. "Just wait till I get Pony fixed up and I'll cut you a piece."

I heaved myself out of the saddle, feeling exhaustion in every bone in my body and cursing those dreams. I'd been up all last night turning that calf in the womb and seeing it came out right. Wasn't I entitled to a little rest? But no. Here was that damned woman again. That woman, that damned damned demon woman, breaking my sleep as she had broken it every night for the last week and many nights before.

I unsaddled Pony, still cursing.

What sort of new torment was this? I hadn't dreamed of Andre/Bedazzer in six months and now, just as I was hoping he had forgotten me, this horrible vision of some demon world came. Was this sent intentionally, or was it just some delightful new side effect of the link that had been forged between us that time we had fought together? Sometimes lately I'd been too scared to go back to sleep afterward for fear that I would wake again and find Andre standing by my bed as I both feared and longed for. Would this never end?

"Good morning to you Enna Dion," said a voice. "It seems you have bad dreams."

On the chopping block before the woodpile sat a pale-haired man, his knees drawn up to his chin.

He was a Wanderer. At least I thought he was. He wore black, whereas most Wanderers wear shades of green or brown, but the holy symbols of the Wanderers—cups, candles, and circles of leaves—were embroidered all over his garb.

Despite Maria Prima's remarks, which were to a certain point true enough, I liked the Wanderers I had met immensely and even had a particular friend among them. Almost every month, a half-blind woman called Causa would come to call, led by her young daughter, and we would drink tea and and she would tell me of the news from Gallia City. It was a strange relationship, for she was a warm, kind woman, always interested in my problems, and yet she never told me anything of herself. I was not sure why she—or any of them, for that matter—called on me. They had no need of my healing skills and in fact sometimes gave me advice. Maybe it was because I was a mage and they were a people steeped in magic. Perhaps we were simply drawn to each other in the way exiles are, for like me they had been exiled from Moria after the Revolution of Souls five years ago. We were on the very border with Moria here in Cardun, and that must certainly have been what attracted them to the district.

Though in my restricted childhood I had had little to do with Wanderers, even I could remember the breath of fresh air that had seemed to pass through our district when the Wanderers came. They brought news and trade goods and they mended things or helped with the harvesting. People believed them to have uncanny skills of foretelling, and bought little magics from them which were far cheaper (if a little less reliable) than the magics my foster father sold. Yet even in Moria where the Wanderers used to have their place in the scheme of things, even if it was a place as outsiders, people felt ambivalent toward them. Not only were they traveling folk who looked different from the great dark-haired mass of Morians, but many of them did drink and lots of them were addicted to the dream drug hazia as well. And Wanderer women had great hordes of hungry children following them about and it was never clear who the fathers of these children were.

Wanderers looked like fallen angels, white-haired, raggle-taggle people with dark eyes in beautiful fine-boned faces. When I saw them in Cardun, their children always looked hungry and so I gave them what food I could. Sometimes my parishioners scolded me for feeding them.

"They know you are soft-hearted now," they said. "They're thieves and trash, Madame Dion." The Wanderers were even less liked in Gallia then they had been in Moria.

Causa told me that the Wanderers were, as the legends said, the remnants of a great race of mages who had lived beyond the Red Mountains of Moria when our ancestors had come from Aramaya four hundred years ago. Their homelands had been destroyed in Smazor's Run a hundred years ago, leaving them homeless, a hopeless wandering remnant many people assumed would die out. They worshipped the spirits of nature and of place, and so the loss of their homeland had been a great blow to them.

Even drunk or dazed by hazia, however, they always seemed a gentle people, and though I was taken aback by the sudden appearance of this man, I was not afraid.

"Greetings," I said. "May I help you?"

"It is a beautiful morning, is it not? I have a foretelling especially for you, Enna Dion."

He spoke Morian and used the Morian honorific.

"Today is a new beginning. After today, everything will be different. Two men will come to see you today, Enna Dion. You will do well to follow them. Is that cheese?"

"Yes," I said, caught out by his sudden change of tone. "Would you like a piece?"

"I love cheese," he said.

Cheese. As I took the knife out of my belt to cut it, I found myself glancing up at the woodpile. The raven was no longer there.

"The raven disappeared when I came," said the Wanderer. "But his loss is my gain."

Uncanny how they always did that. I hadn't mentioned the raven. I watched him eating the cheese. He was better dressed than most Wanderers, cleaner and more healthy looking. A strange face. The wrinkled face of an ancient boy with dark clever eyes. I could not be sure of his age. His hair was white-gold like all pure-blood Wanderers.

"This is fine cheese, Enna."

"Good," I said. "Would you like a piece of bread as well?"

He looked at me. His eyes glittered.

"We are going home soon, Enna Dion. Back to Moria. Back to our homeland."

His words touched me. Our homeland.

I should like to see Moria again, especially the hills around Mangalore where I had grown up. I shook off the melancholy feeling.

"Not while the Church of the Burning Light rules in Moria, friend," I told him. "They hate mages like us there. They'd burn us both."

He smiled up at me and repeated, "We are all going home soon."

This was an odd conversation, even for a Wanderer. He looked so elated and yet so mysterious that he must have been chewing hazia.

"I'll just get you that bread," I said, thinking to maybe set him on his way by doing so. Then I could get some sleep.

As I came to my front door, however, it suddenly occurred to me that he might know Causa and that she would be someone to help me with these dreams. I turned back to ask him.

He was already gone. The clearing was empty of everything but cool morning light; even using magic I could not sense him anywhere.

Somehow it was as if he had taken the evil phantoms in my head away with him. I went into my hut and slept dreamlessly, to wake refreshed just before midday. I completely forgot his foretelling.

That day two men did come. They came in the late afternoon when the sun was turning warm and gold on the leaves. I was chopping wood for kindling. I had plenty of kindling already, because Gill Swineherd had come just the day before and chopped me some, but I was in a bad temper. I'd remembered sometime earlier that Parrus had been back from Gallia for four days now and there had still been no sign of him here. I accepted that he didn't care much about me, but did he have to make it this obvious? These things bother you when you are overtired. I've always found chopping wood to be a good outlet for anger.

I really should break with Parrus. I had no business bedding down with anyone, let alone him. He was just sowing his wild oats among the local women as the sons of great families always do and I. . . . What was I doing sleeping with anyone, especially a man I was fairly certain I didn't love? Whore. It was just. . . . Sometimes the future seemed an endless straight road stretching boringly out into the distance with me trudging along it all alone. I could not imagine anybody ever wanting to marry me, with my powers and my past, so what point was there in keeping myself pure and denying myself these small passing excitements?

"Now come on, my girl," I said to myself in that stern voice my foster father used to use. "You've had your fair share of excitement. It'll take you this lifetime at least to pay for those mistakes."

But the answer came as it always did.

"So is this all there is and will ever be?" And then, plaintively, "I'm only twenty-one."

Curse it. Now I was getting myself in a state. I threw the

kindling into the wood basket and grabbed another log. Hard work was the best answer.

"Hullo," said a voice behind me in Morian.

Two men, strangers, were standing in the shadow of the trees. Two men. Like the Wanderer had said. How strange.

They were not Wanderers, but ordinary Morians. It was not as unusual for me to see ordinary Morians as you might think. Sure, all nonpriestly magic was forbidden in Moria since the Church of the Burning Light had called forth the Revolution of Souls, and sure, when they were healthy many Morians regarded healers like me as little better than witches, fit only for burning. The practical fact, however, was that the Revolution of Souls was still so new that there were not enough priests or nuns around capable of doing all the healing that ordinary people required. Increasing numbers of Morians had been coming over the border to seek healing from Cardun's Morian healer. The Cardun parish board allowed this as long as the Morians paid something. I always healed them whether they could pay or not. I even healed the ones who made signs of protection against witches when they thought my back was turned. What else could I do? I'm not the kind of person to turn away someone with a broken leg, just because they believe I am evil. I couldn't help hoping, no doubt misguidedly, that my kindness might sow a small seed of doubt in their minds.

So I hardly gave the men's nationality a thought. It was the words that were spoken next that shocked me.

"That's very mundane work for the Demonslayer of Gallia," one said. "Why don't you just magic them apart?"

I almost dropped the axe.

The Demonslayer of Gallia? Angels! How did he know about that? After the pains I'd taken to hide it.

I tried to put on my professional healer's face.

"Who are you? What do you want?" I snapped.

The men came forward. They looked alike enough to be brothers and were both fair-haired. Fair is a common enough coloring among lower-class Morians like myself. A sign of Wanderer blood, some say. One of them was not much older than me. He was tall and well-built, with a placidly hand-some face. The older one, the one who had spoken, was smaller and wiry. He had a beaky nose and bright dark eyes in a good-looking weather-beaten face. His riotously curly hair was dark enough to be called brown.

Their shoes and clothes were greyed with dust and in their hands they carried felt travelers' hats.

"We're looking for Dion Appellez, previously known as Dion Michaeline," said the older one. "That's you, isn't it?"

I stared at him, unsure whether to tell the truth or deny everything.

"Who's asking?"

"My name is Tomas Holyhands. This is my half-brother, Hamel," he said. "If you think about it, you will know who we are."

Holyhands. Should I know that name?

"It's the name of an inn near the Annac monastery in middle Moria," he continued. "The Inn of the Holy Hands. The bastard children of the maid who worked in that inn came to be called Holyhands for their family name because, having no fathers, they had no other name."

I just stood and stared at him. I had been born in an inn, an inn near a monastery. I was the bastard child of an inn maid, one of several. And the name Holyhands. It was fa-miliar. So the man who stood before me must be. . . .

I looked into the man's bright eyes and the strong magic within me knew him for who he was.

Knew him for my brother Tomas!

I sat down hard on the chopping block.

"Tomas Holyhands!"

"Aye little sister. We've come a long way to find you."

I had so much to ask them and yet I could think of nothing to say. I had not seen them for seventeen years. I had given up on ever seeing them again a long time before the Revo-lution of Souls had exiled me from Moria. When I was four years old, my mother had sold me to a mage to be his ap-prentice, and that was the last I ever saw of my disreputable family and the inn where I had been born. A long, hard time ago now, I had come to the conclusion that my family had forgotten about me and I had set out to do the same to them. Now here was the past returned, clothed in flesh.

The minutiae of hospitality covered my initial confusion. There was a hut to invite them into, chairs to offer, food and drink to bring. Tomas sat down gratefully and pulled off a shoe.

"This foot is blistered to hell," he said, rubbing it, and I ran to fetch him a poultice.

Of all my siblings, Tomas was the one I remembered best. He was the oldest and had always been the one to pick me out of puddles and, with a story and a kiss, tuck me into bed in the small dark room at the top of the stairs where we children slept in two big beds. My adored elder brother had always seemed so big and strong. Now I was almost as tall as he.

The other brother, Hamel, did not sit.

Instead he took my hand and squeezed it tight. His hands were huge and covered in calluses.

"We are very glad to find you, Dion, and to see you so well," he said, smiling with such sincerity that despite the fact that I wasn't sure which of the others he was, I warmed to him instantly.

"Aye," said Tomas. "We've been on the road for almost three weeks now. We've been to Gallia and back. I spoke with your friend Kitten Avignon. In fact she gave me this letter for you. Here!"

He reached into his coat and passed the small white packet to me. I turned it over in my hands, uncertain about opening it. A letter from Kitten Avignon was normally a great happening for me, but brothers. . . . That was even more so.

Tomas smiled at me for the first time. "We heard stories of your power to make a brother's heart proud. They still speak of your fight with that demon with awe. You're almost a legend in Gallia." He grinned. "As you were in Annac. Do you remember that time when you were three and you flung Arvy Ironmonger into the horse trough because he threw a horse turd at you?''

"Yes!" I cried, my shyness chased away by delight. My memories of that time were the fuddled memories of a very small child, but one of them fitted what Tomas had said. "Was he a mean boy with black hair that stood up in the front? Who used to always call us whore's spawn? Oh yes! Did that really happen? That was great. He ran off bawling, didn't he?''

"Aye! And Aunt Minnette begged Marnie to put you in a witch manacle before anything worse happened. Sweet Tanza, Dion! Even when you were small you were so powerful. Magic used to just flow out of you. Do you remember how the others used to get you to pull the sugar tin down from the mantle? Marnie had to put an iron chain round it in the end.''

"Marnie?''

"Our mother," said Hamel quietly. "Dion looks like her, doesn't she, Tomas?''

Tomas shrugged.

"How is . . . our mother?" I was not sure I really wanted to know. When I had asked my foster father about that half-dreamed mother at that half-remembered inn, he had told me that being careless, foolish, and of loose morals, she had had more children than she could feed and had happily sold me for a minimal sum to a passing mage. In the end I had come to believe him. That didn't mean I wanted the story con- firmed.

"Ah Dion. I'm sorry," said Hamel. "She's been dead these three years.''

"Oh!" I felt disappointment deep inside me. A door closed forever.

"And she never got to know of your success," said Tomas regretfully. "She would have been so proud and happy. She agonized about sending you away.''

I blinked in surprise.

"Well don't look so surprised. What mother wouldn't?" said Tomas sharply. "She had to send you. You had to learn to control your power. You were a danger to yourself and others as you were. She was trying to get the fee together for the healer's college when that Michael came and offered to take you. Even offered money for you, which we always needed. But that didn't mean she liked doing it. She never even spent that money in the end. She buried it under the statue of the Blessed Mother in the Holy Way with a prayer for your protection. So have a bit of gratitude for her. You were lucky. You got away."

"Oh yes?" I snapped. His anger came out of nowhere and it made me angry. I could feel how much I wanted to believe this nice little story, a story which didn't fit with the heartless, promiscuous woman I had long believed my mother to be.

"Tomas, don't be such a bear," said Hamel easily. "You don't know what it's like to be sent away. And you know Marnie said she would be full of doubting. Why shouldn't she be? Dion has no way of knowing any of these things.

"Marnie sent me away too," he told me. "When I was eight my father, Jean Miller, took me away to be his apprentice. His wife was barren and he had no other child. Even though he told her not to, Marnie used to walk almost seven miles to see me. At least once a month. Even just to wave at me in the street. Now I will be a miller after him. A respectable profession with security. I missed her so much then and hated her sometimes, but it made my fortune. As it made yours. Can you not see?"

I was filled with the most astonishing and bitter jealousy.

"She never came to see me. All those years and not one word."

"That pig Michael insisted on that," said Tomas. "Miserable fellow that he was. He told her that if she ever contacted you, he'd send you back. He believed that contact with a disreputable woman—he actually called her that to her face, can you believe it—could only do you harm. Possibly he was right. She believed him right. But that doesn't mean she didn't think of you often. She disobeyed him almost immediately. That day he took you away, we all watched you go, and the minute you disappeared over the hill it was as if a kind of panic took her and she turned and told me to follow you.

" 'Find out where he's taking her,' she cried, 'and if there's aught ill about the place or how he treats her, steal her away and bring her home to us.' So I walked behind you all the way to Mangalore, almost eighty miles that was, and I slept with the Wanderers under a hedgerow there for a week and every day I'd creep around his house watching how he treated you, till he caught me, boxed my ears and sent me away with a harsh message for her. I saw no reason to take you away. There was nothing for you at Annac.''

I was silent thinking of my foster father, that hard, judging man, of my childhood with him, the endless study, the tasks that never pleased him, the continual threats of abandonment when I displeased him. Of how I'd always thought I'd failed him.

"She knew you were safe," said Tomas. "She had the power of knowing these things. She knew Michael was honest.''

"Michael of Moria was a cold man. He was no parent.''

It looked as if Tomas was about to snap at me again, but instead he swallowed his anger.

"Aye! I can guess. But believe me, Dion. I've seen what might have happened to you if you stayed in Annac and you were much better off with him.''

"Why did you never get in touch with me? You didn't even come and tell me when she died.''

"We're here now," said Tomas gently.

"Dion." Hamel took my hand and squeezed it again. "You must understand us. Marnie was only an inn servant. And she had seven children, most of them out of wedlock. Those who didn't call her worse names thought her mad. She had no chance of respectable work. The only reason she kept her job at the inn was that Old Hallie was her half-brother and couldn't bring himself to see her starved, though he didn't treat us all that well himself. She believed that you were better off forgetting us all. Think of it, Dion. You were the bastard daughter of the village scandal and that is all you ever would have been in Annac, no matter how great a mage you were.''

I knew what he meant. Small villages have long memories. They never let you forget where you come from.

''You had a chance to be respectable,'' continued Hamel. ''To be someone more than a servant's daughter, to have proper training, to maybe even be important, to make your own money, to have the power that money brings. The choice was so clear for her. But don't ever think it was easy.''

It was as if the color of the sky had changed. I stared at him, my head full of churning thoughts. Had she cared after all? Suddenly I felt such grief that I would never know her— and suspicion. I had been brought up to be suspicious of people but I wanted so badly to believe him. The desire to believe is a trap. I wanted to put my hand on his head and enter his thoughts just to be sure he was telling the truth, but it was hardly polite to do so.

Now as I stared at him a shadow crossed his face.

''I do not think you did too badly. Others have not been so lucky.''

His bitter tone stung me out of doubt and into caution.

I took my hand from under his and put both of them tightly in my lap.

''So what has prompted you to come now?''

The two of them exchanged glances. Hamel's at least was guilty.

''To tell you the truth, Dion, we are in need of help.''

I couldn't resist saying it. I suppose I was angry.

''I might have known.''

''Well and why shouldn't we ask you for help?'' snapped Tomas. ''You sit here all day helping strangers. We're your family, damn it.''

Hamel rounded on him.

''Look, will you shut up, Tomas. Why are you so shit-tempered anyway? Dion has every right to be suspicious. And you're just making everything worse. She's not Karac.

Any fool can see that. But you'll turn her into him the way you're going. So just sit there and shut up. Aumaz!''

Tomas boggled at him. Obviously the placid Hamel rarely spoke to him like this. For a moment I thought he was going to shout at him. Then a rueful grin spread across his face.

"Aye, fair enough! I'm sorry, Dion. I'm behaving badly. We've had a great disappointment and it has made me very hasty tempered. Come on then, Bubba.'' He poked Hamel derisively in the ribs. "You're the big man now. Take the floor.''

Hamel gave a long-suffering roll of the eyes.

"Dion, I apologize for us both,'' he said. "You must understand. Marnie made us promise not to bother you.''

"Though she also said we would break that promise,'' muttered Tomas. "And she told right as usual.''

"Yes, yes.'' Hamel dismissed him with a wave of his hand and turned back to me. "We would not come now if we were not desperate. But we have a great need of magery and we have no one else to turn to. It concerns our sister Tasha.''

"Was Tasha the fair-haired girl who liked sugar?'' I asked. I was not going to let my feelings make me act badly. As Tomas said, I spent my life helping strangers. I wanted to help them if I could, and maybe in return I could . . . I wasn't sure what. See them again? Find out more about them? Ah! Here was another trap.

Hamel laughed and the whole atmosphere of the room lightened.

"No, that was Silva. She's the family beauty now. No, Tasha was dark. She and Karac were twins. Do you remember?''

"Oh yes, I remember now. They were very dark. Not just in coloring, but dark people somehow. Strange. Moody and secretive.''

"Aye! That's them,'' said Tomas. "Sweet Mother only knows what their father was like. Marnie always laughed at life and so do the rest of us, more or less, but Tasha and Karac were made completely differently. When people called them bastards and our mother a whore, it was hard for them to forget it. They were like.... Well, when Tasha became old enough for men to start bothering her, she used to smile and lure them away to a lonely place, and then she and Karac would beat them up. The villagers learned to be afraid of them.''

''After you, they were the ones with the strongest magely powers,'' said Hamel.

''And the rest of you, do you have magic too?'' I asked, excited by the thought of other mages who might also be related to me.

''I've got none that I've discovered. Tomas and Silva have a very little. It was you three who had enough to become mages or healers.''

''Though it wasn't so obvious in the twins,'' put in Tomas. ''But they were little swine as children and they got worse and worse, fighting, making all kinds of devilry all the time, drinking. Eventually Marnie worked out what was troubling them. When they were fifteen, she took them both to see the local healer, Auntie Agnes. Auntie took one look at their auras and agreed instantly to teach them the arts of healing magic.''

''So they became magic users too?''

''For a time there was talk of sending them to the Colleges in Mangalore if money or a scholarship could only be found. But then they had one of their fights and Tasha and Silva ran off with a band of traveling players, and a few months later Tasha came home alone and pregnant. You would have thought Karac was her father the way he reacted. He never spoke to her again. He just left with the next band of Wanderers that came through. Then Tasha refused to leave her baby so young, and later the Revolution of Souls closed the Colleges. So they never went. I'll never forgive myself for not going after Karac and smacking his head and bringing him back. It must have all started when he left.''

''What?'' I said, fascinated and frustrated by this meandering discourse.

Tomas leaned towards me. ''Have you been dreaming lately? Bad dreams? The statue of a woman trying to suck your life out? A sky full of eyes above a row of arches?''

He caught me completely off guard. I couldn't help letting out a gasp.

''There,'' he said to Hamel. ''You see. Karac took special steps. I told you so. Heartless swine!''

''A couple of months ago Tasha went away again,'' said Hamel. ''Following a priest—his name was Darmen Stalker. He was secretary to Hierarch Jarraz. It is fearful enough to think of how Tasha might have fared at the hands of a zealot like Jarraz. But now these dreams. We all have them. Tomas and me and Silva and now you. Even Tasha's daughter has had them. All her family. We can feel her behind them. We know something is terribly wrong. We have to find her.''

I was suddenly back in that dream feeling the terror. If that vision did not come out of the mind of a demon, but out of a person . . . out of a reality . . . oh sweet Tanza have mercy!

''You must help us, Dion. She might still be saved.''

I looked down and saw my hands shaking. Pull yourself together, Dion. Pull yourself together. But for this to be reality. . . . Was Andre/Bedazzer involved? No. I wasn't even going to think of that possibility.

''We must have a Bowl of Seeing,'' I cried.

''It won't go far enough,'' protested Tomas.

''It's a start, Tomas,'' said Hamel.

''I can see over a hundred miles in any direction in the Bowl, Tomas.'' I strode over to the water pipe and magicked the water up the pipe and into a jug.

Hamel's jaw dropped, but Tomas smiled.

''Why Dion. You're quite the star, aren't you? Come on then, where are your Prophecy Cards?''

He helped me arrange the wide low bowl on the table with the Prophecy Cards and fill it with water. Without being asked, he produced a woman's kerchief wrapped in a white cloth from his bag.

''You know a lot about mages,'' I said, impressed by the way he had wrapped it correctly.

"Magecraft is strong in our family, sister. This kerchief is Tasha's. She wore it for special occasions."

"I must warn you," I told them as I sat. "I have good range but my ability to find people through their belongings is not strong. Though I've worked on this spell, I still often get no result."

"Just do your best. If you also have been feeling Tasha's dreams, it may make a link between you," said Tomas.

I took the kerchief and began the ritual. Since I had been working in Cardun I had been practicing magic largely without the spells and rituals I had been taught as an apprentice, because it seemed quite easy for me and was quicker. Now, however, I was glad I had been trained to know the words. They helped clear my mind, which churned with thoughts and emotions.

The Bowl of Seeing is the way we mages spy on each other. You can detect all magical activity for as far as you are able to see in it. It looks like pinpoints of light in a black sky. The Cards of Prophecy will tell you things about the individual lights. If used by a mage with psychic powers, the Bowl and Cards in conjunction with a personal object belonging to the target can be used to locate anybody, even when they are not using magical powers. This was what I was going to try to do now.

For a moment after I cast the spell, however, I was too surprised to do the locating spell.

"Where is the grid?" I asked Tomas. "There's so little magic."

"Be fair. There aren't many mages left in Moria," said Tomas.

"But the priests and the monks should show up. And surely the Burning Light still accepts priest-mages. They told the Prince's Council they were maintaining the grid."

"And they aren't?"

"Well, look at this."

I changed my direction and showed Tomas how a properly protected country should look. Gallia was a mass of pinpoints of light, but even in the darker areas there were little pinpoints of light at regular intervals—magical watching posts carefully manned and guarded, watching always for necromancy. The geography of the Oesteradd Peninsula meant it was small and densely populated enough to be thoroughly watched, making it very safe from that terrible, destructive magic. Necromancers use the power of demons to make themselves powerful, and in order to draw this power from the dark hellish plane that demons normally inhabit, they make regular sacrifices. Animals sometimes, but usually people.

I turned back to Moria. Since Smazor's Run when all of eastern Moria had been destroyed, the country had been divided into three parts, North, South and Central. Since the Revolution of Souls, each of these areas was overseen by a leading Burning Light priest known as a hierarch. These hierarchs had been members of the original seven-man council who had begun the Revolution of Souls, though doctrinal arguments had since reduced their number to five.

All over central Moria were the rosy diffuse lights of priestly magic, marking monasteries and churches at regular intervals for as far as my spell could reach.

"But look down here," I said. "Here in the south. This grid is full of holes. Anything could flourish here. What is the Church of the Burning Light thinking of? Stupid fools."

"Well you'll get no argument from most Morians," said Tomas.

"Oh yes?" I said tartly. "And where were they when the mobs were throwing stones at us and the witchfinders were manacling and burning us?"

"True. But people are beginning to see the error of their ways. Now there are not enough priests to do healing and their children die of small things. . . . Anyway, the South is very strange. They say Hierarch Jarraz has run mad. It's almost impossible not to be charged with blasphemy. People are scared and stay indoors as much as they can. I imagine even priests are nervous about practicing magic there. When I was looking for Tasha I got arrested for vagrancy, and I was in prison two days before they accepted my travel permit.''

"You've been South, then.''

"Aye. I set out after Tasha as soon as I got home from my trip. You have to have a travel permit to travel in Moria nowadays, and she didn't have one. I went all the way to Beenac to Darmen Stalker's house looking for her. His servants said he would never soil himself with women and tried to arrest me for slander. It's a mad place there, I tell you. No sign of Tasha. It was on my way back that the dreams started. By then I'd realized it was too dangerous to look for her in the South without some idea of her location. Can you see her?''

I began the ritual for magical location. Tomas put the faintly perfumed kerchief in my hand. I was surprised at the strong impression I got from it. I could see Tasha quite clearly in my mind. A strong-looking woman with olive skin, coal-black hair and sulky red lips. She was beautiful in the savage way a hawk is beautiful.

I closed my eyes and dipped my hand into the Bowl. In the very first moment I felt a tiny tingling in my fingers. Yet as I reached my mind out to find the exact location of it, it was gone. I searched and searched, cursing softly under my breath. It had been there. Curse it.

"What is it?'' hissed Tomas.

I waved him down.

I wiped my fingers dry on my dress and tried again. It was the same, a small tingling to start with and then nothing when I put my finger on it. This time I sat still for a long time, just letting the influences of the Bowl flow over me. Every now and then I would feel a faint frisson on my fingers, but I couldn't pinpoint it. Damn it. It was like trying to scratch an itch and not quite being able to find the place.

Finally I threw down the kerchief in disgust. It was not a very gracious gesture but I was not used to failing at magic.

"What is it?'' cried Tomas. "Can't you find her?''

"Oh, there's something there all right. I can feel her. I just can't find her.''

Then I uttered the fatal words.

"If only I could get closer."

"You can get closer," cried Tomas. "You must get closer. Come with us back into Moria, to Annac."

"What?!"

"Come with us to Annac. Cast a Bowl of Seeing there. You'll be able to see much further into Moria from there. That's what we've come here for. To beg you on our knees if need be."

I couldn't believe what I was hearing.

"You're mad. They'd burn me. They'd burn me the instant I set foot on Morian soil."

"Not if you don't practice any magic. It's safe enough just to travel if you have the permits."

"But you are asking me to do magic."

"People do magic in Moria all the time. Healers are smuggled in all over the place and we hide them from the witchfinders. I've hidden many myself. You come into Moria, you perform the search, we whisk you away into hiding till it's safe to come home. Easy."

Easy! Easy! I could have hit him. *You smooth villain!* I wanted to scream at him. But he who shouts first loses. I learned that from my foster father.

"If you think you can come here and I'll fall on your neck just because you're family. Do you think I'm stupid? I might go into Moria for a friend, but you are nothing to me. Nothing!"

"Look, I'm sorry, but you must. . . . Please Dion. Listen to me. It will be safe. I'd give my life for you if need be. Dion. Listen."

He caught hold of me and suddenly yelped and let go.

In my anger, I had let out a little spike of power and burned him.

I swore and put my hand over my face. Except when threatened mages are forbidden to use any kind of magic on nonmages unless requested. It was our most basic rule. What was I coming to?

"Dion, I know you're angry at me. Look, burn me as

much as you want to. I'll understand.'' He held out his hand. The pink welt was already showing. "But please listen to me."

My heart turned over with guilt at the sight of that welt, and he would know it. My bitter thoughts returned.

"Tomas," said Hamel. He pulled Tomas' hand away. "Leave her alone. Everyone is getting too upset. Come now, let us talk of something else. Or perhaps a walk. Perhaps you'd like to go for a walk. Think things over."

I turned on him.

"There's nothing to think over. Oh, you're so nice, aren't you, Hamel. Well don't think I don't understand. I can see what you and Tomas are doing. Him so nasty and you so nice. Save your breath. It won't work. I want nothing to do with either of you. Why don't you just get out and leave me alone?"

"It's not like that," he snapped. "Aumaz, you're just as bad as the rest of them. Just calm down. Tomas has gone rushing in like a mad bull and now everyone is upset and not thinking straight. We won't talk of it any more. Look. Read your letter. We'll go outside and come back at dusk. Maybe everyone will be calmer then and we can come to some sensible compromise."

"I don't have to do anything for you," I cried, still upset, frightened at what they might ask of me, and at what I might give if I let down my guard.

"I know that, Dion. Nonetheless, we need you. And so we will come back cap in hand and on our knees, and ask again more politely. And then we will abide by your decision."

His words made me feel cruel. So did Tomas' disappointed face. I tried to remind myself they were probably meant to. I tried to rescue my pride.

"Here's some salve for burns," I said, pulling out the pot and giving it to Tomas. I wasn't going to rub it on for him. I was keeping my distance. "Look. I would be happy to help you in any way I can. I want to help you. But I don't want to go into Moria. I don't think there's anything unreasonable about that.''

''I understand,'' Hamel cut in quickly before Tomas had a chance to say anything. ''But I still don't think this is the time to talk about an alternative. I think Tomas and I should go and give you some time to think about things, to get back your calm. I'm sorry we've been so tactless. Come on, Tomas.''

''No,'' I said, feeling guilty. ''Please, you've traveled far and I . . . I'm the one who needs a walk, I think. Please stay here. Eat. Drink.''

I pulled bread and cheese out of the cupboards and a jug of apple wine off the sideboard and plonked them quickly on the table. I wanted to avoid any more talk.

''I'll go and read my letter. If anyone comes, tell them to ring the bell. I'll hear it. It's enhanced.''

I went outside and began to walk along the forest track outside my hut. My words had been calm as I left them, but my mind was full of confused and angry thoughts. I walked as fast as I could. How could they expect . . . ? I couldn't believe. . . . They had tricked me into becoming concerned about their sister and now part of me felt guilty because I must refuse them. How could I go into a Moria ruled by the Church of the Burning Light where five years ago I had been forced to watch many of my foster father's friends burnt at the stake for witchcraft? The same might easily happen to me now.

Suddenly I felt like weeping. My family. So this was my family. Who would happily spend *my* life to get back one who was really dear to them.

Well, I wasn't going to cry about it. I wasn't going to give them the satisfaction of caring. I was going to read my letter. I opened it resolutely and after about five minutes of staring blankly at it, I managed to make myself read it.

I felt instantly better. It was full of the most warm and affectionate messages from both Kitten, the courtesan for whom I had worked as a magical bodyguard, and from Genny, Kitten's healer and friend, who was writing the letter for her. Experience had shown me that their affection was genuine. It was they whom I had thought of as my family for the last few years. It seemed ironic now that it should be Tomas and Hamel who had brought me their letter and even more ironic that that letter should congratulate me excitedly on having found them.

However, the news it contained was so extraordinary that I forgot my brothers and their machinations.

"Great matters are afoot in the city of Gallia," wrote Kitten, or rather Genny for Kitten, since Kitten could not write. "The Duke of Gallia's strange interest in Julia Madraga has suddenly become clear and those of us who admire his flair for strategy are once again filled with admiration."

I had heard in previous letters how the Duke of Gallia, who at twenty-nine was still unmarried, had, to the astonishment of all, begun to show an interest in marrying Julia Madraga, the last surviving member of the family who traditionally ruled Moria. His unmarried state was a result of his desire to make the most advantageous match, rather than any lack of interest in women, as Kitten Avignon, who had once been his favorite mistress, had reason to know. He'd shown and lost interest in most of the major heiresses on the Peninsula. That was why his interest in Julia Madraga was so surprising. Her chances of ascending the throne of Moria were very slim. When her grandfather, Duke Argon, had died, Moria had passed into the hands of his deeply religious cousin, Ayola, who had ceded all power to the hierarchs of the Church of the Burning Light. That was the beginning of the Revolution of Souls. The Church of the Burning Light was now firmly entrenched in Moria. They had the support of the Holy Patriarch of the Orthodox Aumazite Church and thus of all loyal Aumazites, and that included, nominally at least, Duke Leon Sahr of Gallia. Or had this changed?

"Three weeks ago," continued Kitten, "The Patriarch announced that he had withdrawn his support from the Church of the Burning Light. It seems conclusive proof has reached him that the Burning Light has been having congress with necromancy, though we lesser mortals can't help suspecting that the fact that many of Hierarch Jarraz's recent visions are critical of the Patriarch and his continuing tolerance of mage-craft may be the real reason for these accusations. It was enough for the Duke, however, who immediately announced his plans to free Moria of this curse and to 'regain our be-loved Julia's throne.' Those who underestimate our dear cun-ning Duke are astonished at the speed with which he has assembled an army of invasion. It is likely they will set off soon. A small city state like Gallia would be considerably enhanced by the great territory of Moria. There is even the possibility of a crown.''

After this momentous news, the rest of the letter had faded into insignificance. The words ''conclusive proof of necro-mancy'' burned in my mind and wiped out all other thought. Necromancy! By all the Angels. The morning's dream came back to me then, the great statue with red eyes leaning hun-grily over me, and I began to tremble again. Even the fact that Kitten seemed to think it was all just politics was no comfort. The hungry stone woman was definitely some kind of demonic vision. If my brothers spoke true then Tasha had come into contact with a demon somewhere in Moria. And how else did demons touch this plane but through necro-mancy? So were her dreams proof of necromancy? The con-clusion seemed obvious. The tall trees that leaned over the track suddenly seemed to loom darkly at me. This missing sister of mine, had she stumbled on some necromancer? Was she even now being used to fuel some terrible spell?

''Dion,'' said a voice behind me.

I almost jumped out of my skin. Then I saw it was only Parrus, Parrus Lavelle, finally come to see me.

◆2◆

Trust Parrus to pick this highly inconvenient moment to show up.

Parrus Lavelle was the son of the local noble family, employed much against his will overseeing his family's estates while the rest of them lived in the city currying favor with the Duke of Gallia. He was also a mage and since I was the only other magic user in the district we had naturally been drawn together, with perhaps predictable results. There had been a time when I could have fallen seriously in love with Parrus. It had been Parrus himself who had put a stop to that. He made sure I knew that there was no future in our relationship, that it was just a physical thing. It was for the best, really. I couldn't see any relationship surviving the fact that I had once loved and possibly still loved a demon.

We had a kind of teasing friendship with an extra element of passion thrown in, which had lasted for over a year. Parrus must have at least wished me well, for he was very discreet about our relationship. When I had first become involved with him I had not considered that such a course of action might lead to my disgrace and dismissal. To be a male sower of wild oats is a very fine thing, but Cardun is like every other place in this world in that the female half of this crop-sowing team is regarded as a scandalous whore. Fortunately—though I suspect our involvement was well known in many quarters—as long as we weren't too obvious, most eyes were resolutely turned the other way.

Parrus was tall and slim and, although he was a little stooped, very good looking in a rather cool way. He was wearing a new set of blue mage's robes which set off his dark hair and eyes admirably. He looked startled at my reaction.

"Is something wrong?" he cried. "You look like you've seen a ghost."

"Oh Parrus. Yes, yes. No. Nothing's wrong."

I made it a rule never to tell Parrus anything important, but at this point I was too churned up to be silent.

"Just a letter. Parrus, you've just been to Gallia. Is it true what they say? That the Morian Burning Light have given themselves over to necromancy?"

He looked even more surprised at this. "By the Seven, who's been writing to you?"

"Oh, just a friend." I crushed the letter into my pocket. "So it's true then?"

Parrus shrugged. "They do say so, but as far as anyone could tell in the college of mages it has more to do with religion than magic. Perhaps you've heard of Hierarch Jarraz and how he has a statue of Karana that sends him visions and messages from God? Well, you know how the church is always suspicious lest such things come from demons or evil spirits deceiving the Holy. It seems the Patriarch has decided that Hierarch Jarraz's Karana is an evil necromantic spirit."

"So that's all it is. There's nothing else?"

"Oh you're so pretty when you're serious, Dion."

"Parrus!" I pushed him away.

He shrugged.

"I don't think so. There are all kinds of wild rumors about hierarchs fleeing the country, people being killed by necromancers, and fiery angels battling demons over the sea for the souls of the Burning Light. I called on some fellows in the college while I was in Gallia. The White College doesn't seem overly concerned, though of course they are sending regiments of mages with the Duke's invasion force. It's just politics, Dion. Hierarch Jarraz has been saying very critical things in his prophecies about the Patriarch. The Patriarch is head of the Orthodox Aumazite Church. He might be sympathetic to the Burning Light's desire to reform that church, but he cannot be seen to tolerate it when they go so far as to criticize him personally.''

''So the Duke has known about there being necromancy in Moria for some time.''

''No, Dion. He's been saying he knew. It's quite a different thing. That's politics, not fact.''

Duke Leon was a well-liked ruler and it was unusual to find a Gallian being so cynical about his motives. However, Parrus' late father Tirus had been involved in an early plot to put the Duke's brother Dane on the Gallian throne and the family was still laboring under the punishments they had received. For instance, Parrus had been forbidden to attend the White College in Gallia and had had to be educated in the northern state of Borgen well outside Leon Sahr's influence. This was also the reason he was ''rotting in this God-forsaken backwater'' instead of holding a mage's position somewhere.

I thought again of the dreams. Horror filled me. What if it was not just politics and the Duke and the Patriarch knew more than they were saying?

''Necromancy in Moria. It's terrible. We . . . we must all go and join the army, join the fight.''

''Well where do you think I've been? But it was all for nothing. My mother says three of us is enough for the army and I've been sent back here to rot while the others get to go . . . You're not upset then? I've been being so discreet and now it seems you know all about it.''

''Discreet? Upset? Why should I be?''

''You're Morian. The war's against Moria. I thought. . . .''

''I've got no objection to the Duke kicking the Burning Light's arse for them. The quicker the better.''

''And then. . . .''

''Well, he's been a good ruler to Gallia. It's peaceful. People are left alone to get on with things. That's all you can hope for from a ruler.''

''What a little cynic you are, sweet Dion,'' grinned Parrus.

''I can't help thinking I should go to Gallia to offer myself for the army. I mean, necromancy. Every mage should . . .''

''Dion, Dion, surely you're not going to fall for their words. I doubt if there is any real necromancy in Moria. It's just an excuse for the Patriarch to put the Burning Light back in its place and for the Duke to increase his power. Anyway, you're only a woman. I know you've trained as a mage, but fighting's no place for women. I mean, what could you do?''

The problem with Parrus was that I'd never told him what I was really capable of. Certainly he knew that, unlike most girls who were trained only as healers, I'd been privately educated as a mage, but he had no idea of the extent of my powers or that I was the so-called Demonslayer of Gallia. It was something I'd wanted to forget, so I hadn't told anyone. Besides, men don't usually like women to be better at things. Even I knew that.

So I'd been dishonest. Only in a sense, though. I mean he'd never asked, after all, and I could imagine the scoffing my claims would have earned me. Anyway, as Parrus continually reminded me, our relationship wasn't really serious, so there was hardly any need for him to know.

Deep down I knew that I just didn't trust him enough. My time as Dion the Powerful Mage had been marked by betrayal: the discovery that my foster father had purposely kept me ignorant of what I could do, an assassination attempt arranged by a close friend, and later—and much more bitterly—betrayal by a lover, if Andre/Bedazzer could be called such a thing. I had thought about it often in the last three years. How can the powerful ever really know the motives of those who claim to love them? Did my brothers back in my hut really care enough to protect me, or was I just a tool to them? No wonder the Duke of Gallia, who had sipped from the cup of power and betrayal all his life, was such a cold man. Better to be perceived as nobody particularly useful—then you could be more sure of sincerity.

Of course all this meant it was impossible to discuss the issue of what I should do about my brothers, what this suspected necromancy in Moria really meant—and even my disturbing dreams—with Parrus or with anyone in Cardun. Except maybe my Wanderer friend Causa, who had guessed something of my past. And who knew where she was?

"My brothers took me to see the army," Parrus was saying now. "It's huge. Most of the mages in the White Colleges of Gallia and Ishtak are going. There are four platoons of fighting mages. Then the Ishtaki merchants have hired three companies of Soprian mercenaries in addition to the normal soldiers. And all of them have groups of healers in attendance. In all that company they're not going to miss you. Or me, unfortunately. Say what you will about Leon Sahr, he doesn't go into battle half prepared. He must have been planning this little trip for months. Anyway"—He waggled an admonishing finger at me—"your duty is first and foremost to the Parish Board who employ you. And to your parishioners. You can't just run off and leave them to fend for themselves. Duke Leon will do fine without us, I tell you."

I stood there wringing my hands. I really should tell him. I needed to talk this over with somebody. I had no doubt he was right about the Duke being well prepared. If there was more to the reports of necromancy in Moria than a fight between the Patriarch and Hierarch Jarraz, the Duke could be counted upon to know about it. The Duke would have sent for me if he'd felt he needed me. He knew where I was and what I was capable of. To tell the truth I had no desire to become Dion Michaeline the mage again. It wasn't cowardice. Or was it? But I'd been so unhappy living among the court—out of place and always wondering who was and wasn't my friend. It was just that I was one of the few mages on the peninsula who had any experience with necromancy and I was powerful. Possibly I could be useful.

"So who are those two in the hut, Dion?" Parrus asked with studied casualness. "I saw them go in so I thought I'd wait till you'd finished. Are they patients? They don't look like locals.''

I shrugged.

"Or maybe they're suitors," he teased. But with Parrus everything was half serious. "Is that it. Dion? Am I cramping your style?"

"Oh Parrus! If you must know, they're my brothers from Moria.''

"Brothers! I never knew you had family. How fascinating.''

He looked back down the track a little nervously. I knew what he was thinking. He was my lover, but he had no intention of marrying me and a brother might well be expected to take offense at that.

"So how come you're not back there talking to them?"

"We had a disagreement."

"Ah," said Parrus. "Family quarrels. I know that story so well. I've had quite a falling out with my mother . . .''

"They want me to come back into Moria, of all things," I burst out. At least I could tell him about this. "Would you believe it?"

Parrus was startled. "Seven! They're crazy. You mean they just came in here out of the blue and asked you to. . . . The Parish Board would never allow you to take a risk like that. Aumaz! Look, I'll go get some fellows and have them run off if you like. The cheek of them.''

"Parrus. No! It's not such a unreasonable request." I had wanted Parrus' agreement but perversely, now that I'd got it, I found I disagreed.

"Yes it is. You let people impose on you, Dion. It's outrageous.''

"Well it's not necessarily a death sentence. I've met healers who went into Moria and came out safely. Apparently a lot of people smuggle healers into Moria.''

"Well I hope they have a damned good reason."

"My sister is . . . very sick."

I was suddenly unsure of how much to let Parrus know. Was there any need for him to know anything? If he found out I was the illegitimate daughter of an inn maid he'd never stop teasing me.

"Mind you," he said now, "with that huge army coming their way, the Morians would hardly be much interested in catching mages at the moment. It might be safer than it has been for some time."

"That's true." It was a thought. It was definitely a thought. I stared at the folded letter in my hands.

"Well," said Parrus with mock displeasure. "Here I am come specially to see you and all you can talk about is going off to Moria. Didn't you miss me while I was away?"

His hand came to rest on my waist.

"Did you miss me?" I couldn't resist chiding him. "I notice it's taken you a few days to come and see me."

"You weren't pining for me, were you? Counting the days? I'd hate to think I was cutting up your peace."

Curse Parrus. It was always the same little game. You care more than I care. If I had a gold coin for every time he started telling me about the respective merits of some high-born maiden his mother wanted him to marry, I'd have been a wealthy woman. This was a game I had no desire to be the loser in. I'd had quite enough of unrequited love for a lifetime. Yet his hand resting on my waist felt really very pleasant. Parrus was a good lover, for all his shallowness, and it had been several weeks.

"Oh no," I said. "I've been busy."

"So no pining." He bent forward and kissed me softly on the lips. "Not for anything about me?"

His hand slid round my shoulders and almost casually began to rub the back of my neck. I loved that touch and he knew it. I felt desire rising in me surprisingly quickly. Thus do we seek to forget.

When his mouth came down on mine I kissed him back hard.

The next moment the bell was ringing. A moment later a man appeared around the corner of the track. My brother Tomas. Parrus jumped away.

"I'll see you later," he said, moving quickly away down the track.

I went back towards Tomas.

"Who was that?" said Tomas. "He went off very quickly." There was just the hint of a smirk in his eyes.

I scowled at him. In Moria even more than in Gallia, a brother is responsible for his sister's virtue. I hoped he wasn't going to take it upon himself to ask a brother's questions, because if he did there would be trouble.

"There's a patient for you," he continued. "I'd say a broken wrist."

Tomas was quite right. Gerdie Tora had fallen out of his loft and hurt himself and typical of the man, who was as pig-headed a soul as you could ever meet, he'd bound it up and finished the morning's work before coming to me. The wrist was now nastily swollen, so it took some work.

After he had gone, I went outside again without speaking to either of my brothers. What with the letter and Parrus, my thoughts were even more confused than they had been. In truth I was glad Tomas had interrupted. It was hardly the right time for lovemaking. I was annoyed at myself now for even wanting Parrus. Sometimes I wished I was the respectable woman I was supposed to be. I knelt down in the vegetable garden and started pulling out the weeds.

To my surprise I realized that I was no longer angry at my brothers. Now that I had distanced myself a little from my own feelings of hurt, I could see they had acted quite reasonably. They needed help and they had come to the most obvious source. Those dreams. . . . I felt better about the fact that they probably didn't come from Andre/Bedazzer. But if they came from my sister Tasha in some way. . . . The stone woman was certainly some kind of demonic vision. Necromancy? It was likely to be involved somehow, since demons and necromancers went hand in hand in this world. Sometimes so-called good mages had listened to the tempting voices of demons and slipped into necromancy. Somehow I doubted Tasha had. The dreams were too desperate and frightening for that.

I remembered Norval, the necromancer I had fought against in Gallia, Andre/Bedazzer's master, a man of such inhuman malice that he had happily tortured small children to death simply so he might send malicious messages through a protection barrier. Human beings, beings who lived and loved and were important to those who loved them, were nothing but fodder to such people. I saw once again the hateful look of pleasure on Norval's face as he had lifted that steel-headed hammer to smash Kitten's fingers. Suddenly I was trembling with rage and hatred, my fists clenched. Such people deserved annihilation. I wanted to hurt, to burn. . . . While such people lived, could I really sit here weeding vegetables and doing nothing? I was one of the few mages on this heavily protected peninsula who had had any contact with necromancy and demon magic. Surely it was up to me to use that knowledge now. I must at least go and investigate. Find out what was happening to this unknown sister of mine. If I didn't and something happened to her . . . wouldn't I be in some way guilty of her death? Wouldn't I be in some way guilty for all the other deaths that might be taking place while I sat here dallying?

Stop it, I told myself. You're being too emotional.

I shook myself. It would not do to become the old emotion-driven Dion again. That had only led to disaster. I must think calmly.

Right. I tried to think how it would be if I did go with my brothers into Moria. The imminent invasion would change things, no doubt about that, but there would still be witchfinders.

In Moria, when it became against the law to practice magic outside the church, bands of priest-mages called witchfinders were formed to track down renegades so that they could be burned at the stake, a fate usually reserved for necromancers. They used spells that made the sum of the magical powers of the participants greater than their powers separately. Thus four or five fairly weak mages could work together to capture a much stronger mage, who was then chained in an iron collar and manacles known as witch manacles. Iron round our necks robs we mages of our power and makes us just like any other mortal.

But how powerful would a group of witchfinders really be? Would they be able to contain me? There were those who had said I was the most powerful mage on the peninsula. I was strong enough to fight and overcome a demon. Surely I could stand against.... No! Only a fool would put that needlessly to the test.

Well then, what about going secretly? I had met healers who had been into Moria and been smuggled back out without being captured again. How safe were Tomas' methods of smuggling healers into Moria?

At this point, the door of the hut opened and Hamel came out. I wondered what heated discussions had preceded his appearance.

"May I help you?"

"No. I'm just weeding."

He sat down on a stump, took out a clay pipe, and lit it.

"What did you think of your letter?"

"It made interesting reading. Relevant. Very relevant." I changed the subject. "What did you think of Kitten Avignon?"

His face lit up. "Oh. Charming. Charming. A great lady. Truly, I was surprised. I'd expected.... If she's a sinner, some of us would be better for a little damnation."

"And how did she receive you?"

"Graciously, but she is a good guard to you, Dion. It took two days before she would tell us your whereabouts, and she kept us under close eye while she decided. She handled Tomas beautifully. I wish I could do it half so well. He was impatient to the point of rudeness. We had had a great disappointment."

"Disappointment?"

"Karac. Tasha's twin. They haven't spoken in years, but we were so sure that now when she was in such danger he would finally forgive her. We came to Gallia to ask his help. He's part of the retinue of Julia Madraga. He's a great man.

But not to us. He told us . . . well, he told us that he'd never help us."

"In those words?"

"No! If you want to know exactly what he said, ask Tomas. I was more gently brought up than Tomas and it still embarrasses me to use certain words before women." He spoke with a mixture of primness and self-mockery, but under it all was definite anger.

"It is not planned the way Tomas and I are together, Dion," he went on. "It is just that he is hasty and I am not. He sparkles, does Tomas. I used to think of him as a silver sword and envy his daring. But since we began this journey, I see that my own nature, which I used to consider so wooden, has definite advantages."

"So when Karac refused you, you looked around for me?"

"Aye! Marnie had told us you were in Gallia when she lay dying and Tomas had guessed that you were this Demonslayer we had heard so much of."

"How'd she know?"

"Marnie knew things. She was half Wanderer."

Half Wanderer? So I was related to these people who so fascinated me. I had wondered about where I got my fair coloring and it was exciting to have my speculations confirmed.

"She had their gift of foretelling," continued Hamel. "And she often knew what was the right thing to do. She would say it was destiny that she do such and such and so she'd do it and after everyone was done scolding her, they'd turn round and see that she'd done something good. I'd give my right hand for a gift like that, wouldn't you?"

"I would indeed." Especially now. It seemed the right moment then to take the plunge, so I took it.

"So how safe is this route Tomas has planned to get me into Moria?"

A look of hope crossed Hamel's face. "You're thinking about it then."

"I'm thinking about it. It seems to me that these dreams

which you say come from Tasha and these reports of necromancy may well be linked. And if they are. . . . I can hardly
sit here with a clear conscience and do nothing, can I? So
tell me.''

''Tomas has been running healers across the border for
almost four years. The money's very good for those who are
prepared to take the risk. There's a whole ring of them with
hiding places and everything. Tomas' father is in on it, and
his half-brother. They're both very important people. Tomas
has a flair for dangerous enterprises. He says he's never lost
anyone.''

''Is that so?''

''I know he's never been in trouble. I wouldn't knowingly
lead you into danger.''

I went over to him. ''I know nothing of you and you
nothing of me, whereas I can see how attached you must be
to Tasha. I fear that might blind you.''

He grinned ruefully. ''To tell the truth I used to avoid
Tasha. She was a hard person to love. Last time I saw her
she was blind drunk and called my wife a cow. But I can
see why you would think that. Trust is a hard thing among
strangers. You can't even know if we are telling the truth.''

''But there are ways I can find out, aren't there? I was
wondering if you and Tomas would be prepared to submit
to a mind search. It will hurt you terribly, but it will help
me decide.''

''Of course,'' said Hamel. ''Tomas and I have already
talked about this and we both think it would be best. We can
start now if you wish. I'll get Tomas. Tomas!''

The door of the hut burst open.

''What?!''

''Dion would like us to submit to a mind search.''

Considering how unpleasant and painful mind searches
are, Tomas' reaction was entirely inappropriate.

''Yes!'' he cried, clapping his hands with delight and he
flung his arms round me and swung me up into the air, laughing.

''Dion, you little honey.''

* * *

When you search a person's mind his first emotion is usually fear, fear of the pain, fear of the intrusion. Often, too, people's minds will leap guiltily to the most embarrassing thing they can think of. I heard a mage once tell a class that it was astonishing how often the first image you received from a searched mind was a picture of yourself with no clothes on. It is caused by the search itself, he said, and is quite irrelevant. You must learn to direct the mind away into more relevant channels so that you can glean the pertinent information out of the great mad mass of images and thoughts that fill a healthy mind.

When I pressed my thumbs to Hamel's temples, closed my eyes, and slid my mind into his I was not greeted with any embarrassing pictures, but there was the fear and that usual whirlpool of images. It was easy for me to rise above them. Using magic is very calming, which can be a useful side effect.

Hamel's mind was a straightforward one. He had a wife and a little son and was full of happy memories and cheerful thoughts of his life with them. Entwined among these memories were others of Tomas and Tasha and an older fair-haired woman with a lovely, loving face. From the warm but confused emotions involved with this image, I knew this must be our mother. I moved quickly away from it. I had no wish to get caught up with her at such a risky moment.

To Hamel a good intention was the same as a good act. He had no grasp of political subtlety. But a major limitation of a mind search is that you cannot tell how a person will act at a given moment, only how they intend to act. It was easy to see that Hamel meant only good to me, that he understood my doubts and that he would strive to do his best to see that I came to no harm. I could not really tell how this would translate into action.

It was only at the end of the search that I saw something I did not like. I asked him about Tasha and suddenly I saw the stone woman with glowing red eyes reaching toward me in the darkness. I was loathe to see that vision again. I pulled out of his mind more quickly than I intended and hurt him more than I needed to. As he slumped forward, I quickly pressed a pain-relieving spell into his head.

"Ah, sister. You really do have a strong touch," he said, squinting up at me through eyes hazy with pain. "That's better. I thought my head was going to explode for a second there."

"I'm sorry to have hurt you," I said. "I can send you to sleep for a time. You'll feel better when you awake."

"Yes," he said. "That will be best."

As I turned from Hamel's sleeping form to Tomas I was suddenly conscious of apprehension. I had never doubted Hamel, I realized, but I had doubted Tomas. Now I would find the truth.

When I reached out to take his head between my hands he did not bow down as Hamel had, but caught my hand in his.

"Dion. Before you begin . . . I have a confession I should make. I would be loathe for you to find it out by chance. I feel . . . I have much anger in my heart against you."

He took my hand and squeezed it as if to soften the words.

"Your friend, that charming Kitten Avignon, she tried to explain it to me and I tried to understand. Yet I cannot and still I am angry. You have had everything we, Tasha especially, never had. A chance to escape your birth, honors from those who matter. . . . You have great power, Dion. I know how mighty one must be to slay a demon. And yet you are nothing. You live here in this poor little hut. You are nothing but a village healer in the poorest of poor villages. Surely that Duke of yours offered you honors and wealth when you slew that demon."

"Yes," I said. "But . . ."

"Our mother wept when she gave you up. Were her tears for nothing?"

I was dumbfounded by his words. There were so many things I could not bring myself to tell him. My first contact with Bedazzer, the demon I had defeated, had happened during a foolish hazia experiment a long time before the battle.

The contact had marked Bedazzer out for slavery by Norval the necromancer I had been hired to protect Kitten Avignon from. Norval had been able to draw sufficient power to bring Bedazzer into this world as a slave. The demon had masqueraded as Andre, a tall, handsome Aramayan lord. Demons can read your most secret thoughts and Andre/Bedazzer had made himself into everything that was most attractive to me so that I would leave myself open to betrayal. As I had. I did not want anyone to know my guilt in this matter, or how I still longed for Andre. I had been a foolish woman driven by emotion and desire. Tomas would despise me forever— as I still despised myself. Yet I had to make some attempt to explain.

I tried to form words.

"There are things . . . things that happened. . . . I have power, that is true. But you must have more than power to be the great mage in Gallia. You must have the eye for politics. I do not. You must have wisdom, understanding of people. I . . ."

"But you have gained nothing. Surely you have a right to be part of the White College of Mages. But you don't even have that."

"Tomas. I'm a woman. There is no place for women to act as mages on the peninsula. Would the Duke let himself be advised by a woman? Would students let themselves be taught by a woman? I was useless in Gallia as a mage. I am useful here in Cardun as a healer."

"Power is power no matter who wields it, Dion. You could have made your sex irrelevant had you the will to. The courage to."

He was right there and the knowledge stung a little.

"Tomas . . ."

"They look on you as some kind of wonder, the common people of Gallia. They almost worship you. The innocent young girl whose purity and power saved Gallia from a Demon."

Purity, I thought ironically.

"Tomas . . ."

"Yet you've even changed your name so that those who would honor you do not know to do so."

"I was confused. I needed time to think . . ."

"About what? Who needs to think about glory and wealth and opportunities. Surely you just take them with open hands? I don't understand. It was a great victory you won and yet you've thrown it all away. Made it into a defeat."

"It was a defeat."

"How? How? Tell me that?"

"I would if you would just let me speak," I snapped.

He was silent for a moment.

"I want to understand," he said quietly. "Tell me."

"Tomas I . . ." I was lost for words again. I did not want to tell him anything.

"So when you slew the demon," he said gently. "It was a defeat for you? Not a victory? Why?"

I suddenly saw my way clear.

"There would have been no demon to slay had I not through one act of foolishness upon another caused it to be freed in the first place."

He stiffened.

"Did you dabble in necromancy, little sister?"

"Oh no, no. Nothing like that. No, these were errors of judgment. I trusted the wrong people. I was irresponsible. I showed myself unworthy to wield great power and that is why I have hidden from it. Do you understand now?"

There was a long silence.

"I think I understand better," said Tomas. "That's not to say I agree, mind you. There are plenty of fools with power in this world. You at least have the wit to know and heal your mistakes."

He smiled at me, ruefully. "Don't look on me so anxiously, sister. We are one blood. That means a lot to me, however angry I may be. I will stand by you always from now till my death."

"How can you say that? You hardly know me."

"We are both the bastard children of Marnie Holyhands. The world has little time for bastards. Now she is gone, we

have nobody else but each other. Even were you a necromancer, still you would have my loyalty. When you look
into my mind you will see that for yourself. Come now. You
know all that I have to hide. The sooner you do this search,
the sooner the headache will be past.''

I lifted my hands and pressed my thumbs to his temples.

I think part of me hoped that Tomas would prove to be a
villain, part of some crazy plot to lure mages in exile back
into Moria so that they could be executed by the Burning
Light, perhaps. But his truthfulness was quite clear and his
loyalty to me was, if anything, even stronger than Hamel's—
strong because I was a stranger to him and thus needed special care. The only fearful things I saw were his ambition for
me, which was writ large in his mind, and his frustration that
I did not share that ambition. And images of the stone
woman. It seemed she loomed large in all our minds.

Afterward when Tomas lay asleep, I went outside and sat
under a tree at the edge of the forest and tried to think calmly.
But our dreams, so similar, of the stone woman kept coming
back into my mind and I found myself shivering again. Now
that I could be sure that my brothers' intentions were honest,
and I had to seriously face the possibility of going into
Moria, I was horribly afraid. For a moment I toyed with the
idea of waiting for the Gallian army to come and joining
them as they passed. If Tasha was being fed on by the stone
woman, however, and if she was enduring the kinds of tortures necromancers inflicted on their victims, I was amazed
she had survived this long. Surely she could not go on much
longer. And others might be there with her. No. Armies
moved slowly and something must be done as soon as possible.

I knew I could not refuse to go with my brothers and keep
my self-respect. But what about the witchfinders? What terrible things might I find following Tasha's dreams?

Your fears are not relevant, I told myself sternly. You
know the right thing to do. You must simply do your best
to do it.

As I sat staring at my home, breathing deeply and trying

to still my fear, a magpie flew down into the garden and began waddling importantly about, searching for snails. A family of blue and red honey parrots squabbled raucously over the sweet oil blossoms above me and away in the forest I heard someone cutting wood. I had been so happy here in Cardun. Was I really going to leave it now?

But under all these miserable and confused thoughts I was aware of another emotion. Excitement. Part of me was actually looking forward to the adventure, to hunting down this necromancer and to being a proper mage again.

·3·

$\mathcal{I}$f we had all followed our own wishes, we would have set off the very next day like heroes in some old tale. First, however, there was the matter of how to be safe in Moria.

Here Tomas took control. As I had discovered under mind search, he was indeed experienced at smuggling magic into Moria and since he had no guilty memories of failure, I had to assume he was successful at it. Certainly he seemed to know what he was doing.

The following morning, he sent Hamel into the village to find a horse and some suitable clothes for me. He asked to see my hands and was torn between disapproval and relief that they were much more work-hardened than the hands of mages normally are.

"Don't you use magic for anything, Dion?"

"If most mages have nice hands," I said tartly, "it's because they get servants to do everything, not because they choose to waste magic on household tasks. As it is, my foster father and tutors would be most disapproving of the mundane things I use magic for."

Most magic users needed to marshal their powers or they quickly became exhausted and were unable to call on those powers in emergencies. I had never had a problem with this. Magic seemed to just flow and flow from me, and so I used it for unpleasant tasks like cleaning out Pony's stable, or bringing wood into the house on cold nights. I had a positively luxurious system of transporting water. A small stream ran through the nearby forest and I had set up a pipe to it. I could magically draw water up through it at will and even heat it on the way.

Other things, however, like weeding the garden or picking apples, I did by hand, partly because I enjoyed the physical exercise and partly because old habits die hard. My foster father, for mysterious reasons of his own, had never told me that I was more powerful than other mages, although he'd never had any qualms about telling me I was more silly. Isolated under his care, I had no way of knowing otherwise, and so for the first seventeen years of my life I had nurtured and rationed my strength just like any other mage. I still felt uncomfortable taking it too much for granted.

My brother shrugged at my forthrightness and, changing the subject, asked for pen and paper.

He seated himself at my table and began writing, copying from a paper that he spread out before him. When I had finished my chores, I came and watched him. I felt better now that the decision had been made. My mind felt free to think about other things, like my mother for instance. The memory of her had been even more present in Tomas' mind than in Hamel's. In Tomas' mind she shone brightly, surrounded both by love and admiration, almost like the icon of a saint. I was interested in her despite myself. As I watched him writing, I wondered how to bring up the subject.

Tomas wrote in a fine and aristocratic hand and he wrote in old Aramayan, the language of legal documents.

"You speak Aramayan?" I said, surprised, and wondered then if I had been tactful.

He smiled at me.

"No. I only know some phrases. Like those suitable for travel documents, which is what I'm copying out now. Nice handwriting, isn't it?"

"Aye, indeed it is."

"It's my brother's. I came to writing very late, but I've really taken to it and I must say I think I do a very creditable job of forgery."

"Your brother's?" I asked, mystified.

He grinned.

"Aye, Lucien Sercel, my half-brother. Our mother furnished me with a very nice class of relative. So just you show a bit of respect."

"So he's related to *the* Sercels? The Lord-Electors of Middle Moria?"

"My dear little sister. He *is* one of the Sercels. My father is Sandor Sercel, the Lord-Elector himself. Now don't you look so doubtful. It's not proper to question your big brother."

"But how . . ."

"Marnie used to work as a chamber maid at the White Tower of Lammerquais. You know the story. Hot-blooded young master, pretty young maid. Along comes Tomas. I'm his oldest son. His first misspilled seed. And he's proved to be a good enough father. He's taken good care of the rest of Marnie's children as well. If he'd remembered my existence when you were four, we could probably have sent you to school instead of off with Michael. But he didn't discover me till I was fifteen and came up before him for stealing. Lucky for me. And for him. A bastard son is just the kind of person you can ask to do those little tasks that aren't quite honest. Like forging travel passes or smuggling mages into Moria."

He grinned at me again. "You don't believe a word of this, do you?"

"Oh, I . . ." I was flustered. The Sercels were one of the most powerful families in Moria. The Lord-Elector Sercel was one of the five great leaders who elected the Dukes of Moria. Still it was not inconceivable that he could be the father of an inn servant's child or that he would acknowledge the fact.

Tomas reached out and pulled a battered tin water flask out of his pack.

"Old Sandor only ever managed to have one legitimate son," he said. "So he was pleased to acknowledge me. Look!"

He turned it upside down and pressed the bottom. It slid away and beneath it was a small cavity. There was a ring fitted neatly into the cavity.

"Look at this. Do you recognize the seal?"

Two snarling wolves against a background of lilies. Any Morian child could recognize that device.

"He trusts you with his seal?"

"Sandor Sercel is a great and powerful friend. I would never do anything to jeopardize that and he knows it. Anyway, if I misused it, I've no doubt that my father could have me sent into slavery before the wax was even dry."

"Sandor Sercel is in exile in Floredano," I pointed out. "The Church of the Burning Light has pronounced an anathema on him."

"He signed his lands over to his son before he went. Lucien Sercel is Lord-Elector of Middle Moria now. The family lands are largely intact. The Burning Light has no quarrel with him. Don't worry, little sister. I use this seal with my half-brother's approval too."

He pressed the seal into the dab of wax.

"Yes indeed, I learned my lesson. It is better to be a nobleman's bastard than an inn servant's bastard. There was a time when I would have nothing to do with him for all that he paid to have me taught to read and write."

"Why not?"

"He ruined our mother, didn't he? He made her pregnant and she lost her place and he did nothing. Except go off to Mangalore and get engaged to some well-born maiden the following year. While she got pushed into a miserable marriage."

"Our mother was married?!"

"Oh yes. Our grandfather Joseph Holyhands Senior was a respectable fellow for all he was a drunk. He wasn't going to have any unmarried daughters around with bastard children. So he fixed up a deal with an old farming crony who owed him money. Francois Cremer. A sour old sod.''

''He was cruel to her?''

''No. Marnie told me they tried to have a proper marriage at the start, but they never had a single thought in common. She was only eighteen and he was almost her father's age, over fifty, and very set in his ways. Probably a bit obsessed with being cuckolded, too. At the end it was just two polite strangers living in a house. Marnie worried that she had made him unhappy, but me, I think it almost killed her trying to fit into his idea of a proper wife. Her gift for foretelling was a continual embarrassment to him, although he was happy enough to make use of it when it suited him. She never sang or even smiled if he was in the house and he used to have the maidservant spy on her.''

A possibility had occurred to me.

''So how long . . . ?''

''They were married over five years before he died. They had two daughters together. Silva is his daughter, and so was Byrda. Byrda fell off a horse when she was ten and broke her neck.''

''So I was born after this Cremer died.''

''Oh yes. You and Hamel and Tasha and Karac. But even before you lot were born, she was the village scandal. She said she wasn't made for respectability and that she was tired of having to do what people told her. So she refused to live with her stepson till she found another husband like a respectable widow should, and she came back to the inn and worked there as a drudge for her half-brother. Spent any spare time she could find with the Wanderers. Her father was dead too by then and Uncle Jos. . . . He never let us eat with them, but he would never have let us starve either.''

Another possibility had occurred to me.

''Do you know who my father was, then?''

''Who can say?'' he said absently. Then he caught sight of my face. His own softened. ''Ah, Dion, don't look so disappointed.''

''I'm not,'' I lied.

''I'm afraid she never told me. Though I don't doubt it

was some Wanderer man, from your powers. She went on a journey with them just before you were born. Ah. Now that reminds me. I do have something that she gave me. Something for you. She did think of you."

He began digging around in his pack again. "She talked of you while she was dying. She told me that you were in Gallia at the College of Magic there. When I heard the stories of Dion Michaeline the Demonslayer, I knew she was right."

This all sounded very nice, so it was probably a lie. Though I remembered her warm-hearted face in his memory.

"How did she know where I was?"

"Hard to say. Someone might have told her. She was very close-mouthed, was Marnie. Comes from a lifetime of being the odd one out. She may just have seen it in a dream or vision."

He brought out a cloth-covered bundle and placed it on the table.

"I'm afraid I've been making use of this even though it's yours, which is why I carry it. I hope you'll forgive me, but it has come in mighty useful on occasion."

Even before he had unwrapped the bundle, I felt the dread. When he had spread it out on the table I saw why. It was an iron necklace. And such an iron necklace. It was not an odd thing in itself. In the interests of preventing them from becoming too powerful, mages on the peninsula are not allowed to inherit lands or titles. Wearing iron around the neck prevents the wearer from practicing magic, so therefore thin necklaces of iron links are a common feature of aristocratic wear, proclaiming, as they do, the wearer's lack of magery and fitness to inherit. I, on the other hand, being a mage, felt a kind of cold dread on seeing it, a dread filled with memories of powerlessness.

The necklace itself did nothing to lessen that dread. It was a thing of old and arcane design, of short iron spikes covered in runes and wound together so that it looked like a necklace of thorns. It was a savage-looking thing.

"How do you like it?" said Tomas. "It's very old and, I think, valuable."

"But. . . . But why? Why would a woman who had magic powers give an iron necklace to a daughter with magic powers?"

I'd hoped for, I don't know what, some small token of affection. Instead here was this hateful thing.

Tomas picked it up. "It's not as bad as it looks, you know. Look."

He put it over his head. "See. It just looks bad. The spikes don't ever stick into you even if you sleep on it. It won't show under your clothes and strangely enough it can't be felt by anyone either. I've sometimes wondered if this thing doesn't have some magic of its own."

"It's iron." I snapped. "Iron hates magic. How can you wear it? I thought you had some magic."

"I don't find it very comfortable, it's true, but my powers are very slight and I'm used to not using them. On the other hand, I've given it to some of the mages I've had under my care and it's been very useful. Wearing it seems to cut you off from any magic you've recently performed, disguising the traces. And it helps to confuse searchers using magic, too. I think you should wear it when we are in Moria, Dion. For safety's sake."

"What?" I was appalled. It was like suggesting I tie up my hands and feet. "Of course I'm not going to wear it."

He took my hand. "I know you don't like it, but your best protection against witchfinders is their ignorance."

"I'll be a helpless target."

"Well if that happens it's easy to take off. It's not a witch manacle."

"It might as well be."

"Dion, what about last night?"

Last night, waking in panic from dreams of the stone woman, I had thrown out a mage light without even thinking twice. Last night my brothers had been happy enough to be woken from similar dreams by the light.

"Could you stop yourself from putting forth that magic light when you wake up with a fright? Can you honestly say that?"

"No," I said. It was second nature to me, something I had learned to do as a child afraid of the dark.

"Then you see the sense of wearing this. You don't want to bring the witchfinders down on us before we've even got to Annac, do you? And you know how they are trained. They'll come for you in a group, maybe more than one group, and even you may have trouble beating them in an open battle. Once you're a couple of days' ride inside Moria, it won't be easy to escape."

"No," I said glumly because he was right. Unfortunately.

"It is possible Marnie foresaw this need when she gave me this necklace for you," said Tomas.

This seemed a little farfetched, though I tried to let it make me feel better. I agreed to wear the necklace. I even agreed to try out sleeping in the necklace that night. Though I did not much like it, I saw the sense in Tomas' scheme. It had also occurred to me that the necklace might be useful for my own purposes.

Although I was known as the Demonslayer, I had really only banished Andre/Bedazzer from this plain. He was still very much alive in his own demon world and like all demons was closely in touch with the worlds of magic. He had the ability to reach me in dreams or through mirrors, and he longed to get back into this world. As I was his only connection here, it was unlikely that he would forget about me. For the last three years I had hidden from him in a house without mirrors and slept behind walls covered with the runes of Protection, Distraction, and Blindness. Traveling in Moria I would not be covered by the protective runes and I would be unable to make more. Maybe the necklace would make it harder for him to find me. He was certain to be looking.

I dreaded the thought of seeing or hearing from Andre/Bedazzer again. Dreaming of him reminded me of my shameful failure, but worse than that it filled me with longing. Andre had been the first man I had ever loved, and I had come to Bedazzer's attention in the first place because demons and their power had fascinated and excited me and still on some level did.

A parish healer cannot in conscience just up and leave her parish. I had to inform the Parish Board that I was going, arrange for the neighboring parish healers to cover for me, and see to the patients who I was supplying with long-term treatments.

So later that day, I set out on Pony to do all these tasks.

I called to see Parrus first, but he was not at home. I managed to catch a couple of the other board members at home, however. The Parish Board consisted mostly of owners of the district's larger farms who had clubbed together to raise sums of money for community improvements such as bridges and healers. The ones I spoke to were horrified when I told them I was going. They were both of them good-hearted men who agreed that yes, indeed I must go back to Gallia to nurse my ailing sister (this being the story I told them). Both of them begged me to return as soon as I could in a way that made me feel both proud and guilty. Cardun was such a poor parish, as far from the city of Gallia as you could get and still be in the same country. It had been eighteen months without a healer before I came, and they had been desperate enough to take me even though I had not had the proper healing training and had no degree. They would have trouble replacing me, and once I went the nearest official healer would be ten miles away in the next parish.

I did not call on this healer, Adalane Fourizzi of Assi-Verdi, though I did send her a letter. She was a very fine healer, but she was not a warm person. She always made her patients feel guilty about taking her away from her beloved herb garden. Because of this and because she was such a distance away, I knew most of the healing work would fall on the shoulders of Jerusha Aretto at Castelnuovo Farm, where it had rested before I had come.

Dear Jerusha. She had taken me under her wing when as a raw half-trained healer I had first come to Cardun, and she remained my closest friend. She was a healer who had come to a neighboring district years ago and who had married and settled down with a well-to-do farmer in my parish. The paid position of village healer was forbidden to married women as interfering with their proper duties. In practice, however, it meant that in places like Cardun when there was no official healer, these women did the work of healers informally on top of the considerable work involved in being a farmer's wife and a mother, without receiving either the honor or the wage for doing such work. People would probably pay Jerusha with gifts of food as they always had, but she was getting old now. In the last two years her hair had become very white and her joints pained her in the mornings. With her last child soon to be married, she should have been looking forward to a decrease in work, not the increase my leaving would bring her.

She did not show any resentment when I told her I was leaving, but asked kindly after my sister.

I had invented a salve for her to rub on her joints by combining a painkilling salve with an antiinflammatory salve, using a binding spell that I had learned in my mage training. I had made two barrels full of it the previous evening, and I brought them to her strapped to the back of Pony. Though I had tried to teach it to her, Jerusha could not manage the power needed to bind the two ingredients effectively together. It was one of those moments when I had realized to my surprise just how unusual my level of magical strength was.

"Promise me you'll hoard this salve for yourself," I said to her, knowing that she wouldn't. "I will try to send you some more from Gallia."

"You will not be sending me any more if the witchfinders get you," she said, sweeping away all my lies in one sentence. "Don't make the same mistake others have made. Don't assume that you are strong enough to take them on. Be careful and stay alive."

She had obviously guessed more about me than I had ever told her, and it seemed an insult to her now to protest that I was only going to the city. I simply nodded and kissed her good-bye, promising that we would see each other again.

I felt thoroughly depressed by the time I left her. To make it worse, I met the parish priest, one of the few members of the Parish Board whom I did not like. Mages and priests never get on well, but our feud was a particularly strong one. Basically the priest, as is the way of his kind, believed that chastity was the highest feminine ideal. Since it was a quality that seemed to be somewhat lacking in my nature, however, I took the more practical view that it was a nice ideal, but if any local girl asked me to dispense a potion to prevent her conceiving a child, I wasn't going to ask any questions. Unmarried motherhood was not something I'd wish on any village lass. The parish priest was outraged at my "encouraging immorality" among the local people, especially since the other healers had never gone against the church in this respect. (It was one of the few issues Jerusha and I disagreed on.) He had even preached a sermon against me. I promised to stop, but I just kept on doing it behind his back and everybody knew it. I could tell by the big pleased grin on his skinny face that he'd heard the news, though he was polite enough to try and conceal his triumph.

On the way home I felt thoroughly gloomy, and only the certainty that I must go and find my sister held me to my purpose. The people of Cardun had treated me with great warmth and acceptance over the years. I knew this was the reason I had changed from a scared eighteen-year-old terrified of disapproval to someone who was brave enough to disobey priests and indulge in illicit love affairs. How could I abandon these people like this?

The last thing I needed was difficult questions from Tomas. They came anyway.

"That fellow who was here yesterday came round again today. Parrus. So what's going on between you two?"

"Nothing," I said, a little too quickly.

"Oh yes? It's just from the guilty way he acted I felt sure you must be sleeping together."

"Tomas!" Brothers, like priests, were notorious for valuing chastity in womenfolk, if not in themselves. I'd been seventeen years without a brother and I was going to nip this brother thing in the bud before it got out of hand and Tomas got the idea he had the right to defend my honor.

His next remark was disarming, however.

"Look, I don't mind, Dion. I never interfere with the loves of my sisters. I'd be a fool to try. I was just wondering, that's all."

"I see." If I didn't protest and didn't admit to anything, I figured he'd lose interest quickly enough.

I was wrong.

"I just kind of wondered if it was just a casual fling or if there was anything to it, you know. . . . He'd be quite a good match, young Parrus."

"What! What are you talking about? He's a Lord's son. Don't be ridiculous."

"Not so ridiculous. It's not such a great family and he's not the oldest son. If nothing else, you could breed some pretty powerful mages together."

"Tomas! You're talking rubbish. Anyway Parrus doesn't even know about my magecraft."

"Yes, so I gathered. Oh don't worry, I didn't tell him."

"You gathered? How long were you talking for?"

"Oh, I invited him in. He's very interested in Moria, isn't he? His Morian's not half bad either."

That was how Parrus and I had met. He'd come to me initially to learn Morian. Things had gone on from there. We'd both come to desire each other and after Andre. . . . It seemed kind of pointless to go around saying no to men, just because that was what a nice woman was supposed to do. Life's too short and I was hardly a nice woman to start with.

"You had quite a little heart to heart then," I said sarcastically.

"We had a few drinks," said Tomas, smiling blandly as he slid away.

They had had a few drinks too. One of my bottles of wildberry wine was completely empty.

I was relieved that the whole subject had been dropped, however, and thought nothing more of it. There was much to do to make the hut ready for a long absence, and a long line of patients had begun to come calling with gifts and requests for medicine.

It was only on the evening of the next day, the evening before we were to leave, that I discovered just what the few drinks had led to.

We were going over my disguise.

"This stuff is a bit nice for a maid servant, isn't it? And this scarf. This is Borgenese, not Gallian."

"Yes," said Tomas. "We had a bit of a change of plan. We thought it might be better for you to pass as the wife of a Borgenese merchant. A married woman will attract less suspicion. Here, I got you a wedding ring."

I knew something was up. Hamel was looking nervous. Tomas, on the other hand, had the same bland look on his face that he'd had the day before when we'd been talking about Parrus.

"Why Borgenese?" I asked.

Tomas shrugged.

"Actually, it was your friend Parrus' idea," said Hamel suddenly.

"Hamel!" said Tomas in warning tones, but it was too late.

"You see he wants to come with us and we thought he'd be very useful, and he could be a Borgenese merchant because being Gallian wouldn't be a good idea in Moria at the moment and he speaks very good Borgenese, and so he could be your husband and you could be . . . Look, I know we should have discussed it with you, Dion, but you were busy and . . ."

"You what . . . ? Take Parrus into Moria. . . . Are you insane? You'll get us all killed."

"It could be very useful to have two mages, Dion," said Tomas. "Parrus really wanted to come. He could be very useful to us."

"No! It's crazy. I don't want Parrus tagging along. It won't work, Tomas. They'll know he's not Morian. They'll throw him into jail just for being a Gallian."

"Well I judged it would be well," said Tomas as if there

was no point in this discussion. "And so I decided he should come."

"You . . . well, I think it's a stupid idea. I . . ."

"What do you know about it, anyway? I'm not interested in your opinion. You know nothing of Moria and what will work and not work. For God's sake, Dion. Stop wasting my time with things that aren't your concern. Do I tell you how to perform healing?"

I just gaped at him. When someone you hardly know speaks to you so sharply, it's always a shock.

Tomas rounded on Hamel. "We agreed to say nothing. You said you'd back me up on this. Thanks very much, Hamel."

"We should have discussed it with her. It just wasn't right."

"What else haven't you told me?" I said, anger blasting through my shock.

"Nothing," snapped Tomas. "Stop fussing. It will be all right."

The way he spoke, that long-suffering tone of a man dealing with a fool; that was the last straw. This insane plan, the fact that they hadn't even asked me, they'd just assumed they could force it on me—the whole thing went off like a firework in my brain.

"That's it," I shouted. "If Parrus goes, I'm not."

"Oh that's just wonderful," shouted Tomas. "Stay then. We'll take Parrus."

"Fine!"

"Dion, don't be like that. Tomas . . ."

"And you shut up," snapped Tomas. "You've done quite enough, Hamel."

Silence in the room. The fire crackled in the hearth.

"Tomas, you'd be angry too, if someone just sprung something on you like this. Let's just talk it over."

Tomas snorted.

Hamel continued. "Listen, Tomas, women have just as much mind for reasonable discussion as men, no matter what you think."

"Oh, listen to Mr. Expert," sneered Tomas. "You know all about how to handle women."

"Well I handle my wife well enough, don't I?" said Hamel levelly.

"You . . . you shit!" shouted Tomas. He spun round and in a madness of anger made as if to hit Hamel.

"No! Stop!" A surge of panicky power came out of me and Tomas froze mid-punch. A second thought and I made his arm come down and stick to the tabletop so that Tomas had to crouch beside it.

"Sweet Tansa's mother!" said Tomas wonderingly.

Hamel blinked, then turned away, suppressing a smile.

"That was well done, little sister," said Tomas admiringly.

"Don't 'little sister' me. It won't work." I turned to Hamel. "I don't think we should take Parrus. It's too dangerous."

"It's dangerous whether we take him or not, Dion. But a married woman with a husband there with her. . . . They're less likely to be looking for a healer in those circumstances."

"But two mages, that's pushing our luck. And one of them a Gallian. Moria is at war with Gallia now."

"Well I said so too, and that's when Parrus said he could pass for a Borgenese. Do you think he's lying?"

I didn't think Parrus was lying. He had been five years in Borgen and he was good at languages. His knowledge and fluency in the Borgenese tongue was no doubt very good.

"He just has to pass for three days," said Tomas. "Until we get home."

I scowled at him.

"You could let me go," he said politely nodding at his wrist which was still stuck to the table.

I turned pointedly back to Hamel.

"Are you allowed to do this? Use magic on helpless people like that?" said Hamel doubtfully. "Doesn't the White College forbid it."

"Tomas Holyhands isn't a helpless person. He's . . . he's a dammed snake."

Tomas grinned.

"Two mages would be very useful in Moria," said Hamel. "It's likely that Tasha has got herself mixed up in something very bad. We might need a mage to help get her back. And you'll be in hiding after doing the searching spell."

They had a point here. It was something I had thought of myself.

"You'd be better to take me than Parrus," I said.

"Oh Dion, it doesn't sound like the South is any place for a woman."

"Dion is the stronger mage," said Tomas. "We would be better to take her. But we'll see how the land lies in Annac before we make any decisions. You can see the point of our plan, can't you, Dion?"

I looked at him with annoyance and then sighed. Curse Tomas. I was already considering Parrus' coming as a possibility.

"But can it be done safely?"

"I really do not think it will be any more dangerous than just taking you alone," said Tomas. "I've done this before. Many times. You must trust me to know, Dion. Now be fair. I don't tell you how to do healing, do I?"

"Why on earth would Parrus want to go into Moria?" I wondered, though part of me knew the answer already. It was not much of a life for a well-trained young mage to be hanging round on the family estates, overseeing the farmwork. And possibly Tomas had worked on him a little. My respect for Tomas' powers of persuasion was rapidly growing.

"You just don't want him to find out about you," said Tomas. "You're afraid he'll go off you."

It occurred to me at that moment that Tomas might be matchmaking. No. That was too insane.

"You shut up, Tomas," I said briefly.

"Look, he knows about our mother now. We told him. He seemed amused more than anything else."

That sounded like Parrus.

"But we haven't told him about the magery. And we

won't either, till you're ready. Not many men take kindly to being outdone by a woman. Come on, Dion, let me up. My knees are killing me.''

"When was I going to find out about this wonderful plan, as a matter of interest?''

"Parrus is going to meet us tomorrow at the border cross-roads.''

"Not till then!''

"You'd have been less likely to turn back then. I've always found it best not to offer people too many choices.''

"You are a snake.''

"But I'm a smart snake. And I'm a snake on your side. You'll come home alive, sister. Don't worry. Come on now, please let me loose.''

"You should have asked me first," I said. "Then none of this would have happened.''

But I let him loose and I let them persuade me that Parrus should come with us. I didn't see that I had much choice. I had no intention of withdrawing from the expedition and I suspect Tomas knew as much.

Later when Tomas was outside checking the horses, I asked Hamel, "Why did Tomas get so angry at you before?''

Hamel shrugged guiltily. "The issue of marriage is a sore one with Tomas.''

"Why? Tell me, Hamel. Is it a subject I should avoid?''

"Several years ago Tomas was in love with a woman in our village. For him it was the great love, though he's always been something of a ladies' man before and since. In those days, he just took life as it came. He worked at the inn looking after the horses. He and I and Lucien Sercel used to go fishing together. And there was this woman. Marie-Louise. She was a wealthy farmer's daughter and was courted by most of the village, but she favored Tomas— loved him, I think. A loving passed between them and she became pregnant. Tomas was overjoyed by this. He thought her father would be forced to let her marry him, a thing that would not have been possible before. But Marie-Louise wasn't about to marry the ostler at an inn and have all the village laughing at her. Or to bring her father's wrath and maybe his disinheritance down on her. So she accepted one of her other suitors, the right suitor, another well-off farmer's son. I heard her tell Tomas that to marry an inn whore's bastard would shame her too much. I don't think Tomas had ever given such ideas any thought before then. It broke his heart. He changed and became bitter. He left the inn and went to work for the Sercels, and Lord Sandor began to make something of him as he'd always wanted to.''

''It must have been very hard on Tomas.''

''It wasn't the worst thing. The worst thing came a few years later. Tomas had hardly been back to Annac in that time, but one day Marnie sent for him. The two of them went out to see Marie-Louise and when they came back, they came back with Tomas' son. It seemed that her new husband had never forgiven her for being pregnant by another man. He'd taken to beating the both of them, but especially the 'cuckoo in his nest.' The poor child was but three and yet he was near to death when Tomas bought him home. They healed him as best they could, but he will always limp and he will never hear again in one ear. Tomas loves his son. Since he has had care of Martin, he has become even more hungry for things. I can understand what made him so but sometimes I cannot like this new Tomas. This was the only time he ever spoke badly to our mother. He told her she had made him believe in a way of living that was just not practical, that his illegitimacy had ruined his life and now his son's. Marnie wept.''

He stared into the fire. ''Part of her believed him.''

''But they made up?''

''Oh, yes! Tomas adored Marnie and she cared for Martin until she died. She had a way with children. In some ways she was much like one herself.''

''What did you think of our mother?''

''What does a person think of their mother? You love your mother. But to tell you the truth, for a long time, I tried not to think of it at all. The world, people round Annac, my father even, could not decide if Marnie was a whore or a fool, bad or mad.''

This was the question I badly wanted an answer to.

''What do you think?''

''She was just Marnie. Her rules for right and wrong were different from other people's. It may have been the Wanderer in her. Tomas told you about her marriage? She used to say that people are who they are and shouldn't have to try to be something else just to please other people. She's still a mystery to me.'' He shrugged. ''Perhaps parents are always a mystery to their children.''

''But why did she have so many children, by so many men?''

''And you know the thing that still puzzles me is she didn't have to have any children at all.'' He looked a little embarrassed. ''I suspect you may have discovered this yourself. A woman with magical powers often can prevent herself from conceiving. Marnie told me she chose to have us all.''

''All except me,'' said Tomas.

Both Hamel and I jumped guiltily. Tomas came into the room and sat down beside the fire.

''You're wondering why Marnie had so many children, Dion?'' said Tomas. ''When Marnie was working for the Sercels, she was trying to be respectable. She was trying to forget that she was the bastard child of a passing Wanderer woman and our grandfather, trying to live the way people in our village and her father and half-brother thought proper. But she fell in love with Sandor Sercel and she loved him so much that I was conceived—unintentionally with intent, if you can understand that. And I ruined her.

''Of course she meant nothing to Sandor, and when she realized this she was heartbroken. She went down to the wild side of Lake Lammer, with desperate confused thoughts in her head and me growing inside her. She told me both our lives hung in the balance then, for she was not sure who to do away with. She liked the thought of throwing herself in the lake far better than the more sensible thought of getting rid of me.

"A storm came across the lake. The sky was thunderous grey, so heavy she felt as if it would crush her, and the lake was black and angrily thrashing at the shore. Yet where she was, a patch of sun had broken through the clouds. It was like another world, and like a voice from that other world she heard the sound of someone singing and she saw a man coming along the lake's edge. He was a Wanderer with hair like milk and he was dressed all in rags. His feet stuck out of his tattered shoes. She had not spoken to a Wanderer since her mother had left her at Grandfather's door as a six-year-old child, and the sight of him filled her with a strange joy. He came up to her as she stood there and said, "Do not destroy the child within you. Foretelling has shown that your children will repay all the ills you will suffer for their sakes and be your most abiding joy."

The was silence in the room except for the crackling of the fire. I could almost see the lake, with the angry black clouds rolling over it, the strange unearthly sun, and on the shore the fair-haired servant girl and the tattered man with milk-white hair. I felt so sad for her, this betrayed girl with the now familiar face. She was so young when it happened.

"She followed this man to the Wanderer encampment and stayed with them for several days. I'm not sure what happened there, but somehow they comforted her so that she was able to go on. She always said she felt completed when she was with them. Part of the problem between her and old Cremer was that he forbade her to see them."

"She never thought of traveling with the Wanderers?" I asked. It was an idea that sometimes appealed to me.

"It seems appealing in summer, doesn't it," said Tomas, "but in winter. . . . Such a life is very hard with a small child. Sleeping under hedgerows and begging. People are not good to Wanderers. Look how many leave the Wandering life. Only the real wild Wanderers keep wandering all their lives, and they are not always the easiest of companions."

I nodded, remembering the drugged or drunken Wanderers I had seen in the forest.

"To answer your question, though, in my darker moments

I have thought that she got the rest of us simply so she could get you, Dion. Because it had been foretold that her seventh child would be special.''

I stared at him in horror.

"Tomas," cried Hamel. "That's an awful thing to say. You know you don't think any such thing. Our mother would never have let her life be driven by foretellings like that.''

Tomas grinned and I realized that he was scratching at me. It seemed to be his way.

"I have thought that thought, but it's not so. Marnie loved children. She liked men, too, she loved men, but children. . . . To her men were but a fleeting pleasure. That is the way among Wanderers. They don't bother with husbands much. Brothers are the ones who care for their sister's children, just like Uncle Jos, despite his grumbles, cared for us. After Sandor Sercel and then old Cremer, she didn't expect much more than fleeting happiness from men. So her children were the real source of joy for her. And the men she chose to be our fathers, I think they were the ones she loved most. We are souvenirs, Dion, remembrances of happy times.''

◆ 4 ◆

We left Cardun the following morning, while the sky was still pink with dawn. It had rained earlier and it promised to do so again. The bell birds were tinkling out their morning songs in the tall sweet oil trees. A tremendous feeling of sadness came over me as I pulled the door of the hut closed. I stood there before it with a lump in my throat.

"Come on, Dion," cried Tomas. "The day's a-wasting."

Hamel put his arm round my shoulders and drew me toward the waiting horses. It was surprising how quickly our relationship had become this easy.

"Sorry, little sister?"

"Aye," I said. "I feel as if I will never see this place again."

Tomas snorted. "Well, since you've no talent for fore-telling that probably means you'll be home within the month." He pinched my chin. "Did you think of that? Now up with you."

The quickest route over the border was through the forest and over the river, but it was a very stealthy route, not entirely legal, and Tomas had decided against it.

"The border will be crawling with patrols at the moment. Everybody will be on edge because of the war. We are cer-

77

tain to get picked up going through the hills. It's the smugglers' natural path and that will only look doubly suspicious. It's best if we go respectably along the main road.''

This plan had the added advantage of disguising our movements from my parishioners. There were more than the usual number of people working round the village street that morning and the fields by the roadside seemed very busy too. Everywhere people waved cheerful farewells, but their eyes were curious.

It was only after midmorning when we were well into the next parish that we stopped seeing people I knew. I was glad. I could see only trouble stemming from Cardun coming to know that their village healer had not taken the safe turn toward the city of Gallia, but the illegal and highly dangerous route into Moria instead.

It was chilly and every now and then soft rain fell. I leaned against Tomas' back and tried to relax, but I was unused to riding pillion; by midday when we reached the crossroads, I was saddle sore and looking forward to getting down.

''There's Parrus,'' Tomas cried back at me.

Parrus was sitting on the ground beside the shrine to Tansa. He was dressed in the sober blue robes of a Borgenese merchant. It had been agreed (not by me of course, because I hadn't been consulted) that he should call himself Ren Parrus Latrides, making me Enna Dion Latrides.

He greeted us with relieved pleasure. It was only when I got down from the saddle and could finally see more than Tomas' back that I realized why he was so relieved.

On the other side of the crossroad, sheltered by the trees, sat a big group of Wanderers. There must have been thirty or forty of them, just sitting or lying on the grass by the road.

''What are they doing here?'' said Tomas.

''How should I know?'' said Parrus defensively. ''They were here when I got here. Just sitting about. Damned Moonies. Give me the creeps.''

''Parrus!'' I said. It was a pretty common term of abuse for Wanderers, a reference to their moon-white skin and pale hair, but I'd never liked it and now, knowing what I did about my own family, I was ashamed to hear it in front of my brothers.

Tomas just shrugged. "Well you should have asked them, you foolish man. They don't bite, you know."

He had turned on his heel and was crossing the road before Parrus had time to let out an outraged noise.

"Well, to hell with you too," muttered Parrus at his back.

"Just a word of advice, Parrus," said Hamel gravely. "There's a lot of Wanderer blood in our family, as there is in a lot of Morians." Then he turned and followed Tomas.

"I wouldn't admit to it if I were him," said Parrus to me softly. "It's hardly a badge of honor."

"Well, some Morians don't admit it and some do. I'm surprised at you, calling them names like some badly educated lout . . ."

"Well you kept pretty quiet about your Wanderer blood," said Parrus. "In fact you kept quiet about a lot of things. Didn't you trust me or something?"

I couldn't think of anything to say to that, because the answer was no, I didn't trust him. I felt myself turning red.

"Not to worry," said Parrus almost kindly. He stroked my arm. "Your secret's safe with me."

We watched my brothers on the other side of the road. They made the traditional five-movement gesture of Wanderer greeting and bowed.

"Huh!" said Parrus crossly. "Here I was sitting politely enough, minding my own business, and one of them came over and gave me one of their stupid foretellings. Then I had to sit here the rest of the morning with them watching me."

I suddenly remembered the Wanderer man in black. His foretelling was coming true. How odd!

"What was your foretelling?" I asked, interested.

"He said I should follow my heart, not the Duke. When I asked him what he meant, he just turned and went away."

"Strange," I said.

"Dammed annoying is what it was. Anyway, enough of

that. Sit down. How did it go? I think I managed to get away without anyone seeing me.''

This reminded me that I had words to say to Parrus.

"Why on earth do you want to come with us?" I said. "And why didn't you ask me?"

"Your brothers said it would be all right."

"So?" I said sharply, annoyed at his presumption.

He shrugged. "They seem to know what they're doing."

"But why?" I said again. "The danger of the witchfinders. . . . It's not nothing."

He shrugged. "I don't know. You're not the only one who's worried about necromancy in Moria, you know. I'm a mage, for God's sake. And I'm sick of rotting at Cardun. Anyway, what sort of a fellow would I be if I let you go off into Moria just like that?"

Was he actually worried about me? How . . . odd. I found myself looking at him curiously. He reddened slightly.

"You're the best healer Cardun has ever had," he said quickly. "And they are my parish."

"Dion!"

Tomas was calling me, beckoning me to come over.

Hamel came to meet me.

"They said they were curious to see you, Dion. It seems you've got a good reputation among them."

I could not help being flattered by this, but it was an odd meeting. The leader of the Wanderers got up as I approached and bowed and greeted me with their special gesture and I followed as best I could. Then they all sat there looking at me for a moment, their dark almond-shaped eyes expressionless and unreadable and as deep as silent wells. I could understand how Parrus would have been unnerved, waiting here all morning alone with these people. They were real wild Wanderers, the type that didn't even try to blend in with the rest of the peninsula folk. They wore Wanderer-brown garb and their hair was plaited and intertwined with twigs and feathers. In their ears were heavy rings of metal or bone. They were an unusual group for Wanderers. Wanderers mostly travel in family groups and there are always children playing about among them, but this group had neither old people nor children.

"The omens are good for the Duke's journey into Moria," said the Wanderer to Tomas, continuing the previous conversation.

"Is that a foretelling?" said Tomas quickly.

The Wanderer smiled thinly.

"The future changes even as we begin to live it," he said. "Let us call it simply a well-founded hope. We wish you luck on your journey, Enna. The omens are promising for that also."

He bowed and sat down with his face turned away, indicating that the conversation was finished.

"Well," said Tomas later as we rode away down the road. "This bodes well. They say they're planning to follow the Gallian army into Moria. They expect them in the next three days."

"Are they going to join it then?" I asked, thinking again of how there had only been young people in the group.

"Possibly," said Tomas. "Usually they regard any kind of violence as an abomination. Even skill in fighting is disliked by them."

He had changed horses with Parrus so that now, as was proper, I was riding pillion behind my supposed husband. This meant I could see Tomas and Hamel's faces but not Parrus'.

Still I knew very well what he must look like as he said scoffingly, "So they are just going to sit there for several days doing nothing, are they?"

My brothers exchanged a tolerant but amused glance. I couldn't help feeling embarrassed at how narrow-minded Parrus sounded. I resisted the strong temptation to poke him in the ribs.

"I imagine there'll be a few more of them when the Duke does come," said Hamel. "I got the impression this was a general movement. He must be going to win. Otherwise surely they wouldn't follow him."

"Humph," said Parrus, earning another amused glance

from my brothers. This time, however, I was too interested in what my brothers were saying to worry.

"Do you really think so?" I asked. I had always been fascinated by the Wanderers' powers of foretelling, which were very much respected, even in Gallia where they were not well known. Wanderers were very reluctant to talk about such things to outsiders, but it seemed my brothers knew something about the subject and I was determined to get it out of them.

"So do you think it is a sign that he will win?"

"Now, be careful," said Tomas. "There's nothing certain about foretelling. Like that Wanderer said—our actions now are forever changing the future. Just because they say it's their fate to follow the Duke doesn't necessarily mean he's going to win this war, though it is a good sign."

"Well, it would be pretty stupid to follow the Duke if they've foreseen he's going to lose, wouldn't it?" said Parrus.

"Foretelling isn't as simple as that," said Tomas. "It's not like the foretelling of our mages where they cast a spell, and if they are lucky get a vague idea of the outcome of events. Though Wanderers do that and do it well, their foretellers have the ability to see visions of events in the future. But they have no idea how those events will come about."

"What do you mean?" I asked.

"Well, take those Wanderers we just passed. They may be waiting at the border because one—or more likely several—of their foretellers has seen a vision of their following the Ducal Army into Moria. And other foretellers may have seen visions of them living happily in Moria in the future. But they can't really be sure if it is the first vision that leads to the second. This war may end in a terrible rout for the Duke and they may wind up living happily in Moria for completely different reasons in the future."

"Well it hardly seems much good then, does it?" snorted Parrus.

"It is a thing to be very careful of, and the Wanderers are. 'The truth is not the truth till it comes true,' they say. They only act on prophecies after careful discussion with each other and with people called Judges—those to whom it is given to be able to see when a prophecy should be acted upon. Our mother is supposed to have had this gift. She was much respected among them for it.''

I remembered what Hamel had said about her knowing the right thing to do. I wanted to ask more but Hamel interrupted.

"Glassybri ahead," he said. At that moment we passed a troop of Gallian Horse Guards standing on the roadside and clattered onto the bridge that crossed the river between Gallia and Moria.

I froze. I had been so interested in what Tomas had been saying that I had forgotten that this ride was taking us into Moria. Now I was committed.

As we approached the high whitewashed walls of Glassybri we passed many people going back toward Gallia. They were almost all Gallians, but here and there was a richly clad Ishtaki merchant. If the Ishtakis, those angels of commerce, were leaving, the future must look bad for the Church of the Burning Light. It was difficult for me to see ahead, riding as I was behind Parrus, but finally I could see the tall walls of the town before us. About that time we were forced to halt. A great crowd of people was lined up on the road waiting to enter Glassybri, and we joined the queue. The sound of crying babies and complaining donkeys came from the line before us. Every now and then one of the gates seemed to swing open for a short time and the queue would move forward. Our horses snorted restlessly and moved their feet. As we waited my palms became sweaty with fear, though I kept telling myself to be calm. Behind us the line of people grew. In front of us a group of traveling masons and a mercenary played dice in the dust of the road.

Eventually we got close enough to the gates to see that they were letting groups of people through ten at a time.

Once there was shouting behind the gate, and the tingling feeling of magic. I craned my head to look but Tomas pushed me back.

"Don't draw attention to yourself. And act like you don't know us. You two will be safer that way."

At that moment the gate swung open in front of us, revealing a dark, narrow street within. The soldier at the gate counted ten of us through and the gate swung shut behind us.

Inside, the street was cordoned off and groups of soldiers and hard-faced women in the black and grey garb of Sisters of Light, the nuns of the Burning Light, stood beside it. We were ordered to stop and dismount. Tomas and Hamel had moved away from us, so that they stood at the other side of the group. A man in grey and black had approached them.

"Well, well," he was saying, "if it isn't Tomas Holyhands." Then I stopped watching them because the same kind of official had come up to us. He looked over the papers Parrus handed him with a disbelieving air.

"Borgenese, hey? Very convenient. Ren Parrus Latrides. A merchant? Why are you coming into Moria?"

"My wife has a sister deathly ill in Annac. She wants to see her before she dies," said Parrus in his halting Morian.

The official had lost interest in Parrus even before he stopped talking.

"And you," he barked at me. "Answer. Where were you born?"

He questioned me quickly in Morian. Had I not been a native speaker, I might well have got flustered and made some mistake. As it was I was glad I'd spent three days speaking Morian to my brothers. You lose fluency in any language, even your own, if you don't speak it.

Then he lifted up a crystal ball and pressed it against my forehead. I knew that ball. It turned blue in the presence of any trace of magic. I hoped Parrus had been careful not to use magic for the last ten hours. I had been. Still I felt frightened. What if they decided to do a mind search?

He turned and barked at the waiting soldiers, "Search this lot. Jacques, Woody, take the woman."

I was seized and pulled ungently towards the cordon. I squeaked in fright and might have used magic against them, but I was wearing the necklace and could do nothing.

"Hey! What are you doing with my wife?" shouted Parrus.

"Stand still," said the leader. He was running the ball over Parrus while one of the soldiers patted him down. Two soldiers began to pull our bags roughly from the saddle.

"Don't worry, girlie," said one of my captors, not unkindly. "We have to search for healers."

He pushed me through the cordon where I was seized by two of the hard-faced women and hustled into a nearby alley.

"Am I being arrested for something?" I cried, too scared to think clearly.

"Maybe!" said one of them, a tall dour woman with extremely white curly hair. "Have you got something to confess?" Then, without waiting for an answer, she said, "Now stand still and shut up."

The she began rubbing a crystal ball over me while the other woman pulled the scarf off my head and and began running her fingers though my hair. A body search! My blood turned cold. Oh Aumaz. The necklace. She was sure to find it. And wearing such a strange iron necklace was going to look very suspicious. In fright I put my hands over my face and stood so for the whole search, shaking, in a state of the most shameful terror, while they patted over my torso and then lifted my skirts and felt over my legs and through my petticoats. I tried to bring to mind what I must do when they brought in the witch manacles but my mind was too filled with panic. Why did they go on? Why didn't they just get on with bringing on the witch manacles and dragging me off for a mind search? They were just getting a perverse pleasure out of tormenting me.

Then suddenly they had finished.

"That's it, then. You're clean," said the tall one, and the other one pushed me out of the alley. "Put on your scarf," said the tall one as she passed me going back to the cordon. "What kind of slut are you?"

I stood there bemused with fear and relief. They hadn't found it. Why hadn't they found it? It was so pointy. I put my hand surreptitiously to my chest. Strangely enough I couldn't feel it either, although I could feel the weight of it. Then, finally, I remembered something Tomas had told me about how it couldn't be felt. I had been too busy being revolted by the necklace itself to really pay attention at the time. What a fool! All that fear for nothing. Yet how fascinating. An iron necklace that couldn't be felt. And it couldn't be magic either, or it would have shown up in the crystal ball. So how?

There were two priests seated on horses near the cordon. One of them, an extremely handsome fellow with a finely sculpted face and chestnut hair, glanced lingeringly at me, and there was something in that glance that reminded me that I was standing here with my hair all uncovered and coming down. Quickly I smoothed and tucked in my hair, tied my scarf back around my head, and started looking for the others.

A moment later the priest caught my attention again when one of the officials came up to him and said, "This lot's clean, Priest Stalker."

Stalker! Why did that name sound familiar?

I wondered about it as I stood at the edge of the cordon waiting for the other travelers to file out. Parrus came over leading our horse and looking very shaken. We squeezed each other's arms, both too relieved to be pretend detachment.

Then I heard Tomas' voice.

"Priest Stalker?" asked my brother, politely addressing the handsome priest. "I wonder if I might speak with you."

The priest inclined his head in much the same way as a saint would graciously accept our homage.

"My name is Tomas Holyhands. You visited our inn in Annac. The Inn of the Holy Hands. Near the Monastery of the Healing Holy Hands of St. Belkis."

"Ah, yes, I remember it. A lovely place. That explains your colorful name, my brother."

"You spoke with my sister while you were there. Tasha Holyhands. Your words were an inspiration to her and after you left she decided to follow you South. Since then I have not seen her. It's been almost three months, Holy One.''

A strange expression came into the priest's eyes. Then I felt something, a frisson of magic. My blood ran cold and I turned away quickly lest he see the knowledge on my face. Priest Stalker was obviously a very powerful priest-mage. This spell was strong but very subtle. What was he doing? I relaxed into the magic and a wave of liking for the priest washed over me. How sinister. He was using magic to make us like and trust him. I was a little shocked. Such magical tricks were forbidden to normal mages and would have brought a severe reprimand and maybe even jail if reported to the White College in Gallia. But here in Moria, of course, the Burning Light made its own rules.

Even though part of me knew quite coldly what he was doing, it was difficult for me to resist the feeling now I had let it in. I found myself nodding and smiling at him. Just like the other three were.

''I do remember Tasha Holyhands. Poor troubled creature. She wanted to become a priest-mage, but of course that's quite impossible for a woman. Forgive me, I know nothing about her. She never caught up with me, I'm afraid. Your inn is the last place I saw her.''

''But you told her of a place. A place she could serve the Church and use her powers.''

''Did I? I wonder what I can have said.''

There was something in the priest's manner that was not right, but I could not work out what it was because I liked him so much.

''And who are these good people?'' he said suddenly, running his eyes over us. ''More of your family? I remember they were numerous, weren't they?''

''Just some people I met on the road,'' said Tomas. ''My sister, Priest Stalker, can you remember nothing?''

''No, I . . . Wait, I may have told her of Sanctuary.''

''Sanctuary?''

''Aye, it's a community of holy people started by Hierarch

Jarraz whose prayers support our efforts to reclaim the Great Plain of Despair. Yes . . .''

There was a shout from inside the cordon. A new batch of travelers was being searched. The priest turned.

''I am needed. Tomas Holyhands, I would be glad to help you. If you call on me tonight at St. Agnes Church House, I would be glad to tell you more.''

He turned and spurred his horse away.

As we were mounting our horses, they brought a couple through the cordon wearing witch manacles. Behind them rode the other priest, a very fat man. He was holding up a magic lens, the kind healers used to look at the life force of a patient, and crying, ''Behold these sinners. Be warned by their disgrace.'' The soldiers and the women searchers cheered. The malicious cheering reminded me of my flight from Moria back when I was sixteen, and I shuddered.

''Let's get out of here,'' said Tomas, and we set off. We threaded our way through the narrow streets. I had forgotten the conversation with Darmen Stalker in my distress at seeing the couple in the manacle, and so I was surprised when a short time later we halted outside an inn.

''I'll bespeak us some food and some beds,'' said Hamel as he jumped down from the horse.

''No, Hamel,'' said Tomas. ''Only the food for the moment. I'll see to the horses.''

It was early afternoon and the dining room of the inn was almost empty. Hamel found a seat by the fire and by the time Tomas came in from seeing to the horses, the maid was bringing out bowls full of savory-smelling stew and a plate of bread and cheese.

Hamel waited till the maid was gone before he asked the question that was obviously most urgently on his mind.

''Are we not going to stay here tonight? What about this meeting with Darmen Stalker?''

''I'm not fully sure that I should go and see him,'' said Tomas.

I sat quietly and ate my stew while the men argued in low voices, Parrus adding his urgings to Hamel's. All of them felt that they were closer to finding Tasha than they had yet been, but Tomas was mistrustful of Darmen Stalker, who was after all Hierarch Jarraz's secretary. Though initially I had planned to let the men decide because I thought my fear of the witchfinders might be clouding my judgement, I gradually became more and more certain that Tomas was right and that I must stop him from going to see Stalker.

"That man was using magic to make us like him," I said, breaking into the discussion. "I don't think we should trust him."

There was a stunned silence.

"You can't know that," snapped Parrus. "I didn't feel anything."

It was on the tip of my tongue to tell him that I was more powerful than he, but instead I said, "I've felt such things before. It's not an unusual technique for witchfinders to use if they can."

"You speak like some kind of expert," sneered Parrus crossly.

"Well I'd obviously know more about it than you," I snapped, stung.

"For God's sake keep your voices down," hissed Tomas. "Dion's right, Parrus. I wondered why I liked him so much all of a sudden. I'd been dreaming of punching his face up till then. I knew something was wrong."

"You might ask yourself what kinds of things I saw before I fled Moria five years ago, Parrus," I hissed, unable to resist snapping at him. "I've dealt with witchfinders before. They're very cunning. Why was that Stalker man so interested in whether the rest of us were family? Because magic runs in families and they know it. It was always their habit in Mangalore to round up the blood relations of mages and put them to mind search."

"There is no sin in having magical powers," said Hamel. "Only in using them outside the church."

"All they need to do is subject Tomas to a mind search and all will be revealed," I went on. "They might not have the manpower to mind search everyone who comes into

Glassybri, but put that Stalker in a room alone with Tomas and what's to stop him? He could do it himself, you know. He's a priest-mage of some power.''

"Aye," said Tomas. "Right then, I say we keep going. We've found out the main thing. That she may be, or may have been, in the Great Waste at this Sanctuary place.''

"If the dreams take place there," I said, "this Sanctuary is no sanctuary.''

Hamel was silent for a moment.

"You're certain? That he was making us like him, I mean?" he asked.

"Oh yes.''

"So am I now," said Tomas.

"Aumaz! How underhanded," Hamel said. "I'm with you then. We'll go.''

Parrus shrugged his shoulders irritably. "Well, if you want to go about this the most difficult way . . ." he said. "She's not my sister.''

Tomas pushed his chair out from the table.

"Finish your meal. I'll go see to the horses." He squeezed my shoulder as he passed. "Thank you for backing me up, sister. I feel we are doing the right thing.''

"Yes," said Parrus crossly. "I'm sure you've been a big help, Dion.''

Hamel smiled sympathetically at me.

I couldn't help being hurt by Parrus' remark, and it was not until I was following him out into the courtyard that I realized why he was so annoyed at me. Of course. I had bested him in magic and his pride was hurt. I'd had experiences like this with Parrus before, each one of them confirming that I had been right not to tell him about my powers. Apart from his pride, mages also tended to be very touchy about the difference between healing magic, practiced mostly by women, and the far more highly regarded magic practiced by male mages. It was probably the reason he was so scoffing about Wanderer prophecy, too.

When we joined him in the innyard, Tomas was standing

by the horses, talking heatedly with a small man with pro-truding rabbitlike teeth.

"No!" Tomas was saying.

"So who's she then?" said the small man, nodding at me.

"This is my sister," said Tomas sharply.

"Don't look much like you."

"She's my half-sister," snapped Tomas. He grabbed the little man by the shirt and pulled his face up to his. "Look, Nab, just push off. The place is crawling with traps and I've got nothing for you."

Parrus looked questioningly at Tomas as the little man disappeared into the crowded stable yard.

"Customer," muttered Tomas.

We mounted up and left Glassybri as quickly as we could.

·5·

It was only after we had been traveling for two hours that I started to feel we had got away and stopped looking back for pursuers. That afternoon I rode behind Tomas, in order to give Parrus' horse a spell. Parrus' sulks did not last long and he began pointing out interesting sights and chatting to me, which I knew he meant, and I accepted, as an apology.

It stopped raining, though the sky was still cloudy. The country we were traveling through was not so very different from the area of Gallia we had left behind. Low rolling hills were topped with stands of mountain ash and sweet oil trees. I had never traveled in this part of Moria before. I had spent most of my life in the north near the capital Mangalore, where the countryside was far less fertile, and my foster father and I had left Moria by traveling through the wild and sparsely settled mountains there into the Tyronic Duchies. Here in Middle Moria the wide valleys were full of villages clustered around churches or monasteries, and small neat farms surrounded with great wheat fields and fruit trees covered in blossom. Morian houses were noticeably neater and whiter than Gallian houses. In fact, they were noticeably neater and whiter than I remembered them being up north, too. It did not take me long to realize why. Almost everyone we passed on the road wore the grey and black of the Church of the Burning Light. The presence of so many of these aggressively respectable people had affected the whole look of the countryside.

We passed troops of militiamen, all of them in grey and black, marching along the road or assembling in the fields. After we had passed the fifth or sixth group, I asked Hamel, "Surely there were not always so many Burning Light worshippers in these parts. I'd thought it was a northern sect."

"Ah, but they have made many converts since the Revolution. The hierarchs have seen to it that the monasteries hereabouts favour Burning Light believers as tenants. No doubt it is the hierarchs' plan to have as many loyalists as possible here to act as a bulwark against Gallian influences, but rents are low and it has been an opportunity for many of the landless. And the countryside looks well for it, doesn't it? It's never been so prosperous or so heavily settled."

"Aye," said Tomas. "But don't be fooled by the fact that no one seems interested in us. Their beady little eyes are watching. The local witchfinders will have a very good idea of our movements."

His words took the shine off the pretty countryside. I could not help thinking of the witchfinders peering out from behind the shutters of the neat little villages we passed through, like hungry cats peering through the bars of a birdcage.

The Church of the Burning Light. They were a sect of extreme Aumazites who believed we could bring about the Holy City of Tanza on earth by following his teachings to the letter. They wore only black and grey and lived strictly and simply, avoiding finery, drinking, and other forms of wild living, and attending church several times a week. More importantly, they believed that all magic not used by the church was evil. When they had come to power five years before, they had forbidden all non-church mages and healers to practice magic of any sort, and had arrested and burned those who had disobeyed. Eventually the only sensible course of action had been to go into exile. What a bitter time that had been. Even when we were refugees in the city of Gallia, in the days when it still welcomed members of the

Burning Light, they had made my life difficult. When they realized I was a Morian mage they had spat at me or cursed me. One or two of them had even sought my death.

This made me think of Darmen Stalker and something he had said.

"What was it that priest said about reclaiming the Plain of Despair?" I asked Hamel.

"Apparently the Church of the Burning Light has a project to make it fertile land again," said Hamel. "I wish them luck with it. I don't doubt it must be a hard task. Have they got very far with it, Tomas?"

"I can't say. I asked about it when I was down South. Supposedly they are building a monastery out there on the site of Ruinac, the old capital. I've never met anyone who went there by choice. It's one of the things they do with all the prisoners the Hand of Truth takes, and in the South they have surely taken a lot."

"Hand of Truth?" asked Parrus

"Aye, the branch of the witchfinders that deals with blasphemy that is not necessarily related to magic."

"This Great Waste, this is the place they also call the Plain of Despair, isn't it? The place where Smazor's Run occurred?" asked Parrus. "Why haven't they tried to reclaim the land before? It was the best part of Moria before that disaster, wasn't it?"

Even though Parrus was a Gallian, he knew all about Smazor's Run, when a slave demon had accidently been set free by his master's death and had killed nearly half Moria's population. Much of Morian history since then, its poverty, its backwardness, its dislike of mages, even the rise of the Burning Light, stemmed from that dark day.

"Well, it's the worst part of Moria now," said Tomas. "After a fire, plants grow back in the ash, but after Smazor's Run, though it's been over a hundred years since then, there is still nothing but ash in the Great Waste, great clouds of it blowing in the wind. They say Smazor sucked the life out of the very soil and it needs magic to put it back in. I never met anyone who went there by choice. That's why the Burning Light are using convict labor. It's a fearsome place. Only ghosts and nightmares live there.''

"In Gallia I heard the Duke intends to try to reclaim the Wasteland when Lady Julia regains the throne,'' said Hamel. "I will be glad if he takes that on.''

I heard Parrus laugh. "That'll be interesting. I doubt that cunning Leon Sahr will feel any shame about taking credit for something that the Burning Light has started for him.''

It was almost dark and we were already talking of stopping for the night when we came upon a disturbing sight. On a lonely stretch of road a young woman had been taken with a fit.

I will never forget how helpless I felt as I sat beside her watching her lying there, thrashing the ground with her arms and legs, bashing her head back and forth on the cloak I had placed under it. Grit and blood flecked the foam at her mouth. Her basket lay tumbled at her side and broken eggs littered the ground.

One spell, I thought sadly. *One little spell would lift this.* I did what I could to lessen the fit, preventing her from hurting herself too much and holding a phial of soothing oil under her nose, but all we could really do was wait for it to run its course.

Hamel had gone to see if he could get help, but Tomas stood beside me.

"I hate this,'' I said to him. "I wish I could do something more.''

"I know,'' said Tomas. "But don't, please. The girl's probably lived with this for the last five years. She can surely live with it a few more weeks.''

"Aye,'' I said miserably.

Five or six treatments with a specialist healer and possibly the woman might never have another fit again. She would certainly have fewer of them. It would be useless suggesting it to her, however. She wore black and grey and no doubt her family would never hear of such a thing. I wondered if there was any priest in Moria capable of performing such delicate healing.

"Isn't there anything more you can do?" said Parrus in a distressed voice. He was holding the horses nearby. "Honestly," he went on. "This is an insane country. What sane person would choose to have falling sickness?"

If it had been Tomas who had said that I would have agreed wholeheartedly, but somehow I felt a need to defend my countrymen to Parrus.

"They haven't turned their backs on healing completely," I said. "It's just that they believe that all magics should be performed by priests or nuns and there are not enough priests with the right training to go around yet. In time it could be a workable system."

"And in the meantime, people suffer from curable things. Great!"

Just then the woman began to come out of the fit. She was weeping and distressed to find strangers leaning over her. I did my best to reassure her in my best healer manner as Tomas and I wrapped her in a blanket. I dosed her with a little herbal sleeping potion and she soon fell into an exhausted post-fit sleep with her head in my lap.

Shortly after that Hamel came back, bringing with him a tall man driving a light pony cart.

"I met the lady's brother coming to look for her," he explained.

The two of them gently lifted the woman onto the cart.

"Mortality here has offered us lodging for the night," said Hamel.

"Well, thank you," said Tomas. "We would be very glad of that."

"What?!" I hissed in Gallian. Parrus looked horrified. Tomas squeezed my arm warningly.

"Have a heart, sister," he said cheerily in Morian. "It's growing dark and there's more rain coming."

I could equally cheerily have strangled him.

Mortality Genez was a gentle, dreamy man not at all the sharp-tongued sharp-eyed zealot I associated with the Burning Light. I could not imagine him cursing or spitting on anybody. He insisted I ride on the cart with him, fussing over my warmth and comfort and showing a genuinely sympathetic interest in my journey to the bed of my sick sister. It was hard not to like him.

He lived in a thatched farmhouse set around a courtyard. As we turned into the courtyard, a group of women came rushing out of the house, exclaiming over the woman in the back of the cart.

"My mother Juba, my sister Mercy of Thy Hands, my brother's wife, Great Light Shall Return," said Mortality by way of introduction.

His sick sister's name was Voice of Grace. His brother, Obedience, carried her into the house with the mother fussing around her like a hen around a chick, but the sisters waited to draw me down from the cart and took me into the kitchen to stand before the fire, where they took my damp cloak, plied me with refreshments and food, and asked me all about Gallia, forcing me to elaborate on the story we had worked out. I wished I could be with the men in the stableyard where I could see them unsaddling the horses.

It was not to be, however. Men and women among the Burning Light seemed to lead even more separate lives than normal people did, and so I sat in the kitchen until it was time for dinner. Even then we did not sit with the men, but served them at the table, waiting till they had finished before we ourselves ate in the kitchen.

Parrus was highly amused by the situation. Had I dared, I would have kicked his shin several times during the meal, for he winked and carried on, ordering me about and calling me "woman."

"My wife has a servant," he told the others. "No doubt she thinks such tasks beneath her."

"The care of men for women finds its echo in the care of women for men," quoted Mortality as if from a holy book. After that gentle criticism Parrus toned it down. The Burning Light men were unfailingly polite and addressed all the women with the honorific Enna.

Though the conversation flowed over dinner, oddly enough the invasion, a topic which must have been on everybody's mind, did not come up. The Burning Light people probably thought, and quite rightly, that we were from the part of the Morian population which would welcome the return of Julia Madraga with open arms. Although references were made to the fact that Mortality, Obedience, and the two hired men had been training for several hours a day in one of the parish militias that would be defending Glassybri, most of the talk was of crops and the price of good horses. I had a sense that they were not sure when, or even if, the invasion would come.

Despite my bitter past, I could not help liking them very much. I wished that they all lived in Cardun where the invasion of Moria was so irrelevant that we had not even known of it last week. After dinner, when we women sat in the kitchen again, several people came to the door begging and were all given a warm welcome. Juba washed and dressed the wounds of an old man. Till then I had not thought of Burning Light people as capable of being good and kind. I could not help feeling guilty at deceiving them. I had to keep reminding myself that it only needed a small slip on my part to turn all that warmth into vitriol.

Voice of Grace, having been ill, was to sleep with her mother. I was offered her bed in a room she shared with her sister. I dreaded sharing a room with one of the Burning Light and wondered whether I should insist on sleeping with my "husband" in the hayloft, but I found that they had placed a screen between the two beds so that I had my own private little cubicle and I was able to undress for bed without fear of my iron necklace being seen.

The next morning as we were leaving, Voice of Grace came to bid me farewell and to thank me.

She was a pretty young woman, but she was probably doomed to be the unmarried sister in the households of her brothers. Only a very committed man would have wanted to marry someone with falling sickness.

"In Gallia, they have healers who could cure your condition," I said softly to her, leaning down from my horse.

Her face lit up for a moment, then her head dropped. "Healers," she murmured.

"We pray often for my sister," said Mortality sadly. "It seems to be the will of Tansa that she suffers so. Perhaps she bears the burden of some family sin. Perhaps Tansa will release her one day."

"Mortality," said Tomas suddenly, "I saw the Gallian army of invasion when I was in Gallia. It was a very big army. It's a hard fight you'll be facing. I urge you to get your womenfolk as far away from here as you can, and soon. They expect the army at the border in a few days."

"I thank you brother," said Mortality. "But the Church has taken steps for the care of our womenfolk already. When the invaders reach the border, they will be setting out for the South and Sanctuary."

"Sanctuary," cried Tomas. "Good God! No! Please don't send them there. We have heard rumors of Sanctuary that bode ill. Reports from one who had been there. Statues that spoke and signs of demons and necromancy. It is in the Wasteland. A trap. If you mean to send them somewhere safe, send them to me. My family has an inn in Annac called the Inn of the Holy Hands. I swear to you I'll try to keep them safe for the sake of your generosity to us."

"Necromancy," smiled Mortality. The word had relieved rather than worried him. "Those who wish to discredit people always cry necromancy at them. I have seen no such thing in our Church and I doubt it exists. Do not be afraid for us. Our faith has never let us down. God and his Holy Son will protect us as is best for us."

Although Tomas repeated his urgings, he would not be swayed.

"Religious fanatic!" muttered Parrus. "What a fool!"

Yet I could tell that, like the rest of us, his heart was darkened with forebodings for these kind people.

The following day's travel was uneventful. The weather cleared. Rain was replaced by soft spring sunshine. The country became wilder. There were fewer farms and more woodlands and the houses we passed were not as pristinely whitewashed. We saw fewer and fewer Burning Light followers and more and more ordinary Morians.

The low rolling hills continued. Except for the mountainous region around Mangalore, which formed a strong barrier against the Holy States and the Tyronic Duchies, most of Moria was low rolling hills. Then the Red Mountains formed a kind of spine down the middle of the country and beyond that was the great coastal plain that had once been the richest and most populous area of Gallia and was now the Great Waste.

It was such a clear night that we did not stay at an inn, but stopped under a low spreading pine tree by the roadside. We built a large fire and ate the food that Juba had given us that morning. I for one was glad of the privacy. Though there were fewer Burning Light people about, plenty of ordinary Morians disliked mages and you could not tell who was your friend. Here we could talk about things. For the first time I showed Parrus my amazing iron necklace. He handled it gingerly, but with fascination.

"Do you think it could have some magic?" I asked him.

"I don't sense anything," he said. "Have your immensely superior senses felt anything?"

I stuck my tongue out at him.

"It's Wanderer make," said Tomas. "Look at these runes on it."

I had not really looked at the runes before. Most of them were completely new to me.

I asked Tomas if he knew the meaning of them, but he shook his head and said, "I never learned anything of runes."

"Marnie used to say that Wanderer magic works differently from ours," said Hamel. "She said they used more runes and that it was more powerful for that."

"Rune magic?" said Parrus, looking skeptical but nonetheless interested. "What do you mean? The Wanderers are just fairground fakes or hedge mages at best. They wouldn't have the skill to use runes. And magic is magic. What on earth do you mean by different magic?''

''More runes I suppose,'' said Hamel, looking uncomfortable. ''Look, I don't know much about it. All I know is that Marnie told me Wanderer magic is much more powerful than we give it credit for.''

''Oh, come on, that's just a legend, isn't it?'' said Parrus. ''Like that story about Wanderers being a great race of mages who sat at the right hand side of the old kings of Moria. Where has that magic gone, then? You never see Wanderers at the White Colleges.''

I'd heard those legends too and was still unsure whether to believe them or not, but Tomas seemed to have no such doubts.

''That's no legend,'' he said. ''Anyone who has studied history will tell you it's a fact. When our people came to the peninsula from Aramaya, the Wanderers were here. They were a tribe called the Klementari, a tribe of very powerful mages. The New People, as they call us, could not defeat them, so the kings of Moria were forced to deal with them. The Madragas sometimes formed marriage alliances with them. There's a lot of Klementari blood in the Madragas. The Klementari in their turn helped the Madragas to forge a kingdom when all the other rulers on the peninsula could only control small dukedoms and principalities. Four hundred years of continous rule is quite an achievement for one family. As a symbol of this alliance, it became the custom for the Klementari to place the crown on the head of the ruler, using an iron regalia that they had made for the Madragas. A form of this custom has survived Smazor's Run. Up until the Revolution of Souls, the fact that the greatest mage of the realm always crowned our ruler often caused trouble with the Patriarch.''

''Presuming you are right,'' said Parrus, ''what happened to these wonderful Klementari to make them the drunken layabouts you see nowadays?''

''Smazor's Run is what happened,'' said Tomas. ''See, the Klementari had a very special relationship with their homeland Ernundra. Some say there was a race of spirits who lived there and guided them. Ernundra was on the other side of the Red Mountains along the Basane river, and it was destroyed by Smazor—and most of the Wanderer race with it. Some of those who survived killed themselves. The rest wandered bereft and became called Wanderers. Since then many of them have tried to forget their heritage and become like the rest of us. You see Morians with Wanderer faces all over Southern and Central Moria—the product of marriages or of people who settled down and tried to become Morians.''

Tomas nodded at me.

''It must have been what our grandmother hoped for when she left the six-year-old Marnie with Joseph Holyhands. But the old people say bloodlines will show and it was certainly true of Marnie. She never really managed to become one of the New People. In the end she turned her back on trying.''

He turned back to Parrus. ''I've spoken to learned men who've seen this in books. It's not just legend. And don't think that because the Wanderers don't go to your White Colleges that they have no powers. I've seen Wanderers do things that would surprise you.''

''Fair enough,'' said Parrus, uncomfortable at Tomas' intensity. I could see he was still unbelieving, but fortunately he was too polite to say so. A slightly strained silence fell on the group.

After a few minutes Hamel thoughtfully brought up a new subject. ''I suppose with the Madragas back on the throne, things will be back the way they were with magic in this country,'' he said.

''That can only be a good thing,'' I said, but I was interrupted by Tomas, who said a little grimly, ''It won't be the Madragas, brother. It will be the Sahrs of Gallia on the throne.''

''Surely the Duke will just be a consort,'' said Hamel. ''He won't actually rule. He's a foreigner. The electors would never stand for a foreigner.''

''Well it's unlikely that they would put a woman on the

throne," said Parrus. "And believe you me, Leon of Gallia is not going to spend all that money and manpower just to give a present to his betrothed. He's not a man who shares power."

"There have been woman rulers of Moria before," said Hamel.

"There always seem to be woman rulers in legend," said Parrus gently. "But can you see the Lords of Moria nowadays minding a woman ruler? The Lords of Gallia mind Leon Sahr well enough, though, and the Lords of Moria will too."

"Parrus is right," I said. "Duke Leon is good at keeping the peace, and that is the most important thing a ruler can bring a country. What do any of us know about Julia Madraga?"

Parrus grinned at me and patted my cheek.

"Bless women," he said. "They see things so simply and practically."

We did not set a watch that night.

"We'll be safe enough," said Tomas. "Now that you need to have a travel pass to move around the countryside, most of the robbers are in Burning Light prisons. It's about the only good thing the Burning Light has done for this country."

Yet when I awoke with a start later that night, Tomas was sitting awake.

I had woken out of dreams I could not remember, feeling uneasy. Someone was looking for me. I awoke suddenly and lay as still as possible for some moments, looking for the watcher. I was glad when I saw Tomas awake, though I couldn't seem to convince myself that he was the watcher I had sensed. He wasn't even looking at me. He was staring grim-faced into the fire.

"Is all well?" I asked.

He started. "Oh, aye! I could not sleep."

"Did you dream?"

"No, nothing like that," he said. "In fact I could almost

wish I had. At least when I dreamt of the stone woman, I knew Tasha was alive.''

It was difficult to answer this remark.

"What kind of woman is Tasha?'' I asked him, thinking it might comfort him to talk of her.

"Difficult,'' said Tomas. "Sometimes she was very difficult to care for. Once Karac left and there was the child . . . she was often angry, often in black despair. She drank. Yet when she was in a good mood . . . oh, Dion, she sparkled. Even in her cups she was a fine healer. She might have been a fine mage had she had your opportunities. If only she'd been more lucky.'' He was silent for a moment.

"But there was something about her, something that seemed to almost grab onto ill-luck, to magnify it. To be an estranged twin, to have a bastard child, to have powers of magery when such things are forbidden—they are all things that can be got over or lived with. They are things other people lived with. But they tormented her, and the torment was what made her so difficult. I knew it and it used to make me crazy. If only I could have been more patient with her. Maybe she wouldn't have gone.''

Three years of being a healer, attending the grieving and guilt-stricken living as much as the sick and dying, had made me familiar with such monologues, but not hardened to them. I still felt a terrible inadequacy in the face of others' mental anguish. I suspect it is inevitable. I did my best.

"Don't blame yourself,'' I said. "Do you really think you could have made her happy? You can't make other people be happy.''

"Aye, you're right, of course. But I can't help feeling. . . . I am the oldest brother—the head of the family, for what it's worth.''

His voice trailed off.

"So why did she go after this Stalker man?''

"All that unused magic was becoming a torment to her. She said once that it was like having your spirit filled with congealed porridge. In the last year I've thought several times that she was losing her mind. I think she did too.

Sometimes it was as if she didn't know where she was. She went off into the forest once and after two days I found her hiding in a fox's den, covered in dirt and dead leaves, out of her mind, babbling something about angels of vengeance made of fire. I should have found some way to send her into Gallia, but somehow. . . . Well, she wouldn't go anyway. I never understood that.''

"Sounds like you did what you could.''

"You know, she joined the Sisters of Light at one stage,'' he went on. "That's right, your sister was a Burning Light nun at the convent in Lammerquais. They work as healers, so it seemed like a good place for Tasha. At first. That was a year of troubles—well, not a year. She only lasted there eight months. She was always being given penance for disobedience. It was a very strict place and she just couldn't seem to knuckle under.''

"What happened?''

"What happened? She got pregnant, that's what happened. And they threw her out, of course, because chastity is one of their watchwords. Oh, Tasha. I mean, I would have thought it took real effort to get pregnant in a convent, but Tasha. . . . Sweet Tanza, she was infuriating sometimes. Of course she must have wanted to do it. To escape. She didn't want to disappoint me by just leaving, I see that now. I was worried about her and I pushed her to stay. I thought the discipline might give her some sense of place. What a fool I was.''

"You did what you thought was best, Tomas.''

"I should have done better, Dion. Then she might not have gone.''

"No,'' I said. ''I'm sure not.''

He shook his head and went back to staring into the fire.

I judged it best not to push him. There seem to be times when it is better to leave people with their own thoughts.

I got up and ducked out under the low-hanging branches. It was chilly beyond the firelight, but clear and crisp, sparkling on the skin. The pale white moon shone high and full in the black dome of the sky. There was a small track leading past our campsite. I wandered down it a little way and stood staring back at our campfire through the trees. The moon was so bright it was almost like day.

"Was I not right, Enna Dion?"

I almost jumped out of my skin.

Beside the track where I stood was a high tree stump. A man sat perched upon it. I jumped back so that I was well out of reach.

"Who . . . !?"

"So you don't remember me, Enna Dion? I told you that we would be returning to Moria and here we both are."

The raven. The Wanderer on my woodpile. Yes, it was that same old, young face.

"What's going on?" Tomas had come out from under the pine and was coming towards us, his hand on his knife hilt. "Who the hell are you?"

The man jumped lithely down from his perch. He drew himself up and pushed the great dark cloak he wore back over his shoulders.

"I am Symon," he said. "I am the Raven."

I was startled by the strange coincidence of it, but Tomas' reaction was even more startling.

"Aumaz!" he cried. He caught my arm and tried to whirl me round at the same time as he pushed me behind him. Naturally I stumbled and almost fell.

"What business has the Lord of Ill Times with us?" said Tomas, pushing me back towards the cover of the tree.

"My, my, Tomas Holyhands," said the voice of the Raven in the darkness, admiringly. "You are knowledgable."

"What's going on?" I cried. "He wasn't hurting me, Tomas. I'm sorry about my brother, Ren Symon."

"Don't speak to him, Dion," said Tomas. "The living should not speak to those defiled by blood."

"It's too late for either of you," said the man. "Those people you spoke to at the border crossroads were not ordinary Wanderers but a group of the Dead. And Enna Dion is most certainly defiled. She has killed two men."

By the Seven! He knew about Norval and my would be assassin.

"How do you know that?" I cried.

He tossed back his cloak again. It flapped like the wings of a great black bird.

"I am the Raven," he said simply. "I know many things. Among them, I know that it is cold and I have traveled far and you have fire and food over there and yet you have not invited me to share it."

I could feel Tomas' tension beside me. He looked nervously around at the darkness.

"What are you doing here?" he said. I could not get over how unfriendly he was being.

"Just passing," said the Wanderer. "Calling upon Enna Dion, who is an acquaintance. Don't be afraid Tomas. If I wished to call down my hordes upon you, don't you think you would already be dead?" He turned and smiled at me and his eyes glittered in the moonlight. "I could not hope to take Enna Dion except by surprise."

And then he was moving past us and toward the fire.

Tomas looked anxiously back into the darkness and hurried after him, pulling me behind him.

I studied Symon in the firelight. That ancient boy's face. It was not that he was young. The skin stretched over his cheekbones was soft with age, not youth, and there were wrinkles around his eyes. He simply had a guileless quality about him like a boy does, except that his guileless quality seemed at the same time to speak of great cunning.

Hamel was already sitting up, not showing any surprise at the sudden appearance of this strange Wanderer. He just watched. I suspected he was armed beneath the blanket round his waist, for I noticed that the sheath of his sword was empty. Parrus too was tensely awake.

I opened one of the packs.

"I remember you liked cheese."

"I dote upon it, Enna Dion," said Symon. "And I will have a little bread this time, if you have any."

He tore the pieces of bread and cheese off with long white

fingers that reminded me of claws. He was a tall, thin man, but he sat hunched in a way that disguised his size. His stance reminded me of a raven. Was he some kind of shape-shifter? I had felt no frisson of magic in his prescence.

"Who's he?" hissed Parrus in my ear as I sat down.

"I am the Wanderer Raven," said Symon.

"What . . ."

"The Raven is the Wanderer war leader. A defiled bird of ill omen and destruction," said Symon calmly.

Parrus blinked.

"Surely the Wanderers don't. . . . They are a peaceful people. Everyone knows that."

"And that is what we would have you think. But since your people came to the peninsula, war bands have always existed among the Wanderers. They live separately from the families, so that they might not pollute them with their knowledge of violence. They are called the Dead, because only the dead should live among death."

"But a Raven is only ever elected to the Council of Six when the Wanderers are at war," said Tomas. He offered the Wanderer a cup of ale. "Are the Wanderers at war?"

"The Wanderers are moving to return to our homeland. We will fight anyone who dares to try and stop us."

"Surely you can rely on the Duke of Gallia to fight the way back into Moria?"

"No, Tomas Holyhands, you do not understand. We are going back to Ernundra, our true homeland in the place you call the Plain of Despair. We have been Wanderers long enough. Only the homeland can cleanse the sickness in our spirits and make us back into the Klementari."

"But isn't that place a wasteland?" I said, too fascinated to be formal with this obviously important person. "It's barren. Nothing lives there."

"Oh, things can be made to live there with enough work and power. That is not the point. It is our homeland. We should never have abandoned it. All this . . . wandering, living like fairground fortune tellers, the exile, even from Moria, it is punishment for our wrongdoing. To be blessed again we must cease to be disloyal to the place where we belong. We must return to it.''

"So what are you doing here?'' said Parrus. He too was fascinated, too fascinated to be his usual sarcastic self. "Won't they burn you for a witch?''

"If they catch me indeed they will. If they can spare the time from Duke Leon Sahr. He will be across the border in a few days' time. And they won't catch me before he comes. The Wanderers were once a great people, Parrus Lavelle, though I know you and your kind doubt it. We still have the seeds of greatness in us. Once, the New People married us, became our allies, and relied on our power. That time is coming again.''

He stood and his shadow fell darkly over us.

"I thank you for your hospitality, Enna Dion, and look to the day when I shall be able to repay you.''

He shrugged his great black cloak over himself and turned to Tomas, who had risen with him.

"You are worried for your sister, Tasha. But you shall not have to worry much longer.''

He stepped away from the fire, out through the branches and was gone.

"Raven,'' cried Tomas, pushing out after him. "Tell me! Wait!''

But there was nobody out beyond the branches.

Tomas was searching around the tree. I stood looking out over the empty field still white with moonlight. A dark bird was flying low across the trees. Was that. . . . No. This was Moria under the witchfinders. Nobody could cast that kind of magic here.

"Impressive exit,'' said Parrus at my elbow. "Fellow should have been an actor. That was really peculiar. Where did he come from? And what did he come for?''

"He said he was passing by,'' I told him.

"Just dropped in for a chat, did he?'' said Parrus wryly.

"It was as if he came to tell us those things,'' said Hamel. "He left when he finished.''

"Do you think he meant it as a foretelling? What he said

about not needing to worry about Tasha much longer?'' said Tomas.

"Now, brother, what were you telling us about foretellings? Don't get your hopes up.''

I caught Parrus grinning at Tomas' remark and scowled at him. He dropped his eyes discreetly, but I could tell the whole incident amused him. *Typical superstitious Morians* was what he'd be thinking now. I couldn't say I blamed him. I had heard of the Klementari and their powers as a child, but my foster father, even though he had been a Morian, had told me they were the stuff of legend, not something educated people believed in.

Yet when I lay down by the fire again, I could not sleep. I was conscious of a certain exhilaration. It wasn't just the way he had talked of returning to their homeland, of fighting anyone who attempted to stop them, though there was a sense of heroism in that which caught my imagination. I felt as if I had seen something strange, as if I had been touched by the weirdness that is a proper part of magic but too often dispelled by the White College of Mages and all the mundane rituals of everyday life. While I knew it was ridiculous, I kept thinking of that great black bird flying across the moon.

We traveled hard for the next two days, starting early and finishing after dark and staying at inns, which gave Parrus and I the joyful opportunity to make the most of our supposed status as a married couple. By this time I was almost certain that Tomas hoped that Parrus and I would eventually make a match of it despite our considerable social distance. I didn't let myself worry about what he thought. I knew perfectly well that Parrus would never care for me that much. Tomas would find out soon enough, foolish fellow, and for the moment he was too concerned about Tasha to try anything embarrassing.

I couldn't help being glad Parrus had come, and not just for physical reasons. I'd known him for much longer than my brothers and sometimes it was good to have someone to roll my eyes at. Sometimes Tomas could be very bossy, and as for Hamel, he finally revealed that his beloved wife, Radiance, was a member of the Burning Light and that he had given permission for her to bring up his son Shine in her faith.

"But what does she say about your family background?" I said. He just shrugged and said there was a lot to be said for having the Church control magecraft.

The last morning of our journey Tomas was in a fever. He'd been persuaded to stop overnight only by the strongest arguments. He would have preferred to have continued through the night to Annac, which was only half a day's journey away, and he roused us out of bed well before dawn the next morning.

It availed us nothing, however, for halfway through the morning we became caught up behind a prison caravan and were forced to follow it for several miles. Tomas was bitterly impatient, but there were deep ditches on either side of the road and beyond stretched muddy fields of new wheat that would have made even slower going. The heavily guarded wagons were impossible to pass, and whenever we went through a village, people gathered by the road to watch. Sometimes small groups of people, most of them Burning Light but some of them not, would start singing hymns about Holy Tansa and his healing fire, but mostly people just stared with fearful eyes. The sight of those white-faced prisoners with heavy iron manacles around their necks and wrists filled me with dread. I had come to Moria to perform an illegal act, and maybe next week I'd be in one of those wagons too. I was glad when we came to the turnoff to Annac.

As we came closer to our journey's end, I scanned the countryside trying to recognize things. Nothing looked particularly familiar. I had expected to feel excited at returning to a place so long in the past, but my main feeling was apprehension. It was not just that I would soon have to do that searching spell. It was Annac itself. What would it be like? Perhaps I would hate it. Maybe the rest of my family were terrible people. What if they didn't like me?

·6·

Finally we crested the hill and there was Annac, the village where I had been born, a cluster of whitewashed houses snuggled around the spike-roofed church and huge white-walled monastery which stood at the top of the high hill before us. The hill and valley beneath it were like a hundred we had seen before; dotted with sheep pastures, wheat fields, and orchards. The gaily painted shapes and the white pathway of the the Holy Way of Annac winding up the hill made the only real difference.

We did not have long to look at it. Suddenly Tomas let out a yell.

"Aumaz! She's back. She's back."

Without stopping to explain, he dug his feet into his horse's flanks and set off at a fast gallop.

"Look," cried Hamel to us. He pointed to a long low building at the edge of the village. White sheets hung out of the windows.

"Silva said she'd hang out sheets if Tasha came back. Come on! Let's see!" he cried as he too dug his heels into his horse.

Parrus urged our horse on. After coming so far and with two of us on its back, however, the poor horse couldn't manage more than a fast trot and we were soon well behind.

Down the hill we went, between the fields, and then suddenly we were trotting up the hill between small white houses with thatched roofs and people were turning to stare at us. We had completely lost sight of my brothers.

But just after entering the village we saw the unmistakable sign: a painting of two severed hands, dripping vividly painted red blood at the wrists: the Holy Healing Hands of St. Belkis. It hung over a gateway and we turned sharply and went through two tall gateposts and there, surrounding a courtyard, was the whitewashed inn where I had been born and spent the first four years of my life.

It was a long low rambling building with a dark wood balcony along the second storey. I had remembered it as being huge. My first thought now was *How small it is*. My second was the slightly panicky realization that we were alone in this strange inn courtyard and, apart from the two sweating saddled horses standing in the center of the yard, there was no sign of my brothers.

"Your relatives are the end, Dion," said Parrus. "Which door do you think they've gone in?"

"Hello, can I help you?" said a voice.

A man was standing at the door of a stable. He was quite young and he wore a rough shirt and breeches.

"Yes," said Parrus. "We came in . . ."

"Aumaz!" said the man softly, blinking in surprise. His pleasant blue eyes were fixed intently on my face as if he recognized me. I couldn't remember ever having seen him before. He was very plain with a big nose and and slightly buck teeth, but there was nothing threatening in his stare.

"Who are you?" he asked me.

"I am Parrus Latrides," said Parrus, remembering his Borgenese persona. "And this is my wife, Enna Dion Latrides."

"Dion," said the man. "By Aumaz, little Dion. Well, you do have the look of your mother, cousin." He took my hand.

"And who are you to call my wife cousin?" said Parrus stiffly.

"Oh, I beg your pardon. I'm Mouse. Mouse Holyhands. Do you remember me, Dion? How we used to play ball on those balconies till . . .'' His voice trailed off. Since the incident involved magic, this was hardly surprising.

"Yes," I said quickly, "I remember it well. I remember you too, Mouse, though I would never have recognized you now. We came with Tomas and Hamel." I pointed at the two sweating horses. "Is it true that Tasha's come back?"

"Aye," said Mouse, and a shadow crossed his face. "But there's no reason for rushing off. She's asleep, as Tomas will be finding out now."

Something in his tone made me ask, "How is she?"

"Not well, cousin. Someone has used her very ill. Indeed we've wondered if she'll ever wake up. There seems to be some head injury. I only hope she has not come home to die."

"Perhaps Dion should see her," said Parrus. "She has some skill with healing herbs."

Mouse frowned. It was unwise to make too much of such skills in Moria. "She has a healer with her now."

"A priest?" I said, looking pointedly at Parrus. "Of course. This is Moria, isn't it?"

"Aye. He's an old friend of the family. But you must come inside, Dion. Come in and meet Silva and the rest. I'll wager it must all seem very strange to you after so long. I'm afraid Sonia has gone. You used to be such friends. She married some foreigner from Mangalore, would you believe it? Oh, and Shad. You must meet Shad Forest. He's the fellow who brought our girl home. Shad, come out here and meet Tasha's sister."

A man with dark curly hair stepped out from the darkness of the stable. He was quite a small man, not much taller than me, but he was well built and the hand he offered me was strong. He wore gold rings in each ear in the Wanderer style and there was something that spoke of Wanderer about his face, but otherwise he looked like an ordinary Morian. His shirt hung loosely off his body, showing a tanned hard chest, as if he'd just pulled it on, which no doubt he had. Smiling dark eyes looked into mine.

"Shad found Tasha unconscious by a road somewhere

down South and he was kind enough to bring her home on his way. The man's a saint, quite honestly.''

Shad grinned at Mouse. "Hardly," he said. His voice had the soft lilt of the South. "I would have been a villain to leave her there.''

"And modest with it," said Mouse. "And he works as well. Can't seem to stop him. If only I could find some way to marry him into the family." He smiled good-naturedly, his trouble momentarily forgotten, and put his arm around Shad's shoulders. "Now you come along with us, Ren Forest. People like you should be sitting by the hearthside warming their feet and eating honey cakes, not mucking out stables.''

We followed the two of them across the courtyard. Mouse pushed open a door and before us was a large whitewashed kitchen. There was a huge fireplace at one side, filled with all kinds of pots and pans, and on the other side was a large table flanked by benches. Sitting on one of these, her face in her hands, was a woman. She jumped up the moment we entered, dashing her hand across her eyes. She was stunningly beautiful. Parrus' jaw dropped.

"Silva, look who's here. It's Dion come back to see us. Uncle Louie," Mouse called to an elderly man who was sitting at the seat in the fireplace. "It's little Dion. See, something good has happened. And this is her husband Parrus. He looks a fine fellow, doesn't he?''

Silva took my hand wonderingly. "Dion? You mean my sister. Dion." She stared at me as if she could not believe it. She was tall and slim with deep blue eyes, a little reddened from weeping, and a beautiful fine-skinned face. The hair showing under her kerchief was golden.

"Sweet Tansa, I never expected. . . . Oh, but what I fool I am." She flung her arms around me. "Welcome. Welcome. Dion, you are most welcome. Oh, but it's good to see you. I never expected to see you again and here you are. Well, you find us in a crisis at the moment, but we are still able to give welcome to such wonderful guests. Please sit down. You must be Parrus. I am your sister-in-law, then.''

There was a shaking of hands all around and Silva herded us onto benches and capably plied us with refreshments. As she brought a jug of ale and glasses, her every movement flowed with grace. I could tell Parrus approved of her.

We were introduced again to Mouse's maternal uncle, Louie Greve, who everyone seemed to call Uncle Louie, and the six of us sat at the bench and made stilted conversation, stilted on their side because it was obvious my family were all listening for movements upstairs and on our side because both Parrus and I were embarrassed now about our false marital status and reluctant to trot out the lies Tomas had formulated for us. The presence of Shad, who was a totally unknown quantity, made it necessary, however. He on his side told us that he was a woodcarver on his way to seek employment in the Holy States.

Suddenly, Tomas erupted into the room.

"Sweet Tansa, Silva. Who did this to her? How did she get here? Tell me!" His face was tight, his eyes full of anger and grief.

"Shad here . . ."

Shad stood up and offered a hand.

"Shad Forest. A friend and I found your sister about a month ago. Near the Red Mountains."

Tomas grabbed Shad's arm and almost pulled him over the table.

"Who did this to her? I'll kill him."

"Tomas!" cried Mouse and Silva anxiously.

There was sympathy in Shad's eyes. He gripped Tomas' arm firmly and looked him in the face.

"There are a lot of bandits in the Red Mountains," he said calmly. "I'd say it'd be them. I found her left for dead this side of the mountains near a place call Memit. But there's no point going down there looking for revenge. They'll be long gone now."

"Bandits? She's been gone three months."

"I know," said Shad grimly. "Doesn't bear thinking of, does it? I myself have wished I could kill men who do such things."

His eyes were full of understanding as he stood calmly in Tomas' grip and for a moment it seemed to calm my brother. But only for a moment.

"Aumaz! Is there nothing to be done?" he cried suddenly, lashing out and throwing a jug onto the floor.

"Now Tomas, don't start breaking the place up," said Uncle Louie sharply. His thin face was dour and stern. "Stop acting like a wounded bull. You're no more to blame than I am."

Hamel came into the room. "Dion," he said. "I wonder if you could take a look at Tasha and . . ."

He stopped short, seeing Shad.

"I'd like very much to see her," I said, getting up and going out of the room with him.

"Isn't there some priest with her?" I hissed, stopping him in the hallway.

"Priest? Oh, Brother Alcumund. There's no need to worry about him. He knows all our secrets."

I hoped he was right.

Tasha lay in a little whitewashed room off a long narrow corridor.

A grey-haired man in the rough brown habit of a monk was leaning over the head of the bed, and a girl of about fourteen or so was hovering at its foot.

"This is Dally, Tasha's daughter," said Hamel, waving at the girl, who hardly looked at us. "And this is Brother Alcumund. This is our sister Dion. I think she might be able to help you."

"Dion?" said the monk, startled. "The baby sister?"

"Aye. We ran into her in Gallia. Persuaded her to come home to help search for Tasha. She's been a healer."

I could have kicked Hamel for telling the monk that, but Brother Alcumund just moved aside with a measuring glance.

I looked down and was instantly filled with leaden horror. It was not the fading remnants of the scars that covered the pale face of the sleeping woman, or the bandaged hands that looked disturbingly shapeless as they lay on the blanket; it was the sleep, the heavy, almost deathlike sleep she lay in that made her chest heave painfully as she breathed. I had seen this same white-faced sleep of deep exhaustion before. One summer in Gallia City, the poor had been plagued with it.

"What is it?" said the girl urgently.

"How long has she been like this?"

"We've been unable to wake her since she was brought home yesterday morning," said Brother Alcumund. "I can't understand it. The injuries to her head do not seem to warrant it. She's not unconscious. She's just deeply asleep."

"Have you got a healer's lens? Have you looked at her life force?"

"Yes." Brother Alcumund pulled a lens on a chain from over his neck. Being a member of the clergy, he was allowed to carry such things. "It is terrible to see. She has almost no life force left. It's as if she's about to die."

I did not need to look through the glass to know what he said was true. My heart was freezing within me. I already knew what my half-sister was suffering from. The exhausted sleep and the spent life force were not an illness. Something terrible had happened to Tasha in the time she had disappeared; a terrible thing with terrible implications.

A demon had fed upon her.

I couldn't suppress a gasp. Here was cruel proof of necromancy, of the truth of those dreams. Maybe it was only a servant demon, still trapped in its own world, being rewarded with tidbits like poor Tasha. Then again maybe it was bound and living in this world as Andre/Bedazzer had been, waiting to maneuver its master into a fatal error so it might be free— as Smazor had been freed.

"Do you know this sickness?" demanded Tomas from the doorway.

"Yes. I have seen it before." I looked around the room. What could I tell them? I didn't want to tell them anything. It would have made it true and it couldn't be true. I looked at Tasha again. It was true.

"Dion," said Hamel, touching my arm.

"What is it?" cried the girl again. "Tell us!"

"It's ... called Summer Sleep," I said, mentioning a harmless name that had been used for it and not the more insulting and common name of Whore Sleep. "It doesn't have to be fatal. I've seen it in Gallia. She'll wake up in a few hours now. When she wakes you must milk a cow and then you must cut one of its small blood vessels and put some fresh blood in the milk. The illness destroys the life force. It needs replacing."

"Sweet Tansa, Dion! You mean she can recover?"

"A little, Hamel. Not fully."

"They've had this in Gallia then?" asked Brother Alcumund.

He was a Morian monk. I looked uncomfortably at him, or rather at his feet. Somehow lying made it worse.

"There was an outbreak four summers ago." I could not bring myself to tell them why, not now. Not without thinking it over. Demons were not the business of ordinary people, especially people bent on revenge like Tomas. "We were never really sure of the cause. But we found this regimen of fresh milk and fresh blood improved them."

The woman on the bed stirred.

"She's waking," cried Tomas. "Tasha! Tasha my honey."

"Gently, Tomas!" said Hamel.

Tomas bent over.

"Oh Tash, girl, what have they done to you?"

He touched her face. Her head turned toward his touch and her eyes opened slightly. She stirred and for a moment I recognized the strong-faced woman I had seen when I had touched that lock of her hair back in Gallia. Then she moaned a little and closed her eyes again.

Tomas was desperate to bring her back. He reached out and drew me to the edge of the bed.

"Look, Tash girl. Here is our little sister. Here is Dion come just to see you. Open your eyes and look at her. Dion would love for you to do that."

A sudden great shudder passed through the woman's body

and her eyes started open wide. They were a deep velvet black, as black as night. Her hands thrust out.

Tomas was startled, but eagerly he thrust my hands into hers, crying delightedly, "She wants to look at you, Dion."

Tasha's grip was cold but fierce. She had looked like a fierce woman in my vision. And strong-minded. She must have been strong-minded to have survived so long with her injuries.

She dragged on me, struggling to rise.

"No! Lie still," cried Tomas. "Save your strength."

But somehow she was sitting. She was looking into my face, struggling to speak. A series of grunts was all that came out. There was a terrible emptiness behind her teeth where her tongue should have been. Tomas stopped protesting and took her shoulders, gently supporting her.

She gasped, breath rattling in her lungs, and lifted her heavy bandaged hands to my face. Her eyes were full of grim intent. It was like looking into the face of a bird of prey.

Her damaged hands cupped my cheeks. Her thumbs clamped into my temples like the jaws of a vise. I had taken off the iron necklace, but I could not bring myself to use magic against such a sick woman until it was too late.

Her voice slid into my mind. Suddenly a great flood of noise filled my head.

Voices, voices yowling and wailing, sobbing and screaming. Someone, somewhere, was screaming a terrible scream of agonized terror.

A voice spoke above the roar, a savage magical voice that sounded as if it came from a throat full of thorns.

"Little sister. I waited for you."

"Tasha," said Tomas' voice, far away. "You mustn't! That's magic. They'll see."

God and angels. Her mind was a great blackness, gaping and bloody. I struggled to get away from it, unable to breathe, gasping, drowning, going under into agony.

"Care for my little girl, sister Dion. You must save her from my fate. You can. You must."

The terrible screaming was so close. Coming closer. I was

afraid. Something too terrible was coming. Away. I had to get away.

"You weak bitch!" howled the thorny voice. "You had what I never had. Use it. Use it as I would have used it. Revenge me! Revenge me!"

Oh sweet Mother, the terrible agony. For a moment I felt someone pulling on me; then there was only darkness and screaming.

"Revenge me," howled the voice again and again, and visions began flashing through my head as I fell into that wounded blackness.

A field of green trees . . . a lake full of bones . . . a huge savage dog picking among them. Slaves toiled in a ditch full of blood . . . a great cathedral rose in the distance . . . bone cracked, claws slashed . . . a stone woman, red eyes, a line of arches . . . pain, oh such pain. A man's face staring back over his shoulder, grinning with cruel amusement. Another man, his eyes full of savage animal pleasure. A knife covered in blood, a mouthful of agony, a huge spiked club raised over me, smashing down, smashing, smashing.

A scream ripped through me. Agony. The whip, the fist, the great spikes. Those vicious laughing eyes, the ravenous faces of stone saints. Screaming and screaming. The blackness and the pain, the drawing, wrenching pain, I tried to scream it all away but still it came on and on, an agony that would never stop, never.

Then, *snap!* the darkness fell away. Something hit me hard. The floor. Me. My guts writhing in agony, retching and choking on sobs and vomit, astonished that I was not choking on blood.

In the darkness a voice was calling.

"Dion! Dion! Where are you, little mage?"

I knew that voice. But . . . Who was it? I would answer and find out.

No! Bad idea!

"Dion. Little mage. I know you're there. Come out, come out wherever you are."

It was closer now. Suddenly I was very frightened. It mustn't find me. I crouched down as small as I could . . .

And opened my eyes to light.

I was in a strange room lying on a mattress. There was a killing pain behind my eyes as if my head was twice as full as it should be. My mouth tasted bad and I felt as if someone had kicked me in the stomach.

Someone was kneeling beside the bed. I struggled to rise, but firm hands held me gently back.

"You must be quiet," a voice breathed softly in my ear. "The witchfinders are here and if you make a noise they will know you are here and want to see you."

Witchfinders! I was in Moria, in Annac. Tasha! I saw again the spiked fist, the club, heard the screaming. . . . A hand was clamped over my mouth. A heavy weight came down on my chest.

"No!" hissed a voice. "Stop it. Stop it. You must stop it or witchfinders will kill us both. Calm now."

I clenched myself up, trying not to scream, pushing the memories away.

"That's right. Calm now," whispered the voice. "Calm. Gently." A hand was stroking my hair and my cheek. It was comforting. The weight lifted slowly off my chest. "That's right. Better now?"

The hand stroking my cheek was rough, but pleasantly so. I looked up and saw it was Shad who was leaning over me.

"You mustn't make a sound," he whispered. "Understand?"

I nodded and he pulled his hand carefully away from my mouth.

He helped me sit up, wincing as the change of weight on the mattress made the floor creak slightly, and handed me a cup of water. I drank some of it gratefully and patted the rest over my face.

Shad was listening to something. Voices, the sound of heavy feet a few rooms away. Witchfinders? God and angels! Tasha had used magic and they must have seen it and come. Probably from the monastery. It was horribly close.

We sat there.

A pair of feet came heavily down the passageway towards us. There was the sound of a door being tried on the next room. We tensed.

Then a woman's voice, loud and clear. Silva's.

"You'll need a key to look in there. All these rooms are locked until the Great Pilgrimage. Shall I try and find it for you?"

"No!" The voice was clipped, disapproving.

The woman's voice dropped. "Please, Ren Benis, won't you tell me what you will do with my sister's body? When can we have it back to bury it?"

"You'll not get it back," said the first voice.

Then another voice broke in from further down the hallway.

"She shall be burned, Enna Holyhands! She was a witch and must be burned to purify the land of her pollution. Her ashes will be thrown into a pit of lime. And just consider yourself lucky. We are satisfied for the moment with your tales. But we may well return with a Priest-Mage tomorrow to put you all to the mind search."

A pair of footsteps turned and clumped away.

The first voice spoke again. "Do not fear, Enna Holyhands. I doubt we will return. Brother Alcumund has spoken well for you. But give up this idea of getting your sister's body back. She died deep in sin. She could never lie in hallowed ground."

The two of them moved away from the door and though I heard Silva speak again, I could not hear what she said. Instead I heard another noise, soft and far away. The sound of a man weeping. Somehow I knew it was Tomas.

Shad pulled a relieved face at me.

"Parrus," I hissed at him. "Is he safe?"

"He was in the stable unloading your horse when it happened," murmured Shad. "Hopefully he had the sense to stay there."

I hoped so too. I lay back down on the mattress, listened to my own breathing and resolutely thought of nothing.

* * *

Dark was coming in through the windows. Shad had settled himself at my feet, his back leaning against the wall, and he seemed to have dozed off. My head still felt as if it were stuffed with wool. I had managed not to think about the things I'd seen in Tasha's mind, but now I was having other thoughts that frightened me and they concerned this Shad.

Footsteps came down the passage. Shad's eyes sprang open, but it was Hamel who unlocked and opened the door.

"How are you both? It's safe to come down now."

He helped me up and led me down the stairs. He would have carried me if I'd let him, but I insisted on walking, though if the truth be told my legs felt as shaky as a newborn lamb's and I was glad to lean on him.

He helped me into one of the fireplace seats, tucking a blanket about my legs. "You've had a shock, sister. Stay here and rest and get nice and warm."

Shad had slipped off ahead of us and was now nowhere to be seen.

A savory-smelling stew was bubbling in a pot on the fire. Hamel served me up a bowl of it. I ate slowly. It tasted as good as it smelled. From nearby rose the sounds of a noisy taproom. Silva came rushing in the doorway, ladled stew into two bowls, smiled quickly at me, and rushed out with them. Otherwise the kitchen was empty.

"Taproom's full tonight," said Hamel. "People have heard we had an outbreak of witchcraft here, so of course they all just happened in for a drink. Silva gave the maid a few days off yesterday. Lucky as it turned out. Fewer people really in the know the better."

A fair haired girl of about thirteen came running in, cut a hunk of bread into slices, put it into a bowl, and darted back out again.

"You'll be safe enough here," said Hamel, "but stay here. We don't want too many people seeing you, or there may be difficult questions. I'm going to go home to Medane now. I don't want to leave my family alone any longer. There's been talk of punishing the Burning Light before the Duke comes." He hugged me and kissed my brow. "Take care, sister. I hope to see you again soon."

"Where's Parrus?"

Hamel grinned.

"He's out serving at the bar, would you believe it? Having the time of his life."

He pulled open the door and was gone. I sat there staring at the fire. I was tired to the bone, but otherwise felt nothing more than a vague dismay at Tasha's death. I hardly knew her, I told myself a little guiltily, though unless I kept my thoughts well under control, I knew her better than anyone could wish. I put my too-full head in my hands. Why had she done this to me? It seemed so cruel.

Silva came bustling in again, followed by the fair-haired girl and a small boy of about ten. She brought the children over to me.

"Look, children. This is your Auntie Dion come all the way out of Gallia."

It was odd to hear myself called Auntie. No one had ever found me old enough to do that before.

"These are my children," said Silva. "Needra." The girl bobbed her head respectfully in my direction. "And Derrum." The boy pressed himself against his mother's side. "Don't be shy, my love," she smiled at him. "You will like your Auntie. But now it's time for bed." She turned toward the stairs.

"Silva, there was another child. Tasha's daughter?"

"Oh, yes. Syndal is her name though everyone calls her Dally. She was there in the room. . . . She's upstairs now. Tomas is sitting with her. It's a hard grief for a young girl. But we'll care for her."

The three of them went away up the stairs. A short time later Tomas came downstairs and sat beside me.

"I'm sorry for what happened, Dion. If I'd known what she intended . . ."

"I know."

"I tried to pull you away and I saw some of her horrors

myself. Poor woman! Poor Tasha.'' He squeezed my hand. ''Poor Dion!''

I should tell Tomás about Tasha's sickness. I should. But I wasn't sure that it would be wise. He had shown himself hasty before and this situation needed tact. Instead I sat quietly and listened to him talk about Tasha, apologizing and making excuses for her actions until he had talked himself out. Then I sent him to get Parrus.

A few moments later, Parrus came out of the bar red-faced and grinning cheerfully.

''Whew!'' he said, plumping himself down beside me. ''Tomas said you wanted me.''

I told him what I had recognized about Tasha's illness and its cause.

He stopped grinning.

''By the Seven, Dion, are you certain?''

''I was working as a healer in Gallia then. We didn't know what it was. We called it Whore Sleep until after the demon outbreak, when we found out what it really was. It's the same thing. I'm sure of it. Parrus, I'm worried about that Shad person. He brought her back and that's well enough, but what if he's connected with her illness in the first place?''

''Now come on, Dion. Surely he wouldn't stick around here if that was so. And why would he bring her home? It's not sensible.''

''Victims of Whore Sleep never remembered how they got it. It would be safe enough for him. I know it sounds outrageous, Parrus, but . . . it's an incurable condition. We have to be careful. There are children here. We don't know anything about him. And if he's a necromancer or even a bound demon like that other one, how would we know?''

''Magic, the witchfinders. . . .''

''If he was a bound demon, they couldn't detect him the normal way. Do you understand? Any magic he performs would be completely invisible to them.''

''You seem to know a lot about it,'' said Parrus in an unbelieving voice.

''They took care that we should, afterward.''

I didn't bother telling Parrus that I had taught myself the long and magically exhausting ritual you could use to tell if a person is a demon. There was no way I could use it here without calling the witchfinders down on us.

"It's not logical, Dion."

"I know, but think, Parrus. It is possible. A necromancer might find bringing a victim back to her family very humorous. How can we know what motivates such people?"

He was silent.

"You haven't told your brothers about this."

"No."

"Good. He might be a perfectly innocent man."

"I know, Parrus, but it was Whore Sleep. And he is afraid of the witchfinders too, remember."

"Aye. Well, I don't think much of your reasoning, but I suppose we can't be too careful. We'd best keep an eye on him."

Shortly after, Shad came in from the stables, chatted to us pleasantly and went upstairs to bed. Parrus followed him.

·7·

Parrus spent most of the night sitting outside Shad's door. In the end it might just as well have been me after all, for though I was exhausted, I slept very badly. I did not take the sleeping draught Silva offered me, in case Parrus should need me in the night. As a result, every time I drifted off, the darkness behind my eyes was filled with those horrible faces. My ears rang with screaming and I would start awake again, my heart fluttering like a bird. In between such dreams, I lay there in the darkness, wondering if I was being a fool for suspecting Shad and tempted to call Parrus back into the room and tell him to forget about it. Parrus was right. It wasn't logical that Shad would have been the one to harm Tasha. It was much more likely that he was afraid of witch-finders for the same reasons as we.

This Shad with his kind smiling eyes did not seem cold enough to be a necromancer. And demons. . . . The only demon in human guise I had ever seen had been Andre/Bedazzer, who was so vivid, so super-alive that in hindsight it was amazing no one had suspected him. He'd also been incredibly handsome, powerful, charismatic, charming, and amoral, all of it used to lure humans so that he could feed on their emotions and life forces. Shad was good-looking, but otherwise he seemed determined to fade into the background.

If nothing else though, my experiences with Andre/Be-dazzer had taught me to doubt my own perceptions, and Tansa only knew, there were whole worlds of things I didn't know about demons. I lay there staring at the ceiling, trying to work out a way I could question Shad about my sister's illness without giving myself away as a mage, yet still get to the cast-iron, indisputable truth. I almost hoped he would run away during the night.

Finally in the early hours of the morning, when I saw how it was going to be, I got up and woke Parrus, who had fallen asleep with his head on his knees, and helped him to bed. It was easy to see Shad's door from ours so I left our door ajar and lay down next to Parrus with my head at his feet so that I could see the door. Listening a little enviously to Parrus' peaceful breathing, I waited for the long night to pass. Yet just before dawn I must have fallen asleep, for I had a strange dream that was half dream, half memory.

I dreamed I was awake and lying in the same bed and the grey predawn light was coming in the same window. Except the bed was enormous, or I was much, much smaller.

A woman stood before the window plaiting her long fair hair. She picked up a string from the windowsill and tied the plait up with it. Then she turned and caught my eye and her own twinkled fondly. I squirmed down under the covers till only my eyes showed. I was only very little.

She laughed.

"Oh, no! Where has Dion gone?" she cried with mock distress. She began to look for me, peering under the chair and in the cupboard, calling "Dion, Dion! Where are you?" I huddled under the bedclothes and giggled from excitement and delight.

"Aha, what's this lump here?"

A finger poked me in the ribs and I squealed with delight.

"I can see you, little slugabed." She pulled back the covers. "Hey little snail. What are you doing lazing around, hey! Little snail!"

She tickled me gently as she said it and I squirmed with delight under her hands, rolling away from the tickling fingers, but at the same time reaching up for the hug which I knew was coming next . . .

. . . And woke suddenly and regretfully in that same bed with the grey predawn light coming in the window.

I groaned, pushing down a sudden sense of loss. It had been a pig of a night and I could only be glad it was over. To make sure it was over, I got up and padded over to the window and stood looking out at the damp, dawn world.

From here I could see the first few statues of one of Annac's main attractions, the Holy Way, a path lined with huge wooden statues of saints and martyrs, which was one of the things pilgrims came in summer to see. I remembered the statues quite well—statues of women with their breasts on plates and men with stakes nailed through their eyes and heart, as well as things like St. Racidan turning an unbeliever agonizingly into a tree. They had made a big impression on me as a small child. I remembered quite clearly now that my mother had forbidden me to go there because I always had nightmares. As well forbid a horse to eat hay. We children had all been fascinated by those statues—the more gruesome, the better.

As I was standing there trying to work out which ones I could see, I saw Shad Forest walking along the path that led between the Inn and the Holy Way. He must have got up when I'd dozed off. Damn! I scrambled into my clothes, took off the iron necklace, and tucked it into my bodice. I didn't want it stopping me now.

I didn't wake Parrus. I was by far the more powerful mage and if by some strange fate there was something ill about Shad, it seemed better to keep Parrus out of it.

It was chilly outside, but I could not help enjoying the sweet scent of damp grass and sweet oil trees.

Even though I had been a small child when I had last seen them, the statues of the Holy Way still looked huge, larger than life size. Perhaps it was the lack of sleep but they filled me with sudden, horrible memories of hungry stone statues with red eyes. Shad was standing in among them looking intently at one of them, which pulled me up short. He turned and walked a little further and stopped in front of another one, moving up closely to it and touching its hands. I went closer.

He spun round, his hand going to his knife.

"Enna Latrides! You surprised me."

"What are you doing?" I said, trying to make it sound like innocent curiosity.

"I'm looking at the carving on these statues. There's some fine work here." He smiled at me. "To visit the Holy Way at Annac is every woodcarver's dream. It's a famous sight. So many different carvers worked on it, and each of them had a different style. I would have come here anyway even if I had not been bringing your sister." He traced the fold of a robe gently with his finger.

"About my sister . . ." I said and stopped, having no idea how to proceed.

"I am sorry for her death, Enna Latrides. She was a very unfortunate woman."

"Did she tell you anything of who hurt her?"

"No," he said, looking me straight in the face. "She could not speak. She had to scratch pictures in the dirt if she wanted to tell me something. You probably know more of what happened to her than I do."

"Um . . ."

"I do not doubt that it was bandits. There are some brutal people hiding out in the Red Mountains. Even the Burning Light cannot seem to control them."

If he was a liar he was a good one.

"You should try to persuade your brother that revenge is useless," he continued, "for I fear he would only get himself killed. The South is no place to be living now."

"Ren Forest, my sister was suffering from an illness."

He looked surprised. "An illness?"

There seemed no way to go except forward. I reminded myself that Shad seemed to be avoiding the witchfinders too. Probably he was in no position to betray me to them. I stepped closer.

"Have you ever seen that illness before?" I asked.

"What illness?"

"The one which made her sleep so much. It's an illness. I've seen it before in Gallia. When did it come upon her?"

His eyes widened, but his voice contained no surprise.

"If that is an illness, then she had it from the time I found her. If anything she'd improved. We nursed her for two weeks before I brought her here."

"Then you've never seen it before."

"No."

Dead end. The man wasn't giving anything away. I must know. Time to try something more shocking.

It came out in a rush.

"My sister was suffering from an illness that could only be caused by necromancy."

He gasped, and I thought I saw some kind of concern in his eyes.

"Sweet Mother. Don't speak of such things."

"I will speak of such things. I think you know more than you let on about this. I want to know what you know."

He sighed, an infuriating, long-suffering sigh.

"Listen, Enna Latrides. This is not Gallia. We do not speak of magic here in Moria, especially with strangers. And as for what I know, I have told you everything. And if you were not a woman who had just tragically lost a sister, I would be very angry at these suspicions."

"I must know. Listen . . ."

He turned on me suddenly.

"No, you listen to me, you foolish woman. You and your husband should go back where you came from right now. It's quite obvious what you are. Neither of you have any gift for stealth. You're looking to get yourself and the rest of your family burned at the stake the way you are going."

His voice was soft, loaded with anger and contempt. Part of me quailed at it. Another part of me saw a way in.

"Tomorrow we shall go back where we came from," I said. "When I get there I shall tell others, many others, that my sister died of necromancy."

He stared at me, his face unreadable. What was going on

in his head? I had hoped for some stronger reaction.

"And will they listen?"

"I know people who will listen, yes."

"Then we must hope you get home safely."

It was infuriating. I could sense nothing in this remark, no threat, no admission, nothing. I should never have started this conversation. I was useless at this kind of subtle maneuvering.

I tried again.

"Ren Forest, where was my sister when she caught this illness? We are quite alone. No one will hear us."

He stood for a moment, head bowed. The he said quickly, "The Burning Light is building a fortress in the Waste Land. It is called Sanctuary. They use their prisoners as labor. I have seen others who escaped from that place. All of them had been tortured, but your sister is the only one I ever saw alive. That is all I know—and all I wish to know."

He turned to walk away from me.

"Perhaps you should come back to Gallia with us."

He turned back, his face showing bland surprise. "Why? I am a loyal son of Moria. I have business with the Holy Mother Church in the Holy States. Why should I want to go to Gallia?" He bowed a little. "Though I thank you for your offer. Good day to you, Enna Dion."

I stared after him, pride smarting. He thought me a fool. I had a childish urge to run after him and show him somehow that I wasn't. Well, it didn't matter what he thought of me. I felt more certain than I had that he was just an ordinary person. He had not tried to harm me. And he had even told me something, given me a hint of where Tasha had come from. Sanctuary again! I must try to get there somehow. Perhaps the Duke, when he arrived. . . . Shad had told me of Sanctuary when I told him I had powerful friends in Gallia. Was this some kind of cry for help? If he'd been a necromancer surely he would have tried to make away with me at that point.

Then it occurred to me that there were at least four days between me and Gallia. Oh, I was a fool. Just because he hadn't tried to harm me now didn't mean he wasn't biding his time for some later date. I was no nearer to knowing his true nature than I had ever been and I might have increased everyone's danger. Curse it.

I walked back to the inn carefully, with all my senses alert, but there was no sign of Shad in the courtyard. Instead, as I was crossing it, a horse came charging in the gate. A richly dressed man jumped down from it and ran into the inn. I followed him in closely enough to hear him say, "Tasha! I heard she was back."

There were several people sitting at the table, but Silva was closest to the door, standing over the fire stirring a big pot. A stricken look crossed her face. She put down the spoon and came over to the man.

"Oh, Lucien. You're too late," she said gently. "She died last night."

The man's face went white, shocked. He stared at Silva as if he could not believe what she had said. She put her hand on his arm.

"Aye," snarled Tomas. "So you can take yourself away again, Sercel. There's nothing for you here."

His voice seemed to bring the man out of his shock.

He said softly to Silva, "May I see her?"

"No," said Tomas. "Why? Didn't you make enough use of her when she was alive?"

"What did you say?" said the man in a low dangerous voice.

"You heard me. Now get out of my house, you aristo shit."

"Tomas!" cried Silva.

"I want to see her. Dammit, I have a right."

"The hell you do," shouted Tomas. He leapt at the man and the next moment they were wrestling on the hearth stones.

"Sweet Mother," cried Silva. "Mouse! Louie! Do something."

"Let the silly sods work it out themselves, girlie," mut-

tered Uncle Louie, as the man landed a punch that sent Tomas sprawling.

Silva gave the old man a poisonous look and threw herself
between the two men.

"She's not here," she shouted at the rich man. "The
witchfinders took her."

Much good it did. Tomas pushed her firmly out of the
way.

She seized a broom and held it as if to hit someone.

"Stop it, you stupid men," she cried. "Get out of my
kitchen if you must fight."

Uncle Louie just smirked cynically and went on eating.
Mouse too was eating bread and cheese as if this kind of
thing went on every day. Maybe it did. The children watched
with interest, but no one but Silva was doing anything. I was
glad Parrus wasn't here to see this.

Suddenly the door crashed open. Shad charged into the
room.

"Fire Angel!" he shouted. Then I smelled it—the stench
of sulfur and underneath it the sweet smell of rotting roses.

Demons!

A strange orange glow filled the room. A roaring crackling
sound was coming through the door. Shad slammed it behind
him and threw the bolts.

"Fire Angel!" he shouted again.

He caught Silva and me by the arm. "Quickly! You
women get the children out! This house is doomed. Quickly
now! Run!"

He grabbed the suddenly still Lucien and Tomas.

"Fire Angels hate iron! It'll distract them for a little."

Crump! Smash!

The windows and door shattered. Great jets of orange fire
streamed in. Heat searing my skin. All around were screams
and scrambling people. Black terror and fire burning us all.
It must stop.

The calmness of magic came down like a cloak. I wanted
the fire gone. I made it go.

There was great whoosh as a wind sucked air out of the

room, and with it flame and heat were gone. The room was extinguished. The screaming and scrambling around receded into the background. The door lay on the floor. Through the smoldering door frame, I could see fire boiling in the courtyard and smell the sulfurous sweet demon scent. The heavy magic of it tingled on my skin. The calmness of my own magic was like steel stiffening my spine, filling me with the will to destroy.

I went for the door.

Behind me someone caught at me, shouting. I pushed them away gently without even touching them.

Outside the hot air reeked of sulfur, smoke, and burning flesh. The very stone of the courtyard was melting stickily against my feet. Beyond them the outbuildings were a wall of flame. Terrified animals screamed though the roar of fire.

I wanted the fire out and with a loud crump it went out. The blackened carcass of a horse lay smoking on the ashy cobbles before me.

A haystack in the center of the yard still burned. Then it moved and I saw that it wasn't a haystack but something alive. It was a great being vaguely shaped like a man, who stood on great squat legs, a living flame as tall as a house with the wings of an angel spread out behind it and a head that was a red-orange flame with no face.

Fire Angel!

It turned, and though its face was no more than a sheet of seething flame I could feel a malevolent gaze upon me. It threw back its head and laughed, a high-pitched cackling of evil joy. Its hot stench filled my eyes with tears.

It beat those huge wings and a great fireball roared toward me.

I took it face on. Felt it streaming hot and tingling past me. My skin was as cold and tough as ice and the fire merely tickled pleasantly. I stretched out my arms, filling them with magic, wonderful, wonderful magic. It had been over four years since I'd used magic like this and Sweet Lord of All, how good it felt coursing through my veins. Like swimming in a big surf, like diving through the sky—the hot taste of true power.

The fireball streamed past me. The air cleared. I stretched my hands out to the Fire Angel and willed it to go out with a great rushing, roaring smash of power. I walked toward it, arms outstretched, my flesh singing with that power.

If flame can show shock, it looked shocked. It screamed a shrill scream of vicious anger, a scream like nails on glass. I felt its power heaving and scrabbling against my will. It reared up and back, stretching its substance into the air, towering above me. Then it dived for me, plunging, rushing toward me, a great roaring wall of flame, breaking over me like a huge wave, blinding me.

I staggered under the first impact, pushing through it, willing it to go out, suffocating it. It broke over me and sprayed up into the air in a great fiery cloud. Pieces whirled in the air above, seething, struggling to rejoin, broken into bits that shrank and shrank till they turned into puffs of dirty black smoke hanging in the air, trailing away in the wind.

How weak it was, how insubstantial now that I had come to grips with it, as insubstantial as fog. Snuffing it out had been as easy as snuffing out a candle, and yet somewhere far away I could hear faint echoes of power howling angrily.

I was alone in the silent stableyard with only the stench of rotting roses and the sound of whimpering horses to remind me of the Fire Angel's existence. I was surrounded by wild exhilarated free laughter. It was my voice, laughing from sheer pleasure.

Hands grabbed me from behind. With a great whoop of delight, Tomas swung me up into the air and whirled me round.

"You did it! What a champion! Well done, little Demon-slayer!"

He let me down and all at once I was being hugged and kissed by Mouse and Silva and Tomas and the rich stranger. I was breathless with laughter, praise and relief. It was a moment of pure joy.

Then suddenly there was the sound of horses' hooves and

a horse pranced nervously beside me, and Shad was gripping Tomas by the arm shouting, "The witchfinders, man. You have to get your sister out of here."

Tomas whirled, shock on his face; a man surfacing into reality.

"Silva, Mouse," he cried. "Saddle horses quickly."

He and Shad spoke together for a short time. Then I was being bundled up on to the horse.

"No!" I cried in sudden panic. "Tomas. Where's Parrus? We have to find Parrus."

Tomas cursed.

"Lucien, can you . . ."

"I've got it," said the rich man, running back toward the inn.

"Tomas!" I cried.

"It's taken care of, sister. Now get yourself out of here. Go."

He slapped the horse's rump, then Shad was urging the horse out between the gate posts. There was a group of people outside who scattered before us as we broke into the street.

"Witch," yelled someone. A stone flew past my head. I looked back. At the other end of the long street that led up to the monastery, armed guards in grey and black were running toward us.

They must be slowed. Darkness and dust would do it.

I sent a burst of power out toward them and the next moment a huge muddy cloud of dust had risen, seething and whirling across the street.

"Very nice," shouted Shad. I clutched him as he wheeled the horse around. He dug his heels into its flanks and we were off at a gallop.

Down the cobbled streets and out onto the dusty road we raced, Shad yelling and urging the horse on. We plunged through the valley and up on to the hill. Ahead of us was the forest. I hung on for dear life, flung around like a sack of corn. Behind us, a pillar of brown dust whirled like smoke above the village even though I was no longer holding it up.

Then suddenly we were in the trees. The sunlight darkened to shadow and I could see behind me no more.

The horse was blowing heavily, tired from its run with two people on its back. We slowed to a trot and went on for about ten minutes until we came to a stream. In the middle of the stream, Shad reined in, jumped down from the saddle with a splash, and pulled me down after him. He unstrapped the saddle bags and slung them over his shoulder. I took the iron necklace out of my bodice, unwrapped it and put it round my neck. Hopefully it would cut off some of the aura of magic that would be hanging round me and leaving traces on any Bowl of Seeing that might be watching at this moment.

"Quickly!" said Shad, indicating that I keep on along the stream. "We'll go round the corner and wait. Tomas should be just behind."

I pulled my skirts up through my belt and started wading. I heard him slap the horse's rump behind me. It went off down the track at an easy trot. The bed of the stream was rocky and slippery and the water was moving swiftly—not easy walking at all. Shad caught up to me and put his hand gently on my arm, leading me, seeming to know as if by second nature where the potholes were. We waded forward as quickly and quietly as we could.

Suddenly there was the sound of horses' hooves coming down the track behind us. We pressed ourselves into the shade of the bank.

A single horse came galloping down the track and reined in in the water and then started up again, just as we had.

Shad leaped out from the bank to wave at Tomas.

"Fire and Air!" he cried. He moved quickly back towards Tomas, who was staggering toward us, clutching his shoulder. Something thin and black was sticking out of it—a crossbow bolt.

"Tomas!"

He staggered against me.

"That fucking Arvy Ironmonger. Shot me, the sod. And he was drinking Holyhands beer last night, too. Come on."

"You're bleeding, Tomas."

He staggered on past me.

"Come *on*, sister! We've got to keep going."

Shad shot me a quick worried look.

"Further on," he said. He slid his arm round Tomas' waist.

"Oh leave me, for Aumaz's sake," snapped Tomas. "Look to Dion. I'm well enough."

Shad just ignored him, dragging his arm up over his own shoulders so that Tomas was supported on his hip and hauling him along quickly, stumbling noisily over rocks and stones in the streambed. I hurried along behind.

The stream had carved a deep bed and the banks were overgrown with ferns. Trees overhung the water, forcing us to bend almost double. We were soon out of sight of the track and hidden from anyone who might be standing in the forest beyond the banks. The water was freezing, but it only came up to my knees, which was lucky, for after a while my fear-numbed brain started to work again and it occurred to me that my petticoats would be needed as bandages for Tomas. It was fortunate that they were still mostly dry. As soon as I could, I climbed on a rock, pulled them off and carried them around my neck.

At last the stream broke into a series of cascades. We climbed out onto dry ground.

"Over the bank here," said Tomas. He dragged himself up onto the bank. His shirt was red with blood, but still he protested that we had to keep going. Shad took out his hunting knife and slit Tomas' shirt open. I ripped one of my petticoats into strips and packed it round the arrow. It had lodged in the back of his shoulder, but high up so that it did not threaten anything vital. It was bleeding heavily, however. I longed to put some healing into it to stop the bleeding, but with witchfinders searching for us, it was the worst possible moment to use such magic. Tomas laughed weakly. "I always wondered why women wore so many petticoats."

"It's the only really useful thing I've ever done with them," I muttered.

He was pale, but still able to stand on his feet. Shad had twisted the bloody shirt into a long bandage so that the strips of petticoat could be held securely to the wound. Now he took off his coat and tied it round Tomas' shoulders.

Tomas scowled at him as he staggered to his feet. He tried to push Shad away as the woodcarver made to support him again.

"Stop fussing, man. I'm fine."

"Oh be quiet," said Shad with surprising good humor. He hauled Tomas' arm forcibly over his shoulder. "Listen, you can drop dead for all I care. Just don't pass out on us before we've got to this safe place of yours. You're the only one who knows where it is!"

"Up here along this path," said Tomas. He described how to get to the place we were going as they staggered along. Shad set a good pace for all that he was almost carrying Tomas, and I followed behind. Birds called softly up above, but it was quiet under the trees. Here the forest was tall, straight cooran trees. Brambles, sword grass, and tree ferns grew in a tall tangle beneath them.

We walked for almost an hour, following a narrow animal path up and down a hill. Tomas had stopped talking, but he seemed to be staying upright. The sun rose higher, but the sky was clouding over and the air was filled with the damp that foretells spring rain.

About midmorning we came to a clearing beside the path. Shad called a rest break. He took a water bottle and offered it around. As I drank, it struck me that only a couple of hours ago I had mistrusted this man, and now here we were having to depend on him.

"It's down in the valley below here," said Tomas. "It's a cellar with the entrance covered by brambles and it's protected from magical searches by Runes of Hiding. We'll have to go straight down the hill. There's no path, and we must be careful not to make one."

"Any food in this hideyhole of yours?" asked Shad.

"Oh, aye! It's well supplied. Nothing flashy. Hardtack and dried meat. And blankets and things. I've used it before.

There's a stream nearby. When we get there you must fill up the water barrel immediately. We're still not that far from the edge of the forest and I reckon the place will be swarming for the next few days.''

"Who else knows about this place?"

"As far as I know, only Lucien."

"Lucien? That fellow you were fighting with?" I asked.

Tomas grinned weakly. "That was nothing. Family matter. I'd trust Lucien with my life. Even if I can't trust the sod with my sisters."

Certain things that had been said back in the kitchen suddenly made sense.

"Did Tasha and Lucien . . . ?" I asked

"She had a son by him last year. Sod. He's my half-brother and she's my half-sister. You would have thought he'd have the decency to keep off. And before you start to have bad thoughts, Forest, they didn't have any blood relations in common."

"I was just thinking that no one could have got your sister with child against her will," said Shad. "I had the impression she was quite some mage."

"Lot you know," snapped Tomas.

"I don't know how you Holyhands have survived this long," said Shad. "I thought Tasha was some mage and now Enna Dion here. . . . No doubt there are others. In the South you'd have been dead in the Waste Land long ago, just for the ability."

"This isn't the South. It's not illegal to have magical powers here. It's just illegal to use them outside the church. Anyway, Lucien is Lord-Elector of Middle Moria and the clergy here are mostly his relatives. Even the witchfinders. I can't say it hasn't helped."

"Even though you hit him?" said Shad.

"He's still family."

Shad grinned wryly. "Do you think they'll question him?"

"It's not real likely, is it? The Lord-Elector. He still has a lot of power in Central Moria. Who'd dare?''

Shad shrugged.

It was a long rough climb into the valley. It must have been around midday by the time we reached a place where the trees thinned and were replaced by great hummocks of brambles that rose higher than our heads. Little drops of rain were pattering on the leaves above.

"In there," gasped Tomas, who was looking very pale. "Take hold of that stem."

Gingerly I pulled aside the bramble stem, which pulled aside several other stems with it. Underneath was a trapdoor.

Below that was a big cellar, dark and cold but, from the look of the walls, dry enough. The floor was earth. A number of crates and barrels stood along one wall.

"There's a candle by the wall there," said Tomas. His voice was light and somehow far away. "There's blankets, food, and some healing herbs over there. Oh, and there's a couple of bottles of potato spirit. Bring those out too."

I lit a candle and found the blankets. I spread the cleanest-looking one on the floor. Shad eased Tomas down onto it.

I busied myself lighting the little brazier, heating water, running a lighted match along the blade of Shad's knife to kill possible disease spirits, and tearing up another petticoat for bandages. I tried not to think of the moment when I would have to take the arrow out of Tomas' shoulder. I had never done anything like this without magic to staunch the bleeding, heal the wound, and stop the pain.

Tomas took a few liberal swigs out of the bottle of potato spirit. It seemed he was dreading the moment too. It came in spite of that. I knelt beside Tomas, knife in hand. For a moment I was unable to do it.

"You've never done this without magic before, have you?" said Shad.

"I'm afraid," I said, thinking of the pain I must now cause Tomas. Part of me hoped that Shad would offer to do it for me.

"Oh, for God's sake, Dion," cried Tomas. "Don't be such a baby!"

"It will be well," said Shad. "Just do it. Then it will be over with."

A few nerve-shrieking moments later the arrow was out.

"Grown-up enough for you, Tomas?" I said, pressing a bandage on the heavily bleeding wound.

But Tomas had passed out.

·8·

As I dressed Tomas' wound and brewed a potion to kill his pain and help him sleep, Shad busied himself filling the water barrel. By the time he'd brought the last bucket in, it was raining quite heavily.

"Good," he said. "The rain will wash away any signs of our passage. The witchfinders have been known to use trackers when magic fails them. You don't look so good. Here. Take a swig of this."

He offered me the bottle of potato spirit. I took a small pull. It was savage stuff, but warming.

"How long will Tomas take to get better?" I asked, looking at the inert form of my brother, who had slid into a kind of half-fainting sleep.

"It takes three or four times as long without healing magic. And he will most probably be feverish for the next few days. I shouldn't worry too much, though. He seems a strong man. I've seen people recover from much worse."

"You're not a woodcarver, are you?" I couldn't resist saying.

"I was a woodcarver, once," he said. "Though there was not time to take my master's papers in the end. But the last three years I've been hiding out in the Red Mountains. There was a group of us called the Shattered Light. We've been

146

fighting Hierarch Jarraz, stopping his prison trains and trying to help the prisoners escape. Fighting against Fire Angels this last year or so.''

He turned to me, his face filled with excitement.

''I've seen two mages die trying to do what you did today. How did you do it?''

''I'm just strong,'' I said. ''That's all.''

''Your brother called you Demonslayer. What did he mean?''

I shrugged. It was hard to talk about those times. People never understood why it gave me no pleasure.

''It was back in Gallia,'' I said.

''Gallia. You're the Demonslayer of Gallia. We heard rumors about a young girl who killed a demon. We thought they must be exaggerated. You really are her?''

I shrugged.

''You really did kill a demon?''

''Not killed it. Dispelled it. Sent it back to its own place.''

''Alone! Just by yourself!''

''No, there was another woman . . .''

''Another woman mage! Another here on the peninsula!''

''Not a mage. An ordinary woman. She struck in the right way and in the right place and with a pure heart. That counts against demons.''

I was back in Norval's castle, struggling with the demon in my arms, hearing again Andre's smooth sweet tempting voice, drawing me in, promising me joy. . . . I had not wanted to resist. I had been at the point of giving in and suddenly there was Kitten Avignon, who should have been dead, striking down with the knife . . .

He said something.

''I beg your pardon?''

''You must be a very powerful mage.''

The admiration in his face. I didn't deserve admiration. I deserved disgust.

''There's more to good magery than power,'' I snapped.

I got up and went to Tomas' side. He was heavily asleep but his breathing seemed all right.

"We need certain herbs," I said. "It should be possible to get most of them in this wood."

"What do you need? Feverwort? St. Ruth's balm?"

His voice was quiet now. All the excitement of a moment ago was gone, replaced by quiet watchfulness. Only this morning I had suspected him of necromancy. I still did not know if he had magical powers or not. He had saved us both and I felt disposed to like and trust him, but as I reminded myself now, I was unfit to make those judgments.

"You know these herbs?"

"Aye. Shattered Light could not use magic without giving themselves away, so we had to do what we could with herbs. I'll go see if there's some by the stream now while it's raining. There was a place that looked good for them."

He wrapped a blanket around himself, climbed up out of the trap door and was gone.

I was relieved that he had taken my abruptness so well. I must not offend him with open mistrust, but I must keep an eye on him nevertheless. Caution and care and polite watchfulness were what was needed, not reckless trust prompted by emotions. I should try to keep some distance between us too, though it would not be easy here.

He was not gone very long and he came back down the ladder with empty hands.

"What's wrong?"

"There are people out there."

Alarm prickled down my spine.

"Searchers? Already?"

"No. Wanderers. They told me to come back down here. Said it was safer. Said they'd bring the herbs." He spoke with quick excitement. "Enna Dion, is it true what they say? That Duke Leon of Gallia is set to invade Moria and destroy the Burning Light?"

"Yes."

"But the Patriarch . . ."

"The Patriarch has decided that Hierarch Jarraz's visions are the result of necromancy and has withdrawn his support for the regime. There is more to it than that but that is all I know for sure. What did you say about Wanderers?''

But he was in no mood for that topic. He could not seem to stand still.

''Fire and Earth,'' he said as if it was beyond belief. ''It's over then. Over.''

He paced up and down the room, his movements full of suppressed elation. He did not seem to know what to do with his hands.

''How long? How long will the Duke be in coming?''

''He has already left Gallia. Two or three weeks, I should say, depending on the forces that meet him.''

''Sweet Mother! It's over! Three long years of slaughter. And soon it will be over.'' He threw back his head and let out a kind of laughing cheer. It was an amazing change from the watchful man of a few moments before.

He caught my arms. For a moment I thought he was going to embrace me, but he restrained himself.

''How can you be so calm?''

''Me? I've known since before I came into Moria.''

''Sweet Mother of Us All,'' he shouted. ''We're free.''

''Calm down,'' I said, half-laughing at his joy. ''We still have to survive the next two or three weeks.''

''Hah! That will be nothing. You have no idea what it's been like in the South. People are afraid to go out of their houses lest they be arrested by the Hand of Truth, for singing or smiling on Aumaz's Holy Day or for owning books or for writing. Hardly anyone travels. And for us. . . . People were afraid to help us, because Hierarch Jarraz had let it be known that those accursed angels were angels of Tansa's retribution. Last summer the Fire Angels patrolled the Red Mountains, attacking us constantly and drying up or poisoning all sources of water. Hiding in this snug little hole with the Wanderers to watch over us will be easy after that.''

''What is this about Wanderers? What are they doing here? What did they say?''

He looked startled then, as if he'd only just remembered them.

"Yes. It was strange. Three of them appeared out of the bushes and I'm sure there were more nearby. They told me they were here for you, Enna Dion. To stop you falling into the hands of the Destroyer. You didn't know, then?"

"We met a party of them at the border, and another one alone a few days afterward. Do you think they've followed me all the way from Gallia? Why would they do that?"

"Well, it's obvious to me," he said. "A mage who can kill Fire Angels is a valuable ally. Sweet Mother, ten minutes ago I was trying to work out how I could get you to come South with me so that we could re-form the Shattered Light. If you were to die senselessly at the hands of the witchfinders . . . what a waste it would be! The forces against the Burning Light will need all the help they can get. Hierarch Jarraz, for I think that's who they mean when they say the Destroyer, he has some great power at his command. I've seen five of those Fire Angels together."

Five. There had been demon power in that Angel I had fought . . . was it only this morning? Five. Did that mean one demon or five? Bound slaves or merely power drawn from another plane? What level of power was implied here? The creature I'd fought had been nothing to Bedazzer. It had merely been some kind of projection of demon power. Usually projections could not affect the world around them, but this had animated fire into a shape and had harnessed its destructive force. It represented quite a feat of magic. Yet for all that the Fire Angel had not been very strong, possibly because it had been projected all the way from the Great Waste.

"I wonder what five Fire Angels means," I said half to myself. "And why did it come? For Tasha?"

"Perhaps they knew she was back," said Shad. "Your family made no secret of it. Perhaps Jarraz had been looking for her. I don't doubt she could have told a few tales about Sanctuary had she lived, and your family has surprisingly powerful friends. Even here where he had little power, it might make sense to use a Fire Angel to wipe out your family so that his secret would be safe. Plenty would still be willing to believe such creatures to be agents of Tansa's retribution."

Angels of Tansa's retribution. It was plausible, especially in a place like the Peninsula that had little experience of necromancy.

"People would prefer to believe that than see them for necromancy," muttered Shad.

I looked at him suspiciously.

"You seem to know a lot about necromancy," I said.

"There were mages among the Shattered Light. They knew that the Fire Angels were not holy magic. It was that which made them stay with us when it would have been safer for them to hide out in Seagan. That was why you questioned me this morning, wasn't it? You thought I was in some way connected to it."

"I know nothing of you, Shad Forest," I said carefully. "But my sister had been fed on by a demon. If her dreams had not told me, that illness would have."

He was silent, staring at the floor. I wondered if I had offended him. I had as good as accused him of being a necromancer.

"I am wondering how I can prove my honesty to you, Enna Dion," he said suddenly. "We shall be here together for some days at least. It would be better if we could trust each other."

"Why should you distrust me?" I asked, surprised.

"I am no mage and even were I one, I don't doubt you could snuff out my life as easily as you snuffed out that Angel today. I don't want to give you reason."

I wouldn't do that, I almost said, but stopped myself before I said it. It is bad tactics to appear harmless in the eyes of someone you cannot be sure of.

"You know," he continued, "if I was some creature of ill intent, it's very likely that the Wanderers would know and have made away with me by this time. They regard necromancy as an abomination. Surely the fact that they leave me here alone with you must be an argument for trust."

"I know nothing of Wanderers and their ways either," I

said, although I had heard Wanderers say how much they hated necromancy.

"I was afraid you would say that."

We sat in uncomfortable silence. Only time and experience could persuade me to trust Shad Forest, and I think we both knew that. There was no point in sitting worrying about it. I decided to continue where I had left off this morning and find out what Shad knew about this Destroyer in the Waste Land.

"Tell me how you really found my sister," I said.

"She came crawling out of the Great Waste, naked and covered in wounds and mud. She couldn't have crawled all the way from Sanctuary. It's near the sea on the site of old Ruinac, two days' walk at least, and the area around the Great Cathedral is patrolled by beasts. I can only think that she must have hidden in one of the carts that come out of the Waste Land. I found her near the cart track. She wasn't the first person to escape from Sanctuary that way, although she was the only one who survived for any time. She had a fierce hold on life. In her waking moments she used to scratch little pictures frenziedly in the dirt, until we understood that she wanted to be taken to Annac.

"There was a healer still with us, who nursed her without magic till she was strong enough to travel. What I told you of her this morning was all the truth. We assumed the sleeping sickness was the result of some damage.

"She came at a time when our band had resolved to break up. If she'd come a week later, there would have been no one to find her. But we lingered until she was fit to travel. The others had decided to withdraw to Seagan for the summer. Last summer, what with the Fire Angels poisoning the water, we almost died of thirst. To make matters worse, a few months ago the Wanderers who had been fighting with us left us and halved our numbers. They were our best warriors."

"I thought Wanderers had been exiled from Moria. How . . ."

"They may be a diminished people, but Wanderers have

great skill in woodcraft.
good at traveling undetect
there has been a day since
that there have not been Wa

"I had never even heard
cently," I said.

"You remember how the o
New People first came to the
ago, they could not defeat the Wa
to those tales, but secretly I alway
fighting with them these past two
They are fine fighters. They see be
and can go longer without food or shelter or sleep than us.
All they lack are numbers, and in the old days they had that,
and the kind of mages who would have equalled you, Enna
Dion. Even now I think they could be a considerable nuisance if they took to fighting against a ruler."

Wanderers, I thought. Now here was a mystery. Obviously
there was much more to them than I had suspected. What
else didn't I know about them? I thought I could be pretty
certain that they were on my side against the Burning Light,
and almost positive that they had nothing to do with the
necromancy that drove these Fire Angels. I just hoped that
my judgment wasn't playing me false again.

After a time, Shad brought out a tattered pack of playing
cards and began teaching me black dog, one of those complicated games men play in taverns. I was glad of the diversion for when I wasn't worrying about Tomas—who was
already flushed with fever—I worried about Parrus and if he
was safe.

The rain either stopped or was too quiet to be heard. It
was permanently night in the cellar. Only by the sounds of
the crickets calling could we tell that night had fallen outside.

Shortly after the crickets began, I heard voices calling me.
When I asked Shad if he could hear anything, he said no.

Putting my hands over my ears, I discovered that the
voices were in my head. They were soft, but persistent. I had

...ence before, but then I had never been ...gical search before. I hoped that the Runes ...ld be strong enough to keep them from finding ...Shad what I had discovered.

...whistled softly. "You really must be some mage, to ...able to hear that."

"What a joy it is to be a powerful mage. Especially in a delightful country like Moria," I said.

He grinned. "You're opening my eyes. I'd thought it was all invisible slaves and flying like birds."

"Invisible slaves," I cried. "I should be so lucky."

Suddenly there was a thud as the trap door rose and fell and two figures dropped into the cellar. The cards scattered as Shad leapt to his feet, knife drawn.

Two Wanderers had landed neatly on the cellar floor. One of them was Symon the Raven.

"Greetings, Enna Dion," he said. His ancient boy's face was solemn.

"Aye," said the other Wanderer. "I know him. It's Shad Forest right enough."

"Gunida," said Shad. "It's good to see you well."

He did not put his knife away or relax. The three of them stood looking at each other, ready to spring. I was fascinated by the woman, Gunida. Had she been among the Wanderers we had met at the border? They had been conventionally dressed, the women wearing skirts. Now Gunida wore leaf-brown breeches and a tunic like a man, and her white-gold hair was short. It was wild and tangled with feathers, twigs, and sweet oil berries stuck into it as if for decoration, making her look as if she were a walking part of the forest floor. Her face was hollow-cheeked and somehow alien, but she looked lithe and fit and she held a long knife very purposefully in her strong hands.

"I suppose he knows how to use that," said Symon to the woman, nodding at Shad's knife.

"Oh, aye," she said. Her voice was heavily accented. "He gave good account of himself in the Red Mountains."

"But can we rely on him to get between Enna Dion and trouble?"

"He is an honorable man. He knows the enemy."

Symon snorted unbelievingly. Shad stood watching them. His face showed no emotion.

Tomas sat up, scrabbling at the ground beside him.

"Tomas!" I cried, terrified that he'd disturb his wound.

Symon paid him little attention.

"We bought you healing potions," he said. "And food too."

"Symon," said Tomas. "You swine! What do you want?"

"Tomas Holyhands! With us again, are you?"

"What do you want?"

"To protect Enna Dion, of course. From the results of your recklessness."

Tomas let out a growl.

"You. You told me I wouldn't have to worry about Tasha any longer. You knew she was going to die, didn't you? You devil."

He was on his feet before I could stop him, and then just as suddenly he went white and collapsed on the floor.

With Gunida's help, I rolled him over. He'd fainted. Loss of blood and sudden movement don't mix. I checked his pulse and his wound anxiously.

"Doesn't look too good, does he?" Symon's shadow was over us. "But he'll live. Our dreamers have foreseen him in further acts of recklessness."

I scowled angrily up at him. It didn't seem to worry him.

"The Destroyer is intent on finding you, Enna Dion," he said as if nothing had happened. "Already searchers are combing the forest. You've piqued his interest with your little show at the inn. You'll need to keep as still and quiet as you can."

He turned away and began stalking up and down the cellar in a way which was strongly reminiscent of the bird he was named after.

"We shall not come in here again, but we shall be watch-

ing nearby if you need us. You would be unwise, either of
you, to leave this place.'' His stalking had brought him in
front of Shad. He leaned forward.

"Enna Dion must not fall into their hands. Do I make
myself clear, Shad Forest?"

"As glass," said Shad.

He spoke a few words to Shad in another language. Shad's
face hardened before he replied in the same language.

Symon turned to face me.

"We will leave you here for the moment. It is a good
enough place. With any luck they will come to think that
you are gone. But we have made other preparations if it
becomes necessary."

"Symon," I said, finally finding my tongue. "Why are
you here?"

"For you, Enna Dion. Didn't this one tell you? For you."

"But why for me?"

"Foretelling has shown for a long time that you have a
significant part to play in what is to come. It is not clear
what that part will be, but it is our intention to prevent it
from being an evil one."

"What do you mean?" I asked tensely. "I'm no friend of
necromancy."

"But I think you are familiar with the idea of tapping. The
Destroyer would be a fool, which he is not, if he overlooked
the opportunity you represent."

My spine froze with the horror of what he had just said.

He turned away again, shrugging. "I am not best pleased
with what has come to pass. It would have been simpler if
you had not come within the Destroyer's grasp."

"Why did you not stop me coming into Moria then, if you
feared this?" I retorted, suddenly irritated beyond reason. He
acted as if he knew everything, and yet he had done nothing
practical to stop this happening.

"The road has many branchings, and who can say when
each one truly starts?"

"Will you say that when this Destroyer of yours takes
me?" I snapped.

"I will say nothing because I will be dead before that happens," he said, effectively silencing me.

He turned in a swirl of black and made toward the trap door.

"It is good this Shad Forest is with you. It will be well for you to have a servant of your own people to help you with your brother. Oh," He turned as if it were an afterthought. "We stopped a man a few miles from here. Lucien Sercel. Said he had a message for you and Tomas. Your doubting friend Parrus is well enough and safe, hiding at the White Tower. He'll probably be more comfortable than you. Ever the way with his kind. This Lucien had things for you." He nodded and now I saw that there was a pack beside the ladder. "We didn't want him blundering about here giving your hiding place away, so we sent him home." He turned as gave us a last glittering look. "Just do as you're told and all will be well."

He swung up the ladder, followed by the woman, and was gone.

I kicked the wall, cursing Symon under my breath. He should have told me if he'd known how dangerous it was going to be. If he'd known. At the Mages' College they had always taught us that it was wise to pretend more knowledge than you had.

"Let's see what he's brought us," said Shad. He picked up the pack and the bag of healing herbs, brought it into the light and began unlacing it.

"You took that very calmly."

He shrugged.

"Didn't that man make you angry? Coming in here ordering us around, playing God. He spoke to you as if you were some kind of servant."

Shad grinned lopsidedly. "This is no time to be looking for trouble. If a man takes the effort to put you down, it means he thinks you could be a threat. It's a compliment in its way."

I scowled at him.

"He talked about me as if I was a parcel."

"Who is he, anyway? I never met a Wanderer like him, not even among the Dead."

I told him about the Raven and what he had said to us on the road to Annac.

He whistled softly.

"A Raven, eh? That explains a lot," he said.

"What does it explain?" I snapped, more sharply than I had intended. I was getting sick of significant remarks without explanations.

"It explains why the Wanderers just up and left our band with no warning. We felt betrayed. But how could they deny a call to arms from a Raven? So what is their plan? Have they decided to overthrow Hierarch Jarraz themselves?"

When I told him what Symon had said about Ernundra, a slow almost dreamy smile spread over his face.

"Ernundra," he said. "What a wondrous thing that would be. Ah, It's been a day of good news. If the Wanderers have finally decided to take their land back, things are looking bad for Bishop Jarraz. Nothing will stop them but death."

Death. The word reminded me of what Symon had said about tapping. I shivered, unable to partake of Shad's contentment.

"Enna Dion," asked Shad, almost as if he had read my mind. "What is tapping?"

"I think you should stop calling me Enna Dion, if we are to be here together for a few weeks," I said.

"Very well." He pulled something out of the pack. "Look! Lord Lucien sent you another dress." He put it down in front of me. "You didn't answer my question."

"Tapping is a necromantic spell. It's where a necromancer links himself to another mage and uses his power for his own ends, keeping the mage alive all the time. It's a kind of slavery."

I remembered Norval—how he had gloated when he had told me he intended to tap me. *Like the paralyzed caterpillar a wasp lays its eggs on to feed its young*, he had said. I felt a little sick.

Shad looked grim.

"Damn Symon. If he knew this was a danger, why didn't he try and stop me?"

"Who's to say he did know?" said Shad. "Leaders talk big. At least now you know your husband is safe."

"Husband? Oh, Parrus, yes." All the guilt I'd felt at our deception came back and without thinking, I said, "He's not actually my husband. It was Tomas' idea to make us less obvious."

It was only after I'd said it that I realized I'd thrown away another advantage. A husband, even an absent one, offered some protection against strange men. Oh Dion, Dion. Think before you speak.

There was nothing sinister in Shad's wry grin.

"Well, well," he said. "I did wonder when I saw Parrus sleeping in the hallway last night. Your brother has his cunning moments, doesn't he?"

In Lucien's pack there were meat pasties carefully wrapped so that they were still warm. Famished, Shad and I set to eating them immediately.

After we had eaten he took a needle from a pocket in his pack. He took a long wooden rod that he had found in the corner and began sewing a blanket to it.

"What are you doing?"

"Making a curtain. The trapdoor is not entirely sealed and this will hide any light that might show through—and muffle our voices. I think I will make another, too, so that you might have some personal privacy."

"Thank you," I said, embarrassed at the subject. "Thank you for staying with us."

He shrugged. "What else could I do? Especially now I have been ordered to by this Raven."

"Is that what he said to you in that strange language? Did you learn it from the Wanderers in the Mountains?"

"Aye. He told me to stay here and do my duty, and as for the language, it's his own language. Klementari, it is called, as they once were. I learned it from my Granny. My father was a full-blood Wanderer."

"You don't look it." I was surprised. Most people with

that much Wanderer blood were tall and fair, and he was short and dark like any other Morian. Only his high cheekbones hinted at his ancestry.

"No," he said. "I'm magic-blind too and have no gift for foretelling at all. I take after my mother entirely. She was one of the New People. Pa used to call me Changeling."

I gasped at the cruelty of it.

He smiled and said, "I do believe he loved me the most tenderly of all his sons, as one loves a cripple, and since he called me Changeling, it mattered much less when the village children called me the same."

"But you're not a cripple."

"To be magic-blind in my family . . ." He shrugged. "They were not great mages, but they all used small magics. It cannot have been easy for my mother in a household of mages either, but they were happy together. When the time came for me to be apprenticed, my father would not hear of me following in his footsteps like the others. He was a woodcutter. He considered it too risky a profession for his son to follow if he could not cast spells to stop trees falling on him, though plenty of the New People do it without magic. Anyway, they sent me away to my mother's brother in Beenac. He was a woodcarver and took me as an apprentice."

"You must have been sorry."

"Aye, at first I was. But I found out quickly enough that it was the best thing my parents could have done for me. Beenac was a town of New People who had few magical powers, and so they valued other things, things I was good at, like running and carving. Even though I did not have magic they taught me to fight with my body which I was also good at. I felt I had found my proper place, that I really belonged among the New People, rather than among Wanderers." He paused. "I wonder if Uncle Pauly . . ." He shrugged. "Forgive me, Enna Dion. You cannot be interested in this stuff."

"No! No! Please go on."

He smiled and shrugged and would say no more. I returned to the earlier conversation.

"If you left now I'm sure you could get away safely. It seems hard of the Wanderers to expect you to look after me. It's nothing to do with you."

"Don't be so keen to get rid of me," he smiled. "You may find me very useful. It takes a certain amount of strength to nurse a sick man."

"This is not your duty. And the Wanderers will protect me now."

"Enna Dion, when Hierarch Jarraz's witchfinders came and took my family away, I vowed I would never stop fighting till he was gone from the South. When I came to Annac it was my intention to keep that vow by journeying to Julia Madraga in Floredano to recruit more fighters to the Red Mountains for the next autumn. It seems to me that protecting Enna Dion Holyhands is a far better way to spend myself and keep my vow. You would be the chiefest asset of any army you fought for. And now I know about tapping. . . . It is vital that you be kept safe."

I was not at all worthy to be so protected. I did not feel at all important or useful. I was scared and wished I was back in Cardun. I must not show my various weaknesses in front of Shad, though he was certain to be disappointed in the end.

"You look worn out," said Shad. "Why don't you rest? I'll be finished with this soon."

I rolled up in my blankets and closed my eyes. The voices in my head called softly and hatefully. To still my fear I tried to think about Cardun: the forest and the honey parrots and the hopping mice who sometimes broke into the grain barrel. Such was my frame of mind, however, that I began to think of how for the last three years, while I had been living peacefully in Cardun, too upset about the past to make real use of my strength, people had been tortured by a necromancer in the Great Waste. I had done nothing to stop it. But I had not known, I pleaded with my hard judgmental self.

Would you have done anything? You had turned your back on your gifts, said that judgmental self.

This was ridiculous. It served no good purpose to lie here

scourging myself so. What was done was done. I must simply try to do better.

Behind me, Tomas stirred.

"Forest," he said hoarsely.

"Hello there. You want a drink?"

"Aye!"

I heard Shad come over and give him some water.

"Forest, I don't want anything bad happening to my sister."

There was silence for a moment.

"What? Reckon I'm going to do something unmannerly to her while you're unconscious, do you?"

"I'm just warning you. She's got two more brothers who'll come looking for you, if anything ill happens. Just you remember that."

"Wonderful. And I really make it my policy to offend powerful mages. Life's short. Why not make it shorter, I say."

Silence.

"I meant no offense," said Tomas.

"Aye, I know it. But the right path is obvious to me and you can rely on me to take it. Enna Dion is not the first of your sisters I have cared for."

The voices kept calling all night. They were hard to ignore but I must have fallen asleep eventually, because I found myself running in terrified slow motion through a forest of cold stone pillars that always seemed to be in front of me. I knew the stone woman and her hungry statues were somewhere in the dark shadows.

Then as I ran a voice seemed to come out from behind the pillars.

"Little mage, little mage," called Andre seductively from out of the darkness. "Come here. I will save you. I will not let them get you."

I knew he was just around the corner. My heart lightened with the thought that I would see him again. I felt myself turning toward him.

"No!" I cried, and found myself awake with Shad sitting up nearby.

Even if I'd been mistaken in thinking that the dreams of the stone woman came from him, Andre was certainly in this one. It was the first one I had had of him in some time. Had it come from him or was my overfilled mind simply playing games with my fears? I felt exposed without the familiar Runes of Distraction, Protection, and Blindness around, but I could not make them without giving away our hiding place to the witchfinders. At least there were no mirrors here.

"My head is still full of Tasha's memories," I lied to the anxious Shad.

"That cannot be pretty. Shall I light a candle?"

I told him not to. I did not want to seem like a coward, though it was pitch black in the cellar and I would have liked a light. I lay in the dark the rest of the night trying not to hear rustlings in the darkness and worrying about the significance of that dream.

After what seemed like an eternity, birdsong in the forest above signaled the beginning of the day. Shad got up and lit a lamp.

I had given Tomas a painkiller for his shoulder and it had a sedative effect. Since he was still asleep, I did not bother getting up. It was chilly in the cellar and I was warm in my blankets. The voices ceased for a time and I lay dozing. It seemed I had just dropped off to sleep when the voices started again. Exasperated, I sat up and looked at Shad. He was intent on something.

"What are you doing?"

He jumped and dropped something and an uncomfortable look came across his face.

"You're awake."

His guilty face worried me.

"What are you doing?" I got up and went over to him. He was blushing.

"Ah . . ." he said haltingly. "I was just fooling about."

A kind of leather cloth lay beside him. It had a series of

little pouches on it containing tools. I remembered he was a woodcarver.

"Are these your tools?"

"Aye. I was just trying them out." He was resting his hand on a couple of pieces of wood so that I couldn't see them. I began to feel alarmed.

"What were you doing?" I said, seizing the wood. For a moment we grappled and then he let go.

"In truth, Enna Dion, I'm embarrassed to let you see them. I have not carved anything for three years."

One of them was a flat plank. He had drawn a design of fruit and flowers on it with charcoal and had begun to hollow out around it.

"This is a common piece. Fine folk like to decorate their cupboards with such things, but the lamplight is not really good enough for such work so I gave it up and tried whittling this."

"This" was a lump of wood that was beginning to take on a shape.

"It's a raven!"

His face lit up as if I had given him some kind of treasure. "So you can see that already, can you? I am pleased with how this is going. It seems I still have a little skill left after all this time."

He took it from me and held it to the light and traced the curve of its neck with his finger, traced it again, and then without even thinking, took up his knife and began whittling the line to a more satisfactory shape.

Surreptitiously I examined the other pieces of wood that were scattered about. There was nothing suspicious about them.

"Have you really not carved for three years?"

"Indeed I have not."

"Why not? Surely there must have been times like these."

"Aye, plenty of them. But a carver makes things and a fighter's duty is to destroy."

He smiled at my startled look. "Ah, no. I make a mystery out of nothing. I think it troubled my conscience to do something I loved so much when my family was still unavenged. But I woke up this morning just itching to see if I could still do it.''

"And with the Duke coming and the time of the Burning Light's fall so near, you thought you'd give it a try,'' I said.

His dark eyes twinkled. "You understand me well, Enna Dion. I still feel a little dishonest. I would have preferred you had not caught me at it.''

It was hard to resist his smile. I smiled back at him.

"You really should stop calling me Enna Dion. It makes me feel as if I'm fifty.''

"Ah. I'll try to remember.''

I sat and watched the shapes appear under his long deft fingers. He handled the tools well. As I watched him smiling to himself, it seemed to me that this man carving wood, making things, was indeed really who he was, and the tense fighting man whose knife came so easily to hand was just some kind of useful clothing to protect against bad weather . . . as my being a healer had been. But now the time was coming when I must become who I really was.

The next few days were very difficult. At night I was tired enough not to heed the voices, but the longed-for quiet of sleep was loud with horrors. Though I tried not to remember the things I had seen in Tasha's memories, the stone woman and her hungry statues were always there, and when it was not them it was Bedazzer in his guise as Andre.

I would awaken with a jolt several times during the night and lie shivering in a cold sweat, uncertain for the first few moments whether I was awake or whether I was still in the dream, expecting any moment to see red eyes in the darkness and to feel the searing pain of the stone woman's feeding. The shock of such wakenings seemed to stay with me all day, a shivery shaky feeling in the pit of my stomach.

But the worst dreams of all were the ones in which Andre kissed and held me as I remembered so well. After I had first sent him back to his own plane I had often been tormented by these sweet nostalgic dreams. Even though I squirmed out of his arms and ran away, I felt such longing. If only. I awoke now as I always had, choking on sobs.

The first day or so Tomas had been in pain and very bad-tempered, and twice we had hard words about my throwing away my opportunities and about his ambition. Soon, however, I would have given anything for angry words from him, for he became very feverish. His wound was red and swollen. Since I could not use magic, there was nothing to be done but to bathe his face and arms with cool water and to dose him with feverwort and sedatives so that, although he muttered and tossed, he was never awake enough to cry out and give away our hiding place. In his brief lucid periods he was too weak to do more than drink water.

As a healer, I had always used magic to ward off fever, and so the only fevers I had seen were those where the disease was so strong that it had overcome the magic and would ultimately kill the patient. Though Shad told me and kept on telling me that it was only a mild wound fever and that he'd seen people recover from much worse, I could not get the sense of death out of my mind. Often on that third day I was tempted to take off the iron necklace and press my healing power into Tomas' temples. Crazy thoughts went through my head, of how perhaps I could take Tomas and fly with him back to Gallia. If we had been closer to the border I think in my tired insanity I might well have tried it.

The witchfinders were hunting us. Several times we heard searchers talking softly in the forest around us and once we heard the sound of feet rustling in the leaves above our heads. Shad turned out the lamp and the two of us sat in the darkness, clutching what weapons we had until long after the sounds had stopped. In my head the voices kept up their relentless calling.

Toward the evening of the third day Tomas awoke and did not know who I was. I gave him a drink and he sank back into delirious fever dreams, muttering about his son Martin and once even about Marie-Louise.

Suddenly the thought that he should die here with me standing by afraid to use my power for fear for my own skin was too much for me. The voices, the dreams, this damnable cellar. Suddenly I couldn't breathe. I wanted to run away. I wanted to scream.

"He's burning up. He's going to die, isn't he?" I cried. "Isn't he?"

I found I was sobbing. I turned away, trying to hide it.

Shad's arm was around my shoulders.

"Come now," he said softly. "It's not so. He will not die. Come now."

The sympathy finished me. Suddenly I was really weeping, sobbing uncontrollably into his shoulder while he gently rubbed my back.

Eventually I came back to myself enough to feel ashamed.

"I'm acting like a weakling. I'm sorry."

"I think it's a wonder this has not come earlier," said Shad. "You must be exhausted. I never saw a person sleep so badly as you."

"I'd hoped you hadn't noticed. I'm sorry to have disturbed you."

"I sleep lightly when I am on guard," he explained. "I never heard anyone have so many bad dreams. Even Tasha did not have so many."

I didn't say anything. I wasn't going to tell him what I dreamed about.

He sighed. "What you need is rest."

He picked up the flask of sedative.

"I think it would be best if you took some of this. It would help you get some decent sleep without dreams."

"I don't want to," I said. "What if Tomas . . . ?"

"Tomas will live through the night. He really isn't very sick. I will stay awake and watch him. And if he worsens I'll wake you, I promise."

I was tempted to take the sedative. I was tired to death. If it had been Tomas urging me I would have gladly. But Shad. . . . I was supposed to be keeping an eye on Shad.

"Do you still mistrust me so?" said Shad. "After these three days?"

He was right. It was ridiculous.

"Give me the potion," I said.

I fell asleep by lamplight and awoke to it. I had no idea how long I had been asleep, but I felt much better, relaxed and pleasantly drowsy from the potion. I lay there luxuriating in the feeling.

Shad was awake. He was sitting in the lamplight on the other side of the cellar combing out his long dark curls. They were wet and now I looked I saw that he was naked to the waist. The lamplight shone on his lean hard muscles. Water trickled down from his wet hair onto his smooth shoulders. His skin gleamed like silk and there was a fine down of dark hair on his chest. How soft it must be to touch. What a very well-made body he had—a harmony of hard and soft. He turned to pick up something and I saw a huge white scar, three even stripes across his back.

"That's some scar," I said.

He turned and smiled at me.

"Aye, it's my shame scar," he said. "It nearly finished me, that one."

He picked up his shirt.

"I was a lot sicker than our lad here before it healed up," he said, sliding the shirt over his head and shaking his hair out of it.

"How is Tomas?" I sat up. Tomas was lying quietly asleep.

"No, don't get up. Stay there and rest. He's well enough. I gave him a drink and a bit of a wash a while ago. You've had a good sleep. It's morning now. Feel better?"

"Mmm."

I was glad to lie back down and cuddle into the warm blankets. He came over and sat near the brazier between Tomas and me.

"Dion, Dion," called the voices in my head, but they were a long way away.

"What do you mean, your shame scar?" I asked.

He shrugged. "I got it while running away. It's not a thing I like to admit."

"It looks like a claw mark."

"That's because it is. I got it from a thing we met in the Waste Land."

"You've been down into the Great Waste?"

"Aye, once, early on. After my family was taken. My oldest brother and I had both been living away from home when the Hand of Truth came so we were not taken. We went out into the Waste to try to get them back. There is nothing but dust and ash in the Waste, but when we came into view of the tower of Sanctuary a great field of green stretched before us. Do you know boneseed, that bush that grows in graveyards? That field was all boneseed and as we walked through it, there were bones under our feet."

He was silent and from the look on his face I was tempted to tell him not to say any more.

"It was silent except for a lonely wind, and then suddenly there was a squealing like pigs and this group of beasts came charging out of the bushes. Beasts like hairy men, and yet they had the snouts of wolves. They were on us even as we leaped onto the horses and ran for it. One of them leaped onto my back, which is how I got this wound, but I managed to heave it off. My brother was not so lucky. I heard him go down behind me. He called out my name as he went down, telling me to run. Then he screamed and there was nothing but the horrible grunting snarls of the beasts. To this day I still hear those sounds in my dreams. It took me a long time to forgive myself for not stopping to help him."

His voice trailed off. Then he said softly, "I would not be here now if I had."

His eyes were shadowed, inward looking.

"That must have been hard." I said. I thought of my own life. "We all have things we are ashamed to remember."

"Is this why you left Gallia and went to live in the country as a healer?" he asked softly, surprising me into answering the question.

"Yes," I said. "I was employed to protect someone from

a necromancer and I failed. This woman was the best person I knew. I was only seventeen, newly orphaned, alone in Gallia. She was a friend to me, almost like a mother. And I let her down. I trusted the wrong person, someone the necromancer had sent to betray me. I should have known better.''

"This was Andre?''

"What?''

"You call his name in your sleep,'' he said. His face was a little apologetic. "I could not help but wonder. So this woman, did she die?''

"No, but the necromancer raped and tortured her before I could get to her, and when I killed him I set his demon free and was forced to fight it to prevent another Smazor's Run. Being the Demonslayer just stemmed from my stupidity. I cannot forgive myself for that or for what happened to her.''

"Where is she now?'' said Shad gently.

"She is a famous actress in Gallia,'' I said. "She is rich and says she is happy.''

"Only the dead cannot recover,'' said Shad tentatively.

"I know what you are saying. But great power needs to be driven by great wisdom and I do not have the wisdom. That is why I became a healer.''

"I understand,'' he said.

Shad was not the first person to have heard me calling to Andre in my sleep and asked me about him. The first person was the man who finally relieved me of my pointless virginity. A peddler by trade, Rafe had come to me with a sprained ankle one rainy night and had stayed in the hut. It had rained all night and in the morning the creek was flooded and we were cut off from the village for three nights.

"Who is Andre?'' he had asked me, and, when I told him he was an old love, he had said, "The best way to forget one love is in the arms of another,'' and had gone on to demonstrate. His injury had in no way dampened his enthusiasm.

Dear Rafe. He was a very ordinary looking man, but he knew how to touch a woman. Perhaps he had a woman in every town. If that was so, I was his woman in Cardun. Every three months after that he had shown up at my door smiling his slinky smile, a smile full of promises that were always kept. Lying drowsily in the warm blankets, I was filled with creamy warm feelings at the memory of him, feelings I knew I would do well to suppress in this cellar. In these close quarters I could not fail to notice what an attractive man Shad Forest was.

For almost two weeks I saw no light but lamplight. It was a stale worn-out time. We slept wrapped in blankets on the hard earth floor, and apart from an occasional gift thrown through the trap door for us by the Wanderers, we ate hardtack and jerky. The only exercise was to walk up and down the cellar, which Shad and I did several times a day. Though the searchers up above came less and less frequently, still they were there and the same was true of the magical voices in my head.

Still, things went better than they had at first. Though Tomas continued to be weak and feverish, his wound did not become worse and he became lucid again. Bad dreams still woke me but now I woke to light, for Shad insisted that we should keep a small oil lamp burning throughout the night. By that light I knew the waking world from the dream world and no longer lay fearful, afraid that the stone woman would reach out of the darkness. Sometimes Shad would speak to me reassuringly in those quiet moments.

Telling each other of our disgraces had broken the ice between us. Only with difficulty could I keep a small suspicious part of myself alive towards him. I no longer bothered keeping a distance. During the day, we often sat in the dark to save lamp oil, and we spent hours then quietly talking together.

He was good company, interested in everything. I told him of Kitten Avignon and the court of Gallia, my life as a healer in dear sadly missed Cardun, and even of my childhood in Moria studying under my foster father, Michael. He told me of his idyllic childhood in the Red Mountains and his last three years with the Shattered Light. Yet he spoke of his experience with such humor, and with such an eye for his own foibles and those of others, that I found myself laughing rather than grieving despite the savage struggle implied by these stories. He seemed to be a man who looked at the laughter in life instead of its tragedy, though I think this was courage in him, a way of getting over heavy ground rather than any light-mindedness. He was affected by pain. I remember the time he described the wagonloads of "sinners" that went every few days out into the Plain of Despair, never to be seen again. Despite their efforts, the Shattered Light had only manged to liberate a few. After that conversation we both sat silent for some time.

Shad had been brought up among Wanderers, even though his family had not wandered. He told me a great deal about their customs and even taught me some of the words of their poetic-sounding language. But most important of all, he knew an enormous number of stories and folk tales. When he was awake, Tomas often asked for stories and we would sit in the darkness listening to Shad's wonderful voice telling us some tale of old kings or Wanderer mages. Some of them were stories I had known since my childhood, yet Shad had learned them from his Wanderer granny and so he told them from a different point of view. His story of the conquest of Moria by the New People did not concentrate on the great and violent deeds of Wolf Madraga, their leader, but on the mighty deeds of the Three Sisters, Jani the first of the Dead, Elaina Starchild, and the magical girl Marigoth who had led the Klementari and who had eventually forced Wolf to make peace with them. His tale of Smazor's Run did not end with the suicide of Luisange and the eight other mages who had accidently let Smazor free, but with Henri Madraga's cruelty to the last few remaining members of the Klementari, and how in dazed grief they had abandoned settled ways to wander lost and homeless as the Wanderers under the leadership of Nesta and Kintore.

He did not do funny voices like actors usually did, and yet he had a way of stringing words together that was completely enthralling and his deep voice with its soft Southern lilt was delightful to listen to.

"You're as good as a player," said Tomas once.

I could almost see Shad's easy grin in the darkness.

"'Tis a useful skill in a fighter," he said. "I've spent most of the last three years in little hideyholes like this waiting to pop out and kill something."

✦9✦

I ran between the stone pillars. *Look out!* cried Andre. I heard something scratching and snuffling through the darkness behind me. I turned to look. In that moment someone seized me.

Andre! No! I opened my mouth to scream but there was a hand clamped over it.

"Stay still," said Shad in my ear. "This is real."

Something was scratching in the earth above our heads. *Scratch, scratch, scratch.* It was like listening to a dog digging, but it was something much bigger than a dog. Showers of earth fell rustling on leaves. Then came a loud snuff so close above us that Shad and I both jumped.

Leaves crunched softly under . . . ? What? Feet? I could hear a faint roaring like the sound a fire made in a chimney. A vivid orange glow shone through the weave of the blanket. I smelled sulfur and rotting roses.

Fire Angel!

For endlessly slow minutes we crouched there, gripping each other, while up above something dug into the roof of our cellar, first in one place and then in another. Beside us the heavily sedated Tomas slept soundly and silently.

I put my hand to the iron necklace. If there was any time to betray myself out of necessity, it was now.

174

Shad's hand caught mine. "Wait," he whispered in my ear. "It's aiming to flush you out. Their senses are not so good and they are easily distracted, but once you use magic, it and any others will be able to see you clearly."

Suddenly a human scream came echoing through the forest and after it a kind of ululating cry. The earth shook with a nearby explosion and then with several others. With a sudden crush of leaves and a shoosh of wings something huge took off above us, letting out a shriek of maniacal laughter.

Shad was up and pulling Tomas out of bed.

"Wake up, man!" he cried. "Wake up!" By now the shouts and screams above us were so loud I could hardly hear Tomas' groaning protests.

With a burst of orange light the trapdoor was flung open. Wanderer faces peered anxiously down at us.

"Come on!" yelled Shad. He slung the sleepily protesting Tomas over his shoulder like a flour sack, carried him to the trapdoor, and passed him up into reaching hands.

He grabbed my arm and scrambled up the ladder, half-dragging me behind him. Hands grabbed me and pulled me away from the hole. Up on the hill above us the forest was burning. Black figures were running through the trees with burning brands. There was a spout of blue flame and another explosion. Fiery stars swirled in the sky above.

At the cellar door the Wanderers crouched silently around us in the damp brambles. One of them was heaving Tomas onto his back. He set off at a run followed by two others in a direction away from the forest fire.

I leaped after them. Hands seized me. Voices hissed:

"No!"

"Leave them!"

"It's safer this way!"

Then suddenly evil giggling cackled out above us and fiery stars began to fall from the sky.

"Oh shit! Here they come! Go! Go!"

Someone pushed me and suddenly I was running full tilt through brambles and bushes, stumbling over stones, Shad dragging me along. A great light came roaring down toward us.

"Down!" shouted Shad, pulling me down against stones and brambles. "Crawl, crawl." I crawled, too terrified to feel pain as I dragged myself over the rough stony ground.

A gout of flame shot out over us. Bang! A sweet oil tree exploded. Another burst nearby.

Little pieces of earth and burning wood rained down all around us.

I kept slithering along as fast as I could, mindlessly terrified as a great light came rushing down toward us. Then suddenly figures came crashing out of the undergrowth all around us, shouting and screaming and waving burning brands. Several flashes of blue light burst forth away between the trees to our left. Magic? Was that magic?

"This way," shouted Shad. He dragged me up and pulled me away from the blue lights. "Don't look back."

Then we were plunging again headlong through the trees, clawing through the whipping branches, stumbling over rocks.

From behind us came a chaos of shouting, screaming, and cackling laughter. Trees burned all around us. Shadows stretched and shrank and leaped skywards as the great lights swung and spun around behind us and evil laughter swooped past low overhead in a roar of flame. All around people were running, or pushing themselves waist deep through the tree ferns, faces grotesquely picked out by the light. Someone screamed—a human scream of pure agony that was suddenly cut off. Laughter, evil cackling laughter. I wanted to turn back, to help, to do something, but Shad kept dragging me on, pushing me through bushes and over stones.

Then a voice cried, "Down here!" and someone shoved me into some kind of hole—no, it was a gap under a rock. The cold stone pressed against my shoulders and face and damp earth soaked into my back. Shad had crammed himself in behind me. His lithe body wrapped itself around me. There was the sound of cloth being spread and leaves being scraped around.

"Dammit," muttered Shad. "You've gone in all wrong. Can you turn your face to the rock a bit more? Got to get as much of you covered as possible." He wriggled around so that he was lying over me and the rest of me was pressed against the rock.

"Can you breathe?"

I could, but only just.

"Hide your face in my shoulder," he said. "You must survive."

"The necklace. I have to get it off," I hissed.

"No, you can't use magic. There are too many of them. Just lie still."

"I have to be free just in case. Let go." I struggled but his hard arms were too strong.

"Hush! My body will protect you from the fire if they find us."

"Shad! No!"

"Earth and air! Lie still, damn you! You'll get us both killed."

He was very strong. The struggle to free myself would be hard and stupid.

"Oh no, Shad," I whispered against his cheek, heartsick at what he had just implied. His curls tickled my face. I breathed in the pleasant, slightly smoky scent of his body.

It was hot. Orange light shone through the weave of the blanket. Screams and great explosions rang out everywhere. A great mad cackling laugh was answered by another one and another till the forest was a cacophony of insane laughter. The roaring of flames seemed to come closer and closer.

Suddenly a great wave of panic filled me. I had to get away. I was trapped. Magic was bursting inside me, trying to get out and blow everything away, but it couldn't. I tried to struggle, but Shad's body pinned me down.

"No! No! Hush! Stay still. You're safe. It's only the fear. They do this to flush out prey."

Then he gasped, "Oh Earth," and I felt him begin to tremble.

I could feel the magic now. It was as if I were two people,

the one who wanted to run away as fast as possible and the mage who could taste magic in the sulfurous smell of demons and knew it was the source of her terror.

"Oh Earth," whispered Shad. "Hold on. Hold on."

The smell of sick roses filled our nostrils. The stone grew warm against my back. I closed my eyes and even through my eyelids I could see the hot red light. Sweat trickled down my back. My limbs cramped with fear.

Boom. Something exploded into flame nearby. All around was the crackle and crack of burning trees. An explosion crashed just behind us and another almost of top of us. I knew I was sobbing though I could not hear myself above the roaring of flames all around.

Then suddenly came a great *whoosh.* I braced myself for the pain. But the light was gone, suddenly the light was gone. It was gone, thank God. And suddenly so was the fear. Shad's tense body relaxed. The laughter rang out again, but a long way away, high above and beyond us. There was blessed darkness all around.

We were safe? We were safe! I hugged Shad tightly, full of hysterical relief. Thank God!

I pressed my lips against his cheek, kissing him again and again on the face and lips, and then he was kissing me. Kissing each other hard on the mouth, lips opening, deeper and deeper, holding each other tight, relief changing to something else.

There was another explosion, making us freeze, but it was some way off. A great harsh screeching like the grandmother of all parrots filled the air.

"That's the sound of frustration," Shad whispered. "They'll get bored soon."

He pressed my head against his shoulder. His fingers were tangled in my hair and I lay against him, caught in the moment, stilled by the fear of destroying it. I had no wish to be anywhere else.

The cloth cover was peeled away. Faces lit by firelight peered anxiously down at us.

We scrambled stiffly up. There were several figures on

either side of me as we set off at a quick trot through the glowing and smoking trees. We were probably on a path, for the going was easier underfoot. The others jogged along and I did my best to keep up with them, though I was quickly out of breath. Just as I knew I must call out for a rest, they slowed to a fast walk.

We had climbed a ridge and gone down over it by now, and the burning trees no longer afforded us any light. Still I could hear shouts and screams from beyond the hill and screeching like the screams of giant birds, and occasionally that insane cackling. Once we all crouched down as a great star of flame shot into the air, followed by two others. Yet even with the chaos of fighting nearby I felt oddly safe among these Wanderers.

After traveling for a long while I began to be able to see the faces of my rescuers all stained with smoke and earth. Dawn was coming. In the fresh morning light we stopped at a stream and ate a little food and washed our faces in the freezing water. A Wanderer man rubbed soothing salves on the now-throbbing scrapes on my bruised hands and knees. He told me his name was Taldera.

" 'Twas lucky it is spring," he said. "They would have set the whole forest alight had it been later in the year."

"Is my brother safe?" I asked anxiously, and was told calmly that he would be, for it was not him that the angels had been looking for; when we had separated they would have lost interest in Tomas.

The voices began calling in my head again as we sat there. We were out of cover now and could easily be found. I told the Wanderers and they finished their rest and got up.

"Do not worry too much, Enna," said Taldera. "We don't think the angels will come back so soon. All over central Moria this night the normal Watchers at the Bowls of Seeing were replaced by southern priest-mages from the train of Darmen Stalker. It was that which made us expect they were going to use the Fire Angels. But now the time for the Watchers to be relieved has passed and there will be those watching that would question the color of the magic the Angels use. There are still many honest priests left in the Burning Light, and Hierarch Jarraz does not have enough power in central Moria to work freely yet. Soon enough now we will have you to safety.''

''Safety? Where?''

Taldera smiled and said, ''You shall see.''

A kind of embarrassment seemed to have sprung up between Shad and me in the light of day. He had sat a little way from me during the break and walked a couple of people behind me as we traveled onward. With a sinking heart I assumed this indicated regret for his actions. Well, I was not about to force myself on an unwilling man. Kissing him had just been the reaction to a moment of relief. That was all. Anyway, he had kissed me first. Or had he? Oh dear. Well, I would just try to act normally, so that he realized it had meant nothing special to me. Then everything would be back to nice and friendly between us.

As we walked onward I could not help thinking of the delicious feeling of his lips on mine and his hard body in my arms. I had not wanted to stop holding him. Perhaps he was just suffering from shyness at the moment, as I was. In that case I shouldn't be too cold. My admittedly limited experience with men told me that they didn't like too much open emotion in the light of day. At least Parrus never had. Parrus! Oh God! What kind of promiscuous woman was I? Inwardly I began to scold myself, not only for my inconstancy but for feeling desire now, when we were in terrible danger. I hadn't changed.

We walked for most of the morning. Occasionally we crossed overgrown and disused-looking riding tracks, but we were deep in the forest, walking among tree ferns and dense grass, and saw nobody else.

At last in the late morning we came to a circle of standing stones which stood among the trees at the top of a hill. I had never seen such a circle before, though my foster father had had a great interest in them and had owned several treatises on them. They were Wanderer relics and people speculated that they had something to do with the Wanderers' strange animistic earth religion.

There was no sign of any religious activities at the moment. The circle was overgrown with trees and underbrush. A small group of Wanderer warriors was gathered around the closest stone, and as we came up to them the dark figure of Symon the Raven stalked into view, appearing as usual as if out of thin air.

"I told you I would repay your hospitality one day, Enna Dion," he said abruptly. "We have brought you here for your own safety, but we must beg of you that you do not speak of what you are about to see. It is one of the great secrets of our people. And you." He turned to Shad. "The same goes for you, but you I do not beg but tell. You are here on sufferance because you have given good service. You are not important, so if you betray what you see here, you will be punished."

"What?" I cried, moving toward Shad.

Annoyance flickered briefly over Shad's face, but he said quite calmly, "You know you have no need to take this tone with me, Raven. I have always kept faith with the secrets of my father's people and always shall."

Symon grunted. He turned with a whirl of black cloak and moved down along the side of the rock circle, and the rest of us fell into place in single file behind him. He passed through a narrow gap between the stones and was obscured from sight. I stepped through after him.

There was a sudden tingling jolt and a sensation of falling. I gasped for air, suddenly winded, and then—as if I had blinked for a moment and opened my eyes again, there I was inside the stone circle, momentarily blinded by the bright sunlight, with my body tingling all over.

Symon was there in front of me and Shad coming out through the gap behind me and yet . . . I was somewhere else completely. It was such an odd feeling. Surely there had been more trees among the stones than this. The grass was drier-looking than I had thought. Where had all these tents and small wooden shacks set neatly around the center of the circle come from?

Symon was looking at me with the kind of smile a cat would have had if a cat could indeed smile, a knowing, cynically amused sort of smile.

"Where are we?" said Shad. He too seemed startled.

"You know well enough," said Symon. "Did your father not tell you of the Circles of Power?"

Shad's face was awed. "This is one of those? But the secret was lost with the Istari."

"No longer lost," said Symon. "Well, Enna Dion?"

"Will we be safe here? Will the magic not bring the witch-finders?"

Symon grinned.

"And what magic is that?"

The tingling sensation had gone. I could not feel magic any longer, or if I did it was only a fleeting sense, like a half-smelled scent.

"Rest yourselves now," said Symon. "You will be perfectly safe here."

"I want to see Tomas," I cried as Symon swirled away from us.

"He is with the Council," said Symon. "They wish to see you, but we had planned to wait until you had rested."

"I would like to see Tomas first," I said. Symon's threats to Shad had made me nervous, and so did this stone circle. What reason did I have for trusting these strange people?

"Very well," said Symon. "Come."

I hesitated, reluctant to leave Shad. The Wanderers had collected around him, strange sticklike figures, with their ghost-pale hair like halos around their faces and their dark watchful eyes. He seemed so small among their tall shapes.

"The man will be safe enough," said Symon in my ear. "Leave him for now."

Shad nodded a calm farewell at me and as I watched, he turned to one of the Wanderers and spoke to him, clapping him on the shoulder in a greeting. A smile passed through the group. My anxiety lifted a little.

The stone circle sat lopsidedly on the hill like a hoop care-
lessly thrown over a church steeple. On one side the top
stones were just around the crown of the hill. On the other
side they came down in a wide circle that took up a large
part of the hillside. The hill bulged slightly here, and set in
that bulge was a large stone doorway. The posts and lintels
were all carved with runes, many of which I had never seen
before.

Symon stopped and turned to me in this doorway.

"Three members of the council await within, Enna. One
of them is our High Dreamer, greatest foreteller of our people. Another is our wisest mage. You are honored in this."

He pulled back the dark cloth that covered the doorway
and I followed him into the smoky blackness beyond.

Symon was suddenly gone, leaving me completely alone,
blinded in the blackness. The cloth had fallen back behind
us and I was no longer entirely sure where the door was. I
seemed to be in some kind of enormous space filled with
unspoken whispers. Panic grasped at me.

There were lights, however, deep in the space. Candles? I
moved carefully forward, my eyes adjusting to the darkness.

Yes, candles. A enormous circle of them. Within the circle
were two shapes. One of them was a man lying on his back
in the middle of the circle with his arms spread out and his
eyes closed. He was so still I would have thought him dead
had it not been for the deep slow rise and fall of his chest.
He wore only a loincloth and his pale Wanderer skin seemed
to take on the glowing of the candles. I sensed that he was
the hub of the circle. Runes were scrawled all over the
ground beneath and around him, stretching out to the ring of
candles. The air around the ring was filled with a strange
kind of magic. When I concentrated on it I lost the feeling
of it and yet I knew it was all around, a part of the very air
of this cavern, the source of the unspoken whispering that
seemed to fill it.

The other shape was huddled beyond the man like an afterthought, completely out of keeping with the symmetry of

the whole scene. As my eyes adjusted further to the darkness I thought it might be—yes, it was Tomas. I stumbled around the circle in the darkness and knelt down near where he lay. As far as I could see he seemed to be sleeping normally. I wanted to reach out and touch him, but I knew better than to put my hand into a magic circle.

"Dion," said a voice just beside me, and I looked up with a start.

"Causa," I cried. For I knew this woman. It was the Wanderer who had visited me often, one who I had thought of as a friend. I was astonished to see her here, for Causa was the most ordinary looking of women, brown-haired, short, plump and apple-cheeked, like a comfortable middle-aged nursemaid. She did not even look like a Wanderer. The only unusual thing about her was that one of her eyes was white with blindness. The sight in her other eye was not at all good, either.

When I had first met her back in Cardun I had been speaking to her for some time before I glimpsed the heavily embroidered green dress under her cloak.

"Are you a Wanderer?" I had blurted out in my surprise.

"Yes," she had smiled. "I know I don't look like one but there is Wanderer blood in both sides of my family and I choose that it makes me one of them."

Yet perhaps it was not so strange to see her in this magical place. Causa did know about magic. All over the walls of my hut in Cardun had been invisible Runes of Protection and Distraction, symbols only visible through the use of magic. That first day I had met her Causa had astonished me by touching those runes and saying, "If you want to keep away evil spirits, you should put a Rune of Blindness up with these." Then she had calmly sat down at my table and showed me how to make this Rune of Blindness, a rune I had never seen before. She never asked me why I had such runes on my wall, nor on subsequent visits did she ever mention the subject again. I had never seen any other evidence of magery. It's not polite among mages to ask for demonstrations.

"It is good to see you safe, Dion," she said now, and as always she enfolded me in a warm hug.

"I'm astonished to see you here," I gasped.

"I am the High Dreamer of the Klementari," she said simply.

"You are not a mage, then?" I said.

"No. I know something of magic but I have little power. Such powers are rarely given to Dreamers. But your mother was one of my closest friends. I wanted to help keep her child safe so I asked Beg to give me another rune for you."

It's difficult to talk when the world is rearranging itself around your ears. Causa had never said anything to me about knowing my mother, or anything which led me to believe that she was more than the matriarch of a Wanderer clan. I was beginning to see just how much the Wanderers kept hidden from outsiders.

"You knew my mother?" I stammered.

"Yes. She saved my life. I shall tell you of her later if you wish. But now the other members of the council wish to have speech with you."

"Tomas?" I said.

"He's fine where he is. There is goodness in these runes. They will revitalize his life force."

Causa turned and I saw the orange light of a fire making shadows dance upon the wall further back in the cave. Strange. I had not noticed it when I had first come in. A man and an old woman sat at the fire. A third figure sat a little separately at the edge of the firelight, with his back to the fire and to us. As we came closer I saw that it was Symon with his head bowed, as if he was not part of this meeting and only waited to guard it.

"Greetings, Dion Holyhands," said the woman in a voice that sounded like old millstones grinding together. She was an ancient crone with skin as dried out as her voice. She had a witch's mane of wild white hair. Clawlike hands clutched a stout-looking staff which leaned against her shoulder. A mage's staff; it was covered in runes.

The man, by contrast, was very young, possibly younger

even than I. He had a round fresh face with chubby childlike cheeks. His face seemed bland beside Beg's wrinkled countenance.

"I am Beg, the High Mage," continued the old woman. "This one beside me is Tarwon the Youth."

I sat down beside the fire. The old woman reached out, took my chin in her hand, and turned my face toward her. Her skin had the feel of soft old leather and smelled of sweet oil and caramel.

"So this is the creature who has such powers without having our beliefs," she said. "A sign of times broken and remade. Tell me, Marnie Holyhands' child, did your mother ever give you anything?"

"No," I said, startled by this question. "I never knew her. She sent me away when I was four."

"Nothing?" she asked. "Nothing made of iron?"

I remembered the necklace lying like a secret circle of thorns at my throat.

"Why, yes," I cried, too excited to hesitate. "She gave me this strange thing. It has protected me from revealing myself to the witchfinders ever since I came to Moria."

I pulled the necklace out from under my bodice and showed it to them. There was a gasp of breath from everyone in the circle. Even Symon turned his head and looked.

Beg's sunken mouth gaped with pleasure. She took her hand from my chin and clicked her fingers and in that moment I felt the necklace slithering through my fingers. I pulled back, but by then it was gone. It hung now in Beg's hands.

She held it up in the air and threw back her head and laughed a cackling witch's laugh.

"How like Marnie Holyhands!" she cried. "Where we see the Holy Iron Necklace of Kings she saw only a magical charm to protect her child."

She laughed again while I stared at her. What an old witch she was.

Beside me Causa gasped. Her face had changed horribly into a kind of stiff mask. Her cheeks twitched. Her eyes were half closed and both of them were fluttering, as if she was watching something very fast happening beneath her eyelids. Her hands plaited the air in her lap.

Suddenly she leaped up and thrust her arm into the air as if holding something up.

"Shall brother fight brother now the Electors have chosen?" she shouted. Her whole body gave a great shudder. She drew her hands down over her face with a low terrible groan and crumpled slowly to the ground.

Beg let out another long cackle of witchy glee, rocking from side to side. Tarwon looked on, his face suffused with strange delight.

I jumped up to help Causa, but Symon was already there and he thrust me down again.

"A foretelling is upon her," he said. "No need to fear."

He picked Causa up and disappeared into the darkness with her, leaving me with the other two.

I was bewildered. Surely they were all mad, especially that old witch Beg.

Tarwon took pity on me.

"Oh, Enna Dion," he cried. "It seems only a necklace to you, but to us this is a sign. It is a sign that the Homecoming is certain."

He clasped my hand and pulled me gently back down beside the fire.

"What is that necklace? Does it have magical powers?" I asked.

"You do not know this necklace? How strange are the workings of fate." He threw back his head and laughed. "This necklace is part of the regalia of the old kings of Moria. The regalia which was lost during Smazor's Run."

He took the necklace from Beg's hand and held it up. Its spikes glittered in the light.

"Look at it. Is it not a wonderful thing? The Klementari made it for the kings of Moria. An iron necklace that has magical power to protect its wearer from magical harm. Iron when we are taught from the cradle that iron hates magic.

The power of Klementari magic is symbolized by this sinister little thing.''

Beg spoke.

"Many, many of our dreamers have seen this necklace. A necklace that was lost even when the other regalia was found. And they see you, Dion Holyhands, putting this necklace around the neck of the future ruler of Moria.''

For a moment I was too stunned to speak.

"Me? Why me?''

"You are the most powerful mage in Moria, Dion Holyhands. The most powerful mage always crowns the ruler.''

I stared at them, unable to find words. The firelight flickered across their faces and across the black back of Symon, who was again sitting in his place outside the circle. The Raven, the outsider. I felt afraid. Were they about to try and push me into something?

"Is that why you have befriended me? Because you see that I can be some kind of powerful ally to you? Because I assure you I am no politician. You would be better off not hoping for such things from me. It is not that I am ungrateful for your help,'' I went on, realizing how offensive I had just sounded. "I am very grateful and would happily help you in any practical way in my power. But I have no gifts for influencing rulers.''

Tarwon grinned and Beg said, "That is the very least among many reasons we helped you. You will be a powerful figure in the coming events whether you like it or not. A mage like you cannot avoid influencing events even if it is only as someone's puppet. But you would be a powerful ally to us without our friendship. We all desire to see the Great Waste freed of necromancy. We know your desire is as keen as ours.''

My first thought was that I hoped she was wrong about my being powerful in coming events, but her words about necromancy chased that thought away.

"Then it's not just Church politics?''

"Our people have seen this necromancy. A demonmaster lives in the Waste Land on the site of Ruinac, the old capital.

He is building a great cathedral to honor his demons. The place is called Sanctuary.''

"Then it's true about Sanctuary. But the Burning Light?''

"A great and evil trick has been played on those who worship the Burning Light. One which they left themselves sadly open to, but it is no less tragic for that. Our people have been to Sanctuary and some came back to tell of things there.''

"At first they were glad, for what was once wasteland is covered in plants," said Tarwon. "Then they saw that the plant was boneseed, the cemetery weed, great green fields of it. At its roots, they found human bones scattered on the ground. Beyond the fields rises a huge grey building like one of your cathedrals, though its roof is open to the sky, its arches like the ribs of a dead creature.''

"The Fire Angels rise to flight from out of that building," said Beg. "All around the cathedral the Destroyer's prisoners labor to build the walls and the other buildings around its base. They quarry stone from a great pit at its foot. Slowly, group by group, they are taken into the cathedral and brought out as mutilated bodies. None of our people has yet got into it and lived to tell the tale. No one has returned to tell us what the face of the demonmaster looks like.''

"The prisoners know from the start that they are to die though they do not know why," said Tarwon angrily. "And while they work, they are whipped and terrorized by the guards, and sometimes attacked by beasts. The Destroyer does not need their labor, for he has the power of more than one demon to build for him. It is simply part of his cruelty. What kind of being trades on others' pain for mere power?''

Beg snorted.

"Mere power can lengthen your life well beyond its natural time, boy. It is a seductive call you will hear soon enough.''

She turned to me.

"Fear makes the life force more savory to demons," she said.

I knew that from my own experiences. I also knew that

the emotion need not be fear. Any intense emotion, even pleasure, would do.

"The Fire Angels would have taken you there, child of Marnie Holyhands," continued Beg, "though I doubt the Destroyer would have wasted your substance on demons."

Suddenly I was filled with shame. I remembered the battle last night in the forest, the agonized scream that rang out. These people had risked and maybe even lost their lives to help me. How could I have answered them so harshly before?

"You saved me from that," I said. "How can I repay you?"

"We saved you because we saw what a weapon you would be in the Destroyer's hands. You are a far greater mage than he. Tapping you, he would be twice, maybe three times as powerful and we would have to fight him."

"I shall fight him with you," I cried. "I vow it."

"Thank you, Enna Dion. For the moment it is enough to keep you out of his hands."

There was silence for a while. The fire crackled faintly in the hollow darkness. My mind, always easily distracted from serious matters, wondered why there was no smoke.

"The other reason we befriended you," said Tarwon, "is for the sake of your mother, Marnie Holyhands. She was a great woman of our people. Twenty-two years ago she went into the Waste Land when most of the Klementari were afraid to go. She found the royal regalia and thus began the Homecoming. For that alone of all her wonders would we watch over her children."

"It was Causa's plan to tell you of that journey," said Beg, "but her mind is full of foretelling at this moment. She will speak to you before you leave the circle."

My mind went back to the earlier conversation.

"Was it Causa who saw me in a foretelling?"

"Causa and others. It is a common vision, a sign of truth."

"They really saw me crowning Leon Sahr," I cried, filled with wonder.

The others looked at me with surprise flickering over their faces.

"What makes you think the Duke of Gallia will be the next ruler of Moria?" said Beg.

"Why? Won't he be?"

"The best person will be clear at the time," said Beg. She didn't meet my eyes.

"You saw someone else becoming ruler of Moria?" I asked.

"There are several possibilities," she said again, but it was an answer given to avoid giving an answer.

"What is it that the dreamers have foreseen?"

"It would merely muddy the waters of the fate to speak them all here," said Beg.

"The future is certain only when it becomes the present," said Tarwon.

In other words, they were not going to tell me anything more.

It was soft dusk when I found myself standing outside the Spirit Chamber again. I should have been exhausted, but my mind was seething with all I had learned.

Gunida, the woman warrior who had come to the cellar with Symon, met me at the doorway.

Smiling, she led me to a small wooden bathhouse near the furthest edge of the circle, where water was already heating on the fire and a clean dress was laid out.

I had spent over two weeks washing with a rag dipped in cold water. I immersed myself in the tub of wonderful hot water and felt the excited confusion of my thoughts collapse into a sleepy muddle. The scented soap was creamy on my skin. I found my mind wandering back to Shad and how we had kissed each other. The thought filled me with fear and delight and a longing to see him again.

When I was finished Gunida showed me the place were I was to sleep. It was a little wooden hut with a thatched roof near the top of the camp where we had come into the circle. A generous bed of quilts was made up on a pallet in the center of the floor. A mattress—how wonderful!

"Have you see my companion, Shad?" I asked her as she

turned to go, and she told me she had seen him sitting on the hillock above the hut.

There was no one on the hillock when I went to look. I felt a twinge of both disappointment and relief. Part of me was still half-convinced that this morning had been some kind of illusion. Perhaps I would be wisest to forget the whole thing. Yet the memory of his lips on mine made my stomach flutter with pleasure.

The stones of the circle curved around behind the hillock and I lingered there, looking out through the gap between them. It was strange how silent the moonlit forest outside was. The trees moved soundlessly in the wind and I should have heard the calls of night birds and animals rustling in the undergrowth.

"Dion?" said a voice behind me. A familiar figure appeared out of the darkness.

"Shad," I said by way of greeting. My mouth went suddenly dry and my knees trembled. I had an intense sense of his body moving up to stand behind me.

There was an awkward silence. Then he asked, "What are you looking at?"

"I was wondering about this place, these stones. Where on earth are we? If I was to step through the stones would I find myself back in the forest?"

"I was wondering about that this afternoon, too, so some of the Wanderers showed me. It's really strange. Come."

He moved forward into the space between the stones. I hesitated, remembering how unpleasant the barrier had felt last time I had crossed it.

He seized my hand. "Come on. Try it. It's astonishing."

I followed him between the stones. A buzzing began and a kind of tingling across the skin. Then everything went black. The buzzing became a juddering whine. My very bones seemed to rattle with the power that came jolting through me. I clenched my teeth so that they would not chatter and clutched Shad's hand as hard as I could.

Then suddenly the darkness lightened and the jolting was

gone and there we were back where we had started, facing down into the camp.

"See!" cried Shad, delighted. "The wall of magic throws you back when you try to pass it. You cannot get out of the circle or get into it without going through one of the gates. Amazing, isn't it?"

Nausea gripped me. I clutched my stomach.

"It was horrible," I said. "Couldn't you feel that power running through you? Like riding in a shuddering cart?"

"Earth and air. Oh, Dion, I'm sorry. I never thought. Are you all right?"

"I feel kind of sick," I said.

He put his arm around me and urged me gently to sit on the ground, apologizing all the while.

I leaned against him. His arms felt so pleasant, but the poor man seemed beside himself with contrition, so I resisted the temptation to play the invalid.

"I'm well enough," I said. "It's passed. Actually I think I'm just hungry."

He laughed with relief and did not move away as I had feared he might.

"I've got just the thing for you," he said. "I brought myself a little feast to eat up here, and because I'm a wonderful human being, I'll share it with you."

He had fresh oat cakes still warm from the oven and spread with melted butter and honey. It looked to me as if he had brought enough for two people. We talked as we ate, speculating on where this place might be, but in truth I don't think either of us was concentrating. We sat close together, bodies brushing against each other ever so slightly. He smelled of soap and of woodsmoke and of himself. I wanted to push my face against him and breathe him in, but shyness gripped me so strongly I could barely look at him.

"And the best bit." He put a bundled-up cloth on my lap, untied it and spread it out. "Adra berries," he said. "Have you ever had them? They're magic."

They weren't anything like magic, to be honest. They were delicious, sweet but refreshing to the taste. He kept trying to eat mine till at last I popped one into his mouth. His tongue felt warm and soft under my fingers. I fed him another one and another, more slowly this time, enjoying the wet softness of his mouth.

"You taste of butter," he breathed, kissing and licking my fingertips one by one. The tickling tingling sensation of his tongue on my fingertips made me hot with desire, made my tongue and mouth hungry for his. I kissed him softly on the lips and his arms came around me as he kissed me back fiercely. The berries rolled away, forgotten.

Much later I awoke in my sleeping hut. I was hot and uncomfortable, still in my dress, which seemed to be all bunched up around my waist. When I woke properly I could not help smiling at the remembrance of why I was still half clad. There had been no time for such things. Shad, sleeping beside me, still wore his shirt. I slid carefully out from under the quilt and crawled over to the door curtain. I pulled it open slightly. Outside, the light was the faint grey of dawn and a pale mist softened the outlines of the other huts. The lacings down the front of my dress were all undone. I leaned against the wall and let the cool air play on my hot skin and bare breasts like the kisses of love.

When I glanced back at the quilt Shad was leaning on his elbow.

"By the earth!" he said. "How did I resist you for so long? Truly I must be a saint."

I pulled my dress quickly shut.

"No. Don't!" he protested softly, and when I came to crawl back under the quilt he insisted I take it off. He had taken off his shirt and the hair on his chest tickled my bare breasts as he rolled close to me.

"How cold you are. Tch, tch, Enna Dion."

"You're not going to keep calling me Enna Dion, are you? I mean here!"

He pulled a comical face.

"I must confess I did it to still the wicked thoughts I kept having about you. Not that it did much good."

"Wicked thoughts? How long . . ."

"Oh, since the beginning." He nuzzled my neck. "I've wanted you from the start." His fingers traced gently along my shoulder. "Such beautiful skin you have." He stroked the curve of my breast, sending heat down my spine.

"I didn't realize."

"You weren't meant to. It's not right for a man to seek such a relationship with a woman he is protecting. It seems it has not stopped me."

I suddenly felt an upsurge of affection for him, dear honorable creature that he was. I kissed him. "Well, you don't have to worry about that anymore." I told him. "I've got a whole camp full of Wanderers to protect me now."

"Leaving me to concentrate on the important business of how best to pleasure Enna Dion," he laughed.

He had a wonderful deep throaty laugh. The skin of his hands was hard and felt delightful on the soft flesh of my flanks and sides. There had been no time for exploration last night. Now I ran my hands slowly down his naked back, feeling the play of the muscles and the hard line of his scars. He kissed my neck and breasts and I felt his erection hardening against my belly. His buttocks seemed to fit perfectly into my hands. The skin was firm, but as soft as down.

·10·

Afterward as we lay drowsily among the tangle of quilts, damp skin pressed against damp skin, I told Shad what I had learned in the council chambers.

"So now there can be no doubts that Sanctuary is a place of necromancy. We must hope the Duke of Gallia will go South as soon as possible. I do not love the Burning Light but I would not wish to see them fed to demons. Tell me, will the Duke listen to you if you urge him to go into the Waste Land?"

"I wouldn't think so. I'm scared to death of the Duke. I'm sure he hates me. Or, not hates me . . . despises me. He knows how I failed. I doubt he was blinded by the fact that I slew a demon."

"You are too hard on yourself. Who else could be as hard?"

"The Duke is an autocratic man. He entrusted me with the guarding of his favorite mistress and I let him down."

"Did he tell you this?"

"He did not speak to me in private after the battle. He rewarded me as was expected of him and then he helped me to disappear to Cardun. I do not want to see him again. Nonetheless I will try to speak to him and tell him of what I have found out here."

He squeezed me. "That's courage in you. Personally I'd rather fight ten Fire Angels than have to seek favor from any Duke."

I told him of the Wanderers' foretelling also.

"It's all very well for you to laugh," I said as he chuckled, "but why do they have to be so frustrating?"

"Foretelling is a frustrating business. Truly. The Wanderers call it the bitter gift, because to see the future and have it to fear can blight a whole life. The fable they told us as children warned of this: of how you can see a vision of your brother with a bloody knife and assume he is going to kill you when really he is going to kill the large bear that would have eaten you. By killing your brother you make it certain that you will be eaten by the bear. That's a simple version, but always there were warnings and warnings and warnings about putting too much weight into foretellings, especially before they have been judged. And the future does change. A foretelling is only a vision of what will happen in the future if things continue as they are. The council must like the future they have seen and be afraid of changing it by telling you too much."

Growing up in Moria there had always been Wanderers in the background—seen passing on roads, heard speaking to the servants in the garden, or glimpsed performing at fairs. During my exile in Gallia I had come to know them better; Cardun was on one of the Wanderers' regular routes and they had always called at my hut on their way through. Then there was a certain cheese-loving raven who I had "coincidentally" named Symon.

."Were you keeping an eye on me?" I asked Causa.

We sat together by the fire in the Spirit Chamber.

She shrugged. "Foretellers have seen the seventh child of Marnie Holyhands in the visions of the future for many years. In Cardun one of our people recognized you as her. We Wanderers cannot help but want to hang on to sweet visions."

"So it wasn't to protect me from the necromancer in the Great Waste."

"It crossed our minds, but there has never been any danger. It is only since you killed that Fire Angel that the Destroyer has considered your existence."

I stared at the fire. There was still no smoke in it and now I noticed there was no heat either. I put my hand into it and felt the magic flowing over it like warm water. Was it Hamel who had said Wanderer magic was different? Amazing as it seemed, he must be right. This magic was nothing like the magic I was used to.

"And Symon. Did he visit Cardun too?" I asked.

"You must ask Symon that question," smiled Causa. "I would have come anyway because you were Marnie's daughter. You look so like her."

Now that the moment had come, I felt curiously reluctant to hear Causa on the subject of my mother. I had seen Marnie Holyhands in Tomas' mind and in that half-dream I had had at the inn and I had liked what I had seen. I was afraid to find out anything that might overthrow my contentment. To have so many children still seemed foolish to me, like an unnecessary confession of guilt.

This was ridiculous. I would be sorry if I never heard Causa's story.

"Yesterday you said she saved your life," I said tentatively.

"She did. I did not always live as a Wanderer. I was born among the New People like you."

Causa had been born near Annac. Though her family had Wanderer blood, they tried to live like New People. She was orphaned young and left in the care of her brother and his wife, brutal people who beat her. It was her brother who, with a particularly vicious blow, had blinded her eye. It did not help matters that she had a tendency to go into fits of abstraction.

One day after a harsh beating, as Causa lay hurt and bleeding in an outhouse, a strange woman picked the lock, tended her hurts, picked her up, and carried her away.

"That was your mother. It was the kind of thing she did. It did not matter to her that one does not steal a stranger's child. She only saw something wrong and wished to put it right. She brought me to the Wanderers. Even though they lived poor and hungry, being among them was like a sweet dream compared to what I was used to. They recognized my fits for what they were and valued me for them."

She rubbed the side of her face with one of her plump little hands.

"The Wanderers were very afraid of the New People in those days. The clan leader protested against taking me, but your mother told them that my brother would surely kill me if they left me with them. She also said she had seen visions that showed that I would be very important to the Wanderers. Though she did not live among them, your mother was very respected for gifts of foretelling and judgment."

"Did she really know . . . ?"

"It came true, didn't it? I am the High Dreamer of the Rebirth council. I am one of the leaders pushing them back to their homeland. Mind you, Marnie had her own sense of right and wrong and I think she would have lied so that I would be safe."

This story appealed to the part of me that wanted people to be as neatly happy as possible. I reminded myself sternly that it also showed that my mother had scant regard for the truth, and a certain manipulative cunning as well.

"Why did Wanderers respect her so much?"

"She was what they called a Judge. She had a strong sense of how and when a foretelling should be acted upon. I often asked her for advice on mine and she was always right. Whenever clans of Wanderers came past Annac, she would come to see us. She hankered after the freedom of our lives, but she did not envy its hardship. Your aunt was mortally ill and relied on her, and she had you small children. The Wandering path is difficult, especially if you've no brothers to help you. Only once did she come with us and then it was because she was driven by a vision."

One day my mother had come in great excitement to

Causa's clan with a vision of the Great Waste. Many would not listen, for their minds were closed to anything that concerned the Great Waste. Causa, who had newly become a full Dreamer, did, and as Marnie told her vision, a similar vision of her own possessed Causa and with it Marnie's certainty.

"Marnie insisted that there was something important for us in the Great Waste and that we must go there immediately. You should have seen her. She was utterly convinced. You know little of foretelling, Dion, so I must tell you that such certainty is very rare. I could not help but share her conviction and there were others too who believed her. Only fear kept them from following her. In those days no Wanderer would go further east than Beenac."

Finally in desperation Marnie returned home, and taking my brother Hamel, who was still too young to be left, she and Causa set out alone. It was the middle of winter and it rained every night. Usually Wanderer women traveling alone faced constant harassment from the New People, but that was the easiest journey Causa had ever made. Everywhere people were kind to them and offered them food and shelter. They met other groups of Wanderers. Some of them were brave enough to come with them.

At last with a small band they crossed the Red Mountains into the Great Waste. My mother was in a frenzy and all for walking on through the bright moonlit night, but the rest of the group was exhausted. They were afflicted with a strange heaviness of spirit, and the more sensitive of them were troubled by terrible visions. Causa too had a tremendous urge to fall into visions, but she resisted it as she had been taught, for she was afraid of what she would see. The group made a magical circle to drive away dreams and fell down within it to sleep.

"When we woke Marnie and Hamel were gone. All day and night we followed them into the Waste. In those days it was a plain of ash, for Smazor had sucked the very life out of the soil so that it nourished very little. It made the going hard. Marnie cannot have been far ahead, for dust blows constantly in the Waste and always we could see her foot-prints. Sometimes I even thought I saw her, but it may only have been a ghost. That place is full of them. At night they cried constantly in our ears. Some of the others suffered so terribly from seeing them that they had to turn back.

"At the end of the second day, parched and burned by the sun, we came upon Marnie asleep with Hamel in her arms. Beside her lay three lumps of rusted metal. On her other side a little spring was bubbling out of the dust and running down over her feet. It came out of the hole from which she had dug the regalia. For that was what the lumps of metal were—the pieces of the regalia of the old kings of Moria. The crown, the orb, and the head of the scepter. The recovery of those things. . . ."

For a moment she stared into space, reliving a wonderful moment.

"The recovery of these things had been spoken of in many foretellings. Often there had been visions—I have had visions myself—of the Wanderers returning to their homeland with the old royal regalia in a wooden box cased in gold. But the regalia had been kept at Ernundra by the Klementari who made it, and it seemed impossible that it could ever be found. Yet because of Marnie Holyhands' determination a wooden box cased in gold now sits in this Spirit Chamber, ready to be taken back to Ernundra.

"The hope that this discovery brought us made all things possible. Everywhere Wanderers were suddenly seized with a purpose. Symon, who was with us in the Waste, left shortly afterward to join the Borgenese army and learn the skills of violence. Now he is the Raven. Beg began to travel among the clans to try and rediscover the old ways of magic. Ever since then the Wanderers have braved the Great Waste to start to drive away the ghosts.

"Slowly purposeless wandering has changed to hopeful action. That necklace you brought completes the regalia. The Homecoming will happen soon. I feel the sureness of it in my very bones. It will be a joy beyond belief."

Causa stared dreamily into the middle distance. I felt as if a light had been turned on inside me. I was glad I had had the courage to listen to the story.

"What did my mother think?" I asked tentatively, breaking into Causa's reverie.

"Marnie? She was relieved that the visionary time was over, I think. You must understand, it was not her nature to ponder much on things. She was a doer."

Lucky woman. My foster father would have seen it as a sign of a lack of intelligence, but I knew it was more complex then that. I thought so much on every decision that often I could not decide.

"Also she knew she would not live to see the Homecoming," said Causa sadly. "She returned home to her children and went on with her life."

A thought came to me.

"I was not born then," I said.

Causa smiled. "No," she said, and her voice was amused. "But you were conceived somewhere on the journey home. Hamel was not weaned when we set out, but by the time we reached Lammerquais again, he was. Poor mite. I remember his outrage. He did not like his warm vegetable mash near as much as his mother's milk. When she left us at Lammerquais, Marnie said to me, 'My brother will be displeased at this new child, but it will be the last,' and it was only then I realized she was pregnant."

"So who was my father?"

"His name was Darrah. What a passionate friendship that was. He was one of the Wanderers who braved the visions of the Great Waste with us. Mind you, he was used to visions. He was very fond of hazia."

"Where is he now?"

"By the time we returned they had argued and parted in anger. He was a wild Wanderer and never could settle, and she did not want the wandering life." She reached out and squeezed my hand. "He drowned during a vision shortly after she left, before you were even born."

Thus my father was found and lost again in the space of a few sentences. Such things leave you breathless.

"Are you troubled by the story?" Causa asked gently.

"I do not know what I think," I said.

I had found both parents now. Neither of them was very satisfactory. I wondered if my mother, with her foretelling skills, had known he was going to die. Why didn't she do something about it, if she did? I shook off these thoughts. It was twenty-two years ago. I couldn't know.

"What did you see in your visions yesterday?" I said in an attempt to lighten the mood.

"Among other things I saw you placing the crown on the head of the next ruler of Moria," said Causa.

"Who was it? The ruler, I mean."

"It changes. Let the future reveal itself to you with time, Dion."

"I knew you were going to say something like that."

She smiled at me. "Believe me. It's better not to know such things."

I remembered that a moment ago I had been about to blame my mother for my father's death. I began to see her point.

How little I knew about the Wanderers. In my lifetime they had been undergoing this great rebirth as a people, re-finding their skills at magic, learning how to deal with fore-telling again, and looking forward to a time when they would return to their homeland in the Great Waste. I had not noticed this change, and as far as I knew nobody else had either. Who bothers himself with the activities of a band of wandering beggars, anyway?

Mind you I had no doubt that the Wanderers had quite intentionally hidden their activities. This was wise of them, since their survival depended on the perception that they were inoffensive, and a growth in power and organization is hardly that. Moreover, this desire to reclaim Ernundra and the echo of the old Klementari power in Morian politics that came with it might well have alarmed the Lords of Moria. Even my foster father, who had been a mage, had been torn between approval of a time when magecraft was a ruling force in the Morian state and discomfort with the fact that it was these spirit-worshipping foreigners who had led that force. I could not imagine what the autocratic Leon Sahr would say when the Wanderers retook Ernundra. He preferred to be the only power in his dominions.

Had the Burning Light been aware of the Wanderers' push to return to Ernundra? Was this why they exiled the Wanderers from Moria? I doubted it. They had simply not liked the Wanderers' wandering and had exiled them for that. Wanderers who were settled and not using magic were left alone, only to be picked up later by the Hand of Truth as Shad's family had been. There was no chance that the Wanderers would ever have become Tansites like the rest of the peninsula folk. They had a religion of their own which they held to strongly, no matter where they were.

Always they rose at dawn and prayed to the spirits that they believed lived in all nature. The ritual consisted of kneeling on the ground and drawing five interconnected circles while repeating a chant about the five elements—earth, water, fire, air, and life—and the interconnectedness of all things. Each morning was a renewal of their pact with those spirits and a promise to respect the balance of the world.

It was Shad who showed me this ritual and translated the chant into Morian for me. The other Wanderers sat by and smilingly corrected his mistakes.

"Tch tch," said one called Kindylan. "You have been neglecting your duties, Shad Forest."

"When I went to live among the New People, I learned to go to church like them. I have not said the Morning Chant for many years," he said. "I had forgotten how beautiful it is."

Kindylan reached out and, rubbing his finger in the earth of one of the circles, smeared a line of it down Shad's forehead.

Shad fell into a thoughtful silence. The next morning when I awoke, I was alone. He returned a little later. The knees of his trousers were dusty.

"Have you been doing the Morning Chant?"

"Yes," he said, pulling off his clothes and crawling back between the covers. He was cold from the early morning air, but an immense happiness seemed to radiate from him.

Although I had not known Shad long, I could sense that our time in the stone circle was exciting for him. He seemed to be rediscovering the Wanderers after years of thinking of himself as one of the New People. When we were not together, he would sit around the fire with them, talking in their language or singing their songs. In addition to his other talents, he revealed a considerable skill at playing the wooden pipe. We would dance to his piping, the Wanderers patiently showing me the steps of the strange interweaving dances they did. They were a considerate people and took great care that I would not feel left out. Even when I was sitting on the sidelines watching them doing soldierly things like shooting at targets or wrestling, they would always chat with me. Nargoy showed me how to weave a belt in the Wanderer way and Gunida and her friend Alleena spent a whole morning plaiting my hair into little Wanderer plaits full of feathers and twigs. Despite their alienness, I felt comfortable among them.

"Are all soldiers as pleasure-loving as these?" I asked Shad.

"How so?"

"All this singing and dancing. And yesterday you spent the whole morning playing chasing games like children."

He smiled. "You mages. Nothing is serious for you but magic. Do you not see how we wear our armor and weapons to play and even to dance? They are practicing moving fast with armor on. I never saw such dedicated warriors as these. They are training when I would be throwing dice or playing cards."

"Are those leather things armor?" I asked, surprised. "Surely they wouldn't count for much."

"Oh, they'll discourage an arrow and soften a blow. The Wanderers are fast-moving troops and metal armor would slow them down. I would not like to have to go up against them. They really have changed themselves. Have you no-

ticed how there is no hazia in this camp? I've see no drunkenness either. This lot are as clean-living as a group of
Burning Light.''

I could not help having noticed it. The word Wanderer
was synonymous with one who was always out of his mind
on hazia or drink. Even those Wanderers who settled among
the new folk had a predilection for the visionary drug, or at
least the reputation for such. Hazia and its time-dulling prop-
erties were entirely absent among the Dead, however. Underneath their kindly exteriors was a steely sense of purpose.

The most mysterious of these strange new Wanderers was
Symon the Raven. Had he been the cheese-loving raven who
had visited me so often in Cardun? The coincidence of my
calling this bird Symon in the year before Symon had actually appeared in its vicinity was too amazing to be believed,
and yet I had not picked it for a magical creature. Try as I
might, I could learn nothing from Beg or Causa about the
topic.

They had plenty to say about him otherwise, however.

''A Raven is an abomination to our people,'' said Beg,
and Causa rather more usefully explained, ''The Raven em-
bodies all that the Wanderers most disapprove of. We hate
the organized violence of war. We despise the ways of warriors. It has always been our way to find peaceful solutions
and to fight with magic if it becomes necessary to fight.

''We call the Dead the Dead because as those who study
to be violent, they are dead to all true Klementari life, and
because the true purpose of warriors is to bring death even
if it is only threatened death. How can such unclean people
be allowed near children and families?

''And yet since your people have come to the peninsula,
fighting has become necessary. We need one to lead those
warriors—a Raven who plans violence, and whose mind is
always on the death of others. It is an evil but necessary role,
a paradox. For a Raven is both a courageous protector who
should be a hero to us, and one whom you would never wish

your children to admire. It is a hard role, but Symon fills it admirably.''

Symon was nothing like any other Wanderer I had ever seen. The Dead might have been fighters, but they were still as kindly and gentle as other Wanderers. Symon was stern, implacable, and sometimes cruel. Where they were easygoing, he was passionately strict. His ambivalent role among the Wanderers could not have been easy for him. It could not have been easy for any of the Dead.

A couple of nights after we had arrived, I was sitting at the mouth of the Spirit Chamber talking with Causa. Nearby the Dead were sitting singing songs in Klementari. I had never heard most of the songs before, but they did sing one I knew. It was a sad song which the Wanderers on the road often sang. I had once asked an old Wanderer man back in Cardun what the song was about, and he had told me that it was about the Istari and their loss. He had not spoken Morian well, however, and when I asked him who the Istari were he became quite incoherent. I gathered that they were some kind of old gods who were believed to have been destroyed along with Ernundra in Smazor's Run.

Causa stopped talking as soon as they began singing the song and an uneasy look passed over her face. There was not even time for me to ask her what she was uneasy about before Symon the Raven came charging out of the Spirit Chamber. He stormed over to the group around the campfire and began scolding them in Klementari. Guilty looks came onto the faces of the Dead.

"What is he saying?" I asked Causa.

"The usual thing he says," sighed Causa. "That the Istari are gone and it is time for the Klementari to learn to live their lives without them. He hates these songs. He says that it is not right to sing them during a joyful time like our Homecoming. Now he is saying that these songs have weakened our people for a hundred years and that he will not have them sung by his troops."

Symon finished his scolding and stalked stiffly past us back into the Spirit Chamber.

Causa turned and followed him. Agog with curiosity, I followed her.

Inside, the magical fire was burning as usual. The Raven threw himself angrily down beside it.

"Symon," said Causa. "What does this anger serve? They are only songs. They will always be part of us."

"When we are safely in Ernundra, then we can sing such songs. Till then they are a nothing but a burden."

He turned and saw me.

"Such songs remember the time of childhood in my people's history," he said to me with astonishing earnestness, "when the Istari were like kind and doting parents guiding our steps and judging our foretellings. When they were gone we were orphaned, and we have wandered for one hundred years paralyzed with grief. We cannot survive as orphaned children. We must grow up and learn to do what we can with what remains. The New People have always lived without such kind parents."

"We too have our gods," I said.

"But the Istari were real beings who lived among us. Not wooden dolls to hold when we were afraid of the dark," he said, confounding me completely.

Did Symon really believe that such gods were real? His cynicism had always made me think of him as halfway rational. It was no wonder priests disliked Wanderers so much if they really did see Aumaz the creator, and his Holy Son and messenger Lord Tanza, as nothing but wooden dolls for frightened children.

"It is like this fiendish passion for foretelling," muttered Symon, still talking out his rage. "Because nothing good was seen of the future, we did nothing to better ourselves. It was left to an outsider like Marnie Holyhands to act. Must it always be outsiders who make things happen for our people? Look at the Raven, the most active principle in all Klementari life. Yet he is unnatural, un-Klementari."

A shadow stirred beside the fire and I saw that Beg had been sitting there all the time. Now she spoke.

"The most powerful things in life come from paradox,"

she said. "You cannot turn your back on foretelling, Raven. You owe your power to it."

"Foretellings," snapped Symon. "If foretelling is so useful, old woman, why did the Klementari not foresee Smazor's Run? Why did the Istari do nothing to prevent it?"

"You know the answer to that question," said Causa. "You know of the madness of the foretellers and the mystification of the Istari." She had sat down beside him. She was smiling quite calmly despite the fact that he seemed to be attacking the very foundation of her existence.

"Foretelling is a pretty gift," muttered Symon, "but it has no practical use. Give me action, I say."

"You speak like one of the New People," said Beg sourly. "Hear how he speaks of foretelling, child. It is almost as if he hates it. No true Klementari would speak of anything with such hatred. Raven!"

"I would die for our people," said Symon without heat. His old cynical expression had returned. "Would you bear the burden of the outsider for the sake of them, you old witch?"

"I have taken my risks too," said Beg primly. "Some of what you say is just, Raven. It is time for us to change as a people or to die. But we shall always sing those old songs. I do not understand why you rant and rave against them."

"That's because you are too old to change."

"And you have changed already," said Causa to Symon. "I wonder often if you are what our people will be like when the change finishes."

Beg made a derisive noise.

"God protect us. I hope this thought never occurs to the rest of the council or we shall have to start all over again."

"I am the Raven," said Symon with bitterness in his voice. "I am dead to true Klementari life. I have no business defining the ways of the living. All I wish is that they no longer wander as homeless victims of the New People."

Causa put her hand on the back of his neck and drew his head down so it rested on her lap. She stroked his hair.

"Nonetheless, Raven, it is your actions which cause our

people to be reborn. Thus you will help to define who they are to become.''

This was as tender a scene as between mother and child. I found it acutely embarrassing. I did not like to see Symon the Raven reduced to a little child like this. And yet as I slipped away, I heard him speak in his old cynical manner.

''Is that a foretelling, Dreamer?'' he said.

''It is a truth that will be,'' said Causa.

I longed to understand the Wanderers' magic better. They had made that amazing iron necklace that cast its own magic even as it disabled mine. They had turned our dangerous hideout in the forest into a kind of idyllic picnic, using this miraculous magic circle. The magic I had learned was powerful, but its power was limited by the fact that it could be detected and defended against by the other people using the same magic. The effect of this balance of aggressive and defensive magic was to make magical power little more useful than skill in swordplay. Now here I was leading an entirely civilized life with warm baths, hot food, and healing magic, under the very noses of people who were searching for us by every means available.

Several times I witnessed groups of searchers walking out of the forest into the stone circle and disappearing where the stones began. Shad and I could not resist running to the other side of the circle to see where they came out. This amused the Wanderers to no end. They followed us, laughing and shouting encouragement, and helped us look for the suddenly reemerging searchers. We would all stand at the edge of the circle calling out rude and provocative remarks at their unaware backs. Even the priest mages with their magic crystals were unaware of us.

I examined the standing stones closely and found the same group of runes at the bottom of each. I did not recognize any of them, but I taught myself to copy them exactly as they were. When I was safe again, I planned to try using them with magical power and seeing where they got me.

But as I was practicing these runes in the dust, someone

put a foot out and rubbed them out. I looked up and saw Beg standing over me.

"Knowing just the runes will not do you any good, Enna Clever," she said, chuckling a little.

"Then what will?" I cried. "Will you show me?"

"No," said Beg, plumping herself down in the sun nearby.

It was left to Shad to try and explain something of Klementari magic.

"I do not think you can do magic like the Wanderers unless you believe in the connectedness of all things as we do," said Shad. "My brothers often tried to show me how to do it, but I have not the ability. It begins with the Morning Chants. You must be able to feel the life force in the world around you to begin. You draw power into yourself from your connection with the life force that flows through them."

I could not imagine it. My power came from within me. This sounded like religious magic, which drew its strength from the strength of beliefs of groups of people channelled through power crystals. But religious magic was not a strong magic and it was perfectly detectable.

"This all sounds like a kind of primitive animism," I said without thinking. Mages have no time for religion. "It's just superstition."

He smiled. "I'm only trying to make it easier for you to understand."

"I'm sorry," I said, realizing how unguardedly I had spoken and how rude it sounded.

"No. You are entitled to think as you wish. I simply think you are wrong."

"Then you believe in these spirits in trees and rocks."

"It's not like that," he laughed. "For many years I went to church like a good little New Person, but I could never see Aumaz as a god up in the heavens needing his son Tanza as a messenger, because it seemed to me he was a part of all the things around us and that I could feel him when I was in the forest choosing wood and in the workshop carving it. I realize it's a heresy, but it's a pretty common heresy in the South, especially among half-breeds like me and you. Now that I do the Morning Chant again, I realize that Aumaz had just become the word I used for life force and spirit.''

"I don't know why Beg couldn't just explain this," I grumbled.

"The New People only treated the Klementari well while they had reason to fear them. When that power was gone, so was the fair treatment. Most Wanderers have good reason to resent the New People."

I knew this was true.

"They do not show their resentment often," I said, remembering how pleasant the Wanderers had always been to me.

"No, it's not their nature. But the term New People is not as pleasant as it sounds. In Klementari the word they use for 'new' actually means 'freshly dropped,' as in freshly dropped pile of shit."

"Oh my," I said half amused and half appalled by my own naïvete.

It had been so easy to talk to Shad in the cellar, and now that we had become lovers, that was easy too. In my admittedly limited experience I had never met a man who enjoyed physical contact as much as Shad did. He made love with the same sensuous enjoyment with which he carved wood, using his strong supple hands to smooth the very essence of pleasure out of me. He was not shy either. It pleased him that I liked his body and wanted to touch it. Often I had felt I must restrain my feelings with Parrus, because I had a sense that he was a little shocked when I expressed desire. Shad simply assumed that I was as lusty as he was.

The first day after I had seen Causa in the Spirit Chamber and visited Tomas in the healer's hut, I returned to my own hut.

Shad was sitting outside carving away at a piece of wood. I stood watching his strong chest muscles through the neck of his shirt. The sight of him, the memory of all we had done together, made me damp with desire. I wanted desperately to touch him, but was too shy to make a move.

Shad kept smiling at me from under his eyelashes until finally he put down his wood, reached out, pulled me toward him, and kissed me on the lips.

"What are you waiting for?" he laughed. "A written invitation? You'll waste the whole day if you go on that way."

He pulled me into the hut where we made heated love for most of the afternoon. In between we lay comfortably together, talking idly, touching and kissing each other with slow, delicious sensuality.

My desire for him amazed me. The feeling of his skin against mine gave me irresistible pleasure. Every night in the stone circle I slept exhausted in his arms, and every morning awoke sensuously curled against his body, impatient for him to slide against me again. In that time I did not once dream of the stone woman or of Andre, and I do not think I gave either of them any thought.

There was a window high up on the wall under the very eaves of the hut. Through it we could see the tips of the stone circle and watch birds flying high up in the sky above us. Shad was fascinated by birds.

"Have you ever changed into a bird?" he asked me once. He was astonished when I said no.

"But you can."

"Oh yes, surely."

"It is the only thing I would really like to have magic for. It would be wonderful to be able to fly." He turned quickly to me and said, "When this is all over could you, would you, be able to take me flying? Just once?"

His enthusiasm made me smile. It was easy enough for me to do. I had simply never done it because mages are not accustomed to thinking of magic as purely for pleasure. The request stood out in my mind afterward, because it was the only thing to do with magic he ever asked me for.

The worm in our apple was Tomas. He had been confined to Taldera's hut for the first two days of our stay, but now that healing magic could be used on him, his recovery was quite fast. By the third day he was able to venture out of the hut and walk shakily around for a short while.

Though I went to see him every day, I did not tell him about Shad and me. How on earth did you bring up a thing like that? Anyway, it was none of his business.

Unfortunately, on the fourth day after our arrival, Tomas found out.

We were standing by the practice area, and Shad had just leaned over and kissed my cheek when we heard an outraged bellow and Tomas came charging down the hill at us and took a swing at Shad. Shad ducked the clumsy blow and jumped away from me.

"What do you think you're doing, you villain? I'll kill you," shouted Tomas, taking another swing at Shad. Fortunately he was still not too steady on his feet. Shad ducked his blow, came up from underneath, caught his arms and bore him back hard till together they hit the wall of a hut.

"I'll get you for this, Forest," shouted Tomas. "I told you not to touch her."

"I'm not hurting her," said Shad. He had Tomas securely pinned by both arms. "Calm down, man. She's taken no harm from me."

"Oh yes. I saw you, you filthy seducing swine."

"This is none of your business, Tomas," I shouted, furious and hugely embarrassed by the interested group of Wanderers who had gathered silently around us.

"I'm your brother. Who else is there to protect you? You won't get away with this, Forest."

"Tomas, stop being ridiculous. I don't need your protection."

"Your sister is well able to look after herself," shouted Shad. "Why don't you just leave us alone, Holyhands?"

"You would say that. But you know just what kind of soft-hearted innocent my sister is. It's her power you're after. You're worming your way into her affections and then you think she'll do anything you ask. I'm not going to sit by and let that happen."

How had Tomas learned so quickly where to put in the knife and how to turn it? I felt myself go cold. Was he right?

What was Shad after? Why had he been so nice to me? Maybe . . . What if Tomas was right?

"What pigshit!" shouted Shad. "Oh, by the Earth, Dion, talk some sense into this stupid brother of yours."

"Don't trust him," shouted Tomas.

"Dion?" said Shad. He had turned his head and caught sight of my face. "Dion, what is it?"

I couldn't speak for the cold fear that was welling up inside me.

"Dion?" said Shad. He dropped Tomas and came toward me. Tomas saw his opportunity and struck out.

"No!" I shouted. But even as I shouted and threw out magic to protect Shad, there was a sort of thud in mid-air. Tomas collapsed on the ground.

Symon stood there, manifestly displeased.

"That was a low act, Tomas Holyhands. How dare you come threatening my people and breaking up the peace."

"You told me my sister would come to no harm. What have you been doing, Symon?"

"If I thought Enna Dion was coming to harm at the hands of this man, I would have stepped in. But I saw no harm. Is your sister to be a nun to please you? That is not the way of our people, Tomas Holyhands, and you know it."

"You don't understand," said Tomas.

"I understand well enough," said Symon. "Your sister is mistress of her own power and must use it as she sees best. Now shake hands with this man. And I want your word you will not try to fight him again."

I slipped away through the crowd of Wanderers, too upset to stay. What if Tomas was right? In a way he was right. How can you tell why a man is being nice to you? Perhaps this happiness with Shad was all a deception, as it had been with Andre. Deception and self-deception. God knows I would have happily done anything Shad asked of me before Tomas had spoken those words.

I hid away in the bathhouse, which was deserted at this time of day. It did not take Shad long to find me, however.

"Dion," he said softly. "What's the matter?"

"Nothing," I said, unable to look at him.

"Did you believe what your brother said? About my being after your power? Dion, look at me. Dammit, I never gave you any reason to think such things of me."

I did not want to talk about this. I knew I would not be able to bring myself to believe any protests of innocence and sincerity.

"You have no business suspecting me so," said Shad calmly, though there was an undertone of anger in his voice.

"No. No. Of course not," I said. I schooled my face into a calm mask. "I'm sorry. It was nothing. Please forget about it. And forgive my brother's rudeness."

"Of course," said Shad, looking slightly bewildered.

"I must go and speak with Tomas," I said, pushing past him.

He caught me round the waist and pulled me back against him. His chest pressed against my back.

"Dion, I never wanted any woman as hotly as I want you."

The way his lips pressed against my neck, the feel of his strong arms around me, and his hard body pressed against mine—I felt heat sliding with sharp hunger through my loins. I turned in his arms and caught him in mine, kissed him, made love with him there on the floor of the bath house, body straining against body, teeth biting flesh. Afterward it seemed to me that I would be a fool to give up such wonderful lovemaking, when all I needed to do was keep a small secret part of myself watchful and cautious.

Thus I did not go to placate Tomas. The next day Tomas amazed me by coming to apologize.

This gave me a wonderful opportunity to say reproachfully, "You did say you never interfered in your sisters' affairs."

"But you're different," said Tomas. "You are powerful and men will try to use you for that power."

How well he spoke.

"Do you really think Shad is that kind of man?"

"I can't say. How can we know what ambitions lie beneath that pleasant exterior? I mean, what is he? A nobody, a woodcutter's son with Wanderer blood. You could give him everything, Dion. You could make him a great man. Can't you see what a temptation you must be for him?"

I could.

"You're taking it too seriously, Tomas. It's just a physical thing. A passing fancy."

"Well," he said with a relieved sigh, "I am pleased to hear that. Because really, Dion, you could do so much better for yourself. Although too many of these little affairs will not improve your chances. Not everyone is as broad-minded as I am."

I stared at him. "What on earth are you talking about?"

"You could make a really good match. Don't throw it away on some entanglement with a handsome nobody."

I couldn't believe what I was hearing. This was too ridiculous. I wasn't going to get married.

"Don't be insane, Tomas. Who'd want to marry me?"

"Plenty of people. You're the most powerful mage in Moria and you're good-looking and a pleasant person. Through me, you have powerful friends and if you play things right with the Duke this time—because he'll no doubt want your help—you'll have something to offer as a dowry too."

"That wasn't what I meant. Tomas, I have no intention of marrying. For God's sake, I'm not the kind of woman men want to marry."

"Why not? Because of your power? A powerful man will not care for that. And don't worry that you're not a virgin. If a woman has enough to offer, people will overlook that, especially in a second wife."

I'd meant that nobody would ever care enough about me to want to marry me, of course, especially after they found out about Andre. Tomas was talking as if the whole business of love and care was irrelevant. No doubt if I tried to explain my feelings to him he'd just laugh.

"There is no point in going on with this conversation," I

snapped at him. "It's stupid. I'm not interested in being married so just forget it."

"Why? Is this because of Shad?"

"No," I shouted, goaded beyond endurance by this painful subject. "It's because you are too stupid to understand."

I turned on my heel and left him.

Shad was sitting in the corner of the hut when I returned to it. He did not seem to see me when I came in.

"Shad?"

"Dion," he said. He sprang up and caught me in his arms and pulled me down on the quilts, kissing me so passionately all thought of anything else went out of my head.

Later I woke to find him out of bed and looking at his weapons. Though he had a sleeping place elsewhere, his pack, which the Wanderers had rescued from the remains of the cellar, had, like him, come to live in my hut.

"What are you doing?"

"Seeing to my weapons. Kindylan told me the Ducal army has reached Lammerquais. The Burning Light and its witchfinders have gone—fled south or thrown into prison. The city has opened its gates joyfully to the Gallians and Sandor Sercel is back in the White Tower. He will be receiving the Duke there tomorrow."

"That's wonderful!" I said, though suddenly I was very far from feeling it.

"Aye! If there is a place for me in that army, I must join it. I must see this thing through to the end. I have promised myself and the spirits of my family that I shall see them avenged. I must do it."

It was as if Tomas had engineered the whole world to suit his own purposes. Soon Shad must go and then I would not see him, maybe never again. It was a bleak thought, but I could hardly have expected otherwise.

Shad did not look at me as he polished his sword. I could understand his embarrassment. No doubt he was afraid I would make claims on him now. Well, I was not going to do that. I would do my best to show him that from now on.

"You will not fight with the Wanderers?" I asked, keeping it light.

"I would be better off among the New People. I am more used to the way they fight. Anyway, the Wanderers will not stop fighting till they have regained Ernundra, even if it takes every last man, woman and child of them. I'm still not sure if I can do that. It's something you should think about too, Dion. They may expect the same commitment of you one day."

That evening another band of warriors came. The circle was almost three times as full as it had been. As we sat around the fire, Symon the Raven stood and announced the arrival of the Duke of Gallia in Lammerquais and the overthrow of the Burning Light and its witchfinders.

"Enna Dion Holyhands and her companions may safely leave us now," he said. "She no longer needs our protection. Now the time has come for us to finally turn our faces toward Ernundra."

A cheer rang out so loud I felt sure it must be heard outside the stone circle. Wanderers gathered round us and hugged and kissed us, bidding us farewell, each one promising that we would meet again soon. Joyful songs broke out.

Through the dark mass of people I saw Symon slipping toward the mouth of the Sprit Chamber.

Quickly I followed him and caught him just as he was pulling away the curtain.

"Symon. What do you plan to do next? What should I do?"

He turned and a smiled a thin-lipped smile.

"Come," he said, and pulled me through into the Spirit Chamber.

Today Beg lay in the center of the circle of candles, wearing a thin linen shift and managing to look bent with age even lying flat on her back.

Symon knelt in the light of the candles, one knee drawn up under his chin, looking up at me. I sat beside him.

"Will you be fighting against the Duke?" I asked. "Will you be joining his army?"

"That will depend on the Duke's actions," said Symon. "In a few days all the army of the Dead will come to Lammerquais. We shall call ourselves the Klementari from that time and our return to Ernundra will be made public. But the issue of who will rule Moria is of secondary importance to us. We are not a numerous people and I have no wish to lose precious Klementari lives in unnecessary fighting before we reach Ernundra. Do not tell the Duke of us. I doubt that a connection with us will do you service in his eyes. This is a time of diplomacy and politics. Moves must be made carefully and sides chosen with equal care."

"Could you beat the Duke in battle?" I asked. "If it turns out to be necessary?"

"If the Duke does not fit in with our plans we shall go South without him and retake Ernundra alone. Then we shall defend our rights to it to the last person. But it is likely that Duke Leon will want our help and be prepared to give good terms for it. Two weeks ago an army led by the Holy Patriarch entered Moria from the north and took Mangalore. The Patriarch has his own pretender to the throne, Gerard Hawksmoor, and the Northern Elector, Alceste Rouget, supports his claim to the throne."

"Aumaz! But this will be civil war!"

"We must hope the New People will free the South and end the Destroyer's reign in the Waste Land before they stop to quarrel over the throne. We will certainly not involve ourselves in any struggle between the Patriarch and the Duke."

The Patriarch and the Duke were old rivals, and it was unlikely that this invasion from the north was in any way allied with the Duke's move across western Moria. Would the Duke and the Patriarch be able to ally themselves to save the South? Every right-thinking person must see that wiping out necromancy was the most important priority of all and yet. . . . Would the Duke and Patriarch see it this way, when the crown of Moria was at stake?

Or would it come to Northern Moria against Central Moria like two dogs fighting over a carcass, while the South remained under Hierarch Jarraz's yoke and the prey of this necromancer?

After lunch the following day, Tomas, Shad, and I set out through the forest. We were a subdued group, for I had told the others about the Patriarch's invasion. Kindylan and Gunida came with us to guide us and to help Tomas, who was still shaky on his feet. The two of them called frequent stops, which Tomas grumbled about, claiming he was not in the least tired, but I knew he was finding the going exhausting. Midafternoon we stopped on the crest of a great hill.

"Just over there is the main road to Lammerquais," said Gunida.

Shad and I ran to the crest to look over it and saw that though we were close in distance, we were not at all close in travel time. We were at the top of a steep escarpment. It looked like it would be a long hard climb down in that direction. In the valley beneath us the main road came into view, between two stretches of heavy forest. Along that road a great line of people were marching. Soldiers on horseback were followed by a long line of foot soldiers. Bright-colored pennants fluttered all around them. The sound of pipes and drums floated up to us. This must be the tail end of the Ducal army going to join their leader in Lammerquais. Shad and I stood and waved, but at that distance no one noticed us.

"Can you see them then?" called Tomas, struggling up the hill after us.

"Aye." I turned and saw that we were alone. Gunida and Kindylan had disappeared.

"Damn it. How are we going to get down?" said Tomas, following my gaze.

"Look!" cried Shad. "A company of fighting mages." I could just make out a company of men in mages' robes striding past.

Shad turned to me, smiling. "This reminds me," he said in a mock accusing tone. "I'm sure you promised to take me flying first chance you got. Now the witchfinders are gone, what's stopping you?''

I grinned at him. ''I didn't say anything about first chance.''

''Good God, Dion!'' laughed Tomas. ''Flying?''

I caught Shad round the waist and flung us into the air and over the edge of the escarpment. Shad gave a yelp of surprise and clutched me. Then he started laughing with pleasure, looking at the trees beneath us as we hovered a few feet off the edge of the cliff.

''Up?'' I said.

''Let's go.''

We rose into the air until Tomas was just a small figure beneath us.

''This is great,'' cried Shad, squeezing me around the waist. His eyes shone. ''I can see the White Tower from here.''

Magic surged deliciously through me.

''Tomas is waving at us,'' said Shad.

''Hey,'' yelled Tomas. ''You two. Don't just go off and leave me.''

''Some other time we'll have a proper flight,'' I promised Shad as we went back down to the ground.

The moment the magic stopped a wonderful feeling of joy and freedom filled me. It had been almost four weeks since I'd used my powers. It was wonderful to be free of the fear of the witchfinders. I felt like a room that had been cleaned and cleared of cobwebs. I lay in the grass looking up at the two men and laughed until they both began laughing at me back.

''So,'' said Tomas. ''What about me? Are you going to make your poor crippled brother walk when he could fly?''

Still filled with almost hysterical happiness, I slid an arm round both their waists and pulled them off the edge of the cliff.

The three of us sailed easily through the air vaguely in the direction of Lammerquais. The others both seemed to be enjoying themselves, so I didn't hurry. I floated on the fresh breeze, ignoring the nagging feeling that I was wasting my magic. Nearby a soaring hawk squawked and quickly flew away. Soon, however, I began to sense the presence of magic below. Tiny tendrils of it were licking out and glancing tentatively over me. Of course, some of the mages below in the army would have felt my magery and were sending out spells to see if I was dangerous.

"Oh, Dion, you silly fool," I thought.

Alarming a whole army full of mages was distinctly unwise. Back to the real world. I willed us up over the forest and made off purposefully toward the White Tower.

"Go little sister!" cried Tomas, waving his fist the air and the two men whooped and cheered all the way to town.

As we came over the White Tower, I could sense panic below me and a flurry of magical activity.

It was time to start acting harmless. I dropped us quickly into the courtyard before the tower and we landed with a gentle thud on the cobblestones.

The place was full of Ducal troops: men at arms, priests, mages, and horsemen; but a space cleared about us with satisfying speed. As I was still shaking the windblown hair off my face, a group of mages ran out of the crowd and assumed a fighting phalanx formation before us.

There was a tense silence. Anxious flickers of magic moved over us like a thousand questioning voices. I kept my mind defensively on Tomas and Shad, wondering at the same time what to do next.

A mage stepped forward wearing the blue silk robe of the Ducal bodyguard.

"My Lord Mage," he said, bowing his head toward Tomas. "I am Chief Magus of the Bodyguard of the Duke of Gallia. I bid you and your companions welcome."

It was a natural enough error in a world where women are not usually taught magecraft, and he looked a little offended at Shad's shout of laughter. Tomas merely grinned. I sensed outrageous possibilities moving through his mind and moved quickly forward to grip his arm. He managed to elude me.

"I beg pardon for my companion," he said bowing and speaking in his most courtly Gallian, "but I am afraid you are mistaken. It is My Lady Mage you are addressing. Allow me introduce my sister Madame Dion, already known to you as the Demonslayer of Gallia. She is at your service."

A satisfying gasp of disbelief and amazement went up from the crowd.

It was interrupted by a shout from behind us. A group of men came down the stairs of the tower.

"It's the Duke," I hissed to the other two, and dropped into my lowest curtsy.

"Madame Dion," cried the Duke, holding his hands out in a welcoming gesture. He was quite a short man, not much taller than my brother and slightly built. Despite this he had the indefinable air of command. There was a sharp ruthless mind behind that thin-lipped face with its cold blue eyes. The warm tone of his voice was completely unexpected.

"No, no," he said. "Do not be so formal. We are old friends."

He took my hand and lifted me out of the curtsy.

"Madame Dion, I am so pleased to see you with us again." He took my hands in both of his and patted them in a way that was positively avuncular.

I tried not to stare at him in amazement. I had spent time at court but I could only remember one or two times when he had had just this same friendly tone. Usually it had meant he was having a joke at my expense. To be honest I couldn't help being a little scared now. I thanked him politely and hoped I was not betraying my fear. He drew my hand through his arm, a tremendous honor, and led me toward the steps of the tower to be introduced to everyone. Perhaps he was having a game at the expense of the others. There was enough amazement among the onlookers to please even the Duke's exacting sense of humor. He certainly had Tomas fooled. I could see the look of pure delight in my brother's eyes as I looked back at him. Shad, on the other hand, looked uneasy.

And so began my (mercifully brief) time among the shapers of Morian history.

Politics

·11·

The White Tower of Lammerquais had originally been built as a fortress on the the shores of Lake Lammer. It was a great square castle with towers on all four corners. When it had first been built three hundred years before, the Sercels had been robber barons out of Gallia who had taken advantage of a period of civil unrest to acquire land in the area. Since then their hold on Middle Moria had only strengthened. It was helped by the fact that Lord Sandor's grandfather, who had been a very clever engineer, had built locks at the place where the river Amer flowed into Lake Lammer. Barges could come all the way from Borgen and cross to the other end of the lake fifty miles away without once having to be unloaded. The Sercels had become immensely rich on the tolls and taxes they had levied on this lucrative trade, and Lammerquais had become the most important city in Central Moria.

Two magnificent buildings had been added to the original white fortress, wings that stretched out on either side of it. These had no defensive function at all. They existed only to impress onlookers with the Sercels' wealth and the strength of their hold on Middle Moria, which they did admirably.

When our little group had finally been dismissed by the Duke, I discovered that the inside was as impressive as the outside. Lucien Sercel led us through a low white archway that connected the castle with the left wing. Beyond was the most magnificent hall, its walls hung with brilliantly colored tapestries and handsome paintings. The ceiling rose in elegant arches above us and each crossbeam carried a beautiful chandelier of colored glass. I fell behind looking at it all and had to scamper to catch up.

I rejoined the men as they began to mount the great staircase, just in time to hear my brother saying, "And to think Dion told me the Duke of Gallia disliked her. Honestly, Dion, you're hopeless. Angels would weep."

"Well, I really thought he didn't," I said, knowing I sounded defensive.

Shad cast me a sympathetic look over his shoulder, and so, to my surprise, did Lucien Sercel. He and Tomas seemed to have completely forgotten that they had been fighting last time they had met and were acting like the best of friends. I could only imagine that this was one of those wonders of family life.

"Now, Tomas," said Lucien softly. "Great men have great need of friends in the Duke's situation. Especially friends who are powerful mages. It is enough to make them overlook any past displeasure."

"Humph," said Tomas. "All I know is that my sister has no more sense of her own worth than a newborn lamb and this just proves it."

Lucien changed the subject. "Lammerquais is crowded at the moment. The Duke has brought a large army with him. All the noble commanders and Lady Julia and her entourage are housed here in the tower. And Blanche Shomnee."

"Shomnee! Not the Elector of Southern Moria, Shomnee."

"The very same. Rumor has it that no men of the Shomnee line survive and that Lady Blanche herself is next in line for elector. She came to the Duke after the battle of Glassybri and threw herself on his mercy. Interesting, no? I suspect she'll be trying to get some kind of amnesty for her uncle Bishop Jarraz in return for her vote. But she's only seventeen and she can hardly be expected to undertake such difficult negotiations herself. She's waiting for some kind of negotiator to come from her uncle to help her finish the deal.''

"You mean the Duke is going to make a deal with Jarraz?'' cried Shad. "Hasn't he heard what's going on in the South?''

"Don't worry,'' said Lucien, clapping Shad companionably on the shoulder. "Everyone's heard of what's going on in Sanctuary. The whole Peninsula is outraged and no one more than the Duke. But Lady Blanche is insistent that her uncle is an unwilling dupe, an unworldly holy man, and for his part the Duke believes that the South might be liberated much faster through peaceable negotiations than through war. Especially now he's got the Patriarch on his doorstep. Have you heard that he's in Moria?''

"Aye,'' said Tomas cynically. "Everyone wants to help free us from the Church of the Burning Light these days. Very good of them all to bother.''

"The Patriarch will arrive at Lake Lammer in a couple of days. The Duke's intention at the moment is to stop here to replenish the army and recruit more men. I tell you, Shad, there are suddenly hordes of Southerners in Lammerquais, all wanting to join the army. Lord Quercy is here.''

"Lord Quercy!'' echoed Shad. "Earth and air. He began the Shattered Light. It will be an honor to serve with him.''

"He seems a very fine man,'' said Lucien. "Hey!''

Lucien's exclamation was directed at a small figure who at this moment came plunging down the stairs toward us at a limping run, shouting, "Pa! Pa!''

"Marty boy!'' shouted Tomas, rushing forward and scooping the him up in his arms. He squeezed the boy to him and kissed his face.

"My best boy,'' he cried. "Here, lad, what's this? Tears? Why, did you think your old man was gone for good? There, there now, you foolish boy. You should have known better. I wouldn't leave my best boy.''

The next minute a wave of children came shouting down the stairs: Dally, Tasha's child; Silva's children, Needra and

Derrum; and two dark little children in rich clothes who seemed to belong to Lucien. The wave broke around Tomas' legs.

"Uncle Tomas, Uncle Tomas," they all shouted, dancing around him and hugging him, and Tomas laughed and shouted back, dancing up the stairs with Martin still in his arms, until right at the top he suddenly turned pale and had to sit down in a big chair.

Lucien shouted for the nursemaid to take the children away, but the nursemaid could do nothing with them until Silva came sweeping down the corridor, clapping her hands, crying, "Children, come leave your uncle alone. Can't you see he is tired out? Quickly now, upstairs, all of you."

Clamoring to be visited later, the children were finally threatened and enticed away by the nursemaid—all except Martin, who Tomas insisted must stay to help support his poor elderly father.

Silva kissed us all warmly, even Shad. "You are almost like family to me now that you have saved Dion's life," she said to him. She was as beautiful as ever, warm and smiling, but she had lost weight and there were dark rings under her blue eyes.

"We have been in prison since you were gone," she told us by way of explanation. "I am so grateful to Lucien, Tomas. He cared for the children and it would have been much the worse for us had he not pestered the witchfinders so."

"Mouse? Uncle Louie?"

"Uncle Louie is not so well. They put us to mind search several times. I can't understand why, for they must have quickly seen that we knew nothing. I'm afraid something has broken in Uncle Louie's brain. I was hoping that Dion might be able to . . ."

"Of course," I said. I felt vaguely guilty. Compared with prison, our adventure in the forest seemed positively idyllic.

"As for Mouse, he is well enough. But, oh, Tomas, they set fire to the inn and it burnt to the ground."

"But why?" cried Tomas. "It. . . . Why? How could they?"

"There was no one to stop it. It was punishment to our family for harboring a witch. Mouse is out there now to see if anything is left."

"Don't worry, Tom," said Lucien, patting Tomas' shoulder. "We'll rebuild it."

"Aye," said Tomas, his face hard and bitter. "The witchfinders' time is over now. I am in your debt, brother. I thank you."

"My pleasure," said Lucien. "And I'd feel sufficiently repaid if you could just refrain from mentioning the past more than once a day. Hmm?"

It was obvious from the way the side of his face drooped that Uncle Louie had had a stroke, but when I looked inside his head I found that another healer had already treated him, smoothing over the damaged brain tissue and reconstructing his blood vessels as best as could be done. Healing can do nothing for what has been broken too long. If he had had treatment immediately, much more could have been repaired.

"There is nothing more I can do for him," I said, sliding my power carefully out of Uncle Louie's skull and leaving him quietly asleep. "The other healer has done well. He will get better, but he will never be entirely well. How often did they search you?"

"Every couple of days," said Silva. "They must have done me about ten times at least."

"But why? What did they hope to achieve?"

She shrugged. "There was a priest among them called Zorzar. I think he enjoyed seeing how much it hurt. When he left they did not bother again."

Enjoying people's pain. Now here was the sign of necromancy.

"And how are you?" I asked her. "Your head has ached ever since those mind searches, hasn't it? Didn't you get the healer to look at you?"

She shrugged. "She was overburdened with work. There is much healing for her to do since the Burning Light has left Lammerquais. My headache wasn't bad enough."

Ignoring her protests, I cajoled her into lying down upon my bed and letting me treat her with a soothing sleeping spell.

She must have been glad to close her eyes, for the muscles on her face and neck were very stiff and her mind was tender with the expectation of pain. Her ears must have been ringing with it. It was good to see her face relax.

The calmness of magic left me as I sat by Silva's side, watching her sleep, and I felt overwhelmed with guilt. I was not worth their pain, Louie's paralysis, the burning of their home. Who was I? Hardly even a real family member. I was no one particularly valuable or useful. I must strive to make their sacrifices worthwhile.

There was no sign of Tomas or Lucien in the corridor outside the room, but Shad was there, standing in one of the alcoves that lined the corridor, running his fingers along a border carved with fruit and flowers.

"This is beautiful work," he said. "Beautiful."

He turned and saw my face.

"What is the matter?"

"Oh Shad. They were so hurt. I don't think Uncle Louie will ever recover, and all because the Burning Light were looking for me."

He put his arms around me and I leaned against him and felt him rub my back.

"You did not order the mind searches," he said.

A door banged at the end of the corridor, and as if by mutual consent Shad and I moved quickly apart. A young woman came sweeping purposefully down the corridor toward us. From her rich velvet dress and the fact that an older woman was scurrying behind her in attendance, she was obviously someone of importance. Her bright red hair was uncovered in the fashion of an unmarried aristocrat and hung in a long braid twined with pearls down her back. Perhaps one of Lucien's relatives? Whoever she was, such was her manner that without thinking twice I found myself curtsying and saw that Shad too was bowing.

She did not sweep past, but came straight up to us and held out her hand.

"You are Enna Dion, the Demonslayer?" she asked excitedly.

I murmured my assent, took the hand uncertainly and curtsied over it.

"This is such a privilege for me," she said. "I never hoped to have the opportunity to meet you, Enna Dion. Your actions are an inspiration to Morians everywhere."

"Thank you . . . ma'am."

Who was this woman? Yet even as I wondered I began to suspect who she might be. She spoke Morian like a native, but she had red hair, which was not a common colour among Morians. Surely it couldn't be *her*! Not here speaking to *me*!

"And who is your companion?" asked the lady.

"This is Shad Forest," I said. "He saved my life and protected me while I was hiding from the Burning Light."

Shad bowed low. "Your loyal servant, my lady," he said in an awestruck tone.

"Well done, Ren Forest. We and all of Moria are grateful to you. So you have been hiding in the forest, Enna Dion? Near here? For how long?"

Her questions came like arrows, swift and unavoidable. She wanted to hear the whole story and there was no brushing her off with half-truths. Fortunately, before I got to the part about the Circle of Power, we were rejoined by Tomas and Lucien.

"This *is* an honor, Lady Julia," murmured Lucien, bowing low. So it was definitely her. Lady Julia Madraga! Heir to the throne of Moria and the last surviving member of the Morian ruling family. A Duke of Gallia was all very fine but he was only some parvenu foreign ruler. Our own dear Lady of Moria was scion of the oldest royal family on the peninsula.

I was interested to see that Lucien introduced Tomas quite openly as his father's natural son and managed to give the impression that I was Sandor Sercel's natural daughter. The Sercels were very great nobility, however, and could no doubt afford to be careless with both conventional morality and the truth.

Lucien's arrival put an end to the encounter with Lady Julia, which was perhaps lucky, because the definite knowledge of her identity had made even Tomas lose the power of coherent speech. After a long round of bows and polite remarks by Lucien, she swept away with her lady-in-waiting pattering after her.

"Look at you lot," laughed Lucien. "Anyone would think you'd seen Tanza's own mother."

"Lady Julia Madraga," said Shad in an awestruck voice.

"What a wonderful creature," said Tomas in much the same tone.

"Yes, and very quick off the mark even for her," said Lucien wryly. "Everyone in Lammerquais is crazy to met the Demonslayer of Gallia and lucky me—she's my half-sister."

He drew my hand though his arm.

"Am I your half-sister?" I asked.

"You're my half-brother's half-sister. That must make us some kind of relative."

Despite the fact that the White Tower was full to bursting with the Duke of Gallia's retinue, I was to have a room to myself. It was a little room on the fifth floor up under the eaves of the building. I suspected that it was normally a servant's room, but it had a comfortable bed and that was all I cared for. There was a trunk in the corner for my clothes and a large mirror on the wall at the end of the bed. Almost without thinking, I took the mirror down and turned it to the wall.

Although I had not had any dreams from Andre/Bedazzer since I had gone into the Circle of Power, I was pretty certain that would not last. Though the Duke and Lord Sercel would have teams of mages in this tower maintaining all kinds of magical protections, they were unlikely to be much use against demons and dreams of demons.

I took my chalk from my belt purse and set to work decorating the walls with the runes of Protection, Distraction, and Blindness. Though runes were made with chalk, when they were fused with magic they became invisible to ordinary sight.

Halfway through my rune-making I heard the door creak open behind me. I assumed it was the maid, who would know better then to interrupt a mage at work. When I had finished, however, I was surprised to find myself still alone. I had been sure someone had come in. When I went over to the door it was slightly ajar. I opened it and looked down the corridor, but the only people there were two red-faced maidservants toiling up the stairs carrying copper buckets of hot water for my bath.

While I was bathing, two messengers came. The first came from Lucien, bearing a gown that had belonged to his dead wife. It was midnight blue silk and covered in red ribbons. It was so gaudy that I shrank from wearing it, though I knew that a grand gown would be my expected dress while I lived at the White Tower.

The second messenger was Lady Anne, Lady Julia's companion in the corridor. She bore a beautiful black velvet gown with brocade sleeves compliments of Lady Julia Madraga. Lady Julia obviously remembered her countryman's love of somber magnificence. It was far more to my taste than Lucien's gown and I accepted the gift gladly. The maid who had been scrubbing my back was obviously impressed by this present and by the well-dressed servants who came with Lady Anne. She began scrubbing with much more enthusiasm and even offered to obtain some scented oil to rub me with. Lady Anne, however, quickly hustled her out of the room and set her own servant to washing me. By the time this was finished and I was tenderly ushered out of the bath, I was more thoroughly washed that I could ever remember being in my life.

Lady Anne bundled me into the gown, got one of the maids to measure me for alterations and then bustled away, having organized the other maid to massage me with scented oil while the first sewed.

I lay on the bed enjoying the massage and reflecting that I had changed a great deal from the shy seventeen-year-old I had once been. When I had last been in such grand surroundings I had found such attentions unbearably intimate and embarrassing. In those days I would never have imagined myself sleeping with a man, either. Strange how three years as your own mistress, surrounded by people who look up to your advice, can improve your confidence.

In the old days, for instance, I would have been barely able to speak to the Lord-Elector of Middle Moria without blushing and stammering incoherently. Yet that evening when I was seated beside him at dinner I managed to maintain quite a creditable conversation.

Sandor Sercel was a tall grey-haired man, still very handsome despite his age. His eyes were dark and clever. He had a wonderful deep and melodious voice, which was such a pleasure to listen to it must have been a considerable asset to him, if only in the seduction of servant girls.

I found myself unwilling to like him despite his considerable charm. This was the man who had ruined my mother. Because of him, she had had an unhappy marriage and a life of drudgery. Though I had only been four when I left the inn, still I remembered how hard she had worked and how poor we had been. Sandor had done nothing to help her. He did not seem to have paid at all for what surely was an equal amount of misdemeanor. At the same time, a part of me could not help feeling I was being a little harsh on the Lord-Elector. What had happened between him and my mother was a very common story and he had only acted like everyone else in his position. In fact he had probably been too young at the time to have had much control over his fate.

Both Tomas and Lucien bore a marked resemblance to Lord Sercel. Lucien looked more like him, while Tomas, who was much shorter and fairer, had the same quicksilver cleverness about him. I guessed that Tomas had the same driving ambition as his father, a quality which Lucien quite obviously lacked. I could not say I regretted the lack, however. Lucien sat on my other side at dinner and was charming companion throughout the whole meal.

Despite the fact that the dinner was served on silver platters in a magnificent tapestry-hung room, Lord Sercel called it "an informal family dinner with a few close friends." Apparently he now regarded all of Marnie Holyhands' children as members of his family, though Silva and I had no blood relationship with him. A number of Sercel aunts and cousins who lived at the White Tower were present, along with a formidable-looking matron who was Lucien's older sister and a pleasant-looking monk who turned out to be the Abbot of St. Belkis of the Holy Healing Hands in Annac and who was, fortuitously, Lucien's uncle.

"You will think this scandalous, Dion," whispered Lucien in my ear, "but while you and Shad were dragging a wounded Tomas through the forest, Parrus and I were having wine and cakes with the children in the Abbot's private parlor. After the hue and cry died down, we were given priests' clothes and let out the back gate of the monastery. We strolled home through the forest, a group of children walking with their tutors. Abbot Louis has been a good son of the Church, but he draws the line at the arrest of relatives. Or children."

Parrus was at the table too. It was the first time I had seen him since the morning the Fire Angel had come to the inn, and I was so relieved to see him well that when we met before dinner I hugged him. I quickly realized that this was a tactical error. Though I was not sure what to do about Parrus, I knew that the relationship between us could not continue as it had been before I had left Annac. Parrus, however, had not changed. He nodded and smiled secretively at me throughout the meal. I could only be glad we were not seated together and that private conversation between us was impossible.

I was struck by how much younger and more ordinary he looked than Shad, who was also there, looking extremely handsome in elegant new clothes. It was as if some artist had painted them both, using cool elegant pastels for Parrus and rich bold colors for Shad.

The third non-family member of the dinner party was Lady Blanche Shomnee, possible Lady-Elector for the South. She was only seventeen, tall and very thin, with wonderful smooth creamy skin and huge dark eyes. She hardly spoke throughout the evening. She had been cold when I had been introduced to her, but she probably had no need of my good opinion anyway, for after dinner when we retired to another room to drink hot kesh and sweet wine with little cakes, she was well supplied with male attendants.

I had thought to have used this time to somehow indicate to Parrus that our relationship had changed. By the time he had finished playing the gallant to Lady Blanche, however, the opportunity for private talk was past for we were honored with a visit from Lady Julia Madraga. After the initial round of compliments and bows, Lady Julia seated herself beside me.

Having a brief encounter with a legend is one thing, but having to drink kesh with one is entirely another. However, like most of the great, Lady Julia was adept at putting people at ease and my intial awkwardness soon passed.

Soon the conversation turned to the subject of women's education, which was one on which I had strong feelings. In those days, on the peninsula at least, women had few chances of formal education. The only real schools for women were the colleges of healing, where the women usually had to be taught the skills of reading and writing from scratch as well. Nowhere on the peninsula was there a college for training women in the arts of higher magic. It was widely believed that women were not logical enough to study such magic. I had been trained at home by my foster father as an experiment, and I suspect in the end he concluded that popular opinion was right. Occasionally in darker moments I myself believed it.

So when Lady Julia said, "When I am queen the first thing I shall do is start a college of higher magic for women," my excitement swept away my awe.

"If I did would you teach at it for me?" she continued. "So few women have your qualifications."

"Gladly, Lady Julia," I cried, unable to hide my excitement. It would be wonderful if things could be different for a new generation of girls. Maybe my own nieces would benefit.

"So you approve."

"Yes indeed . . ." Then suddenly I remembered my own experiences as a mage.

"Doubts, Enna Dion?" She was very perceptive. "Do you perhaps agree that women are not logical enough to learn higher magic after all?"

"It's not that, my lady." I paused, unwilling to voice criticism to such an august personage. But she had asked, so I answered.

"When my education was finished there was still much question of how I would use it. There is always work for healers, but nobody then or now would employ a woman mage. If you set out to train women mages you will still have the problem of making their knowledge useful afterward."

"Hmm," said Lady Julia. "I see I must think seriously on this. But you do agree that in principle women are just as intelligent and logical as men?"

"It has always seemed to me that women's minds are not very different from men's."

"You are yourself an example of that," she said. "It is something we have in common. For I too was educated beyond my sex. I was brought up by a maiden aunt who was lucky enough to have her own fortune and she put her beliefs into practice on me. I think I am at least as educated in the arts of politics and rule as my dear Duke." She shot me a sideways glance. "Possibly you are wondering how the art of politics can be an asset to any woman, since we are not destined to rule but to be ruled. I think my aunt dreamed that I might one day be sole ruler of Moria. Interestingly enough, when it seemed certain that I would not ascend the throne of Moria and my aunt sent me to a convent, I found such knowledge applied as much to nuns as it did to states.''

Actually I had not been thinking anything of the kind. To me all knowledge seems useful. What I had been thinking was how similar our backgrounds had been: both raised as experiments, and if I read the signs correctly in Julia's case, when the experiment was over she was discarded as my foster father had often threatened to discard me. For the first time in a long while, I found myself blessing Michael of Moria for his humanity. A nunnery. What a horrible fate.

''I do not see why magical women should have the monopoly on education,'' continued Lady Julia. ''If I become queen I shall open a college for ordinary young ladies as well.''

''May that day come soon, My Lady,'' said a voice beside me.

A man in mage's robes had come to stand by us.

''Ah, Ren Karac,'' said Lady Julia. ''Good. Enna Dion, is it true that your half-brother is completely unknown to you? That you have not seen him since you were four? It is! Well, please allow me the honour of reintroducing him to you. He is acting as my personal mage.''

So this was Karac, Tasha's difficult twin brother. He was a dark man with high cheekbones and narrow black eyes set in swarthy skin. Such looks were unusual and striking, even among the dark-haired Gallians. Perhaps his father had been Aramayan. He was handsome for all that and had a certain self-assured, almost arrogant way of holding himself that drew the eye. If Tasha had looked anything like this in her heyday, she would have been very attractive.

My half-brother took my hand and kissed it politely.

''It is an honor to make your acquaintance finally, dear sister. I have heard so much about you. I hope we will be friends. I'm sure there is a great deal you can teach me. About demons, for instance.''

He made it sound like an accusation, and I was about to trot out an excuse when I remembered that a Demonslayer might reasonably be expected to know about demons. It was just my secret guilt over my involvement with Andre/Bedazzer that made me uncomfortable.

A cynical smile played across my brother's face. He had noticed my discomfiture and was enjoying it. I suspected that he was one of those ambitious career mages who probably saw me as a rival. Well, damn him.

"Will you get me another cup of kesh, Ren Karac?" said Lady Julia.

"A pleasure, my Lady," said Karac.

"Your brother is a fine wizard and invaluable to me," said Lady Julia when he was gone. "But he is something of a tease. I hope you are not offended."

"No, no," I said, astonished that she should care.

Shortly afterward Lord Sandor approached and, bowing low, asked if he might have private words with me. Lady Julia nodded her assent. Was it my imagination or did some kind of knowing look pass between them?

Tomas came with us. I was, at first, glad of his company at what promised to be a very serious interview.

"Enna Dion," began Lord Sercel. "As you are no doubt aware a very serious situation has arisen in Moria."

"Indeed I am," I said. "And I am keen to do anything that will help with the liberation of the South."

"The liberation of the South. Ah yes. That is a dreadful thing. To think that the Burning Light has become a haven for necromancy. I can assure you the Duke feels as much outrage as you on this subject. It makes this situation with the Patriarch just that much more difficult and it makes it all the more important that it be resolved as quickly as possible.

"No doubt you have already heard that the Patriarch has his own candidate for the throne in Gerard Hawksmoor, Lady Julia's cousin through the female line. The Patriarch's army will be reaching Lake Lammer in a couple of days and I have offered him my castle in RougeLammer. It is only fifteen miles from here and gives enough distance to avoid trouble without being so far away as to make negotiations too difficult.

"For this is a very complicated situation which will require much negotiation. Two candidates for the Morian throne now exist: Gerard Hawksmoor with the support of the Orthodox Aumazite Church, the Northern Elector, and many Northern Morians, and Duke Leon Sahr with Lady Julia as his wife with the support of myself and many other Morians who do not want to see the Church dominating this country."

"What about Southern Moria?" I asked feeling that we had got away from the important matters. He did have a point about the church, however.

"We shall have to do the best we can for them despite this situation, of course, but I must tell you, I suspect the Patriarch is willing to fight to see his candidate on the Morian Throne. We may wind up liberating the South only to plunge it into civil war unless this situation is handled with the utmost care. I very much pray that we can resolve this situation by making use of the electoral system. Do you know much about this system, Enna?"

"It's a system by which the five major powers in Morian society pledge their alliance to the ruler by casting a vote in his favor, isn't it? But surely it's only symbolic?"

"It has become symbolic, yes, but it was originally designed as a practical way of resolving precisely the problem we have before us now.

"As you may know, there are only five Morian Electors since Smazor's Run, but that is enough to give a majority to one candidate or the other. There is Lord Rouget of the North, myself in Central Moria, the Shomnee elector from the South, the chief mage of Moria who represents magery, and the Church Elector who is always the highest priest in the land."

"Is Blanche Shomnee the elector of the South?" I asked.

"It seems likely that she will be, although I am waiting for my investigators to return to see if this is really so. She has made it clear that she is still undecided over who she will support in the election."

"But she surrendered herself to the Duke, didn't she?"

"Actually she surrendered herself to my protection," said

Lord Sandor. "I agree it looks as if she favors the Duke's candidacy for the throne, but she has made it clear that certain conditions, one of which is a safe passage into exile for her uncle Hierarch Jarraz, are attendant on her actual casting of her vote."

"Perhaps the Duke should not come to such agreement over one who has so obviously favored necromancy," I snapped, surprised at the anger I suddenly felt.

"Enna Dion, this is the real world. Surely someone as caring as you must see the value of a bloodless surrender over losing men in a series of battles."

"Yes," I said, a little shamed by his steady look. "I beg your pardon. I do see your point."

"In actual fact, Enna Dion, it is the Elector of Magery who is going to give us problems."

I noticed that Tomas suddenly began to look very excited. Nice for him if he knew where things were going. I was still completely in the dark.

"The Elector of Magery?" I asked. "That is the head of White College of Moria, isn't it? But surely he supports the Duke. I met him on the steps this afternoon, didn't I? What was his name?"

"Ren Daniel Devoirs. Oh, yes, he supports the Duke. The problem is that his right to act as Elector has come into question. I know it's been the custom for many years for the Elector of Magery to be the head of the White College of Moria, but in fact the constitution states that the Elector of Magery is to be the most powerful mage in Moria, and although Ren Daniel is an excellent head of the White College, he is not a very strong mage. The Patriarch has a much more powerful mage in his train at this very moment, one who claims the right to be Elector of Magery and who has challenged Ren Daniel to a battle of mages."

"What sort of mage would support the Patriarch?" I cried. The Patriarch had won the undying enmity of all members of all the White Colleges when he refused to step in and forbid the burning of mages at the stake during the Revolution of Souls.

"Ren Bernard was a priest-mage until very recently when he resigned from the priesthood."

I looked at him with horror.

He nodded.

"Scandalous, isn't it? But I'm afraid the constitution does not forbid an ex-priest from being Elector. If Ren Bernard wins the Battle of Mages, as he surely must, then Gerard Hawksmoor will have the support of the Elector of the North, the Elector of the Church and the Elector of Magery, giving him a clear majority. The only answer to this problem is to find a more powerful mage. That is where you come in, Enna Dion."

"Me? You want me to stand as Elector of Magery?"

"You would easily defeat Ren Bernard."

"But I'm a wo . . ." I remembered Blanche Shomnee and closed my mouth, which was showing a distressing tendency to hang open anyway. "So my being a woman is no bar to this?"

"The constitution does not forbid it. You would not be the first woman to act as Elector. My Grandmother Bettine Sercel acted as Elector during my father's minority."

"I'm not sure . . ."

"Oh Dion," broke in Tomas, "just say yes. It's a tremendous honor and my sister is aware of that, my Lord."

"Tomas!" I cried. "Do you mind?"

"Yes I do, actually. This is just your tendency to hide from honors, Dion, and if I don't help you to overcome it, you never will."

"Tomas," said Lord Sercel smiling tolerantly. "Let your sister speak. If she has doubts then it's important that we discuss them. I'm certain that she does not want to see Moria in the hands of the Patriarch."

He was right. I didn't.

"Are there other duties involved in being Elector?" I said. "I don't feel I'm qualified to become Dean of the White College."

"No, and you need not. The most important thing about

the Elector of Magery is that it is he who places the crown on the head of the ruler at his coronation.''

My God, I thought. The Klementari had seen me putting the crown on the head of the ruler and here it was about to come true.

"The only other duty, and there is no need for you to take it up, is that you have a place on the ruler's Council of State,'' he continued. ''The Duke has set up such a council, but it is by no means compulsory for you to attend.''

The Council of State. I quailed at the thought of being a member of such a body, which would no doubt be full of people viciously struggling to gain the attention of the Duke. I knew it did not make policy—for that had always been the Duke's prerogative—but it advised him, which meant that it had his ear. A member of the Council of State was a public figure, open to all kinds of comment and criticism. Perhaps I would even find myself involved in decisions that would affect other people and go horribly wrong.

On the other hand it might be a position from which I could help a cause I believed in. Perhaps I could even help the Klementari when they came. It would be very wrong not to take the chance just because I felt scared.

"I would like to take up my right to sit on the Council of State,'' I said, ''though I am no politician. And I am willing to be the Elector of Magery, if that is what the Duke wants.''

"Hooray,'' shouted Tomas.

Lord Sercel looked strangely startled by my words, but he shook my hand warmly and assured me I could count on his support in the Council of State.

I was stunned by the turn events had taken. The most I had hoped for was to be allowed to join the army like Shad, and now here I was about to become Elector of Magery.

I couldn't face Parrus after such terrifying news, so I did not return to the others but took myself straight off to my bedroom and lay on my bed in the dark, trying to be calm.

A little while later footsteps came down the corridor and there was a knock at my door. I had recognized the step, however, and did not answer. It would be another tactical error to let Parrus into my bedroom at this point, especially since I hoped that Shad would come later.

My hope was rewarded. A short while later I heard Shad's footsteps coming down the hall, stopping and then going away again. I opened the door and called him in.

"I thought you might be tired," he said.

I told him my news. He looked as stunned as I felt.

"Congratulations," he said. "This is a great honor. Now you will be in a position to urge the Duke to do things. Are you pleased?"

"I'm terrified."

He smiled and squeezed my shoulders.

"You will do fine, Dion. I know you can do it."

I had decided that it would be very dishonorable for me to make love with Shad while things with Parrus were still unresolved, but somehow we could not help hugging each other, and one thing led to another. His arms were so firm and strong and he looked wonderful in his coat of rich dark velvet with his silken shirt open enough at the neck to show part of his strong brown chest.

Afterward, as we lay letting the fine linen sheets caress our naked limbs like cream, Shad said, "I meant to tell you that I had exciting news, but yours put it completely out of my mind. After you left, Lady Julia offered to help get me a good position in the army. I am to ride with Lord Quercy tomorrow."

"That's wonderful," I said, though it was like cold water being poured down my back.

"I'm sorry," he said softly. "I must see this thing through. Otherwise I could never live with myself."

"Of course," I said. I turned and put my arms around him. "I'm glad things are turning out so well for you."

I knew I felt no such thing. I didn't want him to go away to the army, but I understood perfectly that he had to see the liberation of the South through as he had promised himself. What could I offer him instead, anyway? Myself? A very poor bargain.

We lay there silently holding each other. Just as I felt certain that he had fallen asleep, he said softly, "Why is Lord Sercel so convinced there will be a civil war?"

"The Duke and the Patriarch have been on a collision course for years. My friend Kitten used to tell me that it was Leon Sahr's ambition to unite all of the little states of the peninsula under the Sahr banner. She was seldom wrong about such things. Moria is one of the biggest states on the Peninsula. Think of what a prize that would be to him.

"On the other hand a united Peninsula might well try to influence the Church, and Patriarch Sylvestus cannot want that. He certainly would not want such a large state as Moria and Gallia combined to be ruled by Leon Sahr, who has a mind of his own. Duke Leon has ignored the Patriarch's repeated reprimands on being too lenient toward heretics and people of doubtful morals."

"Then Leon Sahr cares nothing about necromancy in the South. He is really just here to build a kingdom for himself."

"I'm sure he does care. What normal person wouldn't? But it's not unreasonable for him to have an eye for his own advantage. Most people do."

"I suppose so. I cannot bring myself to like him, though I know it is hardly important. He seems so cold and ruthless. You looked afraid of him the whole time."

I explained that I'd been afraid he'd been having a joke at my expense.

"There now, you see? That would be a cruel thing to do to someone. Why do you like him so much?"

"I don't particularly like him. I just think he's a good ruler. Gallia is prosperous and well-ordered. He favors the merchant class and keeps the nobles well under control. Otherwise he leaves people alone. He does not overtax them, he hardly ever begins wars, and he never tries to tell them what to think. Gallia has more religious freedom than any other country I know of."

"He gives no freedom to the Burning Light. He has ordered them all imprisoned."

"They tried to overthrow him in Gallia. Why should he

give them any freedom if Moria is an example of their work?''

"True enough. But Lady Julia thinks we should try to forgive and forget. She says the Burning Light are still Morians—Morians who have been misled.''

"She is generous. Especially after her experiences.''

"Yes,'' said Shad. "She seems a fine person. I do not understand why you prefer the Duke to her.''

"Prefer? But they are going to rule together.''

"Why? Why does she need to have this foreign man to help her be a ruler? She could be Queen by herself.''

I was astonished that Shad was so naïve.

"But she's a woman. Women can't rule.''

"Women have ruled among the Klemantari. You do things women aren't supposed to do.''

"It's different, Shad. The Lords would never mind her. She wouldn't be able to keep them under control. I mean, they'd fight over who was to marry her, for a start.''

"She could marry Gerard Hawksmoor or Duke Leon and not crown him King.''

"That's crazy. He would never agree to that.''

"There are all kinds of people she could marry. All I'm saying is she might be a perfectly good ruler and she seems a better person than this Duke of yours.''

"Can you really tell what kind of person she is after two meetings? These people always wear a pleasant public mask.''

"I suppose so. But when the Klemantari spoke of the future ruler of Moria they always spoke of a queen. They never mentioned a king.''

"A queen? But Moria is a duchy.''

"If the Waste Land is reclaimed it will be big enough to be a kingdom again.''

"Well then Lady Julia will be King Leon's queen.''

"They never spoke of a king. I was certain it was a queen alone. Queen Julia Madraga.''

·12·

What do the wealthy do in the morning? If my experiences in the White Tower of Lammerquais are any guide, their lovers slip from their beds at dawn and they go back to sleep to be woken luxuriously late by a maid who brings them hot chocolate and rolls in bed.

As well as rolls and chocolate, however, the maid brought a note that spoiled my breakfast. It was from Parrus asking me to meet him in the Green Morning Room in an hour's time.

A dull sense of foreboding filled me as, following the directions provided by the maid, I made my way to the Green Morning Room.

Parrus was already sitting within, looking very elegant.

"Is that a new robe?" I said.

"Yes. You like it? Lord Sercel gave it to me. A very generous man. You must ask him for some new clothes too. Those are a little understated for the Elector of Magery."

"You know about that?"

"I called by your room last night to congratulate you, but you must have been asleep. I must say you are unexpected, hiding yourself away like that. What were you doing in Cardun?" He slid his arm around my shoulders. "You are obviously too modest and we must take you in hand."

His patronizing manner set my teeth on edge.

"Have you and Tomas been talking to each other?" I snapped pushing him away.

"No!" He looked startled. There was an uncomfortable silence.

"Dion," said Parrus. "Didn't you miss me a bit while you were gone? I missed you."

His arms were round me again, his fingers stroking my neck. He nuzzled my cheek. It was actually very pleasant. For a wild moment I wondered how it would be if I kept Parrus as a lover as well as Shad. But only for a moment. Any passion I had felt for Parrus had simply disappeared.

"Parrus. Don't."

"Don't be like that. It's been ages since I saw you. I've been longing to see you again. Come on, don't tease me. Didn't you miss me?"

"Of course I missed you." Oh dear here I was lying to save his feelings. I must think of something more realistic that wouldn't lead to an unpleasant confrontation. This was pathetic. I had to do better. I leapt in.

"Look Parrus. I know we. . . . I think we should let things cool off for the moment, don't you? I mean it's different here now. This is Lammerquais, not Cardun. People are going to notice and say things."

Parrus was silent for a few moments as if thinking deeply about something.

"Yes," he said slowly and deliberately. "Yes, we certainly don't want to set people talking especially now you have become so important. Here a woman has to be more careful of her reputation. That's why . . ." He took my hand with sudden formality. "Dion, I thought about you a lot while we were apart. You know I'm fond of you and now things have turned out this way. . . . Well I think it would be a good thing for us to get married."

"What?" I cried. "My God, Parrus, what are you talking about?"

He looked as shocked as I felt. It was one of those moments when you both realize the other person is a complete stranger to you.

"I'm sorry," I said, striving for a less insulting reaction. "It's very kind of you, I don't. . . . I really don't think it would work out between us."

"What do you mean?" cried Parrus. "I thought this was what you wanted."

I had once, but I stopped thinking of Parrus in that way a long time ago, when it had become clear that I was just going to get hurt if I did.

"Oh Parrus, I am sorry. I had no idea you felt this way. I thought it was just a passing fancy."

I tried to touch his arm.

Naturally the sympathetic tone infuriated him.

"It was just a passing fancy on my part. Of course it was. How on earth could you sleep with me if you weren't serious Dion? Good God, what kind of a woman are you?"

"Well what about you?" I snapped, stung by this remark which hit me right in a guilty spot.

"At least I'm trying to do the right thing here. I know I've compromised your reputation. Think of what people are going to say about you when they find out what happened in Cardun."

Compromised my reputation. That was true, and for a moment I fell back to an earlier time in my life when the idea of compromised reputations frightened me terribly. But only for a moment.

"How have you compromised me? Nobody but Tomas knows what happened between us in Cardun."

Parrus' face reddened.

"Parrus?"

"I let something slip to Lord Lucien, who seems to have told his father. And it seems the Duke found out somehow. I know it was wrong of me." He took my hand and patted it gently. "I was alone and afraid and you know how you share things with people in those circumstances. But I'm prepared to make amends. I have to marry you, Dion. Now that all these people know. Otherwise you'll be ruined."

Ruined. People saying mean and dirty things about me behind my back and maybe even to my face. Not only had I slept with a man I wasn't married to, but I hadn't even loved him. Men did it all the time, but not women.

Ruined. Bad things happened to ruined women. Like my mother cast out from her job, penniless and pregnant. And darker things were supposed to happen to women when men didn't respect them anymore.

But I wasn't pregnant. And with my powers I couldn't see how men could force their attentions on me. Would I care if nobody at the White Tower ever spoke to me again? If they found someone else to be Elector of Magery? Had what I'd done with Parrus been that bad? Was marrying the way my mother had married the only answer? I mean My God, *marriage.* That was a lifetime. With Parrus?

"I really don't think it would work."

"Why not Dion? It's worked well enough in the past. These are just nerves." He squeezed my hand. "We have Lord Sercel's blessing. He told me the Duke has agreed to give me a place at court among the mages. You'll see. It will be fine."

And suddenly I did see. I saw with blinding clarity. Why should the Duke give Parrus, who was the son of one of his enemies, a position at court? On the other hand, the Duke seemed very concerned to be nice to me. It was just as Tomas had warned me.

"No!" I said. "I'm not going to marry you, Parrus. I'll just have to ride out the scandal if there is going to be one."

Parrus went white.

"But . . . but it's all decided. The Duke . . ."

"No Parrus. I'm sorry. It just won't work."

Anger boiled inside me. I made for the door.

Parrus grabbed my arm and whirled me around to face him.

"Now listen you. Stop being stupid. You've got all full of yourself, haven't you? Well it won't work. If you think that just because you're a powerful mage you can go round acting like a whore and getting away with it, you're in for a big shock, my girl. You're still only a woman. I'm not going to stand by and let you do this to us. You've got to marry me.''

I pushed him away. "You toad," I shouted. "You let me go. Stop pretending you give a damn for me. You never did before. You've been trading me for favors with the Duke, haven't you? Haven't you?"

"It's not like that."

"Well looks like it to me. I'd rather be condemned to the deepest pits of whoredom a million times than ever marry you Parrus Lavelle."

"Fine," shouted Parrus. "You'll be sorry just you . . ."

Slamming the door on his shouted words, I charged down the hallway. I wanted to hit something. That pig!

I threw myself down the stairs, saw a door to the outside and made for it. At least in the garden. . . . Maybe I could find something to throw.

It was entirely the wrong kind of garden for my mood. I charged around among the elegant ornamental flowerbeds for a while, but there was not even a flower pot to break, and kicking trees is very unsatisfying. I wished Shad was here so that I could have poured Parrus' villainies into his ear, but of course he was not. Just as I was deciding to go in, I heard someone calling me.

I looked up and there was Silva leaning out of the first-floor window.

"What are you doing Dion?" she asked laughingly. "Why did you kick that poor tree?"

"It's too complicated to explain."

"You just wait there," she said.

She leaned out the window, caught hold of the drainpipe, swung herself out to it with a flurry of skirts, and shinnied down. Sidestepping onto the ground floor windowsill, she seemed to hang there for a minute before she vaulted lightly into the air. Suddenly there she was on the ground beside me, calmly pulling the skirts of her plain workday dress down around her legs.

"I've been wondering for three days if it could be done," she said.

I gaped at her in astonishment, which seemed to please her no end.

"Did Tomas not tell you I was once an acrobat?" she said. "When Needra and Derrum's father was still alive I performed in his troupe. I have some magical powers which I used to soften people's falls. Eventually they taught me all their tricks."

She came forward and slid an arm though mine. "So tell me, sister dear, why have you been stomping about the garden? I've been watching you kicking trees for this past little while. Who has annoyed you?"

All my anger came pouring back.

"It's Parrus. Do you know what he did? He proposed to me, the swine."

"So you mean you aren't already engaged?" inquired Silva.

"No," I cried. "Oh God, has Parrus been telling everyone we were?"

"Lucien told me. I thought. . . . Well, so he proposed. Why are you so angry?"

"Parrus cares nothing about me. He just saw it as a good way to win favor from the Duke. I can't believe he's told everyone we were engaged. How cynical can you get?"

"Are you sure that's why he proposed? Really, sister, you are very attractive. Any man might. . . . He may just have been hiding his feelings. Men do do that."

"Parrus! Parrus 'you're very nice Dion but you're not the only woman in my life and anyway my mother wants me to marry this heiress,' Lavelle. I mean for almost a year, I've been hearing this from him, and now suddenly he wants to marry me. There can be only one reason for that."

"So you're not in love with him?"

"No way. When we were first involved I could easily have been, but months and months of his telling me I was just a passing fancy cured me of that. And you know he had the cheek to tell me he still thought of me that way but felt he should marry me to protect my reputation.''

"Well how stupid can a man be?" she cried. "What woman in her right mind would accept such a proposal? I'm not surprised you're annoyed. I'd have slapped his face.''

We walked up and down for a while, enjoyably ripping Parrus' character to shreds. As my anger cooled, however, doubts began to assail me. I remembered how Parrus had shouted 'You're just a woman.'

"You don't think. . . . You don't think he's right about my reputation, do you? There won't be a scandal?''

"I can't think why. It's your right to refuse him.''

"We were . . . involved.''

"It's not much of a reason to marry him. Especially since he seems to have treated you so shabbily.''

I sighed.

"I should never have got involved with him in the first place. My foster father would say I should be grateful to Parrus—that it was the only way to save my reputation.''

"Reputation! Humph! That kind of thing is so difficult to keep hold of it's hardly worth bothering trying.'' She hugged me. "Don't worry Dion. I doubt if Parrus will say anything. He'd be a fool to tell people about his humiliation. And even if he does, scandals pass. Your friends are much more powerful than his, and your family will stand by you. Lucien and Tomas will probably have Parrus thrown out of town if they find he's making trouble for you.''

It was so easy to talk to Silva. It was as if she had been my sister all my life, which technically I suppose she had been.

Silva had led a very exciting life. Though Tasha had returned after running away with the traveling entertainers, Silva had joined them. She was in love with one of them, and for many years she and Jontine—and later their two children—had traveled all over the peninsula performing at fairs and Holy Day celebrations.

The Burning Light did not like vagabonds and entertainers however, and the troupe was arrested in Mangalore. Jontine died in prison. When Silva was released, she and her children returned to the inn at Annac, where she worked until Tomas in Lammerquais had asked her to keep house for him.

"I knew from experience that it would be easier for my children to grow up somewhere where their grandmother and mother aren't scandals," she said. "In this I have been luckier than our mother."

Yet in her way our mother had been lucky too. The life of a woman alone with seven children could have been disastrously hard. We might all have starved. But my mother had always had the inn at Annac to fall back on. I had met many women in my work as a healer who had not had that fall back and who had starved or been forced into crime and prostitution because of it. Though I had always thought of my mother as careless, I was beginning to see that she was not careless at all—except about things like reputation and respectability.

Perhaps Silva, who had lived with our mother for eighteen years of her life, was like her. Had she been the same kind of warm generous person Silva seemed to be? But no, Silva was more practical. Or was she? She had not bothered to marry her children's father either.

"Jontine and I did not see the need of it," she said airily.

A practical woman would have insisted on marriage, lest she be left alone with two children to feed. But then, just like Marnie, Silva had always had the inn at Annac to return to.

"Silva!" called a voice behind us. Silva turned and I felt her tense. Karac was standing there.

Something was seriously wrong with him. The Karac of this morning was completely different from the poised Karac of the night before. He held his arms stiffly at his side. His eyes were bloodshot smudges in his pale face.

"Silva," he croaked urgently. "Can I speak with you alone?"

"Of course," said Silva. "Please excuse me, sister."

There was a certain reserve in her manner that made me watch protectively as he drew her away down the garden.

When they disappeared under some trees I followed at a distance, keeping them in sight.

They talked urgently for a few minutes. Then Karac's figure drooped. An immeasurable despair seemed to overwhelm him. Silva tried to put her arms around him, but he pulled away from her and walked away quickly with his head down and his fists clenched.

Silva walked back to me with her head bowed and her arms wrapped around her.

"Is everything well?" I asked as she came up to me.

"No. Poor Karac. Poor stupid Karac. Honestly, when I think of the times I just wanted to give those two a good smacking. And it ends like this. Lucien told Karac that Tasha was dead last night and how she had died. Karac had not known. He wanted me to tell him Lucien was lying."

Her face was bitterly sad.

"But he hated Tasha," I cried. "He refused to help Tomas find her."

"The hatred between Tasha and Karac was the hatred of those who love each other too much. There was never anyone else for Tasha, and I see it is the same for Karac. They were twin mages. They could touch each other's minds. I know Tasha sent out her bitter thoughts to Karac and he was forced to close his mind to her. So when she reached out to the rest of us in her distress, he felt nothing. Oh those two. What sad fools they were."

When I returned to my room later, who should I see coming out of it but Dally, Tasha's daughter. The moment she saw me she took to her heels and ran off down the hallway, even though I called after her and told her I wasn't angry.

I hovered in the hall unsure whether to run after her or not. I didn't want to frighten her. The last time I had seen her had been at Tasha's bedside just before Tasha had emptied her memories into my mind and died painfully. The part of me that felt guilty over Tasha's death also wondered what on earth Dally must feel toward me. I had a feeling it wasn't good and was a little afraid of finding out. Unsure how to proceed, I made a mental note to speak to Silva about meeting with Dally. If she inherited her mother's powers, the magic would be making itself known in the next year or two. I must try to help her.

I could not find anything missing and I had so little magical equipment with me she could have come to no harm. Only my mirror was turned back to face the room and that had probably been done by the maid. I turned it quickly back to the wall.

That afternoon I was called to the Duke and in a private audience with him accepted the role of Elector, hoping secretly that Lord Sandor had not led me astray over the extent of my responsibilities.

A private audience with the Duke of Gallia was not terribly private. In the room with us were Tomas, Lord Sandor, Lucien, a couple of favoured courtiers, Ren Garthan Redon— a mage I had been at college with—and Ren Daniel Devoirs, head of the White College of Moria. I was surprised not to see Lady Julia there until it occured to me that she might not have been invited.

The Duke of Gallia was just as friendly as he had been on the previous day, but I knew that he was a complex man, capable of a certain amount of loyalty but also of heartlessly discarding his friends when they ceased to be useful to him. Yet he was a liberal-minded, well-educated man too. As I had told Shad, Gallia had enjoyed an unprecedented period of peace, freedom of thought, and prosperity under the Duke's rule. He was usually kind to ordinary folk but delighted in keeping his courtiers off balance by playing them off against each other. I'd been told it was a ploy to keep them from plotting against him, but now that I was an Elector and counted as a courtier, this knowledge was not much comfort.

I thought I saw surprise flicker across the Duke's face when I said that I would be sitting on his Council, and several other people in the room looked astonished. It was only then that I realized that I had not been intended to take up this part of my Electoral role. I was both embarrassed by my mistake and annoyed that they had assumed I would not be interested in the Council. Despite my past lack of action, I was determined to do all I could to support the liberation of the South.

That evening the Duke held a reception for the Morian nobles and notables. The Great Hall of the White Tower was packed with every important person in Lammerquais, all wearing their dark finery and what looked like every piece of jewelry they could muster. Most of the important people in the Duke's entourage and his army were also there. I recognized several of the mages from my time at the White College of Gallia.

As I stood among the shifting crowd, flanked by Tomas on one side and Lucien Sercel on the other, I was uncomfortably aware of people looking at us. I was not sure why until I heard a woman exclaim, "But she's just a young girl," and turned to see her startled face looking at me. Then I realized that it was well known that I was the "Demonslayer of Gallia." No wonder Tomas looked so pleased and was nodding to so many people.

"Where is Parrus?" I asked Silva during a break in the introductions. I had been hoping to smooth things over with him somehow, but he was nowhere to be seen. I liked Parrus. I did not want to be on bad terms with him.

"Oh Dion," she cried, looking conscience-stricken. "After I left you this morning, Tomas came charging into my room asking me if I'd heard this story about how you were engaged to Parrus and I told him all about the proposal. I'm so sorry, but he caught me off guard. Lucien has just told me that Parrus has left the White Tower and gone to join one of the magical regiments. I have a feeling Tomas arranged it."

I stared at her in horror.

"Tomas can be quite diplomatic sometimes," continued Silva, although she did not speak with much conviction. "And it's not as if he has thrown Parrus out into the street with nothing. Lucien says it's an honor to win a place in the regiments of fighting mages.''

When I questioned Tomas, he told me in a furious whisper that Parrus had managed to embarrass himself so badly before the Duke and Lord Sercel that it seemed kindest to remove him from the White Tower as quickly as possible.

''Don't go feeling sorry for him,'' he hissed at my unbelieving look. ''Look at how presumptuous he's been. It's exactly what I warned you would happen.''

''Tomas, you dragged him here, not me. You . . .''

We were interrupted by a fanfare of trumpets. The crowd parted and the Duke, leading Lady Julia Madraga, swept down the room and onto the dais.

Dressed in a magnificent black gown and with her red hair falling like a cloak around her shoulders, Lady Julia shone like a fiery star from her place beside the Duke. The faces of my countrymen were suffused with joy. To see a Madraga back on the throne was a sign that things were back to normal, after the uncertainty of the Revolution of Souls.

After he had welcomed the company and spoken stirringly of his determination to see Moria freed of Burning Light necromancy, the Duke beckoned me onto the dais and announced that I had been named Elector of Magery. There was much cheering and clapping, while I blushed and bobbed my head and felt like an idiot. Someone, my ever protective brother for instance, might at least have warned me that this was going to happen.

When the speeches were over every mage in that room must have introduced himself to me, all of them telling me of their heartfelt support for the Duke. A surprisingly large number of Morian mages seemed to have come back into Moria in the Duke's train. Seeing them, it suddenly occurred to me that although the Duke had invaded Moria with the support of all these mages and the White College of Moria, he had not sent for me to join his invasion. It suddenly seemed very strange behavior, especially considering how pleased he was to have me here now.

As the stream of magely introductions slowed, I found Ren

Daniel Devoirs, the head of the White College, standing beside me. He was a small neat man with grey hair and an earnest face the color of chalk.

"I was interested to hear that you are going to take up your rightful place on the council," he said. "I will be glad to have another Morian voting with me."

"Thank you, Ren Daniel. I hope I can be useful there."

"With all this business with the Patriarch," he said, "I cannot help fearing that the invasion of the South will be put off. No mage can want the South to be in Burning Light hands a moment longer than necessary."

I was delighted to find that he was an ally and was just telling him so when I saw Shad standing nearby talking to Tomas. When I called to him, he came pushing through the crowd. He was smiling, but the smile did not reach his eyes.

"Where did you go today?" I asked him.

"I went riding in Lady Julia's company this morning and met with Lord Quercy. I am to have command of a company of men. Quite a step up in the world for a woodcutter's son."

"That's wonderful, Shad."

"Aye," he said, "but he has asked me to leave the White Tower this very night and take up my billet with my troops. They are raw recruits much in need of a commanding officer." He took my hand. "It has been a great pleasure knowing you, Enna Dion. I hope we shall meet again. I wish you happy in your . . . future life."

"Oh Shad," I said, unable to think of any appropriate way to show my dismay at this news.

Just then Lord Sandor came up with a group of nobles in tow and the nightmare of curtsying, hand-kissing, and murmured thanks to undeserved compliments continued. When I was at last free to look around again, Shad was gone.

First Parrus gone and now Shad. All things considered, it had not been the best of days.

·13·

Four days after we arrived at the White Tower, news came that the Patriarch had arrived in RougeLammer. He had also taken the town of MontLammer at the furthest end of Lake Lammer and stationed much of his army there. When this piece of news was brought, Lord Sercel put down his goblet in such a hasty manner that the wine slopped on the table. Although this was the only sign of it, I could tell that he was furious.

"As well he might be," said Tomas to Lucien later.

"Why?" I asked.

It seemed that Lord Sercel and the Duke had hoped to contain the Patriarch by positioning him at RougeLammer, which was on the northern side of the widest part of the lake. At the western end of the lake, the Red Mountains, which were impassible at this point, come down almost to the lakeside except for a narrow mile or so of swampy land on the lake's edge which was controlled by the fortress at Mont-Lammer. Had Lord Sercel been able to keep control of MontLammer, the Patriarch would have been cut off from Southern and most of Middle Moria. Obviously, however, Lord Sercel had not instructed the head of the MontLammer fortress properly, for rather than fighting his own country-men, this worthy had surrendered to the Patriarchal army.

"Personally, I don't think the plan ever had much chance of succeeding," said Tomas. "The Patriarch is too good a strategist to accept having his access blocked. It will be interesting to see if he is a better strategist than the Duke."

Tomas' detachment amazed me sometimes. He assured me that he was very concerned about the liberation of the South, but it was hard to see it, if it was so.

Perhaps I was being too hard on Tomas. I myself was obssessed with pushing the army South. What good did my obssession do? By the time the Patriarch came to Lammerquais, I had come to the immensely frustrating conclusion that there was no way I could actually speed the movement of the Gallian army and that all I could do was wait patiently for the Duke's command.

My hopes of achieving some effect on the Council of State were quickly dashed. The meetings of this twelve-member council were unbelievably boring—a series of extended debates on such stimulating topics as the Morian constitution, supply of the army, who was legally responsible for war damages, repair to the walls of Glassybri, and endless discussions about which petitions should be brought to the attention of the Duke. Though there were several other Morians on the Council, we spoke in Gallian. The twelve councilors, all of them important men, argued endlessly over the meanings of single words and the procurement of insignificant supplies like baskets of carrots. I had nothing to say in any of these debates and sometimes had to pinch myself to stop from drifting off to the sleep as this sludge of detail washed over me. Although I daydreamed about leaping up and saying, *Away with these details, let's go South*, of course I did not. I told myself that most of these issues were important in the interests of a sucessful military campaign, as no doubt they were. The real reason, of course, was that I was scared of making a fool of myself in front of the important mages and aristocrats who comprised the council. In the end it did not stop me however.

Lord Matteo Utrello, who was leader of the Council,

seemed to have a enormous interest in ladies. At least he frequently mentioned them. Almost every day he said at least three times that he was glad Lady Blanche was going to let herself be represented on the Council by someone else as was the proper behavior for a lady. I was so unused to thinking of myself as one of these elevated creatures that it took me two days to realize that these remarks were directed at me. Then I was very angry. What had I ever done to him that he should make these nasty remarks? I had been extremely well-behaved on the council. In fact I had hardly opened my mouth.

After two days of seething, I was angry enough to retort.

"It's a pity I'm not a lady. I would like to have some underling bear my responsibilities. Unfortunately I am a mage and the daughter of an inn servant, so the term *lady* does not apply to me."

Everyone, including me, was shocked into silence by my retort. Lord Sercel put his face in his hands.

Lord Utrello puffed himself up till he looked like he was going to explode. He jumped out of his chair, smacked the table, and shouted, "Women are too emotional. The Council of State is no place for them."

"Why?" said Ren Daniel suddenly. "The Duke has seen fit that Enna Dion sit with us. Surely you are not putting your judgment above his."

"I'm sure he would be very distressed to hear that you were, Lord Utrello," purred Lord Sercel.

"Sweet Tanza release us all," cried Lord Utrello, shaking his fist at the sky with the air of a man at the end of his tether. Then he sat down, shuffled the papers before him for a moment or two, cleared his throat, and proceeded to talk on the issue of forage for the cavalry as if nothing had happened.

I felt like bursting into tears and running away, but I was not going to let that nasty man push me out of the meeting. When I regained the courage to look up from my lap, Ren Daniel caught my eye and winked and Lord Sercel nodded kindly. Later, as we left the chamber, Ren Daniel caught up with me.

"Enna Dion, that was bravely spoken," he said.

"Was it? I suspect I have simply been foolish," I said.

"Today has proven just how important it is for you to come. It's good for these fellows to have to look at you across the Council room. In time they will come to think it normal. And they must, for now that you are Elector of Magery you will always be entitled to sit on the Council of State."

"I just feel so useless," I said. "I know nothing of forage and the procurement of camping land for the army. And we seem to spend so much time arguing about si . . . small matters."

"Councils always move very slowly, but we are an invaluable tool for the Duke. We free him from such small matters to see to the important things."

I wondered what kind of big issues the Duke was dealing with, since to me the only issue seemed the journey South which was manifestly not happening. Though there was the Patriarch. That was a big issue that would have to be dealt with.

"I cannot feel I am doing anything useful sitting silently on the council," I sighed. "Is there nothing we can do to make the Duke move South faster?"

"These things need preparation," said Ren Daniel. "I assure you we are going as fast as we can. Please do not get discouraged, Enna Dion. You cannot leave the liberation of Moria entirely in the hands of foreigners, and think what a vindication it will be of your foster father's work to have a girl mage sitting upon the Council of State."

Ren Daniel can have had no idea how matters had really stood between me and my foster father, otherwise he would never have tried such an argument on me. Still, if Lady Julia managed to open a school where women could learn high magic, one day some of them might want to sit on the Council of State. Since there seemed to be nothing I could do at the moment to free the South, I supposed I might as well work at setting this precedent. I only hoped that my actions would provide a positive example and not be used to prove how unsuited women were for the role.

That afternoon at a soiree in her chambers, Lady Julia herself took me aside and congratulated me on my words to Lord Utrello.

"How dare that man say that women have no place on the Council of State. I shall make sure the Duke hears of this outrage."

I wanted to protest, for I did not want people making a fuss over me to the Duke. I contented myself with making an uncomfortable face and saying, "I fear I am no politician, my Lady."

"You get better at these things with practice," said Lady Julia. "If you only knew how much I envied you your place on the council."

"I would happily give it up to you," I said.

"And I would happily take it. After handling nuns, I imagine the Council of State would be easy work. But alas, the Duke will not hear of his betrothed sitting on such a council. He feels that the advice of a consort should be given in private."

Something in the way she sighed as she said this gave me the impression that her private advice was not being sought. "Still, I am glad to have good friends who keep me informed of what is going on in the Duke's councils," she continued. "I hope I can number you among them."

I was not entirely comfortable to have Lady Julia regarding me as a friend. She was clearly someone who knew the game of politics and who seemed to play it well. The company of politicians is no place for us lesser mortals. We are the moths to their candleflame.

On the other hand I could not help liking her. She was immensely capable, energetic, and charming. She listened to what you had to say and remembered it, which is a rare quality in anyone. She reminded me of my friend Kitten Avignon, although unlike the ever-tactful courtesan, Lady Julia was both more forthright and more commanding. Lord

Sercel had once said in my hearing that it was a pity Lady Julia was not a man, for she would otherwise have made an excellent ruler. The more time I spent with her the more I was reminded of this.

I had always excused the Duke of Gallia's cold tendency to manipulate others as the result of his background. Life in the Sahr family had been a snakepit of treachery. The Duke's mother, brothers, and uncles had all plotted against his life at one time or another and he had had to learn to be very ruthless in getting rid of his opponents. However, if anything, Lady Julia's life had been far more difficult.

She was the sole survivor of the family of Bertrand Madraga, estranged oldest son of the last Duke, Argon. When she was eight her father and grandfather had had a falling out, primarily over the Church of the Burning Light. Some said the argument and Lord Bertrand's later death in prison had been organized by the Duke's ambitious younger son Phillipe. Perhaps it was, for Julia's mother had quickly fled with her three children to the Tyronic Duchies. Three years later she and her oldest son Jules were killed when a fireball engulfed their carriage. The guardianship of Julia and her brother passed to their cousin Lord Ayola, the same Ayola who later handed the rulership of Moria over to the Burning Light and who was even then something of a religious fanatic. There is nobody more forgotten than inconvenient royal children. Ayola starved and scourged the children for the sake of their souls, until the tragic death from fever and malnourishment of Julia's younger brother Marcus a year or so later.

There was something of a scandal then and the guardianship of young Julia passed more luckily to her mother's sister Lady Desdema. Lady Desdema, a spinster and, unusually for a woman, a considerable landowner in her own right, was something of an advocate of women's education. The aunt might very reasonably have had ambitions of rulership for Julia. Her father's brother, Phillipe Madraga, had not managed to produce a single living heir. However, when he was killed in the same hunting accident that killed his father, Duke Argon, the throne had passed to Lord Ayola, who had handed it over to the Hierarchs of the Church of the Burning Light, bringing about the Revolution of Souls. Ayola had committed suicide shortly afterward, claiming that now the City of God was about to be created on earth he would not be long gone.

Lady Julia had been eighteen when the Revolution of Souls had begun, and she had entered a nunnery with the expectation of spending her life there. But things change, and now the child Ayola had treated so harshly was back in Moria and things looked bleak for his return to any City of God created by the Burning Light.

I went most afternoons to the gatherings in Lady Julia's apartments. It was the most enjoyable part of the day. No matter how used to living in another country you get, nobody is as easy to be with as your own countrymen. Lady Julia's afternoon parties were gatherings of Morians. Lord Quercy, leader of the Southerners, was a frequent guest, as was Ren Daniel. Lord Sercel occasionally attended. There was also a host of lesser lights, most of whom had returned from exile in the Duke's wake: mages, aristocrats, priests of the ortho-dox Morian church, and intellectuals who sometimes enter-tained the company with poems and stories in praise of the traditions of Moria.

Occasionally I was also bidden to attend evening parties with the Duke, and though Lady Julia and many other Mor-ians were also there, we spoke in Gallian of Gallian matters. Was it my imagination or was it implied more than once that Morians, though amusing companions, had no talent for managing a war or a country? Certainly whenever Lady Julia expressed what seemed to me to be mere platitudes about how grateful she was for Gallian help, I saw serious nods of approval and self-satisfaction all around the room.

Sometimes my conscience would catch me out at these gatherings and remind me that while I was eating cake, peo-ple were probably dying at Sanctuary. I studiously ignored the feeling, for I had come to the conclusion that there was nothing I could do but be patient and trust the Duke, who must surely know what he was doing. At least attending parties made the time go faster.

Shortly after the Patriarch arrived, the city notables of RougeLammer held a banquet in honor of the two last remaining scions of the house of Madraga: Lady Julia Madraga and Lord Gerard Hawksmoor.

"The city notables have not declared themselves in favor of either candidate," Lady Julia told me as we rode out together. "The cunning devils say they will be guided by the Electors. I only hope that we can keep the contest confined to an election."

The banquet was held under large canopies on the green shores of the lake at the village of Quainard, a pretty spot halfway between the two towns. The feast itself was sumptuous and the weather magnificent.

Both the Patriarch and the Duke spoke during the course of the Banquet, each talking confidently but briefly about the conquest of the South and congratulating themselves for their efforts against necromancy so far. Then the many other speakers—the Mayor of RougeLammer, Lord Matteo Utrello, and so on and so forth—spoke, stressing what a fine old system the system of electors was and what a privilege it would be for them to abide by "the will of the people" in this instance.

I was seated next to Lord Lucien, who kept up a whispered and witty monologue all through the speeches of the lesser lights, making remarks about their appearances and telling me scandalous stories about them. He was so witty during Gerard Hawksmoor's speech that I was hard put to keep a straight face.

I had to agree with Lucien. The patriarchal candidate for the throne did give the impression of being "a man of very little brain." Hawksmoor was in his mid-twenties and his rather protuberant blue eyes were glazed as, haltingly and with many anxious glances at the smiling Patriarch, he read his speech. Though he wore somber colors, his clothes were cut in the latest Holy States style, and breeches with frills around the bottom cannot be said to show off long skinny legs to an advantage. Was it my imagination or was there contempt in the eyes of the Lord-Elector Rouget whenever his eyes rested upon his candidate?

Despite Lucien's witty remarks, my spirits were low that day. I could not help wondering if the Duke would really be prepared to take the Army South when the Patriarch was poised at a point where he could take Middle Moria from him?

The moment I had this thought I chided myself for being so cynical. Necromancy was pure evil and must be put down. Yet a small voice inside my head could not help pointing out that with such an immediate danger of losing such a large and valuable territory as Moria, a necromancer who was not at the moment bothering him must be of very secondary importance to the Duke. As for this Gerard Hawksmoor, if events fell so that he became king, he looked like he would be entirely a puppet of the Patriarch. Did I want such a person on the throne of Moria?

As we were mounting up to leave afterward, I came up beside Lord Quercy. A scowl was darkening his weather-beaten face. He was furious, spitting hot vinegar as we say in Moria.

"Those villains talk as if the South is already taken. Do they think it will take itself? They care nothing for us, dirty foreign betrayers. Do you know that since the Patriarch has arrived, the Duke has taken Southern troops and stationed them along the northern edge of Lake Lammer between us and RogueLammer? I tell you, he plans to make us fight our Morian brothers, not Hierarch Jarraz's black-hearted devils."

I tried not to think about the situation too much. Surely the Duke would find some way to sort things out. He was about to begin negotiations with the Patriarch and Bishop Jarraz's negotiator would soon be coming from the South. It would be foolish to waste men's lives moving too soon when a little diplomacy might solve the problem. And yet . . .

Perhaps I was just lonely. Though the days were full of

activity, I felt constrained to be careful with most of the people I saw during the day. Tomas' house had been returned to him after being commandeered by the Burning Light, and Silva had taken the Holyhands children and Uncle Louie and moved back to it, so I lost her company. As for Tomas himself, though he still lived at the White Tower, he obviously had a lot of other things on his mind. When we did have time to speak, he had a tiresome tendency to lecture me.

I missed Shad. I think I missed sharing my thoughts with him even more than I missed the feel of his warm body beside me at night.

I also regretted the bad terms on which Parrus and I had parted. It worried me that after enticing him to come into Moria with us, Tomas and I had abandoned him so thoughtlessly. To check that he was at least satisfactorily taken care of, I went down to the barracks of the regiments of mages one afternoon. I admit that the hope that we might achieve some kind of friendly reconciliation was not a thousand miles from my mind.

Mages fight in phalanxes, a triangle-shaped formation of about forty mages. The mages inside the phalanx channel their power into a power crystal held by the mage at the front, who then directs the blasts of power at an object such as the wall of a fortress or a group of troops. The mages along the outside of the phalanx use the magic of protection to prevent those inside from being damaged by missiles, magical blasts, and arrows being shot at them. Phalanxes were most useful in sieges against fortresses, for fortresses generally had spells woven into the fabric of their walls and strengthened by the defending mages, and these things needed to be overcome before nonmagical troops could enter.

A practice session was going on when I arrived at the regimental barracks. I could not tell if Parrus was among those practicing, since everyone was wearing protective leather helmets. Fighting in phalanx requires enormous concentration and coordination. Though a good phalanx of mages can be devastating, the whole thing can go out of balance very easily. Watching them, I could see clearly that the closest phalanx was a new formation. They were trying to blast some cabbages off a wall, but since the leading mage was getting no power at all out of his crystal, they had obviously not harmonized with each other properly yet. A commanding officer was running up and down the line with another crystal trying to find out where the problem was.

Further away two other phalanxes were running back and forth in front of a line of catapults that shot small rocks at them. At the end of each run they would stop and blast cabbages off stands. Even though they failed to hit them about half the time, a commanding officer would shout at them and drive them back through the hail of small rocks. It looked like exhausting but exciting work. All around the air crackled with magic, not just from the phalanxes but from the mages working the catapults and the commanding officers. I could have watched for hours.

"Come down to see the training, Enna Dion?" said a voice behind me. It was my old schoolmate Garthan Redon.

"I've never seen this kind of work before," I said. "It's wonderful. Is it very difficult?"

"They don't hit the cabbages too often, do they?" he said. "They're mostly raw recruits, Morian mages who have come out of the woodwork since we crossed the border. Not very well trained, most of them, but there's some good raw talent among them. The Gallian mages are much more precise. These phalanxes you see here are about half Morian and half Gallian. They train better that way."

We chatted for a while. I asked Garthan about conditions and rates of pay for the mages serving under him, and was relieved to discover that Silva had been right. Belonging to a regiment of Mages was an honor and, like most elite troops, the mages were very well treated. I was afraid Garthan was never going to leave me, but he wandered off eventually. He was the last man on earth I wanted to ask about Parrus' whereabouts. At school he had had an infallible nose for ferreting out secrets. He was obviously intimate with the Duke, but if he didn't know about the situation with Parrus yet, I wasn't about to put him in the way of finding out.

At last the practice was over and the tired and sweaty mages filed off the field. I called out to Parrus, who came over to me, but the talk did not go well. Parrus was angry the minute he saw me and refused to let me apologize. "You used me, Dion," "I will never forgive you," "I can't believe what kind of woman you are," and more of the same came out of his mouth before he turned and walked away from me. For a moment I was tempted to run after him, but I knew his pride was quite naturally hurt. The only thing I could have done to make him feel better was to agree to marry him and take the blame for the "misunderstanding," which would have been idiotic. I turned and made my way back to the White Tower.

Lucien Sercel was one person whose company I did enjoy. Tomas' half-brother was always full of funny stories and gossipy anecdotes. Horses were the only subject he would be serious about. He went riding or hunting every day, often with the Duke. I sat beside Lucien each night at dinner and always enjoyed the experience.

Lucien and Tomas had been childhood friends long before Sandor Sercel had rediscovered Tomas' existence. Lucien spent most of his childhood living with his sisters at Lammerquais while Lord and Lady Sercel stayed at the court of Mangalore. A couple of years after I had been sent off with Michael, he made the acquaintance of Tomas after slipping away from his tutors to go and play in the forest. The two boys recognized each other as half-brothers (Tomas was not Lord Sandor's only illegitimate child), and since Lucien "was sick of having no one but stupid girls to play with" they became fast—if illicit—friends. Through Tomas, Lucien got to know the rest of my family, and he was a wonderful source of information about them. He was especially fond of my mother, who he said was "the best mother a boy could have. I always wished she was my mother. She never told you off and she knew when to leave you alone."

Lucien had had some experience with my mother's uncanny powers of foretelling. He told me of a time when he was about eighteen when, once again out hunting in the forest against the wishes of his tutors, he fell down an old mine shaft. He had lain there all day, passing in and out of consciousness and calling for help, sorely afraid that no one would be able to find him in this out-of-the-way part of the forest. Toward evening, however, Marnie had brought Joseph Hallie and Tomas to rescue him. When he asked her how she had known where he was, she had replied that she had once had a vision that she would find him in just such a place on the day she had found a red skirt with blue embroidery among the laundry. She had that morning been given such a skirt to wash and had set out to find him.

"I thought myself a devil of a fellow at that age and later there was nothing for it but for me to tell Marnie that if she had ignored her vision, she might have made Tomas' fortune, for my father doted upon him and might have made him his heir. She was furious and told me that visions were not to be used for such a wrong. I think I was jealous of Tomas at that time and she understood that, for she forgave me quickly and always treated me like a most beloved son afterwards."

Lucien was the only person who never said anything bad about Tasha. He called her an angel, the first time I'd heard her described in such a way. I was fascinated by what this easygoing man could have seen in such a savage woman, and one afternoon when we had gone up to the nursery to see their little son Henri, my curiosity got the better of me and I asked him what she had been like.

"A wonderful woman," he said. "Wonderful. There was no one like her. The best rider in the hunt. The wittiest dinner companion. And she could drink me under the table, though many is the night I tried to best her. What a wild creature she was. I remember once a whole band of us raced our horses by torchlight to the top lock of the river and back again, and she won by swimming her horse across the river. She almost drowned, but that didn't stop her drinking half a bottle of liquid fire to celebrate. Ah, Tasha. She burned so brightly."

He looked at me with eyes that were suddenly perceptive.

"You've heard nothing but stories of drunkenness and difficulty, haven't you?"

I shrugged, not liking to say anything against his beloved.

"You seem to have been very happy together," I said.

"I was happy, yes, and I think she was as happy as such a restless soul can be. Certainly she stayed with me. And she gave me little Henri and she didn't have to do that. She was difficult. She had a temper. But unlike the rest of your family, I'm not stupid enough to hang around when people are breaking plates. Her anger was always followed by tears. I'd wait until the anger had passed and she was in the mood to be comforted. She always wanted to have a better temper and be a better person and she was frustrated when she failed. I didn't really care if she changed. I loved the fire in her. Such people always singe others, but they singe themselves much worse."

He looked down at the little boy who was now crawling busily round his feet. He sighed.

"Poor Tasha. She had these dark moods and often during them she would go back to Annac and stay at the inn."

"That must have been difficult for you."

He smiled at me.

"You don't understand, Dion. I'm a dull fellow. Too lazy. I'm content to just to let life flow along. It amazed me that she would come to me in the first place. I expected her to leave at any time. The first time she came back to me, the first time she told me that she had missed me—that was the most wonderful moment of my life. It used to amaze me that someone like me had something to offer this creature of fire. I think I am so dull that it calmed her to be with me."

He patted his son's head.

"I wish I could still hope that she was coming back. But you must know what it's like not to use your powers. When she left the White Sisters, she had no outlet for it. I wanted to send her to my father in Floredano with little Henri. She was considering it. Then that damned priest came to her with his talk of Sanctuary. Curse him. A mild form of madness seemed to come upon her in her black moods. If only he had come when she was happy. She might still be alive.''

At that moment the nursemaid came to take Henri away for his nap. She was followed by Tomas.

"Lucien, I'm looking for . . . Oh, there you are, Dion.''

His face changed from concern to pleasure with astonishing suddenness.

"I see you're making the acquaintance of young Henri. He's a charmer, isn't he?"

"Were you looking for me, Tomas?"

"I just wanted to tell you that I'm going to RougeLammer tomorrow with the ducal negotiating team."

This was astonishing news, for I could not see Tomas as much of an asset at the negotiating table. As he and Lucien talked, however, I realized that Tomas' task was more underhanded. He was going to spy on the Patriarch and keep Lord Sercel informed on how negotiations were going.

"You'll make sure young Dion is kept amused, won't you, brother," said Tomas. He looked enormously pleased about something.

After Tomas had gone, Lucien threw back his head and laughed and laughed.

"What's so funny?"

"Our brother can be very diverting sometimes," was all he would say. I found out much later that after all his anger over Tasha, Tomas had actually suggested to Lucien that I would make him a good second wife. I'm only glad that I didn't find out at the time. I would have been chilled to the core to find that he was already trying to arrange marriages for me.

Lucien excused himself for a moment then, saying he was just going to go help get Henri settled down. I was still wondering what had pleased Tomas so much when the sound of raised voices and Henri's crying drew me out of my reverie. I went to investigate.

"Leave my son alone," Lucien was shouting. "You get out of here."

He was holding a crying Henri away from a figure standing by the cradle. The figure was Karac.

"You were always second-best," snarled Karac bitterly. "Your father loved Tomas better and Tasha loved me better and you know it."

"So what if she loved you better? I was the one in her arms," shouted Lucien.

"You . . ." Karac leaped at Lucien, who swung away to protect Henri.

"No!" I cried, throwing magic between them so that Karac staggered backward. Faint blue runes appeared all over the wall.

"Have a care for the baby!" I cried at them both.

Lucien paid me no heed. "You have no rights to my son and you won't get any. You weren't here when you were needed."

I caught a glimpse of Karac's stricken face as he left the room.

"Is Henri all right? What happened?" I cried.

The little boy was screaming lustily, but he seemed unhurt. Lucien placed him tenderly back in the cradle.

"He was in here disturbing Henri," muttered Lucien. "I will not have it."

"Was he hurting him?"

"No, but he hurt his mother enough when she was alive. I will not have him near her son."

"Oh Lucien," I cried, suddenly seeing that I had mistaken the injured party in this. I remembered Karac's stricken face. Sure now that Henri was unharmed, I rushed out of the room to find Karac.

A servant told me he had seen Ren Karac going into his room. The door was locked when I got there. I knocked and called out Karac's name. He didn't answer, but using magic I could tell he was in there. The moment my magic touched him, I felt the most terrible desperate grief. Afraid now of what might happen if I went away, I kept on knocking. At last I decided to go into the room. The lock was very easy to slide open.

The room inside was a study with a desk and a cabinet for papers. Karac was kneeling on the floor beside the desk, bent over as if in pain. His hands were dug into his face so hard that the knuckles were white.

"Leave me alone," said Karac. His voice came out in a choking snarl.

Was he weeping? I was torn between being afraid that I was humiliating him by witnessing this and a certainty that if I went away something terrible would happen to him.

"Are you all right?"

"No," hissed Karac. "Of course not."

"Then I'll sit here till you are," I said, sitting down upon a chair by the door.

"Leave me alone, you stupid cow," he screamed. A huge blue vase that stood on the desk came flying at me. I caught it easily in midair and lowered it to the ground. Again faint blue runes appeared around the wall, set off by Karac's aggressive magic.

Suddenly he cried out "Oh God," reared up and let out a great howl of anguish and grief. He drew his hands down his face, gouging great red scratches onto his skin.

"No," I cried, running across the room and clutching his hands.

He was in an ecstasy of grief, howling like an animal, howling terrible curses at God and the world.

"I killed her," he cried. "I killed her." I held his hands and knelt beside him until finally the fit passed and he lay silently.

After a time he stirred. He did not raise his head but he pushed me away.

"Why can't you leave me alone?" he said bitterly.

"I'm afraid to leave you," I said. "Tell me someone who can sit with you and I will go."

"There is no one," he said. "There was never anyone but her."

The mind is a traitor. It wanted me to say, *then why were you so stupid as to leave her so long?* I did not say it. I knew full well how it feels to do something that cannot be put right. The mind searches and searches for a way for things to be different—and comes up again and again with proof of your guilt and failure. So I stayed kneeling beside him.

He lay there, shuddering every now and then, with his head on his knees and his eyes open. This terrible empty silence was somehow worse than his howling.

At last there came a knock on the door.

He sat up.

"Lady Julia. Oh . . ."

I pushed him back.

"You can't go to her like this. I shall tell her you are sick."

He stared at me with glazed eyes as if he couldn't remember who I was.

When I returned from giving the message to the servant, the room was empty. He had wandered into the bedroom next door and was now lying huddled on the bed.

"I want to sleep now," he said.

I took this to be a request. Sleep is a good tonic for the grieving, so I rubbed sleeping into his temples.

"No dreams," he muttered as his eyes closed. "Cursed dreams."

The sleep was deep enough that he would dream little and not remember them when he was awake. Gently I healed the scratches on his face.

Now that he was asleep, I felt safe to leave him. I was shaken by Lucien's vindictiveness and by the terrible intensity of Karac's grief. I wanted nothing more than a good strong cup of tea.

Opening the door into the hallway, however, I ran right into Lady Julia.

"What is the matter with Ren Karac? Is he ill?"

I knew instinctively that he had not told her of Tasha's death and I was not sure if he would wish her to know such a personal thing about him.

"He's sleeping now," I said.

"What's wrong with him, Enna? He has been acting strangely since we came to Lammerquais. Tell me please."

The please was a command, not a request, but Lady Julia's eyes were full of gentle concern.

"He is grieving," I said carefully. "His twin sister died before he came here. They were very close."

I was right. She knew nothing of Tasha. "A twin? Truly?" she said in a surprised voice.

"Yes. I hope he will be better in the morning."

She seemed to shake off her surprise.

"Ah, Ren Karac," she said. "I did not think you capable of such softness. The world is a surprising place, Enna Dion."

"I think it is a surprise to him also," I told her, thinking immediately afterward that I was saying too much.

"Do you think he will be able to continue his work?" she said thoughtfully. "Or should I find someone else to do his duties until he has recovered? I have great need of a personal mage at this time."

I wondered why. I was never really very sure what personal mages did for people. I sensed that for Karac to be replaced with Lady Julia would only make things worse for him.

"If you could just wait till tomorrow," I said. "We can see how he is then."

"Of course," she said. "Do you think there is anything else I can do for him? He has served me very well and loyally."

I felt a sudden warmth toward this woman, who was not just another selfish aristocrat after all.

"I don't know," I said. "I hardly know my brother."

"I find I do not either, though I thought I had his measure. I do know that he is a proud man. I do not think he will thank you for having seen him in his weakness. I shall send a manservant to sit with him till he wakes. It may be better if you avoid him for a few days."

I was relieved. I had been worried about what to do about Karac in the long term. I did not think he would like the interference of strangers in his grieving. Since he was as rude and withdrawn as expected the following day, I was very grateful that someone else was keeping a close eye on him as well.

"I do not think you need to worry about your brother destroying himself," said Lady Julia a few days later. It was obvious from the way that she spoke that she now had a much fuller possession of the facts. "I have come to the conclusion that he would not regard it as sufficient punishment."

·14·

I was very glad when I received a message from Silva inviting me to come and visit her at Tomas' house. I had half feared she had forgotten all about me. I have noticed that people often take their families for granted, but I could not forget that Silva was almost a stranger to me despite our blood ties. I had not felt able to go and see her without an invitation.

There was also the issue of Dally. The day I had seen her coming out of my room, I had made a mental note to try and form some kind of relationship with her. When I had first been named Elector I had been very preoccupied however, and it was during that period that Silva had taken the children back to Tomas' house and removed Dally from easy reach. In my heart of hearts I was a little scared of Dally. Aside from guilt, I sensed that she was very like Tasha in personality, with the same passionate, overwhelming emotions.

Enough of such cowardly thoughts! This time I would find out if there was anything I could do, even if it was to be just a supportive aunt.

I told Lady Julia I was going and she must have told Karac, for as I was sneaking down the hallway trying to avoid the escort Lucien insisted I must take, Karac appeared around a corner and handed me a package.

"Since you're so keen to be a do-gooder, you can give this to Dally from me," he said coldly.

What an ungracious man he is, I thought as I put the gift into my basket beside the other gifts from Lucien and the preserves from the housekeeper.

This was the first time I had actually seen the city of Lammerquais. Its broad, well-paved streets compared very favorably with the small, mean streets of Glassybri, and its fine buildings spoke of cheerful prosperity. The bustling activities of buying and selling were going on everywhere, and on the streetcorners balladists and acrobats, whose activities had been forbidden under the Burning Light, were performing to appreciative audiences. Once or twice I even glimpsed some Wanderers walking through the crowds, but always they were some distance away; mindful of Symon's instructions, I did not bother them. Everywhere on posts and over doorways hung garlands made of the Gallian colors of red and white and the Morian colors of black and gold, giving the streets a festive air.

I had thought it ridiculous to make some poor man follow me around all day, when I was perfectly capable of protecting both myself and him, but I quickly discovered why Lucien had insisted on an escort. There were Gallian soldiers everywhere, lolling in doorways, walking with their arms around the waists of women, or reeling along the street, drunk even this early in the morning. It's odd how men feel free to bother a woman walking alone even when she is wearing mage's robes. I held my head up and looked straight ahead and no one actually approached me, but it is annoying to have people speculate out loud on the niceness of your legs or remind you that your chest measurement is not of the largest.

Annoying, yes, but hardly a good enough reason to blow people up, though by the time I reached Silva's I was feeling sorely tempted. Much later it occurred to me that I could have turned their whole bodies—or maybe just their private parts—a kind of iridescent, shining-through-your-clothes, purple. Another good idea thought of too late. Life is full of regrets.

Tomas' house was in a pleasant area very near the town walls. You could see the orchards and fields outside the town through the gate at the end of the street. It was a tall house, made out of timber and whitewashed stone, four storeys high and with a shop on the bottom floor. Very fine for an inn servant's son. Tomas was still in RougeLammer, probably earning the wherewithal to keep such a house, but Martin was playing ball in the street outside and when I saw him he waved and darted inside to announce my arrival. The next minute Silva came bustling out, enfolded me in a hug, and hustled me back into the house "before all those busynoses in the street see you are here."

"This is Ren Avel Mara," said Silva. I had already heard of Ren Mara, who was Silva's particular friend. He was a cloth merchant who lived nearby in lodgings over his warehouse, and who rented the shop on the street level of Tomas' house. Somehow I had pictured the beautiful Silva with someone quite different from this chubby little man who only came up to her shoulder. His eyes twinkled as he shook my hand in his fat little paws as if he was fully aware of the reasons for my surprise.

"Dion," cried a voice behind us. Hamel was standing in the doorway of the shop with his arms spread wide. He seized me around the waist and squeezed me hard.

Silva hustled us out of the shop and up a set of stairs.

"What are you doing here," I asked Hamel anxiously, for I could see a faded bruise around his eye.

"Just visiting," he said, steering me down the corridor and into a sunlit room. Here two strange women were sewing by the window with Needra and Dally.

"Girls, come and give your aunt a kiss," cried Silva. Needra came forward, but Dally jumped up from her chair and ran out of the room. Oh dear, I thought. I tried to tell myself it was just because I was a stranger.

Hamel and Silva exchanged looks and Silva said, "Dally

is very shy at the moment. I apologize for her.''

"This is my wife Radiance," said Hamel, introducing a shyly smiling young woman, "and her mother Jeanne." The older woman nodded stiffly. "And this little beast is my boy Shine," he continued, swinging a crowing toddler up off the floor. "Give your auntie a kiss, brat."

After I had admired the handsome and incredibly energetic little boy, we sat down and ate cake and chatted while Silva bustled up and down the stairs seeing to the midday meal.

Radiance and Jeanne were in hiding because of the Duke of Gallia's decree that all Burning Light worshippers be sent to prison until the whole of Moria was liberated. Hamel was hoping that here in the town where nobody knew them they would escape notice.

It did seem an unnecessarily harsh decree. I could not see what harm women and children could pose to Duke Leon's hold on Moria, especially since Burning Light women had even less authority outside their homes than most other women. All over Moria now, people must be hiding friends and relatives just as Silva and Hamel were.

"Have you had to leave the mill?" I asked Hamel, anxiously pointing at his eye.

He laughed and said he had left the mill in his journeyman's care for a while. In a week he'd go home, so that people would think he had made a longer journey.

At midday I went downstairs for dinner. Ren Mara and his journeyman sat down with us. Only Hamel and his family ate upstairs to keep out of the way.

"It was not wise of you to come in your mage's robes, Enna Dion," laughed Ren Mara. He was a man full of happy laughter. "Three people already have been in to ask me if that was the Demonslayer they just saw coming in."

"Oh no Ren Mara, what did you say?" said Silva dismayed.

"I denied it and told them that they should look at those cheap ribbons that came in yesterday. And every one of them bought some, taking as long as they could because they all hoped to see the Demonslayer." He chuckled again, while Silva smiled fondly at him from the other end of the table.

"Now Dion, I have an important matter to ask you about," said Silva after the meal was over. "It's Dally. When do young mages usually start to show powers?"

"With girls, it's usually the onset of their bleeding. Why, has Dally . . . ?"

"It's not begun yet, but I think she's already showing signs of power. That's possible, isn't it?"

The more powerful the mage, the earlier the onset of the powers. There had never been a time when I couldn't remember being able to use magic, although my powers increased dramatically after puberty.

"I haven't seen her do anything yet, but I know she can sense the presence of magic," continued Silva. "That day when you healed my headache—when I woke up Dally was curled up on the bed beside me with her hand on my head. And later I kept having to chase her out of your rooms. Something there fascinated her. She said you had writing on the walls."

The runes! Dally had seen the runes which were usually only visible using magic. Or had she simply seen me making them? I remembered someone coming into my room behind me when I had been drawing them on the walls, before the magic had made them invisible. Had that been Dally?

"If she turns out to be powerful, do you think you could take her under your wing and teach her? It would have meant so much to Tasha. Dally is a difficult child, though she's sweet when you get to know her."

"I've been thinking I should take a look at her," I said. "Tasha asked me to protect her when she died."

"Let's go up and see her now then," said Silva, getting up from the table.

I remembered Karac's gift to Dally then and I took it out of the basket and showed it to Silva who pulled a face.

"He's still trying, is he?" she said. "Dally was horrible to him when he came here. Tasha always told her terrible things about him. I don't think she realizes how much Tasha loved him and I don't know how to explain it to her. Well, I suppose we should give it to her. I don't know whether to encourage her to be friends with him or not."

Dally had not come down to eat, even though Silva had sent for her. We found her sitting in the bedroom she shared with Needra at the top of the house. She accepted the gift with pleasure. It was a pretty little necklace and she put it on with a cry of delight and ran to the mirror to look at herself. As I watched her preening in the mirror, I saw a look of distress cross her face. She turned quickly away from her reflection and by the time she was facing us the look of distress had been replaced by one of slyness.

"Tell my Uncle thank you," she said. "And tell him it's a lovely color. It was my mother's favorite and I'm sure she would have liked it. Tell him that."

What a horrible child, I thought involuntarily, and pushed the thought away because I could see clearly what pain lay behind her words.

"Oh Dally. A simple, 'no, thank you' would do," said Silva with a long-suffering look. "Must you be so mean?"

"He ruined my mother's life," muttered Dally.

Had I been this melodramatic as a fourteen-year-old, I wondered. I had a vague embarrassing suspicion that I had been.

"And she let him ruin it," muttered Silva under her breath, but to Dally she said, "Well, I suppose it's your business, Dally. Though I hope you won't encourage your uncle just for the sake of being mean to him. Now sit down. Your aunt wants to ask you some questions."

She answered my questions politely enough. Yes she was aware of a vague tingling sensation sometimes when she was in the presence of magic. She denied ever seeing me make runes however. I was not sure I believed this.

"I'd like to examine you now, if you please," I said lifting my hands.

"No," shouted Dally, jumping away suddenly. "I'm not having her touch me. She kills people."

"Dally!" cried Silva.

"Yes she does. Look what happened when she touched Mother."

Horrified, Silva cried, "You know perfectly well it wasn't her fault."

"She killed her," screamed the girl with an edge of hysteria to her voice. "She did. She did." She rounded on me, "You spoiled brat! She was all right before you came. You killed her." She burst into hysterical weeping.

"Oh Dally," cried Silva in a horrified voice, trying to put her arms around the girl. "I had no idea. Stop it. Calm down."

I left the room, partly because I could see I was making things worse, but mostly because I was trembling. I did feel partly responsible for Tasha's death. Part of me wanted to burst into tears and shout back, *I didn't, I didn't.* I pulled myself together. Grieving people say silly things and say them to hurt. That doesn't mean they are true. I hadn't killed Tasha, no matter how guilty I felt about her death. She'd touched me, not the other way around.

Hamel and Needra came racing up the stairs.

"Sweet Mother!" said Hamel. "What's all the fuss? Is that Dally? Good God! Getting more like her mother every day."

There was a crash.

"She's wrecking my things," cried Needra.

"Needra," shouted Hamel. "Stay out of it!" He made a grab for her, but the girl was away and racing down the corridor in a flurry of fair hair and skirts. She burst into the room. There was a chaos of shouting, a crash, and the sound of two girls screaming and, if I was not mistaken, fighting.

I darted toward the room, but Hamel held me back.

"No Dion, just wait. Silva knows more about young girls than either of us. Lord, that Holyhands temper."

The screaming rose higher and louder until suddenly it stopped. There was silence and then the sound of sobbing.

Hamel walked carefully along the corridor and peered into the room. He came back toward me smiling.

"I think it's over now. Everybody's crying and being

comforted by Silva. Come on downstairs. You look like you need a nice cup of tea. Not used to all this family life, are you?"

I could not believe how relaxed he was. I was frightened that someone had been hurt. Silva, however, was perfectly calm when she came down later.

"I'm so sorry for what happened," she said to me. "I had no idea what was going on in Dally's mind. What a nasty shock you must have had. Still, she's stopped bottling up her grief now. You may actually have done her some good."

I suggested we try again later, not because I wanted to but because I felt that as the adult I should be generous. It was ridiculous to be afraid of a fourteen-year-old girl.

Silva sighed and said, "I don't know, Dion. I don't think you should be too kind to Dally. She behaved very badly and she has to learn to respect people's feelings. Otherwise she *will* become like Tasha. I'll teach her what I know and maybe we'll try again in six months or so. Maybe we should just send her to the healer's college like everyone else."

"Why did she call me a spoiled brat?" I asked.

Hamel made a disgusted noise. "You've got Tasha to thank for that. In the last few years Tasha really came to resent you. She felt you'd had all the opportunities she hadn't. When she was drunk she used to rave on about you for hours."

"And of course Dally believed it," said Silva. "She believes everything Tasha said even more now that she's dead. Ah! Tasha was a perverse creature. She managed to botch every one of her own chances."

"Aye," said Hamel sharply, "and she wasn't much a mother either. She was hardly ever there, and when she was half the time she was drunk."

"And when she was sober she was wonderful to Dally and that's what Dally chooses to remember. Have you never noticed how the neglected child clings closest? Children can be very loving and forgiving creatures. I sometimes think that's why we have them."

Later Silva and I took Derrum and Martin out walking

through the orchards and down to the bank of the nearby river. We talked of Karac. Silva had little advice to give me about him, except to tell me not to be frightened of him.

"Tasha and Karac were very alike as children, but even then he had more self-control. All the well-thought-out plans were his doing. He is a very different man from the woman Tasha became. He has had a happier life for a start—he's been able to make good use of his magery and then he doesn't drink."

She agreed with Lady Julia that Karac was not at the moment in danger of killing himself.

"It will be vengeance that he wants," she said. "Though you are right to watch him, Dion. Her death is like a mortal blow to him and he may yet sicken from it. Or do something crazy. Why on earth did he refuse Tomas?"

"You talk as if Tasha and Karac were more than brother and sister," I said.

She shot me a quick glance. "They were very close even for twins," she said. "I think it was to separate herself from Karac that Tasha ran away with the acrobats and bore her child. Unfortunately, when the trick worked, she found she could not bear the separation."

"And now Karac wants to be friends with Dally," I said. If there was something too intense about Karac's feelings for Tasha, no wonder Silva was uneasy for Dally. I would have been.

"For her mother's sake," said Silva uncomfortably. "And I am not sure what that means and if it would be good for Dally or not."

At that she changed the subject and refused to say any more on the matter.

It was lovely to have Silva to talk to after the loneliness at the Tower. We had a delightful walk and Silva showed me a prettier way to get back to the White Tower without going through the town. Dusk was falling by the time we returned to the house.

"I asked someone to dinner," said Silva. "I hope you don't mind. Ah, I think he's here already."

And while I was still regretting the presence of an outsider, the outsider got up from his chair.

"Hello Enna Dion," said Shad, smiling at me.

I was so pleased to see him I had to clasp my hands behind my back lest I embarrass us both by flinging my arms around him.

How handsome Shad was with his dark eyes and mane of curls. He had new clothes on, a black and gold coat that fitted smoothly over chest, waist, and hips and a white shirt that was slightly open at the top. He was obviously familiar with the house and well known to Ren Mara. I tried to find the narrow line between being friendly and being too friendly. I did not want him to think I was pining after him, but he had such an infectious smile, I could not help smiling back.

I lingered after dinner, but Shad and Ren Mara had become involved in a long conversation about the best strategy the Duke should follow for going South. Eventually I decided I must go.

To my horror, Silva said, "I'll just go get Shad. He offered to walk you home."

I protested, but Silva simply made it all happen. In a few moments I was standing in the street outside with Shad standing beside me holding my basket.

"It's a beautiful night," said Shad.

I did not want him to talk. I wanted to feel his arms around me and his lips against my neck. How deliciously he smelled of wood and woodsmoke.

"Yes. It's lovely." I said. "There a nice walk home through the orchards if we can get out the gate."

"Let's try it then."

The gate was still open. In the orchards a warm scent-laden breeze was blowing through the trees. It was quiet except for a chorus of frogs and the occasional call of a night bird. There was just enough moonlight to see the path.

Shad's hand touched my back lightly to guide me and rested there. His hard body was so close. I wanted him so much I could hardly walk, but I did not want to make a fool of myself. It's not a woman's place. . . . Curse it. Who'd be a woman?

He squeezed my hand. I squeezed his back and at that he turned to me and said my name. I looked up at him. My breast and my belly tingled at the closeness of him, the desire to feel his skin, skin against skin.

He reached out and ran a finger up my neck and cheek. I caught it in my mouth and bit it gently, enjoying the rough texture of it under my tongue.

He gasped and his mouth came down on mine, hard and hungry. We feasted on each other for a moment, all hungry lips and tongues. I pressed myself against him, rubbing my body against him, feeling the bulge of his crotch against mine. His hands gripped my back and then my buttocks. I wanted to climb him, to mount him. A moment later we were off the path among the trees kissing, licking, biting each other with frenzied desire. A convenient tree branch. We hitched up my skirts and his hand caressed my thighs and the wet softness between till I was crying out in pleasure. A brief fumbling and he was loose and sliding into me. I gripped him tightly around the waist with my legs, dug my fingers into his buttocks. An ecstasy of thrusting, riding hot pleasure.

Afterward we lay in a tumbled heap on the ground.

"Air and Fire," he groaned. "I thought I was a gentle lover and I've acted like a rutting bull. All I planned was to tell you that I missed you."

"I missed you too," I dared to say.

We talked softly of all the things that had happened to us while we had been apart. After a while Shad said, "I wondered if we might meet again. If you have no other commitments."

"Commitments?" I asked.

"Do you know that every time I've seen Tomas since that fight in the stone circle he has filled my ears with talk of your imminent marriage."

"I'm not getting married," I said.

"He talked so much about it I figured that," he said.

I was torn between outrage and laughter. It was so ridiculous.

Shad grinned ruefully and said, "I don't want to make a scandal or cause trouble for you with Tomas, but I would like to see you sometimes."

I was determined he would have the chance to do more than just see me.

"I shall ask Lucien to organize a pass for you tomorrow. Then you can come and go in the White Tower as you please."

"Well actually, your sister gave me this," he said, holding up a small but official looking paper with the Sercel seal on it.

"Silva? Well, well. Do you know it was she who told me of this particular path home?" I felt laughter bubbling up inside me at the realization that Silva had engineered the whole reunion.

Shad laughed too. "I think I prefer your sister's meddling to your brother's, don't you?"

After that, on evenings when he was not on duty, Shad would send me word. My room became our little secret world, as the cellar had been.

I did not think about what was going on between us, about whether he was making use of me or indeed if I was making use of him. I only knew I wanted him and the time we spent together cast a warm glow over the rest of the days, made textures, tastes, and scents bright and fresh again. Even the Council meetings seemed a little less boring.

Nonetheless, since much of what was discussed in the Council was to do with the army, I avoided telling Shad about it. I need not have mistrusted him. There was only one thing he cared about.

"Has the Duke set a date to go South?" he would ask every time we met.

And I was forced to say every time.

"No, not yet."

*   *   *

Around this time, my intimacy with Lady Julia Madraga suffered a check. Lady Blanche Shomnee had been named as Lady in Waiting to Lady Julia, and they became constant companions.

Lady Julia clearly did not trust Blanche. She was far more formal in front of her and we only talked polite nothings. Lady Julia's rooms became a far more boring place to visit, for there were no more afternoon gatherings. I had heard rumors that the Duke had put a stop to them, though Lady Julia said nothing on the subject.

Still, it was pleasant to read and chat to them as they sewed. I quickly came to share Lady Julia's opinion of Blanche. At first glance, Blanche seemed the most harmless of mortals. She was polite and proper almost to extent of being dull, and she only said bland ''nice'' things.

But she moved like a snake, soft and slippery, and she watched everything from beneath her lashes and she had a way of licking sugar from her finger. . . . I did not begrudge her her sensuality, for it is a fine quality, but it made her bland public face seem so false.

She was no fool either. Those beautiful dark eyes saw everything. I wondered why such an obviously clever woman needed a negotiator to help her conclude a treaty with the Duke. It was her youth, perhaps and, as I had discovered, the fact that she was a woman made a big difference. Probably she did not have the legal authority to negotiate with the Duke.

One day when Lady Blanche had left the room briefly, Lady Julia asked me quickly to meet her the following morning at dawn in the stableyards.

''I have a private errand outside the town and I need someone trustworthy to guard me. Someone who can be relied upon to say nothing to anybody. Will you do it?''

I could not say no to Lady Julia.

''Of course. What. . . . ?''

At that moment Blanche came back into the room, all eyes and ears and polite curiosity and had to be distracted with questions about embroidery silk.

* * *

The following morning I reached the stableyard as night was turning from black to grey dawn, to find a groom waiting with horses. Shortly afterward Lady Julia came running in.

"We have a little way to go," she told me as she mounted up and brought the horse around, "but if anyone asks, we decided to go for an early ride to watch the dawn."

I was agog with curiosity and could not resist asking where we were going, but Lady Julia smiled and said by way of an answer, "I am glad to have you with me, Enna. You are a good friend. I know I can trust you to say nothing of this journey to anyone."

We did not ride through the town, but through the orchards and out into the forest that clothed the hills all around the Lake. The air smelled wonderfully fresh, and the long grass and low branches were damp with dew. The edge of my skirt was quickly dripping wet. This was the wild part of Lake Lammer where my mother had met the Wanderer that day.

We had traveled for almost an hour before we came to a clearing.

Here three priests and a mage were waiting for us. The mage was Karac. The others I did not recognize, though the most plainly dressed of the priests did look familiar.

It was only when we had all dismounted and Lady Julia had gone to the opposite edge of the clearing to speak with him that I recognized this plainly dressed priest. It was Patriarch Sylvestus.

"Close your mouth, sister dear, there's a good girl," said Karac mockingly in my ear. "It's not as if you've never seen a Patriarch before."

I shook off my amazement and looked around the clearing. The groom was rubbing our horses down with some dry grass. The two other priests were huddled near the horses, whispering together and darting glances at us.

"What's going on?"

"With those two?" said Karac with amusement. "They have recognized who you are and I don't doubt they are in mortal fear of some trap. They were sure of being able to take me on, but they know they have no chance with you, sister dear.''

"And the Patriarch?"

"Oh, he's no priest-mage, though I don't doubt he could give you a few bad moments with a cathedral full of worshippers at his back.''

I looked over to where Lady Julia and the Patriarch were quietly talking.

"Actually, I meant 'what is the Patriarch doing here,' '' I said.

"It's not our business," said Karac. "We only serve our Lady. In fact, if you want my advice, it's best to remain as ignorant as possible. Come, sister, let us sit here upon this log and await the pleasure of our betters.''

What on earth were Lady Julia and the Patriarch talking about? Had she come out here to plead the Duke's cause? If so, why the secrecy? Then I remembered what Shad had said all that time ago about Lady Julia becoming Queen in her own right. Was that what this meeting was about?

"Did you know Tasha at all?" asked Karac in a casual tone.

"Not really."

"Dally said you were there when she died."

For a frightened moment I wondered what Dally had been saying to him.

However, he only wanted to know how I had come to be there, so I told him all about how Tomas had come to see me in Moria and what had happened.

He quickly dropped his show of detachment, hanging on every word I said and asking dozens of urgent questions. His avidity scared me, but I did not like to refuse him. He wanted to know all about the dreams so I described them to him as best I could. In passing I mentioned the memories that Tasha had pressed into my mind. This was a great mistake, for once he learned of it he began to ask me if he might do a mind search on me to see for himself what his sister remembered. I don't know whether it was the thought of Karac plunging around inside my mind or the thought of having to remember

Tasha's memories, but the whole idea curdled my blood.

"Such memories are too horrible to be shared. Even speaking of them makes me feel ill."

"I must. You will. I will make you." He caught my arms.

"No," I cried, frightened into replying much more harshly than I had meant to. "You will not make me do anything. You can't, so don't try."

A frightening look of fury crossed his face, then one of misery.

"How can I avenge my sister when I cannot see who harmed her? And she would want revenge. I feel her uneasy soul even now."

I saw the ghosts in his eyes.

"The necromancer in the Waste Land killed her," I said, more gently. "There is no mystery here. The Duke will destroy him."

"It is not enough."

"If the Duke does not kill him," I said, "you and I shall go and do so. But we must wait until the South is liberated. I promise you I will not leave you out if it comes to a personal battle."

"You must . . ."

"Look," I said. "They are finishing."

Lady Julia had knelt before the Patriarch and he was giving her his blessing. She rose and came to us without looking back. Her face gave nothing away.

"How did it go?" I asked.

She smiled. "I cannot tell you, for I do not really know."

The sun had risen now, but it was still very early in the morning. The trees rang with morning birdsong. Karac and the groom fell behind. Lady Julia and I rode side by side. She seemed lost in contemplation of the lake.

I had developed a theory as to why Lady Julia was meeting with the Patriarch. Still filled with curiosity, I tried to confirm it.

"Your cousin Lord Gerard is unmarried, isn't he?"

"My cousin Lord Gerard is an imbecile and if he becomes

Duke of Moria, the Patriarch shall be ruler,'' she said bitterly.

She caught my eye and smiled and I saw that she had understood the thrust of my question.

''The last thing the Patriarch wishes is that cousin Gerard have a strong wife who will disturb the peace of the realm. Now really, Enna Dion, you must try to control your curiosity. It is not a courtly virtue.''

I blushed at her remark, even though I saw that it was advice more than a rebuke.

We cantered back along the road that followed the shores of the lake. There must have been a market that day, for the way was busy with carts of vegetables and herds of cattle and sheep. Lady Julia had pulled the hood of her cloak over her face, but people still stopped and stared. Some cheered and she smiled and waved at them as we passed.

Then suddenly there was a great clap of thunder and shapes shot out of the ground at the crossroad just before us. My horse reared with fright. Several voices screamed. Then suddenly my horse was still and the voices were quiet. A great calm blanket of silence sparkling with magic lay upon us.

Three Wanderers stood at the crossroads. I had forgotten how alien they looked. Among the small dark-haired Morians who stood clutching each other and staring at them with frightened eyes, they looked like the pale shades of the dead, tall and straight as tombstones, heavy with power.

The man leading them stepped forward. It was only then that I recognized him as Symon.

''We salute you, Lady Julia Madraga!''

The second Wanderer stepped forward, a woman tall and fair and unearthly beautiful.

''We salute you who will soon be ruler of Moria!''

The third, another beautiful woman, said, ''We salute you, Queen Julia. Our Queen and ruler. We have come to serve you as our ancestors served your ancestors, in recognition of the ancient pact of blood between our houses and yours.''

Then suddenly Symon held out his hands and in them was an iron crown. It was a black circle against the sun. The second Wanderer held up a sword and the third an iron necklace made of thorns. Such was the enchantment of the moment that I did not recognize my own necklace.

I only saw Symon, who turned with the iron crown held above his head and cried in a mighty voice, "Blessings to she who will wear the Iron Crown of Kings. Blessings to she whom fate loves."

Suddenly all around us the country folk were crying out and cheering and crowding round Lady Julia's horse, touching her hem and her hand. Some too were shyly touching the cloaks of the Wanderers as they stood with the regalia in their hands, silent as gods at the center of the crossroads. Wonder had returned to Moria.

The White Tower was abuzz with excitement by the time we had returned.

The guards at the gate told us that a great host of Wanderers, all armed for war, were drawn up under the city walls. Almost five thousand of them had simply appeared as if out of thin air.

"I did not think so many Wanderers still existed," cried Lady Julia. "Come with me, you two. The Duke will be wanting advice."

I was swept into the council chamber like a little boat in Julia's wake just in time to hear Lord Quercy cry, "I cannot. Most Southerners will refuse to fight them, Your Grace."

"Can you not command your own army?" shouted the Duke, leaping up from where he had been seated at the great round council table. The group of councilors hovering around him moved back nervously except for Lord Quercy, who faced the shouting firmly.

"Your Grace, the Klementari are at the gates," said Lady Julia.

"You do not need to tell me that," said the Duke sharply. "I do not have the mages to fight five thousand and these Morians of yours tell me nothing useful."

He nodded at the Duke of Tanza.

"Very well. Use Gallians if you must. Just get those mages to the walls."

"Your Grace," protested Lord Quercy. "This is not an appropriate . . ."

"Your Grace, the Klementari, the Wanderers as you once knew them, met me while I was out riding today and hailed me as future Queen of Moria. I do not think we need to be afraid of them. The Klementari are traditional allies of my house."

"Do not show them an unfriendly face, Your Grace," said Lord Sercel. "These people were always bad enemies in the past."

"Past. Past. The Klementari are a myth. What is wrong with you Morians? Must your love of legend always blind you to the facts? An army of five thousand appears out of thin air and you expect me to do nothing?"

"It will be pointless," said Lady Julia.

But she was interrupted by Lord Utrello, who came nervously into the room.

"Your Grace, the leaders of the Klementari request an audience with you."

"Yes, well, see they are kept outside the city till I've got things organized."

"Your Grace," stammered Lord Utrello. "They are already in the anteroom."

How could it be? How could the Klementari just walk into one of the best magically and physically guarded fortresses in the country and penetrate as far as the anteroom of the audience chamber without being seen or stopped by anyone?

To do Duke Leon credit he did not show fear, though he had sworn comprehensively when the meaning of Lord Utrello's words had dawned on him.

As we prepared to enter the audience chamber to meet the Klementari, he had called me over and said, "Madame Dion, I ask that you stand on the dais with us. I rely entirely upon your loyalty."

There was a time when I would have melted for the smile

in his cold eyes, but he was mistaken if he relied on my loyalty now. The Klementari were not here to fight, which meant that any fighting would be his fault. In such a case I did not think I would want to take his part.

As the Duke and Lady Julia were seated, the door swung open with a cold blast and Symon, Causa, and Beg came through it and swept down the length of the audience room. They seemed to glow with might and power. An almost palpable sense of otherness surrounded them as if they were beings from the stars. They must have been casting a glamor on themselves. I could feel a slight whisper of magic like the faint scent of perfume in an empty room.

Before Causa had seemed so comfortable. Now glamor made her blindness and Beg's age part of a glorious frightening whole. The two of them strode along with a strength and certainty that I had never seen before. For a moment I caught myself wondering if their previous homeyness might have been the glamor and this might be the reality.

Symon led the way. He still wore black, but now it was of some rich cloth. A great black cloak swirled around him as he came, and he carried a tall staff in his hand as if it were a banner. Atop the staff was a raven cast in gold, spreading its wings. Causa and Beg wore mage's robes in dark green, embroidered in gold with runes and the holy symbols of the Klementari. Behind them came two warriors dressed in brown embroidered garb and leather armor. One of them carried a large golden chest.

Symon bowed, politely but not low.

"I am Symon, Raven of the Klementari, the people you knew before as the Wanderers. These ladies are Causa the High Dreamer and Beg the High Mage of our people. Greetings and good wishes to you, Duke of Gallia. And to you, Lady Julia Madraga. And greetings and praises to you, Enna Dion. We have heard of your greatness. The Klementari give special honor to all mages."

The Duke returned the greetings graciously and asked what it was that brought the Klementari to Lammerquais.

"A terrible necromancer, a murderer and a demonmaster,

has taken possession of the place that you call the Great Waste, and he threatens Ernundra. Ernundra was once the beloved land of our people, before it was laid waste by Smazor. This blasphemy cannot be allowed to continue. The Klementari go to the Great Waste to destroy the necromancer and all his works and to free Ernundra the Holy Land and take her again to our hearts. It is time the Klementari ceased to wander.''

There was a sensation in the room at this announcement. As well there might be. Everyone regarded the Great Waste as a part of Moria, and the Duke had spoken often of reclaiming it and making Moria a kingdom again. Here were the Klementari claiming part of it as theirs without so much as a by-your-leave.

The Duke was made of sterner stuff. Though the knuckles of his hand whitened on the arm of the chair, his face remained calm "I commend you on your mission," he said now. "It is a fine and holy one. If you were to rid the Great Waste of this terrible creature for us, you would earn our undying gratitude.''

Symon smiled broadly and he turned and looked around the room. He was quite obviously amused at the Duke's attempt to turn him into a subject and he made sure the whole room saw it. Something like wonder began to come into the faces of the Morians. The Gallians on the other hand looked angry, and several clutched the hilts of their swords.

He turned back to the Duke.

"It is not the Klementari's practice to interfere with the activities of the New People. Our policy has always been mutual respect. Yet it came to us that you too were set on a crusade to destroy this necromancer. It is a course all reasonable people must follow.''

"Indeed it is," said Lady Julia suddenly. "Southern Moria must be liberated as soon as possible.''

Symon nodded his head respectfully towards her. "It is a task we are committed to with our whole beings. But before us is Southern Moria defended by a desperate Church which has no love for the Klementari. Thus have we come to you to offer ourselves in the traditional way as allies to your house, Lady. We seek a pact of mutual aid with the one who will go South first.''

''With the one who will go South first,'' echoed the Duke in an arrested voice. ''Does this mean that you will also seek an alliance with our brother the Patriarch?''

''The Patriarch is no friend of the Klementari,'' said Symon. ''And Gerard Hawksmoor will never wear the Iron Crown of Moria. The Dreamers have said so and it will be so.'' He lifted up his hand and the warrior with the golden chest came forward. ''Witness now, the truth of Klementari foretelling. One hundred years ago our ancestress, a woman called Nesta, said that Moria would be a kingdom again when the iron regalia was found.''

The warrior placed the chest on the steps of the dais and opened it. The pieces of regalia were as black as night against its golden lining.

''Behold how foretelling has become truth! Behold the Holy Iron Regalia of Moria!''

''My dear, we fear you neglected to tell us of these particular subjects of yours,'' said the Duke through clenched teeth. ''It was most remiss of you.''

We were back in the council chamber we had been in when the Klementaris' presence had first been announced.

The Duke took a large vase from a sideboard and threw it onto the floor. It shattered loudly. He put his heel with savage deliberation on the pieces and ground them into the marble floor. He did not utter a sound through this whole exercise. Lord Utrello flinched every time his heel came down. Julia Madraga simply watched him calmly, though I noticed her fists were clenched by her sides.

''So is this what it means to be a Morian ruler? Having impertinent vagabonds come with armies of thousands and, speaking like kings, tell me they plan to occupy a slice of our kingdom? You told me the Klementari were dead, a spent force.''

''It was not I who told you this, my Lord. I told you the

Klementari smiled on our endeavor. That their Dreamers had told me that I would one day be Queen of Moria.''

From the scowl on the Duke's face I could tell she had told him just that, and he, of course, being the product of a rational Gallian education, had paid her no heed.

''Really Your Grace, I cannot think why you are angry,'' continued Lady Julia. ''The Klementari have offered you the opportunity to finish this war in the South. It is a valuable alliance they offer.''

''Valuable alliance!'' shouted the Duke. ''Opportunity! What? The chance to be humiliated before all your court? You have a very strange idea of the dignity that is due to you, Madam if you value these impudent . . . witchfolk with their flashy fairground tricks. Their demands for land are just another problem. And will they stop the Patriarch from taking Central Moria while my back is turned? Had you thought of that?''

Fire burned in Lady Julia's dark eyes.

''And I say that five thousand troops are five thousand troops. What kind of ruler are you, Sir, to put pride and a tiny piece of barren land before the good of Southern Moria?'' For a moment the atmosphere of the room was like standing in a lightning storm, as the Duke and Lady Julia glared at one another. Then suddenly, as suddenly as blowing out a candle, the Duke's anger vanished. A cynical half-smile spread across his lips.

''My dear, these are hasty words for one who aspires to a throne. As the only ruler currently in this room, I must tell you I did not become so by giving away slices of my kingdom willy-nilly to every passing vagabond.''

He strolled forward, took Lady Julia's hand, and kissed it with exquisite politeness.

''And allow me to remind you, my dear that you will not be any sort of ruler, unless I make you so. I think you may leave us now. There are important matters to discuss.''

I honestly think I would have slapped his face, but Lady Julia was made of the stuff of Queens. She smiled with the same cynical sweetness, nodded her head, said, ''Of course,

Your Grace,'' and swept calmly from the room.

The Duke stood eyeing the door where it had closed behind her.

"Your Grace, she is right in one thing," said Lord Matteo, coming to the Duke's side. "These Klementari are a valuable force. Such magic as they performed today. . . . No one could think you a fool to promise them such a useless piece of land. Think of how it may persuade the Patriarch. Then later . . .''

"This is good Council, my Lord," said the Duke, silencing his adviser. He nodded at the rest of us. "Pray, good folk, leave us now. Lord Urtrello and I would think and talk quietly on the events of this day.''

•15•

The Klementaris' arrival caused a sensation, not least in the Council where the following morning Ren Daniel Devoirs put forward a motion that we urge the Duke to divide the army in half.

"The Duke is secure here in Lammerquais," he said. "The Gallians can defend Middle Moria and we Morians can go south with the Klementari."

"You place a lot of faith in people whom even you would have chased from your door a month ago, Monsieur Daniel," retorted Lord Matteo. "You cannot know their mettle in battle. Dividing the army will only make us twice as weak."

I had not thought Ren Daniel to be capable of passion, but he was passionate now.

"How can you sit there and refuse me? Do you know what is happening in the South? Even as we speak people are dying horribly at the hands of evil. We must go South and release them as soon as possible and with five thousand Klementari troops with such magic as we can only imagine, how could our chances be better?"

All around the table were angry looks and cries of "Hear hear!" Even Lord Sercel seemed to support Ren Daniel's plan. Lord Utrello did not.

"If you want to see your country fall into the hands of

the Patriarch that is your business," he said with infuriating calm. "I for one do not propose to bother the Duke with foolish plans that he has no doubt already considered. Now if we may turn to the issue of Frederic Gaulthier's petition . . ."

By then, however, the council chamber was so charged with anger on one side or another that Lord Utrello was forced to call for a vote. All the Gallian mages voted with the Morians, except Garthan Redon. The ordinary Gallians, however, stood firm with Lord Utrello and the motion was defeated. At this Ren Daniel swore and strode from the room and I followed him shortly afterward, for I was too upset to listen to more foolish talk about a merchant's petition over damage to a sweetmeat stall done by drunken soldiers.

Ren Daniel was not easily defeated, however. Later that day he came to me with a petition of his own.

"I shall present this to the Duke without going through the Council. Even some of the Gallian mages may be prepared to sign this. You saw how they were in the Council chamber. Necromancy is like fire on lamp oil even to them."

As I signed it occurred to me that Lord Sercel might have even greater chances of bringing the petition to the Duke's notice. After all he had voted with us in the council.

"I've already asked him, and he refused," said Ren Daniel. "Though with regret. Humph. He is a political animal, that one, and will not put himself on the wrong side of the Duke."

Ren Daniel did not get the opportunity to present his petition, however. That evening at a public banquet, the Duke spoke of the plan to split the army and go South. He said it was a good plan and one he had been considering, but any plan at this point was premature. The Gallian army had been in Lammerquais less than two weeks and there had been little time to train and equip the Southern troops. Some hotheads might advocate sending raw and ill-equipped troops into battle, but he was not so callous.

We must wait a few more weeks until the army was in

good order. Until then he was doing his very best to reach some kind of agreement or even alliance with the Patriarch so that this dangerous plan of dividing the army need not even be considered. His prayers went out to all Southern Morians and their families for all the danger they were facing. We owed it to them to do our best to liberate the South and not ruin our chances by embarking on hasty plans or sending too small an army.

This well-considered speech, delivered as it was with an air of grave concern, did much to calm people. The unreadiness of the Southern troops was obvious to everyone.

Even Shad agreed.

"Though I would have thought the Klementari. . . . Oh well even they could not be expected to cover for completely untrained troops. I just wish it did not all take so much time."

"Sometimes I wonder if the Duke has any intention of going South," I said.

"I wonder that too," said Shad and we lay there in gloomy silence for a time.

"Perhaps he is waiting for this Southern negotiator," said Shad suddenly. "A negotiated settlement might be a good thing. It might save many lives. I could even countenance Bishop Jarraz going free if something were to happen and happen quickly."

"Perhaps you are right," I said, though I knew my voice lacked conviction. I hoped desperately that Shad was right because apart from the Duke, what other chance did we have of freeing the South? Even the Klementari seemed reluctant to take on Hierarch Jarraz's forces alone.

"I wish there was something useful I could do." I sighed.

"I'll show you something, if you like," said Shad. "I've been meaning to ask you all this week."

The following morning he took me down to the training ground with him and within the first hour he had me flinging lumps of mud and peat at his troop while they attempted to run toward me, dodging them.

"That's right," he shouted, standing beside me, "keep it

fast and hard. It will be like that when they are under arrow fire.''

Shad was a ball of energy during those sessions. His whole heart was bent on making these men into a fighting force. While I rained these small soft missiles down on the cringing troop, he ran alongside them shouting encouragement and abuse, while almost by second nature fending off my missiles with his shield. He was a fine captain, watchful, tough, but always encouraging. I remembered how he had made me feel I could do things I was afraid to do in the forest. What a fine man he was. I could not think of anyone I admired more than him.

At break we sat under a tree together and drank cold ale.

"They have good hearts," said Shad, "but they're raw as raw. I pray His Grace will not use them as front line troops."

"I would not be so sure of that," said a scar-faced veteran standing nearby.

"Jacques," said Shad cheerfully, "come and join us."

Very shortly there was a whole group of Shad's fellow captains sitting around us, laughing and talking in good-natured comradeship.

"Has no one ever thought of training troops in this way before?" I asked.

"This is the standard way to train," said Jacques, "but the army is short of mages. They are all training our mages to fight properly, so they say."

"Magic will be the most important thing in this campaign," said another dusty little man.

"All I know is that if the army were to divide into Morian and Gallian, ours would be far weaker," said Jacques. "Our troops are apprentices and farm boys and are getting little training, and since our mages are training to fight in phalanx only with Gallian mages, once they are divided they will not be able to form a working phalanx at all."

"What a hothead you are," said another man easily. "In two weeks I wager you the Duke will be heading South and the need will never arise."

For the next few days I helped Shad and his fellow cap-

tains give the troops a taste of what it was to be under fire
and magical attack. During this time I met many of the other
Morian officers. All of them seemed to feel that meeting me
was a great thing. The admiration of these blunt, rough men
touched me more than any of the smooth words spoken to
me by those I had met in the White Tower. The thought of
disappointing them was horrible.

How I enjoyed myself. I felt calmly happy all the time I
was using magic. There was no hint of my exhausting my
powers. All I felt in the evenings was a pleasant tiredness.

This happy period ended after Shad managed to enlist the
aid of two young mages from the fighting corps to test out
my ability to defend troops and to give them some taste of
magical attack. The mages were too in awe of me to speak
to me all day, but they obviously spoke to other people. That
evening I received a summons from the Duke.

I went to him hoping that it might even be some kind of
announcement. Negotiations with the Klementari had ended
in a kind of tentative alliance that only applied to fighting in
the South of Moria. Negotiations with the Patriarch were
proceeding with the usual mysterious slowness.

To my astonishment the Duke wished to speak with me
about my work with the new troops.

"Enna Dion, you must not expose and exhaust yourself in
this way," he said kindly. "I cannot like it."

"I am not exhausting myself, Your Grace," I said, and
then, afraid I might seem disrespectful, I said quickly, "I
wish only to be useful to the cause."

"It is not proper that a mage use himself so," said Ren
Garthan, who was the only other person in the room. "I
know you are strong, but you set up expectations by acting
so. You make the other mages look inadequate. And min-
gling so with the coarse soldiery. It is not ladylike."

"Ladylike," I said, startled by such a word—especially
from the lips of Garthan Redon, who had never seemed to
me to give a thought to such things.

"My dear Enna Dion. It is not a question of ladylikeness
exactly. But you are the Demonslayer of Gallia. It is not

appropriate for you to be doing these tasks. You are too important. You must keep a proper distance.''

"Why?" I cried. Ren Garthan looked shocked. "I beg your pardon, Your Grace," I continued. "It is just that I want so much to do something useful to help the liberation of the South."

The Duke was surprisingly pleasant.

"We understand, my dear. And your feelings do you credit, but we must ask you to keep yourself in reserve for the moment. We have a plan for you. Be sure of that. But you are like a secret weapon for us. You will be worth so much to us if you keep yourself an unknown quantity and do not expose yourself or your powers to people."

I wanted to protest, but I could not think of any respectful way of doing so. I was being outmaneuvered.

"As you wish, Your Grace," I said as calmly as I could.

I knew this was not a request but an order. But why did he not want me to work at helping train his troops?

The Duke took my hand. He was close enough for me to smell the oil of oranges he used as a scent. His hand was smooth and cool.

"My dear Madame Dion," he said kindly. "I see you are sorry. You are very powerful, but you are not schooled in the ways of power as I am. Please allow yourself to be guided by me in this matter even if for now you do not understand me. Will you do that?"

"Yes, your Grace," I murmured. I remembered how grateful I should be to this man—how he had forgiven me my earlier bumbling and was going to give me a second chance.

This mood remained long enough for me to agree when the Duke suggested I allow Monsieur Garthan to assess my power for use in this secret plan of theirs. It lasted all through the slightly painful test, which resembled a mind search but was not nearly as deep, all the way back to my room.

It did not survive my telling Shad, however. The moment I spoke to him of a secret purpose, I realized how ridiculous it sounded.

Shad was incredulous.

"What! What secret . . ." A worried look came onto his face. "If the Duke asked you to assassinate the Patriarch, would you?"

"What! Of course not. Do you think. . . . Shad, I don't think I could even if I wanted to. It would be suicidal."

"Just you be careful before you do any secret things for the Duke."

"I don't think there is a secret plan. It's just an excuse."

"I don't understand him, " cried Shad. "What harm could we be doing?"

A sense of my own inadequacy filled me. If I had been any good at politics I would have known how to get my own way.

"I should have refused," I said.

"No, you were right to agree. Forgive me. I am disappointed."

"I've let you down," I said.

"You!" he laughed. "Oh Dion, it's not you I am disappointed in. You have done the best you can. You are an important person and must dance to the Duke's piping. And you have been wise not to set his back up by refusing him in this. This matter is not important enough. It's just this. . . . I try my best to think he is an honorable man who has the liberation of the South at heart, and again and again he proves it is not so."

I put my arms around him and we held each other.

"It occurs to me that the Duke will not easily let you go South if the army is forced to break in two," he said softly.

"I will go anyway," I cried. "How can you doubt me?"

"He could stop even you, Dion. You must be careful not to show too much sympathy for the South to him."

"I think it's too late for that."

"Maybe it will be well to be more discreet in the future."

I knew Shad was right. Then it occurred to me that maybe this talk of discretion meant that he was going to tell me that we shouldn't see each other anymore. I waited, terrified, for the blow to fall, but he said nothing all evening. For which I was relieved.

Having time to visit Silva again was the one small advantage of not training the Southern troops. Amazing to think such a sense of belonging could come from a mere accident of birth. Silva's talk of all the small daily doings of my nieces and nephews fascinated me. She told me news of Tomas, who was still in RougeLammer, and of Hamel, who had returned to his mill in Medane. Most interestingly she confirmed that Karac had been to see Dally again.

"And this time she was prepared to see him. Though I still wonder if that is healthy. She has become obsessed with her mother being avenged, and she nags him about it incessantly."

"What does he say?" I asked curiously.

"He is odd, but then he and Tasha always were odd. He agrees with her that yes, he is wrong to wait and yes, he is a coward not to go to Sanctuary by himself and try to kill this demonmaster. Nonetheless he says he must wait for the Duke of Gallia, because he cannot defeat the whole South alone and he will not spend his life until he knows he can take the demonmaster with him. It never satisfies Dally. She just tells him off again. He still comes to see her, though."

I could not help feeling a twinge of envy at Dally, who felt so free to be so demanding of her elders. At her age, I would not have dared utter a word of criticism to my foster father.

"Do you think Tomas will mind Karac coming here?" I asked Silva.

"Tomas? Tomas wants to close his mind to forgiveness. He's lucky I'm here to pry it back open for him. I don't worry myself about what Tomas thinks and neither should you. He'll run your life if you let him."

Dally continued to avoid me, and when we were in the same room together she pointedly ignored me.

"Just leave her," said Silva. "You cannot make her your

friend. You can only be open to her if she wants to make advances.''

I was happy to take her advice, because in my heart I found it difficult to like Dally. So I turned my attention to getting to know Martin, Needra, and Derrum, who were all delightful young people.

The Klementari had settled into their camp outside the town. They had reached an agreement with the Duke that they would join him in his invasion of the South whenever it began and they rarely came to the White Tower. On the other hand, every time I went to see Silva, I saw them in the town, walking in groups of two or three. They were manifestly different from the Wanderers who had roamed Moria in a drugged or drunken stupor for the past hundred years. The Klementari were more like visiting foreigners whose calm good manners were a marked contrast to the Gallian soldiers who often caused fights and trouble. The townsfolk came to know that they could turn to the Klementari to break up such fights or to put drunken and abusive soldiers to sleep with the judicious use of magic.

They performed other small magical services too and asked only for food or a drink of water in return. Since the White Sisters, who had done most of the town's healing, were now under house arrest for being members of the Burning Light, people were grateful to be able to turn to the Klementari.

It was quite obvious to me that the Klementari were intentionally putting themselves in the way of winning the hearts and minds of the townsfolk and I could not help admiring their grasp of stage management.

The neighbors and friends who were always visiting Ren Mara's shop were full of the Klementari's goodness and of their loyalty to Julia Madraga.

''Do you think it is a sign that the times of Morian greatness are returning? Surely it is a sign,'' they would say one after another, and they would repeat the old tales from the days when Moria was a kingdom and the Klementari lived in Ernundra.

On the other hand, the Duke was becoming less and less popular. There was concern about when he was going to go South. Partly this was anxiety for the plight of the Southerners, but more immediately people were fed up with his soldiers carousing through the streets and anxious lest there be a battle with the Patriarch at Lammerquais. There was even a creeping sympathy for the Burning Light, for many Lammerquais folk had friends or relatives who had joined the Burning Light but who were "very decent folk despite it." Everyone agreed that it was reasonable to put the men in prison, but the women and children? Prison was no place for them.

One night a servant awoke me after midnight with a message from Silva. Soldiers had come to the house and arrested Hamel's wife Radiance. Shad and I dressed immediately and hurried over.

We found the shop on the ground floor of Silva's house open. Clothes and silks were strewn all over the floor and Silva, Ren Mara, and his apprentice were slowly tidying them up. Fortunately the soldiers had not been informed about Radiance's mother, Jeanne, and Silva had managed to hide her in the roof, where they had missed her.

Tears were streaming down Silva's face.

"They took little Shine," she raged. "And him but two years old. They said he was demonspawn. He's just a little boy. How can he be demonspawn? I tried to take him from Radiance and the swine hit me. By God I wish I could have hit him, but they had a mage with them. If I ever find out who turned us in. . . ."

The soldier must have had a fighting gauntlet on, because Silva's face was very badly bruised and she had a mild concussion. It was amazing nothing was broken. She preferred striding round the kitchen cursing to sitting still being tended, however, and her resistance to magic worked against my best efforts at calming her.

The children were huddled in the arms of the cook in a corner of the kitchen. All of them, including the cook, were red-eyed from weeping and pale-faced with fear—except for Dally whose dark eyes were dry but full of silent fury. I tried tentatively to speak with her, but she just scowled and ran out of the room.

When I came back into the shop, Karac had arrived, and he and Shad told me they had decided to go to the jail to see what news they could get of Radiance and Shine.

"I'll come with you," I said.

"I was hoping you'd say that. Having the Demonslayer of Gallia there will surely help us," said Karac. For once he was not being mocking.

"We have sent for both Tomas and Hamel, but it'll be a while before they get here," said Ren Mara. "If you can at least get the boy out of prison, Tomas can hide him."

The Lammerquais prison was down by the docks, in the very worst part of town, and we could smell the stench of it well before it came into view. Luckily no one was stupid enough to bother two mages and an armed man, for I was seething with anger and Karac looked fit to murder someone. How could they take a small child to prison like that?

We suffered a check at the prison gates when guards refused to let us in, saying that no visitors were allowed and we would have to come back when the warden was awake. Not even my pleadings or Karac's threats would persuade them to open the gate for us.

Suddenly Shad, who had been silent all this time, grabbed the guard by the throat. The other guard made to stab him in the back with his spear and I, in fright, thrust him backward a little harder than I should have and he hit the wall with a bang and was knocked out. Faintly glowing runes appeared on the wall of the prison.

"Now listen, you," shouted Shad at the other guard. "This is Enna Dion Holyhands, who is the Demonslayer of Gallia and a friend of the Duke. She doesn't like being kept waiting, especially by scum like you. You've seen what she can do when she's a bit angry. We can try for really angry if you like."

"Fine, fine," babbled the nervous guard. "I'll get the duty sergeant."

He hauled on the bell rope and the gate was opened immediately. Shad gave the guard a mighty heave from behind so that he went sprawling through the gate and then jammed himself into the open gateway.

"Come on, you two," he shouted. Karac and I dived in after him. The gates swung shut behind us.

I felt about for the magic guarding this place. All over the walls pale blue runes were shining, but I did not think the magic itself was very strong. They probably had only one resident mage and if I was not mistaken he was one of the men hurrying across the slimy courtyard toward us now.

Again Shad took charge.

"This is Enna Dion Holyhands, Demonslayer of Gallia, and her brother Karac Holyhands, personal mage to Julia Madraga. They have come to see their sister-in-law Radiance Holyhands, who was brought in this night."

"It's not allowed for the Burning Light to receive visitors," said the duty warden, a skinny little man who looked as if he would break like a dried-up stick.

"Nonetheless Enna Dion will see Radiance Holyhands," said Shad. I did my best to look threatening, though in fact I was now terrified by the enormity of what we had just done. In my experience, those who have magical gifts need to act as harmlessly as possible unless they want to be well and truly slapped down.

The duty warden looked pleadingly at the prison mage, a seedy-looking individual who had spent the whole of our conversation leisurely doing up his disarrayed clothes.

He shrugged and said, "Don't look at me. I can't stop them."

"There will be a report made of this to the authorities," said the duty warden. "There will be reprimands."

"And they might well be to you, if you keep us waiting much longer," snapped Shad. He was formidable. I certainly wouldn't have stood in his way.

"I don't know why you're bothering," the mage called

out after us. "They'd have burned you lot at the stake."

After consulting a large book in the entrance hall of the prison, the duty warden lead us downstairs to a door and opened it. A thick stench hit us like a blow. It was indescribably bad: ammonia and excrement mostly, with the smell of the sickroom a thousand times magnified beneath it. We struggled forward into the smell. Before us was a huge black room. In the light of the doorway we could see it was crowded with filthy piles of rags that had human faces.

Then we were in blackness again as the Warden slammed the door behind us. Immediately I lit a magelight. Karac tried the door. It was locked from the outside.

Shad squeezed my arm. "Don't worry. They always do that. You know you can get us out of here anytime you like. Let's find Radiance."

In the magelight, the place was a white-lit hell. Slime dripped from the walls. The air was thick as fetid glue. I saw now why it was so bad. There was a pile of dung in the corner that was the only latrine in the place. The straw underfoot was soft and damp and blackish. Everywhere women and children turned toward our light, blinded by the suddenness of it. Their faces were pale and bruised or red with crusty sores. A chaos of voices coughed and called out and hands reached out to touch us.

Radiance was sitting over by a wall clutching Shine on her lap. She had the beginnings of a black eye. She could only weep when she saw us, but I gathered from her incoherent sobs that a man had tried to put his hand up her nightdress and she had objected.

She thrust Shine into my arms, begging me for God's sake to take him out of this terrible place. I would have gladly done so immediately, but we had brought clothes and food for her and seeing the avid gazes of those around us, I did not think she would keep the things long after we had gone. We made her change into proper clothes and eat while we watched.

I could not keep my horrified eyes off the mass of humanity moving, coughing, and shivering around us like some filthy carpet. Anger grew and grew in me. These were people reduced to beasts—to worse than beasts, to sleeping on shit-covered straw while roaches and fleas crawled over them. I could almost see the little beings which caused disease dancing in the air around us. Nothing justified this—not revenge, not justice, not anything. If these women were to die, why not just kill them outright, instead of this slow lingering death?

A small voice at my feet said softly, "Enna Latrides. Do you remember me?"

It took me a moment or two to recognize my alias from all that time ago and another few moments to recognize the filthy creature speaking to me. It was Mercy of Thy Hands, one of the women from the Burning Light family Tomas, Hamel and I had stayed with coming into Moria.

"Enna Latrides, you are a healer, aren't you? Please will you look at my sister," she pleaded. "I think she is dying."

Voice of Grace lay on a bundle of dirty clothes. She was far gone with the prison fever and I did not think she had much hope of survival. She had a venereal disease as well.

"We were captured by soldiers on our way here," said Mercy by way of explanation. "They kept us with them till we reached Lammerquais. We have been through so much together. Please don't let her leave me."

I gave Mercy a little of Radiance's food and all of the money that I had in my pocket so that she could buy food and medicine from the guards. Then I set to work on Grace, calling the little disease beings to a place on her arm where they could be easily killed. It is an inexact and painful way to do such healing, but Grace seemed better after it. As I worked on her a clamor for healing rose around us. People were holding out babies and small children, gripping at me, crowding around, threatening to crush poor Grace. I pushed them back but I could not resist touching the children, trying to strengthen and cleanse their systems. I touched and touched and touched. I wanted to help them all.

Suddenly there came a slither of magic around us and the crowd was pushed back. "Stop that," cried Karac, pulling me out of the crowd. "You have to save your strength. Otherwise we'll never get out of here."

Shad took me by the arm and pulled me gently but firmly toward the door.

"You can't help them all now. We will try to do what we can for them from outside, Dion. Come on."

At the door Radiance handed Shine to me. There was no chance of the prison guards not noticing him, for the little boy started to scream as soon as the door closed on his mother.

"Here, you can't take that out of there," shouted the leader of the guards, a very substantial looking man with a flabby red face. "It's under arrest."

"It's a child," I shouted, relieving my pent-up feelings at him. "He's done nothing wrong. I'm taking him out of this hell."

"No you're not," shouted the guard.

"How are you going to stop me?"

There was a sound of flesh thudding on flesh as Shad felled the guard aiming a mace at the back of my head. Karac caught a thrown spear.

At that anger flashed though my body like fire and came bursting out. With a satisfying blast of power the door at the end of the corridor burst open. A flick of my hand left all those brutal men unconscious in heaps on the floor.

"Wait," cried Shad. He pulled open the still-unlocked cell door and dragged Radiance out.

"We might as well take her with us, since we're already in trouble," he said.

Karac seized both Shad and Radiance and I felt a protection spell go up around us. I smoothed one of my own over the top. All around us the runes on the walls were glowing brilliantly and emitting high-pitched screaming sounds. Behind us, women came shouting and screaming out of their now-open cell.

A warding had appeared over the door before us, shimmering like a skin on hot milk. I blasted through it. Outside two mages bombarded us with weak blasts of magic. The magery had calmed me by then and I left it to Karac to knock them over.

Another blast of power and we were through the gate and outside in the street. Ren Mara was standing there holding a rearing horse.

"Silva thought you might need this. Quickly, up with you, Shad. The gate near us is open. Tomas will be meeting you on the Quainard Road."

"This is getting to be a habit with the women in your family," grinned Shad, as he hauled Radiance and Shine up behind him. He dug in his heels and the horse thundered off.

From inside the prison came shouts and screams, but no one had yet come out of the smoking gate behind us.

"Come," said Ren Mara. "We must get you safely back to the White Tower, before reinforcements get here."

Karac and I set off running down the street. It was still dark.

Of course there was a fuss. Of course Lord Sercel sent for me early that morning and asked me angrily what I had been thinking of and where Radiance Holyhands was.

"You have no business making use of your powers like this. The Duke is beside himself. He begins to wonder at your loyalty."

But I was angry too and soon I found myself shouting back.

"He has no business keeping human beings in those conditions. Those women and children sleep in their own excrement. They are riddled with disease and have no healing or proper food. I would not leave one of my family there even if she were a murderer. Does the Duke really think these women ordered witch burnings or tried to overthrow him?"

There was much more of the same before I stormed from the room in a rage, leaving him shouting behind me that I was a fool and had better take on a more humble attitude or I would be very sorry.

With a belly full of fire I strode down to the Ducal apartments, determined to voice my outrage to the Duke and, as luck would have it, met up with a messenger who said the Duke would like me to see him immediately.

I was shown into a small anteroom to wait. Here I waited. And waited. Minutes passed and became half an hour and then an hour.

I knew I must ask the Duke to relieve the conditions in the prison or be unable to live with myself, but after a time this thought became overwhelmed by the certainty that the Duke was very angry with me—beside himself, Lord Sercel had said.

I could understand entirely why he might be angry at someone who had broken into his prison, injured several guards, and provoked a riot and no doubt a scandal. How was I going to make my complaint without making him more angry, and perhaps making the situation even worse for the women in prison? I understood entirely why the Duke did not want members of the Burning Light free behind his lines during a war. On the other hand what could children do. Or women for that matter.

I could not really defend my actions in taking Radiance from the prison either, because according to the law she should be there and no one was above the law. However, if the Duke told me to return her there I would have to refuse, because no one should be imprisoned in such conditions.

I should allow the Duke to pretend he had not known about the conditions, and then I must apologize for everything and state my complaint humbly but clearly. Though I was not sure I could apologize convincingly, because in my heart of hearts, I was certain he should have made it his business to know about prison conditions like he knew other things. I wanted to level that terrible place and let all those poor people go free.

I rehearsed and rehearsed the scene in my mind, trying to find the most tactful yet effective way of saying what I must, but all of these rehearsals ended with the Duke shouting at me. After an hour I found myself trembling as I walked up and down. What if he ignored me? What if he sent me back to Cardun in disgrace? What if he put me in prison myself?

I paced and thought and trembled from fear and anger, and the time stretched out to an hour and a half.

At that point the door of the anteroom opened and Julia Madraga stepped in.

She came over and took my hand.

"Karac has told me everything. My dear Enna Dion, I am so shocked."

I found myself clinging to her hand.

"You were so brave," she said. "I am amazed at what you did."

"I know it was wrong, but how could we leave Radiance in that place? It was . . ."

"I know. And I have come myself to speak with Duke Leon about it. Though these people are my enemies, they are still Morians and my subjects. What kind of ruler would I be if I did not try to relieve their suffering?"

A great rush of relief filled me.

"I am so glad," I said. "Perhaps the Duke will listen if you speak. I'm afraid he may be too angry to listen to me."

"My poor Dion," she said softly. "Are you afraid?"

"Yes. But I am most afraid that I will not be able to help those poor women."

"We must do something to relieve them," she said. "It's villainous that this should have been going on without my being aware of it. I shall speak to the Duke when they call for you."

Thus when the servant finally came for me after two hours, Lady Julia stood and said, "I'm afraid Enna Dion must wait for her appointment for I wish to speak with his Grace. You may go, Enna. I shall have you sent for at the appropriate time."

She swept from the room before the servant had time to object, leaving me greatly relieved and slightly ashamed that I was hiding behind her skirts in this way.

Still, it worked. The following day half the women from the prison were moved to the Convent of the White Sisters to share in their house arrest. The women's prison was cleaned from top to bottom and steps were taken to provide adequate sanitation, food, and bedding to the women remaining there. The men's prison, too, received attention and a complete overhaul, although since fewer of them had survived to become prisoners, their conditions had never been so desperate.

I went with Lady Julia to inspect the reformed prison, and there was cheering for us in the streets, for such generosity to defeated enemies was a popular action. At the prison the women knelt to Lady Julia and kissed her hand, and many of them addressed her as Duchess and some even as Queen. Mercy of Thy Hands was standing among the crowd of prisoners, and by her side stood a shaky but very alive Voice of Grace. I was able to tell them that they could go to stay with my sister Silva when they were finally released.

I did not ever have my disciplinary interview with the Duke. Instead, the next time I saw him, he smiled at me quite openly and said nothing of the prison incident. After I had broken into the prison the Duke's courtiers and even the servants had been very cold to me. Now they returned to their previous warmth. How frightening court life is.

The Duke did manage to punish me, however, though it was entirely unintentional. A couple of days after I had taken Radiance from the prison, negotiations with the Patriarch must have taken a turn for the worse for it was announced that mixed troops of Southerners and Gallians were to be stationed on the southern side of MontLammer thirty miles away, and that Shad's troop was one of them.

The morning after Shad left for MontLammer, I awoke in the grey dawn light to hear a tapping on my window and started awake with visions of Bedazzer in my mind. To my relieved astonishment, Symon was sitting huddled in the window embrasure. When I opened the window, he told me that he had something to show me in the forest behind the castle in half an hour.

I closed the curtains so that I might scramble into my clothes in private, but it was not necessary, for when I opened them again he was gone. A big black raven was sitting on a nearby tower and it cawed imperatively at me as I looked at it, then flew away.

A stone wall separated the White Tower from the forest behind it. The tower itself was guarded by sentries, but the gardens were protected by magic only and so there was no one to wonder where I was going so early. A locked iron gate gave way into the forest beyond. As I came up to the gate a hand reached through and unlocked it. It was Symon again, dark in his old dingy black. He signaled to me to be silent and led me out into the forest that lay below the White Tower.

It was still very early in the morning. The forest smelled wonderfully of dew damp sweet oil trees. Now that it was almost summer the summersnow trees were in bloom. We turned quickly off the path and ducked down a series of narrow animal trails, brushing through bushes and causing showers of the fluffy white blossom to rain down upon us. Near the bottom of the hill Symon stopped and, motioning me to follow, went down on his belly and began crawling though the damp leaf mold under some bushes. Shortly afterward, we came to a place where we could see down into a small clearing below.

Beneath us on a tree stump sat the Duke of Gallia. At his back stood Garthan Redon. Redon stood calm and still as a man on guard should, but the Duke was impatient. His heels kicked at the tree stump and twice he got up and paced up and down the clearing before the person he was waiting for came down the path behind us.

It was Blanche Shomnee, walking her lithe snakelike walk and humming under her breath.

A look of joy crossed the Duke's countenance, which shocked me, for his was not a face I associated with such soft emotions. He took Blanche's hand and kissed it as if it were the most precious thing in the world. They retired to the other side of the clearing where a rug had been laid on the damp grass.

Garthan Redon had disappeared, withdrawn discreetly back behind a tree, no doubt.

Duke Leon and Lady Blanche sat talking for some time, and though I could not hear what was being said, I could tell from the way they sat together, from Blanche's coquettish looks and the way the Duke kept kissing her hand and once or twice her neck, that some kind of seduction was taking place, if it had not already. I stared at Symon in amazement, for I had had no inkling of this. Symon merely nodded and put his fingers to his lips.

I was filled with anger. How dare the fellow? He was not even married to Lady Julia yet and here. . . . Good God, he had even forced her to take on her rival as a Lady in Waiting.

Yet it did not seem that the Duke was having everything his way, for the second time he kissed Lady Blanche's neck, she moved away. This was the signal for an argument to begin. At first they spoke in low tones, but when Lady Blanche jumped up and began to hurry away, the Duke leapt up and caught her shoulder.

"Do not try my patience too much, Madame. There are plenty of women with charms like yours. I will not wait forever."

"Then do not," she said. "I came here throwing myself on your mercy and offering you the chance to put the crown of Moria on your head and what have you offered me in return? A chance to become a whore and to be called so by everybody. I am a gently bred convent girl and was brought up to accept nothing less than the title of wife."

She twitched herself out of his hold and ran back up the path toward the White Tower. After angrily kicking the tree stump, the Duke strode away in the opposite direction. Garthan Redon appeared briefly from between the trees, scooped up the rug, and followed him.

We waited until they had gone. Then the two of us wriggled back through the bushes.

"What was going on? Is Blanche . . ."

"I do not think she is his mistress yet, but as you see, negotiations are going on."

"But that's. . . . How dare the man do such a thing?"

"Why? Because he is engaged to marry Lady Julia? That

is convenience. Many rulers have done the same."

He was right. It was not unusual that a ruler's wife had to tolerate a rival as Lady in Waiting, either. It was the obvious position for a woman at court.

"But he seems quite smitten with Blanche," said Symon. "Would you have said he was normally that kind of a man?"

"No. The Duke of Gallia always let his heart be ruled by his head. She said something about being a wife. . . . Do you think . . ."

"The chances are slim. The Duke of Gallia could not become King without marrying Lady Julia. Yet I wonder how far he would go for Blanche's favor. She already has a hold on him. After the crown has been on his head a few years. . . . Lady Julia would not be the first spouse to suffer from an arranged accident."

"We must warn her."

"You think she doesn't know already? It is you I wished to warn. Be careful of Lady Blanche."

"I've never trusted her. But why me particularly?"

Symon simply shrugged.

"You are covered in mud," he said.

I brushed the mud and blossom off my clothes using a homely little spell, the kind of spell that would not be seen as unusual by anyone who saw it from the White Tower. A slug had found his way up my sleeve and took some getting out. While I did this Symon sat down and pulled out a package. He unwrapped it and offered me bread and cheese.

"I don't doubt we are at an important point in time," he said as we sat munching in the leaf-dappled sunlight. "Now, the future is that Lady Julia will be Queen of Moria. Foretellers see it every day still. But this Blanche could change things. We must make sure she does not." He frowned into space.

Ever since Shad had told me what the foretellings had said of Lady Julia, I had tried to think of her as ruler in her own right. But I was a creature of my time and place. Such things had never been and I found it hard to imagine them.

"So Lady Julia will be queen?" I asked Symon. "Who will be king?"

"There will be no king. She will rule alone and mostly well. She is the best choice, Enna Dion. The Duke of Gallia cares only for conquest and power. He is not a compassionate man. And Gerard Hawksmoor would be a puppet of the Patriarch. Neither of them would give Ernundra to the Klementari. Lady Julia would. Were it not foretold that she would be queen, I still would work to make it so."

I remembered Symon's words in the spirit cave. "You do believe in foretelling, don't you, Symon?"

"Oh yes! I believe that my people can see the future. I also believe that we can make the future happen with our actions."

Later as we were climbing back up the path to the White Tower a thought occurred to me.

"This is a very clever game Lady Blanche is playing. And she is only seventeen."

"She has been well tutored to play just this game. Her tutor will be here tomorrow and then we will see just how clever he is."

"Who is he?"

"You will see him tomorrow. He is someone you already know."

"Who?"

But he only smiled his Symon smile and went away in a whirl of black.

·16·

I tried to tell myself it was better that I be separated from Shad. I was becoming too attached to him and we could never be more than just passionate friends. How he would react if he ever found out about Bedazzer, the basic uncleanness at the center of my being, the moment when I had wanted to become one with a demon? It was too horrible to think about.

Yet I longed for Shad and I was delighted to receive a message from him saying that he was being sent with dispatches to Lammerquais in two days' time, and asking me to meet with him at Silva's.

Lord Utrello gave me a nasty look in the council meeting that day, because I was humming under my breath. Lady Julia commented on my good mood. It was at a time when Lady Blanche was not with us.

"Could this be the return to Lammerquais of a certain handsome Southern captain?" she asked, throwing me into confusion. How did she know?

Lady Julia smiled and told me that she had asked especially for Ren Forest to carry the dispatches in the hope that it would cheer me up. Though I was disconcerted to think that people might actually know of our affair, I was too happy to care much.

The day Shad came, however, I was not able to get away from the White Tower early. Tomas came home from RougeLammer and asked me to come walking in the gardens with him, a sure sign that he had something private to say to me. Living in the White Tower had given me a new perspective on the use of gardens. Every day, when I sat with Lady Julia and Lady Blanche, we could see people walking there in twos and threes. Sometimes we speculated as to what business they might have together.

I had a sinking suspicion Tomas wanted to scold me over Shad and I was all prepared to tell him to mind his own business. He did want to scold me, but it was not over Shad.

"I'm glad to see you have become so intimate with Lady Julia," he said, "but for Tanza's sweet sake, have you no more sense than to get yourself involved in her plottings?"

"What do you mean?" I cried, thrown by the unexpected direction of this attack.

"What do you think I've been doing in RougeLammer? I've been keeping an eye on the Patriarch, as well you know, and it's not very pleasant for a man to be faced with exposing his own sister as part of a clandestine meeting."

"She didn't tell me where she was going," I protested.

"Aye, Dion. But had she told you, would you have gone anyway?"

I could not answer that, because I would have found it hard to refuse Lady Julia Madraga anything. I was coming to see that she would be a better ruler for Moria then the Duke of Gallia ever could be. I also knew full well that the Duke of Gallia would do his best to see his queen had little influence over the way he ruled.

"Julia is a very clever woman," said Tomas. "I can't blame you if you have done things you didn't intend because of her. But for God's sake, be more careful. Her ambitions for the crown cannot come to anything. Don't get yourself involved in them or you may pay a very heavy price."

We walked silently together for a moment. Then Tomas reached out and squeezed my hand.

"I only seek to keep you safe," he said.

"Tomas, I can't blame Lady Julia for seeking . . . other allies. Did you know that the Duke is having an affair with Blanche Shomnee and she is pressing him to marry her?"

"He never will. What could he gain?"

"I never saw him look at Kitten Avignon in that way. I would be frightened if I was Lady Julia."

"You're very well informed."

"I saw them in the forest together. Symon's been watching them," I added unwisely.

"Symon. Symon. Now there's another one you should be more careful of, Dion. He'll make use of you if you let him. Just you wait and see."

"For God's sake, Tomas, does everybody have to be making use of me?"

"You are powerful and you're popular too, even more so after that silly prison thing. Do you think Lady Julia took you down to inspect the prison with her for the sake of your beautiful eyes? It does her cause good to be seen in your company."

"Oh, Tomas," I protested. All the more because I knew he was right.

Yet when I thought about being used later, I realized that I did not mind being useful to Lady Julia. I wanted to help her and it was the same with the Klementari. It was not just because they had helped me, either, but because I agreed with their goals.

"And you be very careful of Symon and his crew," said Tomas now. "The Duke does not like the Klementari at all."

"Do I have to let the Duke decide everything?" I said crossly.

"You would be wise to follow his preferences a little more closely. You have let it be publicly known you think the push South is more important than the Patriarch and caused a scandal over the Duke's management of the prisons. This is a destructive course to follow. In politics it is unwise to put your heart too strongly behind any cause unless it is that of your ruler."

Though I could see wisdom in his words, his patronizing tone annoyed me.

"Maybe you should be a bit more careful of your allies too, Tomas. Do you really think Sandor Sercel wouldn't sacrifice you if it meant the good of his family?"

"He is not the only one with a family to take care of. We will have to stand behind you even if you disgrace us. Have a care you do not bring us down."

As a result of Tomas' scolding, I did not get to Silva's house until dusk.

Shad must have been looking out for me, for he met me on the corner of Silva's street and swept me into his arms, leaving me breathless with delight. I hugged him as tightly as I could and kissed his face as he kissed mine.

The evening passed in a golden haze. Even Dally's grim little face could not dampen my spirits. A tight knot of desire had formed in my belly. I was most shamefully impatient for the time when it would not be too early to retire to bed and shortly after the children were sent off, I excused myself on the grounds I was tired. I heard Shad making exactly the same excuse to Ren Mara in the shop where they sat talking. As I climbed the stairs to my room, I was aware of every movement of my body, of my breasts firm against the cloth of my dress, of my thighs moving soft and slippery against each other. I heard Shad's lithe step running behind me. He caught up with me at the top of the stairs. His hand was warm against my back as he took my basket from me and ushered me in through the door of our bedroom.

We did not bother to light a candle.

"I want to tell you something," said Shad later, "but it is something that is dangerous to us both. Can you promise not to tell anyone?"

It was a bright moonlit light and I could see his suddenly serious face quite clearly.

"Of course."

"There is a plot within the Southern army to split off and

go South independently of the Duke, the way Ren Daniel suggested.''

My arms tighten involuntarily around his body. What would the Duke do if he found this out?

"Everyone would rather go South with the whole army," he continued. "But people begin to doubt that the Duke will ever move. They fear that our lives will be wasted in some stupid fight with the Patriarch, while the Burning Light still works its will upon our friends and families back home. Have you heard that the Burning Light are beginning to round up all nonbelievers?''

I had heard that story. The Hierarch's Soprian mercenaries were arresting everyone they caught traveling north, but a trickle of refugees still managed to reach Lammerquais. There had been other reports too, stories of the mass execution of villages and the removal of children from families whose menfolk had come to join the Duke's army. There was unrest among the Southern troops from men who were anxious about their families.

"Nothing is definite yet. People are simply forming alliances. That is why I am here. Julia Madraga sent a message to Lord Quercy. I'm don't know what it said, but he now believes she would be willing to lead an army South. I was sent with letters to her.''

Here was my chance to use my power to do something useful.

"You will need mages. What about mages?''

"That is the most promising thing of all. Ren Daniel's plan has a lot of support among the mages, both Gallian and Morian. It is likely that we will be able to muster a couple of full phalanxes despite the Duke's mixing Gallian and Morian together. Your kind's hatred for necromancy is greater than their loyalty to the Duke.''

"Please, Shad, when the time comes will you tell me what is happening so that I may come with you?''

Shad kissed me heartily.

"I was hoping you would say that. Just remember, it will be more dangerous for you to be involved in this plot than me. Like it or not you are a public figure and people look up to you. The Duke might punish you more harshly than others if he found out.''

"Then we must make sure he doesn't," I said lightly. I did not feel afraid. Was it because I had the friendship of Julia Madraga and other influential people? I suppose in my innocence I could not imagine being really punished for undertaking such a worthy enterprise.

We talked excitedly about the possibilities of these plans far into the night, until we fell asleep curled up in each other arms.

I awoke. Someone was gently calling my name. The voice drew me and I must not follow. The room was full of golden sunlight and someone was calling tenderly, "Wake up, my darling little mage."

That voice. Who was it?

"Wake up, my precious. I am here."

Oh God, it was Andre! I sat up in bed in terror.

And he was there. Andre's voice, but it was Bedazzer's face leering in through the window, all horned snout and sharp-fanged grin. He was laughing, but he was angry too, very angry. I could see it burning in his cruel red eyes. I tried to scream, but I could not. I cringed back against the headboard, clutching the sheets to me, but there was no cover, nowhere to hide. He was there. Peering through that window. No. It was a mirror. There was a mirror on the wall and he was looking out of it. How long had it been there?

"No use hiding, you little whore," he snarled in a voice like a thousand vicious gods. "I've got you now." His taloned hands gripped the frame of the mirror as if he was about to leap through.

I recoiled. But no no! He couldn't get through.

He laughed at that, his harsh screaming demon's laugh.

"You thought you'd escaped me, didn't you, little mage," he shouted in his grating demon voice. "You thought you were rid of Bedazzer, but I know where you are now. Whore! Did you think another could take Bedazzer's place? You are mine. You belong to me and no one else. No one else shall have you.''

His voice was like a whip lashing and lashing. I wanted to scream, wanted to run, but terror froze me.

''Wha . . . ,'' said Shad, sitting up beside me.

Shad! Bedazzer mustn't see him.

''Get out!'' I cried. ''Quickly, get out.''

''What the hell . . . ?''

I pushed him away with magical hands and suddenly he was gone. Safe! Thank God!

''You are mine,'' yowled Bedazzer. ''I will never let go of you. Whore! You will not go with any other, do you hear me?''

His face was a chaos of howling.

I hurled myself out of bed and, with desperate valor, tore the mirror down from the wall and thrust it face-down upon the floor.

''Oh God!'' I wailed, crouching by it, my hands on its back. He had found me, he had found me. Oh God, God. It had all been for nothing—all those years of hiding. All my caution wiped out in a moment's carelessness.

I wanted to curl up into a little ball and scream and scream until everything shattered and broke.

But I could still hear a muffled yowling coming from the mirror beneath me. I must get rid of him. I must chase him off before someone came and found out. Before he saw someone like he'd seen Shad.

Runes of Protection and Distraction. The Rune of Blindness. Blood. I would use blood this time to make them really strong.

Shad's knife lay with his clothes on the chair. I ripped it out of the sheath and slashed it down my forefinger. It was sharp and I bled immediately. I began speaking the words and summoning up the runes in my mind.

The door crashed open. Shad stood there, stark naked.

''Dion,'' he cried, ''are you all right?'' I mustn't answer him. It would break the spell and I would have to start again.

''Dion,'' he cried, catching at my shoulder.

"Shut up," I shouted. "Let me alone, can't you see I'm trying to concentrate." I saw Dally standing in the doorway. "And get her out of here," I shouted. "Quickly."

I began again. There was movement in the room around me, but my vision had tunneled. I managed to finish the runes this time. Then, trembling, I turned the mirror over. He was gone. Something had worked. I put another rune in blood on the front just in case. The runes connected, strengthened and faded into invisibility. The spell was finished. The calm of magic had deserted me and I felt the sobs coming up at the back of my throat.

Then Shad was kneeling beside me, putting his strong arms around me. I curled up sobbing against him. He had clothes on now. I pushed my hand inside his shirt and felt the warm, soft hair on his chest. His hand squeezed mine.

"My poor poor girl," he whispered, rocking me back and forth. I felt myself slipping.

"You are mine," he had yowled. "No one else will have you." I could hear Bedazzer's voice in my head. I must not.

No! I pushed Shad away and, choking back sobs, got up from the floor.

"What's going on?" said Shad.

"I have to go," I said. I couldn't relax with him now. I had to get away. It was dangerous for him to be with me. Bedazzer did not like it and who knew what Bedazzer might be able to do to an unprotected mortal? I had to be alone to think before the sobs inside choked me. I pulled on my clothes.

"Dion, stop! Where are you going?"

"Home. I. . . ."

What could I possibly say to him?

"Stop this." He caught my arm. "At least bind up your hand. You're bleeding everywhere."

I touched the hand and the wound closed. I laced up my dress, not looking at him.

"Earth and fire. Tell me what's going on," he said. "What was that thing in the mirror?"

"Nothing."

"It wasn't nothing. You were terrified. Now Dion, you tell me. You can't just go off like this and not tell me."

"Please," I cried, and couldn't keep the tears out of my voice. "Please just don't ask me. I can't tell you." I pushed him away. "No! Let me go."

Shoes on. I could make for the door now and did. Silva was in the corridor clutching Dally.

"What's going on? Is everything all right?"

"Yes, Silva, but I must go home now. Sorry."

I fled down the stairs. At the bottom Shad caught me.

"You can't run off like this. You are going to tell me what that thing was."

I got away from him, ran out of the kitchen into the yard, but he was just behind me.

"It was a demon," he said. "Wasn't it? Don't lie to me. I can see it on your face. I can't let you go running off like this, not alone, not with this happening."

"This is not for you to know about, Shad. It's not safe. You have no magic to protect yourself."

You are mine, Bedazzer had said. *Do you think another could take Bedazzer's place?* I was linked to him forever. Linked by that bitter moment of desire I had once felt as I wrestled in his arms. He would not tolerate Shad. He had made that clear now.

"If it's not safe for me, what about you? For God's sake, Dion, let me help you. I love you."

"No!" I screamed. "No!" I felt as if the words would bring Bedazzer back again. I could still hear his voice. "You mustn't, you can't." I tried to talk more calmly. "Shad. Don't. Just forget about me. I can't. . . . We can't go on with this."

"What are you saying?"

"Shad, I can't, I can't love you back, can't you see? I'm not like other people. I'm already tied. Just . . . Don't, Shad."

There was anger on his face now. "I don't believe you," he said. "It's this Andre, isn't it."

"What are you talking about?"

"It's because this Andre broke your heart, isn't it? You

refuse to forget him. You're afraid to care for anyone else because of him, aren't you? Well that's shit, Dion.''

"It's more complicated than that," I cried. Why couldn't the stupid man understand and make it easy for me?

"It seems very simple to me," he said bitterly. "It's a very old and stupid story, Dion."

Anger surfaced in me. How dare he think this was such a foolish nothing? How dare he? I was not *that* stupid.

"It is not stupid," I said. "I'm trying to protect you, you fool. That was Andre. That creature in the mirror. Yes, and I still dream of him and long for him. And my longing brings him back. It's that simple."

I turned away quickly so I could not see the stunned look on his face turn to disgust, and walked away with my mouth full of the bitter ashes of victory.

All day people knocked on the door of my room, but I lay in bed with the clothes drawn up to my chin and ignored them. I wanted to be able to weep out my horror and pain, but all I could do was stare at the floor. *You are mine. You will always be mine.* Those words were like a death sentence, a death sentence that would last life long.

I thought of Shad, too, of how he had said *I love you.* He would have learned his mistake by now, though. He would get over it soon, if disgust had not already driven it out of him.

Slowly it became dark and it was darkness that brought me out of my stupor. I remembered the first time the demon had spoken to me. I had been in a dark room. I had heard breathing coming from within the mirror. . . .

There were no mirrors here. Strange I had not seen a mirror in the moonlit bedroom last night, either. Who had put it there? Silva knew I did not like them. But then I had not really looked. I was a fool. Desire had made me careless and now I was paying the just price for it. I would always pay.

There was another knock on the door and this time I got up and answered it. It was a maidservant accompanied by a page.

The page bowed and told me that Lady Blanche's negotiator from the South had arrived and that there was a reception to be held in his honor. I was bidden to attend. For a moment I was tempted to make an excuse about illness.

But no. I needed to get out of my room, to be among people, to do something that would make me forget the demon. *You will always be mine*, he had said.

I nodded to the page and said I would be there.

Tomas pounced on me as I came into the reception room. "Where have you been? Silva told me everything. What . . ."

His tone made my hackles rise. There was nothing he could do to help so I was damned if I was going to put up with his scolding. No doubt he would be self-righteous about what had happened with Shad, too.

"Leave me alone, Tomas. It's none of your business."

"None of my business? I like that. Now you tell me . . ."

"Oh, Tomas, you are such a grump," said Lucien, gliding up beside us. "Did no one ever tell you that a lady doesn't like scolding? A lady likes kindness. She likes a man to take care of her." He drew my arm through his. "And to bring her good things to eat and drink." He snapped his fingers and a footman came over with a platter of sweetmeats and another with a tray of sparkling wine.

"Here now, eat something. You must be famished."

Though I could not really feel interested in them, I ate some of the sweetmeats. Tomas stood by, silent, thank goodness and watched us with his arms crossed and an irritable expression on his face.

Fortunately there was no time for speaking with Tomas. For some reason the Duke wanted me to stand on the dais with a number of the other mages when Lady Blanche's negotiator came in. The two men had already met earlier that day, but this was the formal reception and required a show of strength.

Trumpets blasted to announce the negotiator's arrival. A procession of priests and other dignitaries came slowly up the room toward us. They were no more than colored chess-pieces before my eyes. The real drama was happening inside my head. *I love you*, said Shad again in my memory. *You are mine,* said Bedazzer with the howl of a jealous demon.

I shook my head and tried to focus on the procession at hand. There was a whole row of young priests carrying great mirrors painted with the faces of saints. The candlelight sparkled in those mirrors, and faces were reflected among the painted saints in a hectic, confusing way. I hoped nothing horrible would appear now to shame me before everyone.

You are mine, yowled Bedazzer in my head.

The line of young priests peeled away to either side. Behind them I caught a glimpse of Lady Blanche Shomnee.

You are mine, yowled Bedazzer in my memory.

Beside Lady Blanche walked a priest mage. I knew him. Curling chestnut hair. Blue eyes in an angel's face. I knew him. Bedazzer was forgotten as I searched my memory for the priest's face.

And found suddenly and horribly a memory of that face, looking back over its shoulder, laughing cruelly while the spiked club came down and bones shattered. I was in Tasha's mind again or hers was in me. Her tortures overwhelmed my sight. Her terrible pain gripped me. I heard someone screaming in the distance.

"Betrayer, Betrayer, what have you done?"

·17·

"It was him," I cried. "I know it as surely as I know you."

"I believe you," said Tomas. "Truly I do. It's just . . . Oh God! Darmen Stalker . . . The negotiator between the Duke and Hierarch Jarraz."

"I'll get Father," said Lucien, grim-faced.

"Lucien. What are you going to tell him?"

"That Darmen Stalker is a murderer and should be arrested for such," said Lucien. "What do you suggest I tell him, Tomas Holyhands?"

"That," snapped Tomas. "Of course that." The two men glared at each other.

"You should tell him that Darmen Stalker has colluded with necromancy," I said. "He handed Tasha over to those who tortured her and fed her life force to demons. He witnessed at least some of it. I saw him in her memories."

Lucien's face became even grimmer.

"Never fear. He shall pay for it if it's the last thing I do."

As the door slammed on Lucien, Tomas pulled up a chair and sat down beside me. They had carried me to this anteroom when I had collapsed during the reception. I was lying on a chaise. My head still ached from the fall; whenever I closed my eyes Tasha's violent memories replayed themselves in the blackness behind my eyelids. I had tried to swallow those memories whole without thinking them through, without chewing them over, and now they returned as strong and savage as when I had first seen them. It was like some horrible play which I could not stop. Only the memories were twice as close as any play. My tongue could almost taste the salty sticky burlap they had bound around it and feel the agony as the sparkling cold knife cut into it. . . . No! I would not think about that. My hands trembled and the water spilled from my glass.

"Dion, Dion," said Tomas. He reached over and took the glass from my hand and held it to my lips. "My poor little sister." He stroked my cheek. I noticed his hands were trembling too.

"What's the matter, Tomas?"

He was silent for a moment and then he said, "You are sure of this, aren't you? This is nothing to do with what happened this morning?"

"Don't you believe me, Tomas? You suspected Darmen Stalker yourself."

"No, no, Dion that's not what I meant." He sighed. "Oh, Dion, I am ashamed. Finally we find the man who is responsible for Tasha's death and after all my cries for revenge, the first thing I think is that I wish it was some other. Darmen Stalker is the Southern negotiator, Lady Blanche's trusted adviser, and Hierarch Jarraz's secretary. What kinds of trouble will our accusations cause for the Duke? Will Lady Blanche countenance her adviser being arrested, or will she take her vote and give it to the Patriarch in outrage? And how will it affect our making a peace with the South to arrest their emissary?"

"You cannot make an honorable peace with necromancers," I told him, angry at the direction his words seemed to lead. "Are you suggesting we keep quiet?"

"No," snapped Tomas. He pulled away from me. "That's not what I mean. Do you really think I would be capable of letting my sister's murderer free for such reasons?"

"No," I lied, for in truth I had wondered for some time what he in his ambition was capable of.

"I suspect my father will be in favor of such a plan though," said Tomas ruefully.

He was right. Lord Sandor was aghast.

"You plan to accuse the Southern emissary of necromancy and murder on the strength of Dion's claims that she has seen a dead woman's memories?" he cried.

"Yes," said Tomas firmly.

The Lord-Elector reasoned and then pleaded. Tasha was dead, he said, and revenge would not bring her back. Could we not at least wait until a treaty had been signed? Tomas and Lucien stood firm, however, and I pointed out that no college of magery would accept a treaty signed by one tainted with necromancy.

Lord Sandor turned on me. "It seems you have become mighty fond of the limelight these days, Enna," he said cuttingly.

"Don't blame her!" snapped Tomas.

"Well, I only hope you are prepared to undergo a mind search, Enna. Your testimony will not be admissible in court. In fact, I would send for Ren Daniel and have him perform one at once if I were you."

"I will go to the Duke publicly tomorrow and accuse Darmen Stalker," said Lucien.

"Must it be you?" said Lord Sandor.

"I will not let Tasha's murderer go unpunished. Will you support me, Father?"

Lord Sandor sighed.

"Of course not. Have a care for our patrimony, Lucien. One of us must remain on some kind of terms with the Duke."

"Then you will stand against me," said Lucien tensely.

"I will not, my son. Remember, this is not the first time we have been on opposite sides. I merely seek to preserve our family, that is all."

"So be it," said Lucien. "I shall send for Ren Daniel."

He left the room.

"I am appalled," said Lord Sandor quietly.

"Aye," said Tomas, "but if Darmen Stalker is a murderer

and a necromancer, he cannot be acceptable as a peace emissary."

Lord Sercel shook his head. Then he smiled crookedly.

"Do you know, this is the first time I have ever seen Lucien intent on more than hunting? All his life I have prayed for this moment. May Aumaz protect us from our wishes."

So began the Darmen Stalker scandal. That night Ren Daniel came with two witnesses and mind searched me. So strong were the visions in my head and so great was the pain during the search that I did not have the strength to worry about what other guilty secrets he might have seen until I had woken from the sedative spells late in the following day.

By then Ren Daniel and Lord Lucien Sercel had gone before the Duke in the public audience chamber with testimony of my mind search, and had asked that Darmen Stalker be confined to the White Tower and requested to undertake a mind search.

"The court is in an uproar," said Lady Julia, who came to sit at my bedside that afternoon. "The Duke is furious. Oh, don't worry. He has some curses for the Holyhands family, but most of his anger is for fate and the Southerners who have sent such a man as emissary. And the mages are behind you. Everyone is calling for this Darmen Stalker to submit to a mind search."

"Will he?"

"He is refusing at the moment. He says you are an insane and hysterical woman and that this must be some kind of plot by Ren Daniel. There is some history between those two. There is not one mage here Stalker will trust to mind search him and tell the truth of what he sees. Considering we are at war with his master, it is a very plausible defense."

"So the whole situation is blocked."

"For the moment. As Hierarch Jarraz's secretary, Stalker was responsible for many arrests and burnings. When he first arrived yesterday, a delegation of Southern captains came to me and expressed outrage at the thought of such a man being allowed to negotiate a peace treaty. Unfortunately for him, they will now push and push until he is properly tried. Duke Leon will not be able to refuse them without alienating much of the Southern army and most of the mages. An interesting fellow, this Stalker. Did you know that he is a Soprian and began life as a nonbeliever? He had risen very high in the Church from such a background. I wonder what it is that brought him to Moria.''

''Perhaps it was opportunities to practice necromancy,'' I said, only half seriously. I did not really feel in the mood for gossipy discussions of Darmen Stalker's past. He was only a minion. The real villain still went free.

Lady Julia shrugged. ''Well, Enna Dion,'' she continued, ''You have caused a bitter drama' to begin unfolding. No doubt you are glad to be out of it.''

This last remark was a reference to the fact that as a woman, and a minor under the law, I was never going to be called to court unless I was being tried. The testimony of women witnesses was always given by the male mages who mind searched them, so in my case Ren Daniel was now responsible for my evidence against Darmen Stalker. Once again the situation was being dealt with for me. This time, however, I was not glad to be out of it. It was vital that Darmen Stalker be mind searched. There was so much he could tell us about Sanctuary, and about the necromancer and his demons. I did not want him to just disappear, released out of political necessity.

After Lady Julia had left, I got up and dressed and stood looking out the window. The terrible play of Tasha's memories had receded from my mind, but it had left behind worries of my own. Had it only been yesterday morning that Bedazzer had appeared in a mirror, spitting his vitriolic curses at me? I had unfinished business here and I must decide quickly what to do about it.

After three years of thinking over the mistakes I had made in Gallia, I knew that the greatest mistake I had made was not seeking help in dealing with Bedazzer. At that time, telling someone that I had attracted the attention of a demon would have disgraced me horribly. Later I had not known who to trust. So with the optimism of the very young I had hoped it would all go away, telling myself that he was safely in his world behind the mirror and could not get through to me. He had been brought through, however, and even the possibility that it might have happened again (twice in my lifetime, this was misfortune indeed) was too much. He had almost beaten me last time. This time I must enlist some help before I found myself fighting him in single combat again.

And there was Shad to consider. It was difficult for demons to perceive and tempt ordinary mortals, but Bedazzer had seen Shad and *might* have reason to have a special vendetta against him. Since little was taught or known about demons on the Peninsula, my main knowledge of Bedazzer came from my experience of him, which I knew to be woefully limited. In theory, if Bedazzer was safely in his own plane he could not get at Shad, but in practice it was possible he might be able to arrange all kinds of torment and harm for him. And if Bedazzer was on this plane, he could deal with Shad in much the same way Tasha had been dealt with. I must make sure that Shad was safe.

Perhaps I had overreacted the previous day. Then I hadn't seen that Shad might well have been safer where I could keep an eye on him. If only I had not told him. . . . It was too late now. He would be too disgusted with me now that he knew my shame.

Anyway, demons were much more attracted to mages, which meant I would have just served to continue to attract Bedazzer to Shad. Now we had parted Bedazzer could well have lost track of him.

I was no longer worried about disgrace. As Demonslayer of Gallia, it was quite reasonable that I might be troubled by a vengeful demon, and there were any number of people I could ask for help without attracting any accusations of necromancy. Ren Daniel was my proper port of call with this problem. But I had already used all the methods that were available to the White Colleges of Gallia and Moria, and I was tempted instead to go to the Klementari and see if their strange otherworldly magic could free me of Andre/Bedazzer.

As I stood staring out the window, a sudden flash of light caught my eye. A great gout of fire shot out of one of the windows of the tower furthest away from me, and then there was another blue flash of mage power. All of a sudden the white walls of the tower turned mottled blue with runes. A magical battle was going on in that tower.

Instantly, I threw open the window and threw myself out of it. I could hear the high-pitched keening of the runes as I flew over the rooftops. Another flash of power lit up the tower's walls, and another, as great gouts of flame and black smoke blasted out of the top windows. I half flew, half fell into the courtyard just as a terrible scream came from the top of the tower, and then silence.

A magical battle inside a protected fortress is no small matter. As well as the runes all up and down the tower walls, wardings—shining blue skins of magic—were over all the doors and windows. They were designed to keep whoever was using the magic trapped inside and to prevent nonmages from getting caught up where they might be hurt.

I was the first mage on the scene, although the courtyard was full of servants and guards. The Sercel children's tutor was there trying to take control of the situation and herd people back indoors. Although the runes and the warding on the door indicated that the fortress mages would already be aware of the situation, they had not yet arrived. The minute I landed in the courtyard, the guards recognized me and came clustering around.

"Enna, it's Ren Karac in there," they cried. "We saw him go in, Enna, and he's not come out."

"Who else is in there? Whose quarters are these?" I cried.

"They're Priest Stalker's," I was told.

It was suddenly horribly clear. Karac had not been there when I had made my accusation against Stalker, nor had he been at the mind search, but he had had sufficient time to find out. Oh no!

For a weak quivering moment, I wished someone else was here to take care of this.

"Don't be such a coward, Dion," I told myself sternly. I turned and raced across the courtyard.

The wardings at the door of the tower were easily broken. Their strength was designed to keep the magic inside, not to impede the progress of rescuers. The guards came in close behind me. I was all set to race up the stairs, but a couple of them caught me by the elbow and told me that we must all keep together. They knew their business. No matter what a mage's strength, it always helps to have ordinary guards to assist in such matters. Not only do they make good witnesses, but they protect your back and fight off any conventional attacks you may not have the time or strength to deal with. My foster father had also told me that ordinary soldiers could be very useful in absorbing magical blows. Thinking of this, I remembered my part in this bargain and spread defensive spells over all of us.

Up the stairs we went, as fast as we could go without actually running, moving in a clump with all defenses ready like some strange, speedy tortoise. It was quiet at the top of the tower now, but we could hear voices up above us. As we broke through the warding into the next floor, servants and priests, members of Darmen Stalker's entourage, came rushing toward us, shouting and screaming, several of them in hysterics. Some of the guards broke off from our group to keep them from following us upstairs, because the last thing we needed was a press of people coming up behind us. The rest of us went on.

It was the same on all the floors except the last. Here, where Priest Stalker's closest aides had their apartments, there were only a few weeping servant girls. The warding to the floor above was already broken, and as we rushed toward the stairs, a group of men came down them.

Darmen Stalker came first. His face was smudged with soot and he wore a loose white robe. It was obvious from the red burns on his skin, chest, and face that his priest robes had been burned off him. He looked like some chestnut-haired angel, and for a clear detached moment I remembered how I had seen him in Glassybri and how attractive I had thought him then. Even though all my dreams of the night before had been filled with his mocking face turning away from Tasha's pain, my first impulse was to rush forward and help him.

The moment they saw us, however, the priests collected behind Stalker let out a cry and huddled protectively around him. They were all of them covered in soot and burns. The defensive magic they put forth was not strong.

Stalker drew himself up and his shapely hand came out in defense, but his blue eyes were full of anger, not fear.

"So, Dion Holyhands, have you come to finish off your brother's work?"

I needed to be very careful here, the more so because now that my first helpful impulse had been swept away, I could hear a small savage voice in my head telling me that here was a wonderful opportunity to revenge Tasha without any of the complications of a trial. But no. Darmen Stalker almost certainly had a head full of useful information.

"We are a rescue party, Priest Stalker," I said politely.

"Well as you can see we rescued ourselves from what the Lord-Elector so laughably calls hospitality."

He walked past me. His aides followed behind, two of them supporting a third who was very badly burned.

"You are hurt," I said. "May I offer you healing?"

"Accept healing from the sister of my attacker?" said Priest Stalker. "Do you think I'm a fool, woman? I'll go to those who can be trusted not to make my hurts worse. Oh, and you'll find your brother above. The villain is not dead. Yet. He didn't watch his back and Priest Jubal hit him on the head with a vase."

"What a rude shit," said one of the guards as Stalker swept on down the stairs to the lower levels.

I did not hear any more, for I was running up the stairs. I found Karac lying face-down on the floor, a few shy remnants of his robes still clinging to his flesh. He was bleeding and unconscious from a wound to the head. His back was badly burned, testifying to Stalker's malice.

In trying to take revenge for his sister's murder, Karac had put himself in great danger of being executed himself. An attack on a diplomatic representative, no matter what the suspicions against him, could not be tolerated. That evening the Duke was in favor of making an example of Karac, whose attack had only served to make a very difficult situation much worse, but I do not think he would ever have carried through a plan that might well have made a martyr of my brother. When Lady Julia interceded on Karac's behalf, the Duke gave in very graciously and just a little too easily. Darmen Stalker then very generously suggested that he would be quite content if my brother's execution were commuted to exile from Moria. He said he had no wish to condemn a young man to death, especially as it would soon be clear how misguided he was. Stalker's performance of being the outraged but still reasonable innocent was faultless.

So exile was the verdict. The Duke thanked me for my part in the rescue, but I noticed his manner was cool, and when he left the room, none of his entourage acknowledged me. Out of favor again. I was not out of favor with Lady Julia, however. She walked from the room with her arm through mine.

The following morning the Duke announced to a full audience hall that negotiations with Priest Stalker must cease until a new negotiator could be sent. The situation in the South was too urgent to wait until Priest Stalker had been cleared. In response to the accusations against him, Priest Stalker had agreed to undergo a mind search, but only at the hands of an outside authority.

It was thus agreed that they would send for the Dean of the White College of Seagan, a state far away beyond the southern borders of Moria.

"What's wrong with his being searched by the Dean of

the White College of Gallia or of Ishtak?'' asked Tomas, who stood beside me.

"Priest Stalker feels that as supporters of the Duke, they can hardly be seen as disinterested,'' said Lord Sercel weightily. "As a member of the Burning Light he is very distrustful of mages. It's a sensible solution. We must do our best to have a trial that is acceptable to Hierarch Jarraz, otherwise the peace negotiations will be jeopardized.''

I wondered if Lord Sercel really believed any of this. It looked to me as if Darmen Stalker was simply putting off the trial for as long as possible. It would take the mind searchers from Seagan almost ten days to get here, even at their fastest traveling. Ten days. While there was any possibility of a peaceful solution, an invasion of the South was out of the question. So the real question was, with the peace negotiations halted, how long would it all take? Would we ever get there?

From the grim looks on the faces of Lord Quercy and Ren Daniel outside the audience chamber that morning, I suspected that Shad's forging of alliances was now turning into a full-fledged plot to split the army. Shad. I pushed the thought of him away. When I saw Lord Quercy in the audience chamber, I had looked around for Shad, but he was not there. I had had no word from him, and though I had expected none, still it made me sad. He had thought he loved me. Now he had discovered who I really was. Unless I kept away from men for the rest of my life, this rejection could easily happen again and again. Perhaps chastity was the best solution. At night I ached for Shad. I could not imagine wanting another man ever again.

In the corridor outside the audience room Ren Daniel was talking earnestly with Symon the Raven, who had also been at the audience. The moment he saw me, however, Symon broke off the conversation and came toward me.

"You have need of us, Enna Dion. But you are taking such a long time asking for our help that I have come to you.''

His words astonished me. I had been sitting at Karac's

bedside all night, and though I had thought often of how I must go to the Klementari over the situation with Bedazzer and Shad, I had done nothing about it.

Symon smiled his Symon smile at me.

Just then Lady Julia stopped and the two of them exchanged courtly greetings.

"Look at her," said Symon as she sailed away down the corridor with Ren Daniel at her elbow. "She has the expression of a pleased cat. The path fate is to take is becoming clear for her. The Duke plays right into her hands."

He turned to me.

"Come," he said. "I shall take you to Causa and Beg. They will help you."

He would not answer any more of my questions.

A little row of earthenware bowls stood on a bench under the canopy.

"It is in this bowl that I saw the demon in your mirror," said Beg.

You can see necromantic magic in any normal Bowl of Seeing even when it is powered by the force of demons, but the magic of demons *alone*—either in their own world on the other side of a mirror, or on the rare occasions when they have been brought through into this world as Bedazzer had been—is not detectable in a normal Bowl of Seeing. But then these were not normal Bowls of Seeing. These bowls were filled with something that smelled faintly herbal and was much thicker than water. I leaned closer.

"Stop that," said Beg, pushing me away. "That's not for foreign mages to pry into."

"These are especially for looking at demon magic," said Causa. "Each one focuses only on the surroundings of a particular person. When I realized what you were afraid of in Cardun, I took a lock of your hair and had Beg set this up. Don't worry. We have not trespassed on your privacy more than is necessary to keep you safe."

I had not even given a thought to my privacy. I wanted to know how it was all done.

"Is it very difficult?" I asked, fishing for details.

"Too difficult for New People magic," grunted Beg predictably.

"It is even difficult for Beg's magic," smiled Causa. "It has a very short range."

Beg made a disgusted noise.

"The magic of demons is part of their nature," continued Causa. "We think that is why they are impossible to perceive in a normal Bowl of Seeing. Trying to see the magic in their actions must be like trying to see magic in the force of a thunderstorm."

"But magic is a part of our natures too," I said. "So why is it you can see our magic and not Klementari magic?"

Beg smacked me hard on the arm.

"You see, Causa. She is too clever by half. You are telling her too much." Her face was not angry, however. In fact I could have sworn I saw a glimpse of pleasure in her eyes. "If you must know, Enna Sticky Nose, our wise men have speculated long and hard on this subject. Human beings are not magical by nature in the same way as demons, but because we Klementari draw on the natural world for our magical force, our magic appears natural. The magic of the New People, however, is most definitely a thing of artifice. You take puny little powers and draw on them in a twisted, unnatural way to make them much greater."

Artifice? What she was talking about? I had been born with magical powers. Surely, therefore, the magic I did was part of my nature. I could not imagine there being any different way of doing magic, either. It was a mystery I must search out. But later. First there were more pressing questions.

"These other bowls," I asked. "Who are they for?"

"This one is for Blanche Shomnee," said Beg with surprising cooperativeness. "Yes, that is right. Lady Blanche. You are not the only person to have spoken to a demon in the mirror. Blanche Shomnee has had a demon in her mirror three times in this past week."

"Blanche! But why have you not told anyone? She must—''

"Having a demon in your mirror is no proof of necromancy, as you should know, Dion," said Causa. "Anyway, it does nothing to regain us Ernundra by exposing her."

"But she could be mind searched. She might know important things. About Darmen Stalker and Sanctuary. And there's the Duke. . . . I must . . .''

"It will gain you nothing to go charging down there now," said Beg. "Blanche Shomnee left Lammerquais for a convent in Quainard last night."

"You let her get away? Why?"

Causa shrugged. "The foretellings have not changed, so her action must serve the future we desire. Lady Blanche is a small fish, Dion. She does someone else's bidding. And that bidding tells her to flee in fear and outrage at her trusted adviser being arrested for necromancy, and to seek safety with the nuns of Quainard and the guidance of the Holy Patriarch. I think she will be able to waver between the Patriarch's and the Duke's sides for some time before either of them tire of the game. Your accusations against Darmen Stalker have actually provided her with a very convenient excuse."

"Are you saying Darmen Stalker came to Moria expecting to be arrested?"

"I am certain he came to delay the Duke's movement South, though I doubt if he expected your accusations. But how useful they have been to him. While so much is uncertain, neither the Duke nor the Patriarch will go South. This bowl is for him," said Causa, pointing to the third bowl. "He is almost certainly a necromancer of some power and importance to the Destroyer, though he did not use necromantic magic when he fought your brother. There are demons in his mirror also."

"Then why do you not come down to the Tower and add your evidence to mine? Perhaps we could force him to undergo a mind search and stop all this messing about. Get the army moving South finally."

"Our plan is to reach Ernundra," snapped Beg. "The pathetic squabblings of the New People are not our concern."

I stared at Beg, aghast at hearing necromancy so described. She grinned as she turned away.

"Don't bait her, Beg," said Causa sternly. She turned to me. "Do you think our testimony would make the Duke try Stalker any earlier? I do not. And don't you see that the South might be liberated faster the way things are going? The Southerners are angry and restless and all set to go South immediately without the Gallians. In that event Lady Julia will go at their head as their candidate for queen."

She took my arm suddenly.

"But I did not ask Symon to fetch you to tell you our latest predictions for Gallian politics. This demon in your mirror. Why do you fear him so?"

I looked at Beg's back. I did not want her unsympathetic ears to hear about my foolish mistakes. A hard knot filled my chest at the thought of talking about it at all.

Seeing my look, Causa drew me out from under the canopy.

Outside, tall trees stretched up to the sky and the shady dimness around us was full of the smell of sweet oil as the noonday sun warmed their leaves. The Wanderers were camped behind Lammerquais on pastures at the edge of the forest. To the casual observer their encampment ended where the forest began. A short way into the forest another encampment began. Beg's green canopy was here, and all around us were camped groups of old people and children. They lived in little shelters built of bracken and branches hidden by trees and bushes so that they were disguised from all but the most curious eyes. I could not recall seeing any children among those Klementari I had seen in the town, but here the raucous sounds of their voices filled the air as they played happily among the trees.

This well-ordered camp reminded me of something I had long wanted to ask Causa.

"How did your people manage to give up hazia so quickly?" I asked.

"Symon said that those who indulge in the dream drug could not help us fight back into Ernundra," said Causa briefly. "Those people are not here with us and hope has made it easier for the rest to give it up. But no more of your stalling. Tell me about this demon, my dear. Perhaps I will be able to help you."

There was no putting it off. With stumbling words, I told her everything. She was the first person I had ever told the whole story to: how as a lonely young mage I had caught the attention of the demon Bedazzer; how I had gone to work for Kitten Avignon as her magical protector; how I had fallen in love with Andre, who turned out to be Bedazzer, brought through as a slave into this world by Norval, Kitten's enemy; and how I had been manipulated into trusting Andre and thereby captured by Norval. I told her how Bedazzer had maneuvered me into killing his master and releasing him, and how I had fought hand-to-hand with the freed demon in a great magical battle. It was hardest of all to tell her of how when I had almost run out of strength, Bedazzer had tempted me with offers of belonging and union. I could hardly bear to tell her how tempted I had been.

I had never told anyone of this moment or of how unclean I had felt ever since, or of how linked I still felt with Andre/Bedazzer. I wept from the sheer shame of it, and yet as I told the story everything seemed to take on much smaller proportions.

"Oh Dion, do you think you are the only person to have loved a demon?" said Causa as I dried my eyes. "They can read our thoughts and know how to make themselves attractive to us as plants make flowers to attract bees. Surely it's no sign of inner evil that it worked. Neither is that fact that he still appears to you in dreams. The link between you is inevitable. He would appear to you whether you wanted it or not. And if he tires of tormenting you, he will disappear again whether you wish it or not."

I was struck by the simple logic of this argument. I had always blamed myself for Bedazzer's continued appearance. It was almost inconceivable to me that it might not be my fault. But it was worth thinking about. Yes indeed.

"Is this why you are so afraid of him?" continued Causa. "Because otherwise you are safe from him. He is definitely on his own plane. He himself cannot harm you, though he may torment you horribly."

"What about Shad?" I cried.

She looked a little perplexed. "Beg will be able to tell us this for sure, but I would have thought Shad was in even less danger than you. Demons have great difficulty even seeing ordinary mortals unless they are connected to magic in some way. When necromancers sacrifice ordinary mortals to demons, they must do so in the presence of magic, otherwise the demons cannot perceive their food."

"But Bedazzer must be aware of him," I cried. "He was jealous. He called me whore and slut and said he would not let anyone else have me."

To my great mortification, Causa threw back her head and laughed.

"Do you really think a demon would care who you bedded down with, Dion? Does that strike you as logical? Beg and I feared that it was jealous of another demon. Does that not seem more likely to you?"

"But there is no other demon. What other demons could there be?"

"The Destroyer has a number of demons allied to him. It could be that this Bedazzer is afraid you will fall into their hands or that you will yield to their blandishments. There have been no other advances?"

I looked at her in amazement. "No. Apart from the Fire Angels, I've seen nothing else. Did you suspect me ..."

"We could see that you had nothing to do with any other demons, but when Shad told us his story we were worried about you."

"Shad told you of this?"

"Yes, he came to us and told us what had happened. He said you seemed terribly afraid."

My first thought was one of hope but that quickly gave way to depression. Shad was a good and honorable man and even if he had washed his hands of me, he would not want to leave me in trouble. It was no indication of his feelings toward me—which must surely be anger and disgust.

"Don't be angry at him," said Causa. "He is one of the Klementari and knows he can come to his council for help. He was worried for you, Dion."

"And I have no need to be worried for him?" I asked quickly, to get away from this painful subject.

"We shall set up a Bowl of Seeing for him too if that is your wish. Then we can be certain. Is that why you have broken with each other? Because you were afraid for him? Because really there is no need to be."

"No," I said. It only made everything worse to realize that I need not have told Shad at all. It was all very well for Causa to say I had done nothing terrible, but Shad's feelings for me had been based on a false idea of who I was and now that he had discovered what sort of person I really was, he would have realized he was mistaken in those feelings as well. I didn't even want to hope that I was wrong about this because hope can only hurt you more.

It was all so much more complicated than Causa could possibly understand. I changed the subject, thanked her for her help and went back to the White Tower.

Events concerning Lady Blanche proceeded much as the Klementari predicted. For several days of the following week the Duke and his entourage were in Quainard trying to persuade Lady Blanche to return to Lammerquais while representatives of the Patriarch, and once or twice even the Patriarch himself, met with her to express concern at her situation and to make heartfelt offers of aid and protection.

Tomas had gone back to RougeLammer, which saved me from more scoldings. For while the Duke was away, the plotting of the Southerners proceeded apace. Twice I helped Lady Julia slip out of the White Tower unnoticed and accompanied her to a midnight meeting with Lord Quercy at the Klementari encampment. The plot was discussed openly between the Lady and myself now that Blanche was not around to spy on us. At first Lady Julia worried about whether by taking part in this plot she was simply turning a two-way struggle for Moria into a three-way one. Her anxieties diminished with remarkable swiftness, however, and quickly turned into practical plans and calculations.

It was a new Lady Julia I saw these days. I had known her to be a strong, ambitious, and determined person, but now I discovered how cool, clever, and well-organized she could be as well. I was astonished at how right the role of leader seemed for her. She had the way of making herself liked by the common people wherever she went but, more importantly, I saw that the other members of the plot, nobles and army commanders, respected her judgements. Of all the candidates for the throne there was no doubt that Lady Julia was the one who had the good of Moria most at heart.

The Klementari, whose ability to gather knowledge was considerable, informed the leaders of the plot that, although there was a fierce barrier of Burning Light and Soprian mercenary troops between us and Beenac, they were a lone vanguard. Behind them, most of Hierarch Jarraz's Burning Light forces had withdrawn to Sanctuary in the Waste Land. It was strange to hear of people seeking safety in a place I was certain was filled with necromancy and demons. Would the necromancer treat these soldiers as friends or were they only fodder?

If the Klementari had made their knowledge known to the Duke, we might have easily been able to persuade him to agree to splitting the army up. They did not, however. Once again they were manipulating events to suit themselves. To be fair, there was a general feeling of disenchantment with the Duke among the Morian elements in the army. I doubt if anything could have changed the intention to go south without him now.

Yet how long had the Klementari known of the weakness of the South's defenses? For the first time I found myself looking critically at them. To a mage like myself, the fact that they had let Lady Blanche go free even when she was obviously colluding with demons was quite shocking.

"How do you know you can trust the Klementari's reports of what is going on in the South?" I asked Lady Julia. "They may just be tricking us into going because it serves their purpose."

"I doubted them too when first your brother Karac came to me at the convent and told me that the Wanderers had foreseen that I would be Queen of Moria," said Lady Julia. "But consider for a moment. The Duke will never recognize their right to sovereignty over Ernundra. The best he will offer them is some kind of tenancy. I, on the other hand, will give them Ernundra because I know that in the days of Moria's greatness, one of the pillars on which that greatness rested was the Klementari living in Ernundra. I am valuable to them, and even if they are lying to us, I am certain they would never lead us to destruction. I have been dealing with them for three years now, and they have never really given me cause to doubt their wisdom."

The Duke must have had some awareness of the unrest, for he issued several decrees declaring that those who deserted would be executed for treachery. Ironically, the only people hanged were Gallians or Morians who had no knowledge of our plot. The Southern members of the army had an inkling that something favorable was about to happen and stayed quietly in their barracks.

I saw Shad once in the distance at the Klementari camp, and the sense of his presence made me feel as if ice was running though my veins. I did not look at him, for I was still certain that I would see disgust in his eyes, and the fact that he did not seek me out confirmed this. The few times he was sent to Lady Julia I found excuses to be elsewhere. I did not miss him so very much, for these were busy days full of fear and excitement. Only the early mornings were really bad times. Then I awoke to hear the watchman calling four o'clock on the walls and I would weep and wish everything had been different. If only I had had the sense to steal a piece of his clothing so that I might have had the comfort of burying my face in it and breathing in his warm smoky scent.

As for Darmen Stalker, he remained imprisoned—if his stay could be called that. Often I saw him walking in the gardens with Garthan Redon and a group of guardian mages. The sight of him filled me with anger. He was not even being forced to wear a witch manacle. Several times, as I watched him from Lady Julia's window, he looked up and gave me a smiling, mocking nod of the head. He was so good-looking with his chestnut hair and blue eyes, and so confident, I could easily have suspected him of being a bound demon on this plain as Andre had been, had it not been for the fact that Ren Daniel and I had already surreptitiously performed the ritual that reveals a bound demon in the vicinity, and turned up nothing.

Yet every time I saw Priest Stalker I couldn't help wondering if the ritual had worked. He seemed almost amused by his situation, as if he was surrounded by ineffectual ants.

Karac's was not the only attempt at assassination against him, although it was the one closest to being effective. Most of the other assassins perished during their attempts. The Duke had left Garthan Redon and a group of his most loyal retainers to guard Hierarch Jarraz's secretary. They took very good care that he would live—and live very pleasantly by all accounts—to see a fair trial.

Every day I went to see Karac in prison. His imprisonment was very real, even if his small stone cell in the cellars of the White Tower was clean enough, and he was well fed and cared for. I came to know my brother much better in those days, for he was now too depressed to be tormenting. He spoke often of Dally. He seemed to regard himself as responsible for her now that Tasha had gone. He mourned his failure to kill Stalker for her sake as much as his own, and seemed certain she would never forgive him for it. His anxiety about this prompted me to ask Silva several times what Dally's feelings now were toward Karac. Dally, smiling, accepted all messages from him politely and without comment and Silva could not work out if this was good or bad.

"That child has become more secretive than ever," said Silva. We were out on a boot-buying expedition for Martin,

Dally, and Needra, but having successfully completed our mission, we were now strolling slowly though the market. The young ones had fallen behind, having caught sight of the puzzles at a woodcarver's stall. This gave Silva and me the opportunity for some private talk.

"She is not the only one who is secretive, either," said Silva. "Shad Forest stayed with us last night, but when I told him you were coming, he went all silent and this morning he went out early and didn't come back. What's happened between you? What did you say to him that day?"

As I groped for some kind of answer to this, suddenly everything began to happen.

The market was loud with shouting that day, but something caught Silva's attention. Suddenly she whirled round and screamed, "Martin!" Even as she turned I felt a blast of magic that threw everything else from my mind. I spun around ready to fight, just in time to see someone sailing through the air and hitting one of the stalls in a burst of flying merchandise. Nearby two men were struggling together.

Silva dropped her basket and dashed back past me shouting Martin's name.

I ran after her, understanding nothing but danger. I could see Needra screaming and pulling at the collapsed stall. Then suddenly there was another blast of power. Two more stalls collapsed and Dally came flying shrieking through the air. I flung out my power and caught her as she fell. As I did, I felt the magic streaming through her. She was screaming with pain and terror. Those blasts of power had come from her, but she didn't know how to stop them coming. I threw a defensive shield around her as another blast rocked her body, and caught her in my arms.

"Relax!" I shouted. "Let go!" Catching her hands, I squeezed the next bolt of magic out of them before it was fully formed. I pushed her down into sleep and quickly smothered the magic that was raging through her body.

But it had been Martin's name Silva had been screaming. The minute Dally was out of danger I looked up, ready to help. It was all over by then, however. Silva and Needra were pulling a shaken but unhurt Martin out of the wreckage of the stall. Two men were struggling in the grip of several stallholders, while a third was slumped at the feet of Shad Forest. Where had he come from? As I looked up, Shad stepped over the body before him and came over to me.

"Are you safe, Dion?" he said. I had looked into his eyes before I realized what I was doing. He looked tense, but there was no disgust there.

I could not speak. It was as if the air between us were made of jelly. I wanted to leap up and run away and at the same time fling my arms around him. I must have moved to get up, for I was suddenly aware of Dally's weight on my lap.

"Dally!" I said to Shad.

"Air and Fire, yes! Is she hurt?"

"What's going on here?" said a rough voice as the Watch came up behind us. Shad turned away and was quickly caught up, along with what seemed like half the market, in explaining what had happened.

And what had happened? Five men had set upon the children as they wandered past an alleyway and had tried to make away with Martin. In the heat of the moment Dally had thrown out a great blast of power and pitched the man holding Martin into a nearby stall. One of the others had gone at her with a knife, but Shad, who had been nearby, had seized him and knocked him out. Two of the villains had gotten away, but other passersby had managed to grab the man who had been thrown into the stall and one other. Tempers were hot against the villainy of attacking children.

Explanations over, the Watch led the prisoners away. Shad picked up the still-sleeping Dally and we took the children safely home. Shad did not look at me again except for a brief glance as he bid me good-bye. I could barely bring myself to look back at him. I had been a fool to hope for anything more.

"Well!" said Silva. "Fancy Shad turning up. He must have been following us. Don't you think, Dion?"

"I don't want to think about it," I told her in a voice I could barely control and went away as quickly as I could.

"Lucien has had the children brought back into the White Tower nursery," I told Karac later. "It's not clear what the motive was for the kidnapping, but Tomas strongly suspects Darmen Stalker is behind it."

"Did the men say anything?"

"Under mind search it's clear they know little of who commanded them, but two are Southerners and one is a Soprian, and they are all loyal troops of the Burning Light. And who would have better motives than Stalker? He could use Martin to force Tomas to withdraw our accusations against him."

"The sooner that bastard burns the better," muttered Karac. "You won't let him get away, will you, Dion?"

I was about to tell him that Lucien Sercel would see that he was burned even if all else failed, when I realized it would simply make Karac feel more of a failure to mention his rival for Tasha's affections. I promised I would see to it.

"I'm worried about Dally," said Karac. "Where did this spell come from? Did you teach it to her?"

"No. Dally will hardly even speak to me," I said. "Didn't you?"

"I would have taught her how to finish it if I had," he said curtly. "And so would Silva. Then who was the fool who taught her that spell?"

This was the first time I had really thought of it. Up until now I had assumed the power Dally had blasted out in that moment of fear had been the magical equivalent of a boy's voice breaking.

When she had awoken from her magical sleep that afternoon, she had been too upset for me to teach her anything. She had sat there with staring eyes while I had described to her how to finish off a spell. I was not sure if she took any of it in, but I felt I must at least tell her as soon as possible, in case anything went wrong before someone could show her. Silva told me she would show her as soon as Dally had recovered, and I promised to come back as soon as I could and practice the technique with her.

"Maybe she just did it," I said to Karac now. "Throwing people around is not hard to do in a panic. You just wish them . . ."

"It's not hard for you to do, Dion. But you are the Demonslayer. You have an abnormal amount of power and have had it since you were born. But I still need to focus on a spell to be able to do anything and so do most other ordinary mages. No matter how much power she will have, Dally is no Demonslayer. She must have learned that spell from somewhere. Find out for me, will you?"

Although I promised him I would look into it, I did not regard it as a very serious matter. Perhaps I had a failure of imagination here, for I could not imagine what it was like not to be able to tap into your powers at will. I figured that there was some simple explanation. Maybe Silva had taught her, or she had read about it, or Karac underestimated the power of panic. So I was only mildly dismayed when events intervened to make it impossible for me to get back to Dally. That evening before dinner, Lady Julia told me that that very night we would be leaving the White Tower and going South.

·18·

Pleading a headache, I went to bed directly after dinner, but of course I could not sleep. I had known for a couple of days that the plan to go south was going ahead and had been secretly impressed by my own calmness in the face of this dangerous step.

Now all calmness was at an end. So far I had managed to avoid taking responsibility for actions that might displease the Duke. This time. . . . I was the Elector of Magery. I was about to commit an act that had already been called treason. I was scared.

I tossed and turned until I heard the watchman cry two. Then I rose and dressed in my strongest and warmest clothes. Outside the window the night looked oddly pale. It was one of the mists that Lammerquais was famous for. What luck!

A few minutes later I was following Lady Julia and Lady Anne down the corridor. It was pointless to try and use magic to help us slip unseen from the White Tower. The guardian mages would be able to detect any magic and through it our movements. Good old-fashioned bribery had always proven a far better option. No doubt the guards simply thought Lady Julia had a lover or some such thing. We did not see them on our way to the stableyard entrance.

The moment I stepped out into the fog, I knew it was not

natural. It was as pale as milk and no easier to see through. All around I felt little sparklings of magic on my skin, but I could not pin down its source. It must be Klementari magic!

Once the three of us had stepped away from the doorway, we were completely lost. We stood still for a moment clutching one another, not knowing what to do.

A figure appeared beside us and a hand took mine.

"Come," it said. "The horses are this way." It was Symon, moving as easily in the fog as if it were bright daylight.

The three of us stumbled after him. Suddenly a horse was standing in front of me. Shadows gathered around and helped me up onto it and put reins in my hand. The fog was so thick I could not see the horse's head, and I had a momentary ridiculous vision of myself blindly mounted backwards. Then the horse heaved forward in the expected direction.

Magic, magic all around. I must have become more attuned to Klementari magic in the Stone Circle, because all my senses were tingling as if they had been newly washed in crystal cool water. This magic was like wind caressing my cheek and hair. All the magic I had ever practiced hit more like a thrown rock. I loved this silken magical caress. I became dizzy with it as we rode slowly along.

I have no idea how long we rode, but it was at least long enough to get saddle-sore. The swirling grey blindness seemed to go on forever. What kind of magic could create such an enormous fog cloud? Surely we were well out of Lammerquais, and yet still the grey wall of fog continued. It had lifted enough for me to be able to see the head of my horse and the haunches of the horse before me. The two of them were roped together. There were slightly darker patches in the fog that I thought might be other horses and riders around us. I had the unearthly feeling that there were many more riders all around me that I could not see. After a time the joy at the magic left me and my eyes became impossibly heavy. Several times I started awake to find myself slipping from the saddle.

At some stage the fog lightened from dark grey to pale grey. Birds called faintly in the distance. Was this dawn?

I had not been told much about the plan and had accepted this as wise, but I did know that all the conspirators were slipping out of Lammerquais in small groups this night, to be guided by the Klementari to a mustering point on the very edge of central Moria a day and a half's ride south. The logic behind this was that any vengeful Ducal troops would not capture everyone together. With this fog, however, any vengeful troops would have trouble finding each other, let alone following us. Were the Klementari going to keep this up all the way to the muster point? Could anyone keep such magic going so long? How incredible that would be!

We stopped briefly to feed the horses. I paced up and down beside my horse to stretch my legs, afraid to let go of its bridle lest I get lost. A Klementari warrior appeared out of the mist and handed me a flask. It was some kind of hot drink mixed with milk that was both bitter and sweet and quite delicious. Energy surged through me, and after we remounted, I found myself staringly awake.

No less bored, however. We rode on and on in the numbing blindness. We must have ridden for hours.

Once I saw a big black bird fly past us. Shortly afterward I became aware of Symon's thin, slightly stooped figure. I called out softly to him and he told me to hush. We rode on.

Then suddenly Symon was dragging me off my horse, hissing, "Quickly, you have to get under cover."

The horse was gone and springy branches whipped at me as he pushed me down into the slimy leaf mold beneath some bushes.

"Stay still," he hissed. "And don't use magic. As soon as you do, they'll see you and all our efforts will be in vain."

He turned as if to go and then suddenly said "Ah!" and seemed to grab someone out of the mist and pull them toward me.

"Here," muttered Symon, a hint of malice in his voice. "You can keep each other company."

At that moment the grey world burst open. A huge fireball roared past overhead, and another and another. The cold grey turned incandescent with fiery orange light and heat. Symon was gone. I crouched as low as I could as the grey was shot through again and again by hot bursts of orange fire. Horses and people were screaming. My nostrils were filled with the demon stink of sulfur and rotting roses.

Fire Angels!

Why had they come? Were they drawn by the magic? Could they see me in all this mist? Cackling laughter screeched out overhead. The sound plunged toward us. Someone shouted and there was a cold blue explosion that shook the earth and splattered us with earth and leaves. I clutched blindly the person beside me. There was another explosion and another further away and then a cacophony of explosions all around.

"It's all right," said the person crouched beside me. "The blue explosions are fire powder bombs. They confuse the angels."

"Shad," I cried, recognizing the voice immediately. There was a strained look in his eyes. I realized how hard I'd been clutching his arm. I let go quickly.

There were still explosions, but they were far away now, and so was the cackling of the Fire Angels. The orange fire had gone, leaving only the swirling grey fog. But the fog was nowhere near as thick as the atmosphere between Shad and me as, covered with damp leaves, we crouched side by side under the bush.

Sweat dried coldly on my back. My hands were trembling. I wanted desperately to say something, anything that would make things right between us.

Instead I said, "I did not thank you for saving Dally."

"I was there. What else could I have done?"

"Nonetheless I am very grateful to you."

"It was my pleasure."

This was a stupid conversation. We sounded like we were sitting in Lady Julia's drawing room instead of in leaf mold and mud.

"I'm sorry," I said, groping for words that were more real. "I'm sorry for what happened."

"It's my own fault," said Shad. "I should have known better."

Before I could ask him what he meant, someone seized me and I was on my feet.

I heard Shad's voice calling my name and his hand brushed mine.

"Shad," I cried out, clutching at the air. Symon pulled me away.

"The Fire Angels have moved on but they may be back. This is no time for lovemaking," he said. There was a teasing note in his voice that was utterly inappropriate, and I remembered then who had put us together in those bushes.

"What are you up to, Symon?" I hissed angrily at him.

"A little harmless manipulation. I can't believe how stupid you are. You obviously still want the man and he wants you. Why deny yourself such a tasty morsel?"

I lost my temper. "Don't speak of him like that," I shouted, smacking out at Symon.

"Oh ho," said Symon dropping my hand. "Temper, temper."

Suddenly I found myself alone in the mist.

"What are you doing?" I shouted.

"Why should I help you? You tried to hit me," came the mock-aggravated voice back.

The obvious thing to do was apologize, but I was damned if I was going to apologize to that malicious sod. Curse Symon. I put out my hands and stepped forward once, twice, thrice. Cold fear slid down my spine, but still I was damned if. . . . My hand met horsehide and I saw that it was my horse. Still furious, I climbed up into the saddle and waited. A few minutes later a Klementari warrior, his face covered in soot, rode up beside me and roped his horse to mine. Anxiously I asked him about the attack and was told that the Fire Angels had flown away northeast. It had not been a serious attack. They had been easily driven off and apart from a few minor burns, no one was hurt.

We rode on. I forgot about the attack in my wondering at Symon's words. He still wants you, Symon had said. Did

Shad really . . . ? No, how could Symon know that? I couldn't imagine Shad telling him. Symon was just mocking me. And yet what if he was right? Shad had not seemed disgusted with me, though this seemed incredible. How could he not be? I had told him I had once loved a demon. I thought about my uncleanness. No, I must have misread Shad. Yes, that was it. That must have been what he meant when he said he should have known better. Yet I had been wrong before about people. How I wished I could see into his head. If he was not disgusted with me, if he did indeed still love me. . . . My God, what would that mean?

After a long ride in the greyness and another stop to rest and eat, the fog began to lift, revealing a cool crisp evening. Great strands of grey mist still floated in the air, but between them I could see the stars in the night sky. Soon I could see the darker mass of the Red Mountains away to the west.

We had been riding since very early that morning yet despite that the horses began to trot, as glad as the rest of us to be able to see again. I had estimated that we were riding in a small company, but now I saw that there were at least two hundred of us. I could not see Shad. He must have been well back. I was near the front. Ahead of me I could make out the the upright figure of Lady Julia, and near her the slighter figure of Lady Anne. On either side we were flanked by Klementari.

Finally we mounted a rise and there before us the light of many small fires glimmered in the darkness. We had come to the meeting point.

I had meant to seek out Shad and talk to him; about exactly what I wasn't sure. By the time we reached the camp, however, I felt too exhausted to have a difficult conversation with him, though I was more than half aware that this was an excuse.

Fortunately I fell into a pit of sleep as soon as my head touched the pillow that night, and I stayed there until Lady Anne roused me shortly before dawn. I was both disappointed and relieved when I looked for Shad and could not see him anywhere. It was not really surprising. The camp was enormous. There were at least ten times as many people as had traveled with us the day before. Many people had left Lammerquais during the previous day and avoided the mist, and throughout the night other groups guided through the mist by the Klementari had continued to join us. Groups of soldiers were still straggling into the meeting place as our advance party mounted up to ride on to Vernede, where Lady Julia was to lodge for a couple of days in the convent of St. Estrella in order to rally what support we could from the Southerners.

Great carts were also rattling around the campsite that morning. They were driven by elderly Klementari and filled with dozens and dozens of cauldrons. Going to mount up, I passed a gang of children loading one of these carts and saw a familiar face.

It was Beg, as bent and witchlike as ever. I went over and greeted her. She smiled sparingly and greeted me back. Then Causa appeared from behind another cart and embraced me.

"That mist was a marvel," I told them.

"Of course," said Beg, in a tone that indicated such remarks were too obvious to bother making. She turned away to wave another cart forward.

"How did you do it?" I whispered to Causa. "How did you make such a thick cover for so long?"

"Ah," she said, "that would be telling, wouldn't it?" She winked at me. "Tell me, do you like our collection of cauldrons?"

Had they mixed that mist up in those cauldrons like smoke?

I was moving forward to see if I could find out anything, when Beg caught me by the elbow.

"I wish to ask you something, Enna Sticky Nose," she said. She leaned closer. I could smell the sweet oil on her skin. "Do you know the true name of that demon who troubles you?"

"No I don't. Why do you want it?" I cried, frightened by the question.

Names are vital in demon magic. If you know the name of a demon, you can force him to give you his magic in return for the life force of creatures from this world. More importantly, if you have enough power, you can bring him into this world to serve you as a powerful and undetectable magical slave, as Norval had used Andre/Bedazzer. Even had I known his true name I would never have given such an opportunity for power into another's hands.

"If we could control it we could order it to leave you and your man alone," Beg said. She gazed into my face with unusually solemn eyes. "Don't be so afraid. That's all I meant. You New People are silly about demons. You must know your enemy to defeat him."

For a moment all the doubt I had felt about the Klementari since I had learned how leniently they had treated Stalker and Lady Blanche came back to me. I had a momentary terrible vision of the Klementari using demon power to take back Ernundra.

As I stared down into her steady eyes, I knew that she guessed everything that was going on in my mind.

"To use demon power for anything else would besmirch the quest beyond redemption," she said softly. "The price is always too high."

"I'm sorry," I said softly. She nodded calmly, seeming unoffended.

"Why did the Fire Angels attack us back there?" I said, trying for a more ordinary tone. "Was it the mist? Did they attack the individual mages controlling it?"

"We did not make it in that way, because we feared the Angels might be drawn to us. The mist itself was meant to appear to them as a single huge being and it worked. Though it drew them, they were easily confused and driven away. I do not think their hearts were in preying on us, if such creatures have hearts."

Her face was thoughtful. "It was as if they had more important business elsewhere."

I was about to ask her what she thought this business might be when a young Klementari warrior appeared at my side and reminded me that I was wanted in Lady Julia's escort.

This time we rode all day in bright sunlight, able to see the rolling green Southern countryside all around us. Lady Julia rode at our head, her hair uncovered and falling over her shoulders in a great flame-colored cloak. A little behind her rode a standard-bearer carrying the great banner of the Madragas, the red dragon which streamed out above us as we rode. Lord Quercy and Ren Daniel Devoirs and an entourage of mages and Morian aristocrats followed us. Lady Anne had been sent further down in the column, for it was my duty to ride at Lady Julia's side. I kept my mind firmly focused on the chance of any danger to her.

A surprising addition to our party was the two phalanxes of priest-mages wearing the colors of the Holy States, following in the wake of Ren Daniel's party.

"They have betrayed the Patriarch as we have betrayed His Grace," Lady Julia had explained with amusement twinkling in her eyes. "Is it not delightful? They came to the Morian commander at MontLammer and asked if they might join the Duke when he went to fight the necromancer in the South. He enlisted them to our cause."

Demons create the strangest bedfellows.

On either side of the column rode a guard of Klementari warriors, dressed not in their drab fighting garb but in the gaudy embroidered coats that proclaimed their beliefs. This was a procession, not a war party.

To see the Klementari dressed so was to see an old legend come to life. I forgot all about my own small problems in my excitment and pride in being part of such a magnificent company. As we rode along the high road to Vernede, people gathered at the roadside cheering, and sometimes they even knelt and bowed in greeting to their ruler. I heard riders behind us calling out to those we passed, saying that Lady Julia Madraga's Army of Liberation would be mustering outside Vernede, and urging all those who wished to see the Burning Light gone from the South to join us there.

The entry into Vernede late that afternoon was a triumph.

The streets were crowded with people and so many surged forward to touch Lady Julia's robe and feet that I was forced to put a magical shield around her to prevent her from being knocked off her horse. In the town square we were met by a delegation of the town notables, who handed her a huge gilt key and urged her to enter the town hall to address the townsfolk from the balcony. By the time our party had climbed the stairs to the second floor, the square beneath was a seething sea of people, cheering and singing the "Song of the Red Dragon" so loudly that I had to use magic to make Lady Julia's voice heard. After a rousing speech, she caught me completely by surprise by seizing my hand and dragging me out before the crowd, there to be introduced as "The Demonslayer of Gallia, my dear friend whose support has given us all so much hope of victory." As the people beneath cheered, my eyes filled with tears at the hope in all their faces and a lump in my throat stopped my voice. I could only nod my head and wave an embarrassed hand.

The most surprising moment was yet to come. Symon the Raven came forward. The crowd in the square fell silent. Many Klementari had settled and interbred in the South and these people had a very good idea what a Klementari wearing plain black garb meant.

"Good people, I greet you in the name of the Klementari. Our foretellers have spoken and spoken strongly. I call upon you to honor and serve Lady Julia Madraga who will soon be Queen of Moria."

Beneath us the crowd went wild.

The Town Hall was full of the important people of the district, all waiting to be introduced to Lady Julia. Wine and sweetmeats were brought into the room. I realized that I was ravenously hungry and went off after the servant carrying food as soon as he appeared. He was waylaid by a couple of other mages, who plucked the food tray out of his hands and retired to the other end of the room with it. Thankfully they were not averse to sharing their prize with me.

"You are missing meeting all the important people,"

grinned one of them. "I'm sure they would love to meet you."

"Yes," I agreed, taking another mince pie. "How full of disappointments life is."

I made up my mind to stay by the food tray. Surely I had done enough to support Lady Julia's cause for one day.

"Can I have a word with you?" said Ren Daniel, appearing at my elbow.

The urgent look on his face worried me. Had Ducal troops appeared already?

Ren Daniel led me out of the room and onto the stairs. Except for the servants racing up and down with trays, it was probably the quietest place in the whole town hall.

"Enna Dion, I thought I was supporting a quest to liberate Moria," he said urgently to me. "But when I heard that Wanderer fellow talking today. . . . Lady Julia has plans to make a play for the throne, doesn't she?"

"Oh my!" I said, looking at him in distress. What could I say to this?

Ren Daniel drew himself up stiffly and said, "I have been tricked, haven't I?"

"No! No! Of course not. I believe Lady Julia's primary aim is the liberation of the South, which is what we all want. To my mind anything else is unimportant at this time."

"Unimportant! She'll plunge this country into a civil war. She can't possibly stand as ruler against Duke Leon. She's only a woman."

Somehow this protest, which I had made so often myself, annoyed me coming from Ren Daniel.

"But you cannot deny she would make a good ruler, and at least she is a Morian."

I could have bitten my tongue off as soon as I had spoken. A horrified look came into his face. I had confirmed his worst suspicions.

"Ren Daniel, there will be time enough to decide who will sit upon the throne of Moria later. Defeating this necromancer is the most important thing at the moment."

"Yes, of course," he said in a voice which seemed only

half awake. "I beg your pardon. I meant no disrespect to Lady Julia. It is just that . . . her bid for the throne is so unbelievable."

"I am sorry," I said, though I felt a bit ridiculous saying so, because it wasn't for me to apologize for Lady Julia's oversights. I had thought everyone knew. Who else among Lady Julia's supporters had not guessed?

"The most important thing is for us to get to Beenac and liberate the south. If you prefer the Duke as ruler there will be time to leave Lady Julia afterward."

"Yes. Of course," he said. "You are quite right. And this is her most important goal?"

"Of course."

"Well, you have put my mind at ease," he said. He smiled. "I'm afraid it's been such a surprise, I haven't had time to think. Perhaps Lady Julia would make a good ruler. Thank you, Enna Dion."

A carriage was waiting to take Lady Julia to the Convent of St. Estrella, and since being female and important I too counted as a lady, I was loaded into it as well. Lady Julia was exhilarated. She flung her cloak off with a great flamboyant gesture and embraced both Lady Anne and me.

"What wonderful day it has been," she cried. "Did you see how those people cheered for me when the Raven announced me Queen? Queen, queen I see it now. I *will* be Queen of Moria and Duke Leon Sahr can go hang himself. There will be no polite going back and begging of pardon now."

No going back. Her words gave me a horrible falling feeling, especially when I remembered Ren Daniel's shock.

Should I say something? It seemed like telling tales, but she really should know. I tried to be nonspecific.

"Have you thought that . . . perhaps there are those among your following who only support your push to Beenac and would still prefer to see the Duke as ruler?"

It was as if a cloth had wiped all the excitement off her face.

"What do you mean? What have you heard? Who has been saying this?"

"No one," I said, frightened by her expression. I did not want to get Ren Daniel into trouble. "It's just that you never announced it and some of the mages are very conservative and may balk at a woman on the throne."

The expression on her face lightened.

"Oh, Enna Dion, you are a misery. And the worst of it is that you are right. It is certainly something to be aware of. Though, I would be surprised if people had not guessed by now. It's quite obvious that this expedition does not have the Duke's blessing and you would have to be very foolish not to realize that this is a good opportunity for me to play for the throne. You would have to be so foolish, in fact, that your opposition would hardly be worth worrying about."

Or so conservative that the thought of a woman ruler was unimaginable, I thought unhappily, wishing I shared her certainty.

·19·

The following day, I and the rest of Lady Julia's train worked hard organizing the recruits. To my relief Ren Daniel joined us and there seemed to be no terrible upheaval going on in the ranks of the mages.

It seemed as if every man within a day's march of Vernede had come to join the army of liberation. Very few came from the South. Those who did come brought the hopeful news that Hierarch Jarraz's remaining troops had withdrawn back toward Beenac. The area a couple of days' march around Beenac was staunchly Burning Light, and no doubt they would make their stand there. Otherwise their news made depressing hearing. For some days now, the Burning Light villages had been heading out toward Sanctuary, and more recently the troops had been forcing the nonbelievers to go with them. Fire Angels, or rather the "Angels of God," were spoken of again and again as being instrumental in this roundup. Those who came from that far South quite often had been hiding in the forest or making their way North anyway, before they had heard of Lady Julia's army.

I worked all day taking names and home villages for the payroll. The gloomy talk of the men before my table made me wonder that there was anybody left to come.

My fellow name-taker was a pale, shy young priest-mage.

We spoke little during the morning, but at the midday he offered me an apple and we got to talking. Like most of the mages in our company he was driven by a deep hatred of necromancy, and just like me he was terrified by the step he had taken. He comforted himself that he was really doing what Patriarch Sylvestus would have wanted him to do had he been free to order it. I made the kind of comforting noises I would have liked to hear about there being no excuse for not doing right and how surely no one could punish us for it. He must have assumed I was just another healer, for when someone came up and pointed me out within our hearing as the Demonslayer of Gallia, he went bright red and I could not get another word out of him.

Shad was working nearby, handing out the weapons that the Klementari had brought into camp. All day I looked at him and sometimes I was certain he was looking at me, though I never caught him at it. I did my best to concentrate on my task.

Evening came down without my noticing and, suddenly ravenous, I took my place in the soup line with the rest of the camp. Again I saw Shad and again we avoided looking at each other. How stupid this was.

I found a quiet spot in the dark shadows under the tree and sat down to eat my soup in privacy. Symon's mocking words came back to me. Perhaps I should try to talk to Shad. If he still cared for me it was foolish to be going around avoiding each other's eyes, especially when who knew what lay before us. A sudden horrible vision of Shad being shot with an arrow came to me then and left me shivering. I wanted to run to him now and say . . .

What on earth could I say? *Please don't be disgusted with me? Please still love me?* Now here was a question. Did I want to be loved? Didn't that mean forever? How did I feel about him? What if I got involved with Shad again and suddenly discovered I wanted to be uninvolved. . . . My God. It would be worse then the situation with Parrus. Shad was no shallow young man. What if I hurt him?

"Have you still not sorted things out with that man of

yours?'' said a voice. Symon was sitting on the low-hanging branch of a nearby tree, with his hands primly in his lap, regarding me with his head to one side. ''You and he should talk. I will send him to you.''

How could he be so insensitive?

''Hasn't the Wanderer Raven got better things to do with his time than bother about others' quarrels?'' I snapped at him.

He shrugged.

''I have a spare moment or two. I decided to put it at your disposal.''

''I'm deeply honored,'' I said sarcastically.

''I don't mind the man,'' said Symon. ''It would be well for someone like you to be safely mated, and he is a good mate for you. A kind man is a rare jewel.''

I began to toy with the idea of pushing this annoying person off his tree branch.

''When it became clear how things were between you and the man, some of us were very concerned. You are a powerful weapon and should not be in the wrong hands. But I saw quickly it would not be a problem. You do not trust the men you sleep with. And so you will miss your chance here.''

And before I could get over the shock enough to tell him what he could do with his opinion, he slid down from his branch and stalked away.

I walked back to the Convent of St. Estrella along the stream. It was a little less then a mile. There were campfires all along the stream bank, for many of the Southerners joining the army had brought their families for safety, having learned from others' misfortune. The night was warm and filled with the sound of crickets.

I was glad to have the darkness to cover my deep embarrassment. That had been much worse than talking about marriage with Tomas. Fancy describing me as a weapon to be placed in the right person's hands. Was that really why Symon so interested in who I ''mated'' with?

He was right about one thing. I was so suspicious of men

after Andre that I had taken neither Parrus or Shad particularly seriously. I had simply enjoyed sleeping with them and, like my mother, had expected nothing more. Even now I found myself wondering sometimes what ulterior motive Shad could have for saying he loved me. I did not trust the men I slept with.

I sighed.

"Dion," said a voice.

Shad was standing on the path behind me.

"Symon told me you wanted to speak with me."

Oh no! I thought. Curse Symon. I wasn't ready for this. I didn't even know what I wanted to say.

Shad's arms were crossed and his body was turned away from mine. He was not standing far away but the distance between us seemed enormous.

"Shad," I started. "Are you angry at me?"

"No more than is reasonable. What is this? I thought you didn't want us to see each other again."

His arms didn't uncross. He stared down at his feet.

"I'm sorry for what happened," I said, more because it was something to say than because I thought it would help.

"You've already said that. What for? What you said? What I said? That you ever met me?"

"No, I. . . ." I didn't know what to say so I said nothing. We stood there in silence.

"Look, what is it you want to say to me? Or don't you know? Because if there's nothing I think I'd best go. I know I did wrong, but it is not fair of you to toy with me like this. Can you not see that?"

He turned to walk away down the path.

"You are disgusted with me, aren't you?" I said.

"I'm not disgusted," he cried, "but I can't be around you. Do you think I can forget everything so easily? Maybe it was nothing to you, but . . ."

How could he believe that? He must not be allowed to believe that.

"No! No. It wasn't nothing to me. It wasn't that."

He stopped completely, stood still for a moment, and then spun round.

"Then what is it?" he shouted. "Fire and air, woman, what do you want from me?"

In that moment I had no idea. I hadn't thought any further than finding out what he felt.

"I miss you," I said lamely, because it was true.

"Aye, well, you'll get over it."

The bitter coldness of his tone went straight through me. I shrank from him as from frost. This had all been a big mistake. Here I was again, reaching out for someone who didn't want me. Well I would stop now and salvage some pride.

"Yes. Of course," I said with what I hoped was quiet dignity. I turned and walked away from him as quickly as possible.

A few moments later I heard him call my name. He came running up behind me and caught my arm.

"Dion, I'm sorry. That was a terrible thing to say. I was angry. It's just. . . . Please. Tell me what you want from me."

"I really have no idea," I said. I was afraid to look at him.

His hand reached out and touched my shoulder gently. He was so close. I could feel his warm breath on the back of my neck.

"But you miss me. What do you want me to do about that? You know I would do anything for you."

"How can you say that?" I cried. "How can you even touch me knowing what I am. I'm tainted. I'm unclean. It was wicked, what I did."

"You said you still loved him and that you didn't want to see me anymore."

I whirled to face him.

"I don't still love him, not like that. I just long. . . . Oh, maybe I don't even do that. I thought that it was my fault he kept coming back, but of course he would come anyway. But can't you see, Shad, I'm linked to a demon . . . tainted."

"But you don't love him?"

How could he be so dense? Demons weren't like people. You didn't *love* them, you *belonged* to them. "Of course not. Shad, how can you? It's not like he is another man."

He began laughing and suddenly he seized me and started kissing my face.

"You refuse to understand," I cried, though his laughter made me too happy to be really annoyed.

"You are not in love with someone else and you miss me," he said. "What else is there to understand?"

"Everything, you foolish man. It's different. For the rest of my life that demon is going to appear to me in dreams and mirrors and you should not be there to catch its attention. It is dangerous."

"So we won't have a mirror," he said, kissing me again more deeply. "Now don't keep telling me why I should stay away from you, because I'm too happy to listen."

The following morning was just the same as the one before. I wrote names in the roll book while Shad handed out weapons. My mind was as confused as it had been the day before, though about different things. Surely this thing with Shad would all end badly. I was a fool to trust another man. As I became more engrossed in my task, I forgot about everything else. Later when I happened to look up and meet his smiling eyes I was suddenly deliriously happy, fighting off a ridiculous urge to sing aloud.

Around midmorning the work was interrupted when a priest-mage came running up to speak to Mark, the pale young man beside me.

"There is a holy emissary come from our Lord," he cried urgently in Mazdana, the Holy States dialect.

"What does he say?" cried Mark.

"No one knows. He is wounded, as is his party." The priest-mage turned to me and said in faltering Gallian, "Madame, I think they have need of you. There are sick men at the convent."

Strange how people will assume a woman is a healer even when she is dressed in mage's blue.

"Dominic, no!" cried Mark, blushing furiously. "She's not . . ."

Too curious about what had happened to wait and hear what he told his friend, I got up and ran down the main road to the convent.

At the convent gate a crowd of people were milling about. Almost all of the priest-mages from the Holy States seemed to be there.

"I heard there is an emissary from the Patriarch," said Shad, appearing at my shoulder.

"Yes. Come on. Let's go in."

I pushed through the crowd and the guards let us both in through the gate.

"I knew there was a reason I liked you," said Shad, chirpily. "You take me all the best places."

Lady Julia had set up her audience chamber in the abbesses' house. Here we found Ren Daniel, Lord Quercy, and the Klementari council in attendance on the Lady. There were also two men, both of them dusty and one wounded. Beg, looking her most witchlike, was bending over the wounded one, who seemed deeply nervous and greeted me keenly with an "Ah, at last. This must be your healer."

His face fell when Lady Julia told him that this was not a healer but Enna Dion Holyhands the Demonslayer.

"Generations of Morians have considered themselves safe in the hands of the Klementari," she continued tartly. "You should consider yourself lucky that this august lady, who is the best healer in our camp, has time to help you."

The wounded man did his best to relax into Beg's touch, though his smile remained strained.

Lady Julia turned to me and held up a letter.

"These two men are emissaries from the Patriarch," she said. "Three days ago the Holy States Army was attacked and destroyed and the Patriarch now seeks asylum with me."

"The Duke . . ."

"No, Madame," said the unwounded man, whose face was grey with fatigue. "It was a regiment of devils, devils made of fire, and terrible things like dogs that ran on two legs, great hordes of them. They came over the Red Mountains behind us and fell on us suddenly just before dusk. We were not prepared for an attack from behind. The mountains are supposed to be impassable there. They destroyed all our mages first—cut through their defenses and outfought them—and left us to fight alone. Those dog beasts. . . . It was a massacre, Lady. The Patriarch was in the camp that night and we managed to get him safely away, but your cousin Gerard Hawksmoor is dead, though he fought bravely. Most of the rest of the army is dead or scattered. The creatures brought clouds of magical terror with them.''

Both men shuddered in unison.

"It was no fight for mortals, Lady,'' continued the first.

"And they took the mages. We found few of their bodies afterward. The evil in the Waste Land flourishes, Lady.''

"I don't doubt many of our men have found their way to Lammerquais,'' continued the first man. "I only hope that the Duke will deal kindly with them. We were set to go there ourselves, but then news came of your march South, Lady, and the Patriarch was determined to offer you what support we had left.''

"I do condole the Patriarch most earnestly on his losses,'' said Lady Julia. "And I thank him most humbly for his support. Return to your Lord in good cheer and tell him a hearty welcome awaits him here.''

She called Symon over to the table.

"This honored gentleman is the Raven, the war leader of the Klementari and my most valued ally. His servants will bring your party to the camp and see that you have food and healing. This afternoon I shall come myself and speak with the Patriarch. Tell me, is the Elector of the North with you? Yes? I am most pleased to hear of his survival. Good day to you.''

Symon ushered the two men out while the rest of us stood there, too dismayed by their news to speak.

The moment the door closed behind them Lady Julia let out a muffled half cheer.

"Yes!'' she cried, shaking her fist triumphantly in the air.

"Fate turns the cards in my favor at last. Oh, Patriarch, you will help me now."

"My Lady?" I said, blinking in surprise at this reaction.

"Don't you see, Dion? Now my cousin is dead, I am the most acceptable candidate to the Patriarch. He would support a three-legged dog before he supported Leon Sahr. He might even stoop to supporting a woman. I shall be Queen. For with you, Dion," and she took my limp hand as if in a courtly dance, "and with the Patriarchal candidate, and with the support of the Elector of the North I shall have three electors. I shall be Queen. Queen in my own right."

"Madam," said Lord Quercy, bluntly reminding the Lady of what was foremost in the rest of our minds. "This is a mighty chance, but you will excuse me if I point out that this army of Fire Angels and other creatures is no small matter."

She turned to him sharply as if angry, but when she spoke it was lightly.

"Etienne Quercy, you are a killjoy. Remind me to make you my highest adviser when I am Queen. You are right. This demon army is no small matter. Do you think it will attack us? And what do you say, Enna Beg, Enna Dion?"

She did her best to look worried, though exhilaration still shone in her eyes.

I was too overwhelmed by a feeling of horror to speak for a moment. A whole necromantic army. We were impossibly exposed. How could we defend against such a thing?

"He will have used much power in this attack," said Beg. "So many will have been killed. It could be that he has not the resources for another."

I felt a chill at her words. Was this the fate of all those people that had sought safety in Sanctuary? Fodder for this attack?

"He has many of the Burning Light people and troops from the South, who are still withdrawing there, to fuel another one," said Lord Quercy. "And he has the Patriarch's priest-mages too."

"Aye, and they will be worth more to him than ordinary

folk," said Causa. "It's likely that this attack has not exhausted him but replenished him."

Lady Julia's face darkened. "Poor souls. What a fate for them. So, people, what are our chances of being attacked by such an army ourselves?"

"I agree with the ladies," said Lord Quercy. "A magical battle seems possible."

"The omens have never spoken of such an army to my knowledge," said Causa. "But prophecy has been silent before concerning the activities of demonmasters. Perhaps they are too much allied to chaos."

"We cannot know the chances of our being attacked in such a way," said Beg. "We have no way of knowing the Destroyer's strength or his intent."

"Then what are we to do?" said Lady Julia. "How are we to react? It is like expecting the sky to fall upon us at any moment." The room was filled with dismay.

"There is nothing we can do but carry on," said Shad, "and be vigilant. Now we are warned, we will at least give a better account of ourselves than the Patriarch's army."

There was a surprised silence for Shad was not part of this council. Then a voice from the doorway said, "You speak truth, Shad Forest, for all that you speak out of turn."

Symon had returned.

"We have fought Fire Angels before," he said, stalking slowly into the room. "There are things we can do against them. We shall make and issue firepowder bombs to all troops."

"We can have the archers shoot pieces of iron at them," suggested Lord Quercy.

"And we must train the mages to shield the troops rather than attack," said Causa. "I don't doubt that was the mistake the Patriarchal mages made."

"And there are runes . . ." said Beg.

As they began to make plans for our defense against an attack by Fire Angels, the air of dismay lifted. Lady Julia spoke with measured confidence and enthusiasm until even I began to feel hopeful.

"And Lord Quercy, we must make these preparations quickly or we must make them on the move," she said. "I am determined to be on the road to Beenac tomorrow. Events have served my betrothed very well. If the Patriarch's army is indeed wiped out, there can be no bar to His Grace's army following us now. We must get to Beenac before him."

"We were allies only a short time ago," said Shad later as we walked back to our posts. "Now they are our pursuers."

"I can understand why Lady Julia would prefer to be Queen in her own right rather than Leon Sahr's queen," I said.

"Aye, but do you not think it ironic that even with the Patriarch's army destroyed we are in just as great a danger of civil war in Moria as we ever were?"

The order was that all regiments that had been formed by sundown that evening were to move out for Beenac the following morning. A small group would be left behind to act as recruiters and send on latecomers. The Klementari had already begun hiding those priests in the Patriarch's entourage who were too wounded to travel. They had become prizes upon which Fire Angels might now leap. I returned to my nametaking and worked as fast as I could. The stream of men coming to join Julia's army, many of them old and some very young, increased as the afternoon wore on. So intent was I on the task that when the man standing before me gave his name as Lucien Sercel I had almost finished writing it down before it actually registered.

"Lucien," I cried, hugging him. "What are you doing here? Is Tomas with you? You haven't come to drag me back, have you?"

"No, no." he said. "I've decided to throw my lot in with Lady Julia's army. As for Tomas, he did not see things my way, so we agreed to differ."

There was something in the way he spoke that made me ask him if everything was well in Lammerquais.

"Well enough. Can we talk?" he said.

"Surely." I sent one of the guards to find someone to take over for me. "Have you eaten, Lucien? Let's get some food, then."

I could not help wondering if Lord Sandor had sent Lucien to join this army because he thought we might have some chance of winning, and as usual he wanted to have a family member in both camps. But when we had settled with our food on a small patch of grass a little way from the rest of the camp and I asked Lucien if this was so, he was annoyed.

"I can act without my father's orders sometimes," he snapped. "I beg your pardon," he continued, more calmly. "The long and the short of it is that I can no longer give myself to the cause of a man who sets murderers free for policy."

"What do you mean?"

"Darmen Stalker has 'escaped' from prison," he said shortly.

"Do you mean the Duke set him free?"

"The Duke insists that he escaped. It is just that I find it impossible to believe him," said Lucien.

Darmen Stalker had escaped the night before Lady Julia had left Lammerquais. I was astonished. Nothing had been said that whole day and I was almost certain that Lady Julia did not know of it.

The night of the Stalker's escape, Lucien had been dining with the Captain of the Guards and had accompanied the Captain on his rounds. They had, of course, checked Darmen Stalker's quarters and spoken to Stalker himself. He could not say what had made him uneasy; perhaps it was something in Stalker's manner, for the Southerner had seemed more mockingly confident than ever, but when Lucien left the Captain's quarters, he felt an urge to check the prisoner again. He was well known to the guards and had no hesitation about going over to the tower unannounced and looking around.

As he climbed the tower stairs, he was struck by a certain quietness. There was no sign of the two guards who were supposed to be patrolling the corridor and the torches were out further up. Thoroughly alarmed now, Lucien drew his sword and made his way cautiously through the darkness to Stalker's apartments. There was a light under Stalker's door and the sound of voices. As he approached the door, he tripped over the body of man. He was bending to see if the man was dead when he was seized from behind and someone hit him on the head.

He came to lying tied up on Stalker's own bed. The servant found him the following morning, when he came with breakfast. By then Darmen Stalker was well away.

"But we didn't hear anything of this."

"No," said Lucien. "You would have if I'd been well, but since I had a concussion, the healer confined me to my chamber till the next morning. It was then I found that there had been no hue and cry for Stalker. There was an uproar about the fog and Lady Julia's disappearance. Most people thought Stalker had gone with Lady Julia, and the Duke, who had returned by then, begged me to let it remain so. He said it would cause him immeasurable harm if the truth were publicly known and that he was trying to get Stalker back on the quiet. Did you ever hear such flagrant lies? But my father swallowed it like he swallows everything. I, on the other hand, checked, and I know that the Duke made no more than token efforts to regain Stalker. I can see no other reason for his escape then that the Duke willed it so. Stalker must know something very embarrassing about His fine Grace.

"I wanted to challenge the Duke in the open Council, but my father begged me not to bring our family to ruin, and God curse me, I am a Sercel for all he says. But by Karana's sweet child, I can no longer support a man who aids necromancers. That much self-respect I still have. If it ruins me, I shall be better ruined than to follow such a man."

Darmen Stalker set free and one day later an army of Fire Angels and magical creatures comes over the mountains and decimates the Patriarch's army. An army that was very inconveniently opposing the Duke's plans to unify Moria under his own rule. My thoughts turned me cold.

"My God," I said involuntarily. It could not be possible.

There was no proof. But I knew how determined the Duke was to have the crown of Moria.

"Who could believe he would do such a thing?" said Lucien, shaking his head.

Yet it became clear to me as we talked further that he had no knowledge of the attack on the Patriarchal army or of the greater implications of Stalker's escape and I was so horrified by what I suspected that I did not want to tell him.

Instead I excused myself quickly and went off to find Shad, to tell him what I had learned so that he could tell me that I was jumping to conclusions in thinking that the Duke had made a pact with the necromancer in the Waste Land. Instead Shad looked just as shocked as I felt. Even Symon's usually controlled countenance changed when I told him Lucien's news.

"That man has made a pact with evil," he cried. "Have you New People no morals at all?"

"You are the ones who kept secret what you knew about Darmen Stalker," I retorted.

Symon, having spent his anger, merely grunted, "He was only the messenger," and turned away.

That evening I dined with Lady Julia and a crowd of other people notable in her cause. Lucien was there, being made much of. The Patriarch, too, was there, for all that he was heavily bandaged and had to be carried in on a chair. He held the table spellbound with the story of how his army had been attacked, and of his narrow escape from death at the hands of the Fire Angels. As he spoke Lucien's eyes widened. He turned and looked straight at me and I nodded, for I saw that now he too shared my suspicions.

When Lady Julia rose to speak after dinner she said nothing of the matter, however, though I had told her myself of Darmen Stalker's escape. She spoke instead of the plans for the coming day's battle and of how we Morians would ourselves win back our own freedom and purity. Her words were so powerful, so inspiring, that all other thoughts and suspicions left my mind and all that remained was an excited impatience to reach Beenac and a determination to win it no matter the cost.

Such impatience makes for bad sleep. I awoke well before dawn and lay stretched stiffly on my bed, wishing I could go back to sleep but too anxious and excited to do so.

At length I rose and went to pace up and down the cloisters. Here I met Lady Julia doing much the same thing. She took me by the hand and led me into the convent's church, and up the stairs into the belfry. It was the tallest belfry in the town, and we could see everything for miles around, all clear in the early white gold light of dawn: the houses of Vernede huddled around its church, the rolling plains to the east and south of us, the Red Mountains towering away to our west, and the army camped in the pastureland beside the convent. Yesterday it had seemed to cover a great area, but now it seemed pathetically small in the great landscape.

We stood watching as the sun rose and the quietness beneath us began to bustle, seeing the smoke rise from breakfast fires and hearing the distant sounds of horses and voices and the clink of metal.

"I hope to God we have enough men," said Lady Julia softly. "This night I was full of dread that I might be leading us all into a massacre. Who would be a general?"

"We do what we must," I said, because that is how I had comforted myself in the long hours of wakefulness. "That is why we are here in the first place."

"Aye," said Lady Julia. She put her arm round my shoulders and gave me a comradely squeeze. "I am glad to have you with me, Dion, truly I am. When I am Queen I shall remember this morning and all the other things you have done to help me. And I shall be Queen. I feel it in the very heart of me."

·20·

*L*ater that morning as the army lined up to be addressed by Lady Julia, it almost seemed as if we might indeed have enough men.

On one side of the field stood the surviving men of the Patriarchal army, the white and gold colors of the Patriarchate fluttering from their rather battered coats and hats. There were only four regiments, but they were crack regiments of the Patriarchal bodyguard, and despite their bandaged and torn appearance they looked it. With them stood the priest-mages, their black robes laced with white and gold. There were three and a half phalanxes of them now that those the Patriarch had brought with him had been added to the phalanxes traveling with us. The Patriarch had publicly pardoned the renegade priest-mages for breaking away from his army.

Beside the Holy States men stood the great mass of Morians. Every Southerner in the Ducal army must have come with us, and a number of Middle Morians as well. Though most of the Morians were infantry, there were several regiments of horse soldiers. There were also a little over four phalanxes of fighting mages, but the drawback with them was that they had never fought together before. Still, all the Morians wore the red ribbons of the Madragas pinned to their coats and helmets, and their excitement and exuberance was palpable. They showed a distinct tendency to cheer and wave their swords at everything Lady Julia said or did. At the front of this group were the new Southern recruits, badly armored and patchily armed and still wearing the garb of farm workers, craftsmen, merchants, or laborers. If anything they were more wildly beribboned and enthusiastic than the other Morians. They had been placed in the front in this assembly, because in most cases this was the first chance they had had to see Lady Julia, but they were to march at the end of the column and to be kept very much in reserve, for Lady Julia had no taste for sending poorly armed and trained men into battle if it could be avoided. Except for a hard core of experienced guerrilla fighters like Shad, few of the Morian troops had seen any combat.

Finally, to the left of the army, the appropriate side for magic and mystery, were the Klementari.

Was it possible that there were more Klementari than we had started with? They wore their drab brown and green fighting garb and were armed with swords and bows, but although they were lightly armed they looked formidable. Their pale, high-cheekboned faces were calm, their dark eyes unreadable. The light morning breeze blew their wild pale hair even wilder. It was as if the very spirits of the forest and mountains had risen up in cold outrage to smite the necromancer and his demons.

Lady Julia sat high upon a white horse. She spoke brilliantly again, so brilliantly that even though it was almost the same speech I had heard last night, I found myself cheering with the rest of the army.

On a horse beside Julia Madraga sat the teenaged Anton Rouget, son of the Elector of the North and his representative. Lord-Elector Rouget was too badly injured to travel and had sought asylum in a nearby monastery—not before pledging his vote and the vote of his son after him to Lady Julia's rulership, however.

Drawn up alongside them was a litter. The curtains had been opened, and from inside the Patriarch, who had been badly wounded in both legs but who was determined to push south with us, nodded and smiled at the cheering troops.

On Lady Julia's other side sat Symon the Raven, his black cloak spread out over the back of a great silver-colored stallion. The new Southern troops' eyes were upon him as much as they were upon Lady Julia, and I saw they felt a mixture of fear and elation at seeing him there.

It was an army imbued with the spirit of determination that set out on the march to Beenac. The weather was hot and thundery and remained so for the next five days as we marched through the beautiful rolling countryside toward Beenac. At the end of that time it was a far grimmer and even more determined army that arrived at those walls five days later.

This was not because we had been attacked on the way.

There was little sign of the dreaded Soprian mercenaries or of any other of Hierarch Jarraz's troops. In fact, from the day after we left Vernede there was little sign of anybody. The countryside through which we were traveling was green and lush even now in midsummer, when the sun beat down with white heat upon the troops and the air felt like it had been in an oven. Tall shady forests of sweet oil and mountain ash stood on the hills, and in the valleys the midsummer crops stood tall in the fields. They were untended, however, and might never be gathered, for every village and town we came to was deserted, completely empty of any life form bigger than a dog. At first there were signs of violence, burned houses and once or twice mass graves. In the fields and in the village squares were the huge charred circles that seemed to mark the landing places of Fire Angels.

Once we came upon the corpse of a creature that looked like a man but was much hairier and had the face of a savage dog. It smelled terribly and had been dead some days, but was surprisingly intact, as if its flesh was too bitter for the wild dogs, which usually fed upon dead things.

Several times I saw the heartbreaking sight of men breaking from the column to run through these burned or deserted villages shouting the names of families or loved ones.

Then as we passed on into the area that had been most

heavily settled by the Burning Light, the signs of violence disappeared and there were only the empty villages, deserted in the bleak white heat with no sound in them except the deafening grating of the cicadas.

There were people to be found, however, and it was from them that we pieced together what had happened. All through the past few weeks, Hierarch Jarraz's troops had been moving through the countryside, rounding up people to be moved to Sanctuary, where it was promised that they would build a new life free from interference by Northerners and their evil magical slaves. Many of the people we spoke to believed wholeheartedly in Sanctuary, but had not been able to bring themselves to leave farms or homes. Only a few from the burned villages at the start of our march had been suspicious of Hierarch Jarraz's motives, and even these had no thought of necromancy. They were people ignorant of magery who thought the Fire Angels were messengers of God on earth. They had had no news apart from what their priests had told them, and since travel had been strictly controlled they had known little of the world outside Southern Moria. What a terrible trick had been played on these people, and how horribly easy it had been for the trickster.

The probable nature of Sanctuary was now well-known among the army. The horror of the fact that we had come too late to prevent the terrible fate of all these innocent fools settled onto us like the heat. At first there was depression and despair among the troops, but as we traveled through the oppressive sultry landscape, that anguish turned to bitter, slow-burning anger.

For days we held ourselves ready for a magical attack, but the mercilessly blue sky remained empty. On the third night Shad told me that he no longer expected one.

"The necromancer in the waste has sucked everything he wants out of the Burning Light and has abandoned what is left to us. He has no more use for Southern Moria and no reason to fight us for it."

Yet I knew the Klementari still feared a magical attack and I knew that I was the reason they feared it.

The night before we left Vernede, Beg and Causa had come to my room in the convent bringing the iron necklace.

"You must wear this on the road to Beenac," said Causa. "It protected you from the angels once. It may protect you again."

"To my mind," said Beg, "that is why he attacked us on the road south that time. It was a wild chance, but he might have caught us unawares and carried you off."

"I am not a package," I said, annoyed by her words because they frightened me.

"You are as big a prize to the Destroyer as you ever were," snapped Beg, "and out in the open with nowhere to hide and only our small army to protect you, you may pose a great temptation to him."

"She is right," said Causa. "We can think of no other reason why he would attack us. Even if he is the Duke's ally, it is nothing to him if the Duke and Lady Julia fall out. In fact such chaos is a friend to necromancy. Wear the necklace and stay with our troops."

On the road to Beenac I slept among the Klementari, under a blanket covered in runes to hide me. All day a group of them followed me around. I found their constant presence an oppressive reminder, but I bore with it. Only once did I try to slip away from them, one hot afternoon after we had made camp beside a river, when I went down to the river to swim. A furious Symon appeared just after I had entered the water and dragged me out onto the bank and berated me loudly as I stood there in my dripping shift.

"How can you be so heedless?" he shouted, "Will you kill us all? Try to rid yourself of the idea that you are invulnerable, Enna. Five Fire Angels could defeat even you."

Meanwhile Causa stood by looking at me reproachfully. It was her stare which really brought me to a sense of my own carelessness. I did not misbehave again.

But throughout this hot, dusty, and oppressive journey, there was happiness.

Shad was there and every night we slept our exhausted sleep side by side.

* * *

The army arrived at Beenac just after midday on the fifth day. It was another sultry day. The overcast sky was the color of metal, though the hot air offered little promise of rain.

The Hierarch's fortress rose like a tall spike out of the flat green plain of the Roussel River. The town that huddled on one side of it was like something built by ghosts, and the silence of the plain was so great we could hear the shutters banging in the wind. All afternoon I was aware of that deep silence behind the hubbub of the army.

However, Beenac's emptiness made it possible to send patrols under cover of the town to the very walls of the fortress. Though Symon reported that there were people in the fortress and Hierarch Jarraz's residential flag fluttered from the central tower, there was no sign that those within were preparing for a siege. The houses at the fortress walls had not been destroyed and it was decided that even though this might be some kind of trap, we should attack from this side where our troops would have some kind of cover.

The attack was set for the following morning, so we spent that afternoon digging trenches on the western side of the fortress away from the town to prevent anyone escaping from the fortress and to provide some cover if we were attacked on our left flank from the Red Mountains. While near Lammerquais the Red Mountains had been almost impassible, here they were little more than low hills, with the Sanctuary on the site of the old capital only a couple of days' ride beyond them.

Then, around mid-afternoon the gates of the fortress opened and a small group of riders came out, every one of them bearing the green flag of peace. Though a muttering arose from among the troops when they saw Burning Light priests among the company, the flag was respected.

The party had come to surrender the fortress to Lady Julia.

"Has everyone gone to Sanctuary?" asked Lady Julia. By now our horror over the fate of the people in the Waste Land had settled into a kind of grey acceptance of inevitability.

From his fresh face, I judged the priest who led the party

to be even younger than me. His responsibilities sat heavily on his stiff young back. He was a true believer, however.

"Aye, Lady," he said. "The Waste Land has been promised to the Holy Ones. We shall cleanse it with our righteousness and build Tanza's holy city on earth there. The Holy Ones have no further need for the places of evil, where the past continues to taint us with its sin."

"And the non-Holy," said the Patriarch suavely. "Where are they?"

If the boy was daunted at speaking with the Patriarch, he did not show it. Perhaps he did not care. The Patriarch and the Orthodox Church were highly compromised in the eyes of the true Burning Light believer. This was part of the reason the Patriarch had finally turned against them.

"There were none left," the boy-priest replied calmly. "They have been cleansed with fire and labor. They went to prepare our way many months ago as the Hand of Truth found and condemned them. Already they have made a starting place for us and hopefully they have seen the error of their ways."

"Then why have you stayed behind?" asked Julia.

"Hierarch Jarraz is too ill to be moved."

"Hierarch Jarraz is there in the fortress?" cried Lady Julia. "Then I shall go this minute and speak with him."

"He cannot speak, Lady. He has been seized by holy visions. He has not known anyone for this month or more. It is a blessed state, but hard upon his earthly shell."

"He is mad, in other words, and they abandoned him," snapped Lady Julia.

A mulish look came into the boy's face. The Patriarch touched Lady Julia's arm warningly. "Indeed, Hierarch Jarraz is most blessed," he said. "Mother Karana speaks to him, doesn't she?"

"Mother Karana has chosen him for her special mouthpiece on earth. He has a blessed statue that she gave him herself. It weeps at the sin in the world and lifts up its hand in blessing. I have seen it myself." The boy's voice became more passionate now. "Lord Patriarch, he is truly a blessed man. But the visions come so thick and fast that he no longer knows me or any of us. He does not eat or sleep. A transformation comes upon him. I fear he is soon to be taken from us. The rest of us are willing to suffer for his sake, but my Lords and Ladies, I beg of you, if you have any mercy in your hearts, please leave him to follow his path."

There was a startled silence. The boy struggled not to weep.

"Yet our mages say there is evidence of demon activity in the fortress," said the Patriarch. "What do you say to that?"

"*Mages!*" said the boy, as if the Patriarch had made an obscene remark, which I suppose in a sense he had. The Burning Light had no trust in mages.

The boy regained his diplomacy.

"Holy father, there is nothing of that kind. I know there are rumors, but I assure you, your mages must be mistaken."

"Have the Burning Light ever looked for demon activity?" said Lady Julia.

"I am certain there is none to find," said the boy.

Lady Julia accepted the surrender of Beenac, but the minute the boy left the tent there was a spirited discussion about whether she should be the one to actually lead the advance party into the fortress. After a short sharp argument, in which Symon was supported by the Patriarch (more strange bedfellows), she conceded that it would be safer if Symon, at the head of a party of mages and soldiers, was the one to take over the fortress. We could not know what necromantic traps might have been left. The Klementari had had the fortress under magical observation since we arrived, and though most of its magic was the weak rosy glow of priestly magic, there was a core of necromantic magic at the fortress' center. Symon's observation had been supported by the Patriarch's priest-mages, and when Lady Julia asked me to cast a Bowl of Seeing, the small point of necromancy was clear for everybody to see.

"I wonder," said the Patriarch thoughtfully. After a moment's pause he said carefully, "Almost three years ago the Council of Hierarchs sent Hierarch Jarraz on a mission to see how the Great Waste could be renewed. He told me later that while he was standing among the broken walls of the old capitol, Ruinac, he had a vision. The vision showed him where to find the statue of Mother Karana. He told me it was promised that she would guide him in creating the Kingdom of God in the South and show him where sin still lurked. Certainly later it seemed to enable him to predict floods, fires, and famine.

"Yet it has seemed to me and others that it was with the finding of this statue that the Burning Light took its wrong turn."

This was not my reading of the situation at all. In my humble opinion the Burning Light had been wrong from its very inception. I did not make this unnecessarily divisive remark, however.

"Tell me Holy Father, did Darmen Stalker appear among the Patriarch's train at the same time?" asked Lucien.

"Darmen Stalker the Soprian secretary? Oh perhaps so. That's right. He was accused of necromancy at Lammerquais, wasn't he? Well I don't remember him earlier. He was a charming man who always carried out Jarraz's orders most efficiently."

I knew what Lucien was thinking. Stalker could just as easily have been the cause of necromancy as the statue of Karana. Perhaps in the ruins of Ruinac he had somehow appeared and insinuated himself into Hierarch Jarraz's party without being noticed. Or perhaps he had attached himself to the Hierarch's entourage and been promoted with advice from Karana.

It was beginning to look as if Jarraz, who had seemed to be the source of necromancy in this land, was just as much a dupe as the rest of the Burning Light. Tomorrow would tell for certain. But if he was not the demonmaster, who was? Darmen Stalker? Surely he would not have put himself in such danger if he were the center of the whole plot.

"Hierarch Jarraz was such a pure soul," sighed the Patriarch. "He had his whole heart fixed on Aumaz and his way. Yet, for a long time I have wondered if he had somehow gone astray. When one of the other Hierarchs from the Council fled to Mangalore six months ago and told me of the Fire Angels, Jarraz's visions, and this statue of Karana and where they all seemed to be leading the Burning Light, I had to withdraw my support."

"So you think this statue of Karana is the source of the necromancy we see in the Bowl of Seeing, Holy Father?" said Lady Julia incredulously.

"It is hard to believe that Lord Tanza would tolerate such a despoiling of his mother's image by evil, is it not?" said the Patriarch. "Nonetheless, Lord Raven, I urge you to give this statue your special attention when you enter the fortress."

The following morning the party to accept the surrender of Beenac set out. It consisted of the best phalanx of ordinary mages led by Ren Daniel, a phalanx of priest-mages, a party of twenty soldiers to guard us, led by Shad, and a similar number of Klementari who were dressed as warriors, but who could have had all kinds of powers. Beg also accompanied us. She had come to me that morning as I was dressing and had insisted on painting an enormous rune of protection on my bare back. I could feel its stickiness now on my sweaty skin. I shuddered to think what substances the paint might contain.

I went too, although initially I had not been invited to join the party. I had insisted on coming, however, for I wanted to see for myself that the Fortress of Beenac was free of demons. It was finally something useful that I could do. Symon was not pleased, however, and as we processed slowly toward the gates of the fortress he and Beg drew up their horses on either side of me.

"You are to stick close to me," he said sharply and without preamble.

"Fair enough," I said, a little put out by his attitude. Did he think I was some raw apprentice?

"I mean it. Do you not think this is a fine opportunity for him to separate you from the rest of us so that he can overcome you? An arrow in the back or a poisoned dart would stop you as quickly as the rest of us. And there are always witch manacles. And you," he said to Shad, who had dropped a little behind to allow them to talk to me. "You will oblige me by watching Enna Dion's back as if your life depended on it."

"I will be like her shadow," said Shad. "I know how much you need Enna Dion even if she does not. Between him and Beg, they have not one half your power, Dion."

Symon scowled fiercely at Shad.

"Thank you very much for that helpful contribution," he snapped. Then he turned and faced me, though I noticed he did not look me in the eye. "What he says is true enough. That is why we let you come. But be careful."

He drew his horse away from us.

"You were very frank with Symon," I said to Shad, amused at this exchange. I had always known that I was more powerful than Beg and Symon, though I would have been surprised if Shad was right as to the extent of it. Both of them were far more cunning and experienced than I, however, and to my mind this counted for much more than raw power.

"Well, he annoys me. He never gives you your due."

"He says a lot worse things to you."

Shad smiled. "That's different."

The high narrow courtyard of the Hierarch's fortress was lined with enormous white statues of the saints. Memories of the long avenue of statues in fevered dark dreams prickled through my skull. Tasha's memories, I reminded myself. They were unlikely to be memories of Beenac.

Those remaining in the fortress had assembled in the center of the courtyard. There were about forty ordinary guards and serving men and over twenty priests, none of whom wore the garb of priest-mages. As we entered, the young boy priest came running toward the party, his face anxious and strained.

He hesitated a few moments at who to approach, for the choice between mage and Klementari can hardly have been enticing for a priest of his calling, before he ran to my side, probably assuming that I was a healer.

"Enna! The Hierarch will not come out of his room! I have been up there all morning trying to get him to come out. We tried to break down the door, but there is some magic involved."

"Can you hear him on the other side?" said Symon, swinging down from his horse.

"I have heard his voice. He sounded weak. I could not hear what he was saying."

Ren Daniel Devoirs made an exasperated noise. "Can't we just leave him there till we get this fortress sorted out?"

"Should we leave a sick man behind a locked door?" I said. "Especially when it is Hierarch Jarraz."

"She is right," said Symon. "The Hierarch is the hub of this fortress. We must see what can be done."

Leaving some of the mages and men-at-arms in the court-yard to search and guard the prisoners, the rest of us followed the boy up the great white marble stairs. He led us down a series of wide corridors until we were on the other side of the fortress. Through tiny slit windows I could glimpse our army camped on the plain below.

"Stay with us," hissed Shad, gripping my arm, and with a brief sense of shame, I realized that I had slowed to look out of the windows.

The corridors were lined with statues, and in between many of them were great gold-framed mirrors.

"A good bit of money's been spent on this nest," muttered one of the men-at-arms, but money was not what I thought of when I saw mirrors and statues. Demons and dreams of demons. These corridors seemed full of vague echoes of magic.

The boy stopped before a pair of huge brass doors. They were most definitely locked and bolted from the inside. He called out to Hierarch Jarraz, but there was no answer. We looked at each other uncertainly, and then Beg held up a flat stone that glowed with sullen red light.

"There is magic here," she said. She did not name it as necromancy, though that was obviously what it was. "Tell me, lad, is this the room where the Holy Statue of Karana is kept?"

The boy-priest nodded.

It looked like the Patriarch was right and this room was the source of the necromancy in the fortress. We had to go in.

"Let me open the door," I said.

The boy protested that Hierarch Jarraz would be alarmed by magic, but he was overruled. Beg and I checked the door for magical traps and wardings, while the mages and Klementari grouped around us and the men-at-arms drew their swords and fidgeted nervously with their magically enhanced armor.

There was no special spell on the door. I slid my power into its lock and clicked it open and then heaved the bar off its supports.

We heard it clatter to the ground in the silence beyond. The door swung open. Shad slid forward to stand beside me.

For a moment we were blinded by the sunlight coming in through the great windows at the back of the room. Then, through the glare, I saw a large hunched shape in the center of the room. I stepped forward, power at my fingertips, but as my eyes became accustomed to the glare, I saw it was just another huge statue: Mother Karana with her dying son Tanza lying across her lap, her hand resting delicately and lovingly upon his cheek. The same tableau could be seen in thousands of chapels all over the country. Yet as my eyes searched the room for the source of the necromancy which even now I could sense in air, the boy-priest behind us gasped and cried out.

He rushed past me and at that moment I realized that the body across the knees of the Holy Mother was not stone, but an elderly man made of flesh, clothed in a long, dirty white nightgown. His eyes were open, gazing with adoration at

Karana's face just as she gazed back at him, but from the way the boy fell to his knees before them, wailing, I knew the man was dead.

I ran forward to comfort the boy, and to check that the man was indeed dead. His skin was dry and powdery under my hands, as if all moisture had been drained out of him, and yet it was still warm.

"Oh Enna," wept the boy at my feet. "He is gone. He is gone."

I put my hand gently on his bent golden head.

"Look out," cried a voice behind me. Instinctively I ducked, covering my head, whirling around. Something huge whistled past my cheek. I twisted toward the source. Someone shouted again and I saw the boy, who somehow was standing now, fall to the ground.

The statue! Mother Karana was moving. One of my arms was in the crushing grip of her great stone hands. She rose before me straight and tall, far taller than I, pulling me up into the air like a limp rag doll. Her eyes were red and they bored into my own, transfixing me. I felt her heat, the great pulling power of her sucking at the edges of my being. Her other stone fist groped at my throat.

Blasts of power burst all around us, chipping the stone of her skin, showering me with grit.

Hah! She wasn't so strong. I had her measure now. I heaved out a great burst of power, pushing her, flinging her away.

There was pain as we separated, as if something had ripped away from my being. *Smash!* She shattered with a great booming explosion. The world was filled with bits of white stone and I was falling. I brought magic up to shield myself from the sharp cloud of stone, and then I found myself sprawled on the floor, Shad beneath me clinging to my waist. Nearby sprawled the boy priest, a knife in his dead hand. The spreading pool of blood around him turned pink as the cloud of white dust settled over him.

I had no thought for any of these things. I leaped to my feet. The demon was gone from the room, but in my head I could hear its laughter. The palace was full of statues, statues and mirrors, and just because I had destroyed the current form didn't mean it couldn't find another to animate.

The red glow had gone out of Beg's stone. I snatched it from her hand and raced into the corridor, the others at my heels.

Suddenly there was shouting in the courtyard below us. Statues! I flung open one of the huge windows. Three storeys below us, the statues in the courtyard were moving; life flickered back and forth in them like a candle flame. The staff of the palace stood stock still, but our party was huddled together like frightened children, men-at-arms' weapons pointed first one way, then another, mages unsure if or where to blast.

Even as I watched, one of the statues at the opposite side of the courtyard seized two of the men and lifted them screaming into the air. Their life force shimmered in the air around the statue's head. Their struggles weakened.

Without even thinking, I leaped up onto the window frame and out into the courtyard.

"No, no, it's a trap," shouted someone behind me, and arms grabbed at me. As I swept smoothly downward, feeling the air whooshing past my face, I discovered someone was clinging to me.

"Shad! What are you doing?" I gripped him around the waist. The hilt of his sword dug into my ribs.

"It's a trap. Look! Defend yourself."

The palace staff were pulling weapons out from among the statues and attacking our men-at-arms. A firefight had begun between the mages and the priests. In range now, I threw out a blast of power that smashed the moving statue, but it was empty even before the blow hit. I caught the captive men as they dropped through the air, but they were only husks now.

Our feet thudded on stone as we landed, but I was already caught up with another statue, which had flung itself forward to crush our men. I smashed it away already empty and whirled to look for the next.

Shad was fighting six men armed with swords and staffs. A blast of magic hit him in the sword arm. I shot out a smash of power that threw all six of them across the courtyard. An arrow whizzed past my head. Someone came at me with a sword and was flung away. Other shapes were floating down into the courtyard from above, and a great black bird came swooping . . .

A huge stone fist slammed into a row of statues and they collapsed toward us. I blasted them backward. Behind me steel rang upon steel. I smashed the moving statue. Another moved behind it and I smashed that too. Behind it the next and the next moved. Life flowed like a stream along a great path of statues leading out through the arch and I followed, running as fast as I could. It was like trying to swat a fly. I smashed and destroyed the white marble shapes, sometimes ahead of the demonic life in them and sometimes behind, but never right on. They could read minds, of course. Would it have cared if I had caught it? Likely not. But it would suck the life out of whoever it could get near so it had to be tracked down and driven out somehow.

There were big brass doors on the far side of that courtyard. I flung them open. Inside was some kind of chapel. Mirrors and statues lined the walls. Only some of them were safely behind iron grills.

The statues were smaller this time and none of them moved. I hesitated cautiously at the doorway, horribly afraid I had lost it. I did not think it needed to travel from statue to statue. Rather, each statue was somehow an opening between this world and the demon's, as were mirrors. Some powerful magic had made it possible for the demon to animate the stone like a hand animates a glove puppet. It was the same kind of principle that allowed the Fire Angels to animate fire. The demon could probably appear in any suitable statue anywhere in the castle, and might even now be back in the courtyard slaughtering our people. And I was alone here and no doubt vulnerable. I shouldn't have run off.

Then as I turned to run back to the courtyard, I looked down and saw I was still clutching Beg's magic stone. I let a little power seep into it. It glowed hot red. Something using necromancy was nearby. At that moment Shad came dashing out from under the arch toward me, a great black bird flying behind him.

There was a smash at the end of the church. A statue had toppled from its pedestal. Without thinking further, I ran down the aisle toward it, keeping myself magically shielded, eyes wide open. There was another smash as I rounded into the next corridor. Large iron gates barred my way, beyond them more statues and mirrors. The stone glowed red in my hand. The iron gates were unlocked and I pushed them open. They creaked. I did not go through but waited.

Something growled. Two stone dogs at the other end of the hall were baring their teeth at me, not together but flickering back and forth with stunning speed. Their growling made the very air vibrate. I stepped closer. Perhaps if I could get a field of magic around them, I could dispel the demon within.

"Behind you," someone shouted.

That voice. I whirled just as a club swung past my head. Suddenly there were men everywhere, grabbing at me, hitting me, open witch manacles coming at me. A numbing blast of power hit me, flung me to the ground. I was drowning in a sea of hands and legs and iron manacles.

Witch manacles reached for my neck. I screamed and let out a frenzied heave of power, flinging them away with all my strength. Away, away. All away. The whole world dissolved in a shattering red mist.

Suddenly it was very quiet. I heaved myself up from the floor. I was bloodsoaked and covered in bits. Bits of flesh. The walls were spattered with blood. Oh God! I hated witch manacles, feared them above all things. I had flung those men away as hard as I could.

But as I sat there dripping with blood and mush, I did not think of the carnage. In the shattered glass of a mirror stood Bedazzer, wearing the body of my beloved Andre.

"Fool. They would have had you had I not called out. Don't you know to be more careful?"

He leaned close to the mirror's face.

"I have saved your life. I have saved your life because you are mine to save. And I will suffer no one else to have you. Remember that."

A huge black bird came sweeping round the corner and flew at the mirror, with great black wings and flapping claws outstretched as if to drive the demon off. But he had already gone.

Shad was there, shouting and reaching out for me. He was lifting me up and now I could see everything, all the bodies in crumpled heaps strewn around like old clothes. Blood everywhere. Red blotches in my eyesight. All the men I had killed. *I* had killed them. I really did belong to Bedazzer.

There was blood on Shad's face and neck where I had touched him. It would always be like that. He would always be touched by my uncleanness.

Suddenly something snapped inside me. A tremendous rage came screaming out. I hadn't wanted this. I hadn't meant this. I didn't want this filthy blood staining me and staining Shad. I didn't want Bedazzer and his way. I wanted to smash those mirrors. I wanted to smash them so hard the shattered glass would blast back the demon plane, blast so hard that it would shatter the foul beast behind them. Tear and rip and smash.

I don't remember much more. There was running and screaming and smashing, savage, satisfying smashing. The air was full of shards of glass and stone as I pulverized every piece of marble and glass I could see.

Then suddenly I was outside standing on grass. The great whirling screaming mass of emotions was gone, leaving me bereft, leaving a terrible emptiness that began to fill up with choking sobs.

Symon appeared at my side and took my arm in a firm grip. I tried to struggle but I was too busy fighting the sobs inside me.

"Come," he said. He marched me up to a big fountain in the center of the courtyard and pushed me into it. The blood washed from my skin to stain the greenish water red.

* * *

Eventually Beg and a couple of Klementari healers managed to get all the shards of glass out of me. They put me under a painkilling sleep. Evening was falling when I awoke. My face, hands, and arms stung.

"No permanent damage," said Beg sourly. "An outcome entirely undeserved by you, Madame. Such stupidity I have rarely seen. Could you not have shielded yourself? Well, your admirers need not sigh. These little cuts all over you will be gone in a couple of days. If you don't forget to heal them."

Her remark reminded me of Shad and I asked her where he was.

"He is in the Hierarch's audience chamber with the rest of them," she said, as if this were the sign of some great moral failing.

The fortress had been taken and the phalanxes of mages had cleansed it of all traces of necromancy. The surviving Burning Light followers had been taken prisoner. All the statues and mirrors had been destroyed and the red dragon of the Madragas was now flying from the top tower. Lady Julia, who had come in to peer anxiously at me sometime during Beg's proceedings, had come to take symbolic possession of the fortress, though she had returned to her camp on the plains outside until the fortress could be made ready for her.

I got up and put on the new mage's robes that had been laid out for me. I felt strangely cleansed after my enraged dash through the fortress church. I did not belong to Bedazzer. I knew that now, no matter what he believed.

In the Hierarch's audience chamber a small group of soldiers were playing dice in the middle of the floor with two mages. A barrel was sitting on a once-elegant table, red wine in a puddle under its tap. Another group of fellows was sitting on the steps of the dais, blearily singing bawdily modified hymns. Mark, the young priest-mage I had worked with, was curled up asleep on the Hierarch's throne with one of the Hierarch's headdresses lopsidedly balanced on his head.

One or two of the more sober and less intent let out a kind of muffled cheer as I came into the room. They seemed remarkably benign for drunks, though perhaps Shad's well-known interest in me was what kept them polite.

"'E's in 'ere, Enna," yelled one of them, pointing to an alcove.

Shad was sitting in a window embrasure with his knees drawn up to his chest and his head back against the wall, eyes closed as if he were asleep. Golden evening light flooded warmly over him.

As soon as he saw me, one of the three men playing cards on the floor beneath him turned and poked Shad's leg with the hilt of a dagger.

"Hey, Forest! Lady to see you."

Then, with elaborate casualness, they picked up their cards and left the room.

Shad blinked awake.

"Thanks a lot, fellas," he said ironically as he watched his companions creep away.

Suddenly I was filled with terrible conflicting emotions, the chief among them being fear. I had no defenses against this man. I was completely at his mercy. What if . . . ?

"How are you, then?" he said, holding out his hand. I was almost afraid to look in his eyes but I took his hand anyway. The feel of his skin was like going home.

"Fine," I said. "Beg says I shall retain what beauty I have."

His eyes twinkled "Good."

He drew me into his arms. "You certainly feel all right."

"Oh, Shad, How can you? After what I did. All those men . . ."

"You killed them pretty throughly, didn't you," said Shad wryly. "But then they were set to harm you after all. They could not expect much better."

"I didn't have to kill. . . . And afterwards I was so out of control. I didn't know what I was doing. Bedazzer appeared. He told me I belonged to him and I couldn't bear it anymore.

Oh, Shad! I could have done something awful. I was out of my mind with anger.''

"Were you?" he said. "I knew you were angry but you didn't hurt anyone. In fact you seemed to be very careful to avoid doing so."

"You're not shocked?"

"Shocked? Why should I be shocked? I always knew what you were capable of." He smiled and put his arm round my shoulders. "And it's always seemed to me that you were the best person to have such power."

He squeezed me.

"You are a wonderful woman, you know that?"

The look in his eyes made me acutely embarrassed. I put my head on his shoulder and tried not to blush like a fool.

"What do you know? You're a lunatic," I said. "You jumped out of a window after me."

"I couldn't let you go into a trap alone," he said.

I put my arms around him and I kissed him and kissed him again and felt him hold and kiss me back. It seemed a wondrous thing to love and be so loved in return.

◆21◆

It was two weeks after we had taken Beenac and I was sitting in one of the fortress tower rooms, looking out over the great golden plain beneath. All around I could see small figures cutting swaths through the ripe wheat. Lady Julia's Army of Liberation was bringing in the harvest.

Shortly after we had arrived, Lady Julia, with the smiling Patriarch looking on, had formally announced her candidacy for the throne. Any who did not support her were encouraged to leave. Few did, and Ren Daniel and the other mages were surprisingly still with us. Since then the fortress had been preparing for a siege.

The Duke had not moved from Lammerquais, but he had sent a negotiating team. Moria was now divided into three parts, with the Duke holding Central Moria, Lady Julia holding the sparsely populated South, and Elector Rouget's troops still holding Northern Moria for the Patriarch. Since the Patriarch had pledged his support to Lady Julia, the North technically belonged to her, but in reality the question of who ruled Moria was unresolved and would remain so until one of the players took the initiative. The only movement was the tiny trickle of Central and Northern Morians who daily came to Beenac to join Lady Julia's army.

The Klementari were no longer with us. Their eyes were

too firmly focused on Ernundra, which was only three days'
ride from Beenac, to linger in the fortress. They were already
beginning to dig in among the Red Mountains and rumor
had it that sometime soon they would begin an assault on
Sanctuary.

The split had not been an amicable one.

Lady Julia had begged and pleaded with them not to go,
and when all else failed she had screamed at Symon. They
say redheads have hot tempers. "They" spoke true.

"You told me I would be Queen," Lady Julia had
screamed, looking as if she was about to bear down on Symon like a fireball.

"And so you shall be. But we must return to Ernundra
now. We cannot sacrifice one foretelling for another. Will
you come with us?"

"You know I cannot. The Duke would take Beenac and
then what would I have?"

"Then our ways must part," he said.

"You promised me. Do not leave me, Symon," she
shrieked. "I need you. The Duke will eat us alive. Please."

But he was gone from the room without another word,
leaving her to weep and rage and then with surprising speed
to dry her face and assume a calm and queenly pose again.

I knew how she felt, for the night before I had asked
Symon when we were moving on to Sanctuary and he had
said, "There is no we, for you are not coming with us."

It was like being slapped in the face. I could only gasp
and say, "Why not," to which Symon told me that they did
not want to make the effort of protecting me.

"I shall protect myself," I cried. "What do you mean,
effort? I can help your cause."

"We do not want to you to come. It is better if you stay
here in the fortress where you will be safe. You are too big
a prize for the necromancer."

"I can help," I said, hurt by being referred to as a mere
thing. "I want to see this necromancer gone. I want to use
my power against him. Linked with the other mages, I could
give my power, I could make a difference."

But I knew as I said it that the Klementari would have already asked for my power had they wanted it. They had their own way of doing things and I was not trained in it.

"You can help us most by not leaving the fortress and not being caught," snapped Symon. "Ever since you have come to Moria we have had the added burden of protecting you when all our hearts were aimed at Ernundra. Do not further hinder us now, by insisting on coming with us and forcing us to protect you."

I had gained great confidence and satisfaction from the feeling that I was being useful. It was shattering to realize that I had been no more than a nuisance.

Later as I wept in Shad's arms, I looked back and saw that despite all my power, I had been too doubtful and confused most of the time to do anything useful.

Shad made comforting noises, but finally he said, "It is true that you would probably be more useful against a conventional army to whom you represent a genuine threat than against this necromancer to whom you might be an opportunity. You might do real good staying here and supporting Julia. When the Klementari go, as go they will, she will be in a very weak position, a very tempting target for the Duke."

"I do not care," I said crossly. "What importance are petty internecine squabbles, when this Destroyer is still loose in the Waste Land?"

If truth be told I was becoming a little disillusioned with Lady Julia Madraga, and her argument with Symon the following day only confirmed my suspicions. She had liberated the South, but I began to suspect that just like the Duke her ambition was more focused on the crown than on destroying the necromancer. Now that she was holed up in the fortress of Beenac, a real contender for the Morian crown, those of her people who might still be alive at Sanctuary had become expendable.

Now it had come to negotiating teams again. The whole situation had much the same feel as the situation in Lammerquais had, for all that the main actors in that drama had been different.

"What was it you once said to me about the Duke?" said Shad when I shared my thoughts with him. "Who can blame her if she looks to her own advantage?"

I blamed her, because if she had had any decency she would have gone with the Klementari. She would have made the destruction of the necromancer her first priority. Then maybe I could have gone, too.

Yet on another level I knew these were only angry ravings. Despite it all, Lady Julia would still be the best ruler for Moria, and part of me understood that her most logical next step was to stay at Beenac and prepare for civil war.

When the Patriarch, who should have been my natural enemy, asked me to help train his mages in the defense of the Beenac fortress, I agreed. He and the young priest-mage Mark showed me how to operate the Bowls of Seeing and to balance and rebalance the runes that protected the fortress, and were satisfyingly impressed when they discovered that I could do the work of a team of mages by myself.

I helped Shad to train the troops in much the same way as we had done in Lammerquais. While I did not really think these games worth anything compared to the battle that the Klementari faced, I did my best to be useful, and my hurt pride was somewhat mollified by the signs of appreciation for my efforts that I saw all around.

For several days Lucien Sercel had been out helping with the harvest, but being a Lord's son he had no experience at using a scythe. His hands were blistered and on the fourth day he had torn a muscle in his shoulder so badly that Shad had begged him to give up.

So that morning Lucien was sitting beside me as I watched the men in the fields below. We were talking of Lady Julia.

"The keeping of power has its own necessities, and good and evil do not play a part in them," said Lucien very wisely. "In the end it is a matter of levels. We know that she has not made a pact with the necromancer and that makes her the preferable ruler."

"Though she is still prepared to marry the Duke, even though she knows he has."

"There now, Dion, you see, you are judging her by good and evil again. Morally it's not the best decision, but politically it's a very wise one. She is letting the Duke know that even if he does not rule, his son will. It might keep him from remaining our enemy, turn him into our protector in fact. It is an excellent consolation prize."

At that moment the door opened and a voice said, "Hello, you two." And there was Tomas standing in the doorway, covered in road dust.

We rushed over and embraced him in delight. Though he returned our embraces warmly, there was something about his manner which made me ask quickly, "Is everything well in Lammerquais . . . ? Did the Duke . . ."

"No, all is well there," said Tomas. "The Duke forgives Lord Sercel for the sins of his sons and Lord Sercel remains a friend to the Holyhands family. When I last saw her Silva sent her love. No, I did not come south for you, sister. I've come looking for Dally. You haven't seen her, have you?"

"Dally? No!" I cried. "What . . ."

"Shortly after you left Lammerquais she disappeared. Karac and I tracked her south as far as we could. But she traveled surprisingly fast for a girl on foot and we never caught her."

"Karac?" said Lucien. "How could he be with you?"

Tomas smiled, though it was only a shadow of his usual smile. His face looked worryingly tired.

"We broke him out of jail. Silva and I knew we needed a mage. He was desperate to come. All the love he should have given Tasha he feels now for Dally. He helped track Dally to the Red Mountains."

"Oh, no, Tomas, you don't think . . ."

"Aye, sister, it looks as if Dally's taken these new magical powers of hers and gone into the Waste Land to avenge her mother's death. It is just the kind of thing she would do, I'm afraid. The kind of thing Tasha would have done. And now Karac has gone after her."

"Oh, no!" I cried.

"He would burn himself alive for her. I thought I had talked him out of it. We had seen what forces were arrayed against us. The Fire Angels were attracted every time we used magic to search for her, and we were almost caught several times. The last time, we would have been burned to cinders had not a patrol of Klementari rescued us.

"They took us back to see Symon, and I agreed, and I thought Karac agreed too, that we would join them when they made their push to Sanctuary. But in the morning Karac was gone. Oh God, Dion. He will never make it to Sanctuary alone, a mage like him. And part of me feels I should have gone with him."

Lucien and I both protested loudly that it was insane to go into the Waste Land after Dally and Karac, and Tomas nodded solemnly and agreed that there was no reason to throw his life after theirs. Nonetheless I could see he still felt it.

He still intended to go into the Great Waste with Symon as planned. Since Symon had told him it would be a few days before the push began, however, he had ridden over to Beenac to see us, and when I asked him if he would stay for a while he agreed readily.

Tomas had changed. It was as if a heavy curtain of sadness had fallen behind his eyes. He was unfailingly polite to Shad and did not once bully or lecture me. It got so that I would have welcomed one of his scoldings or the knowledge that he was plotting a marriage for me with fifteen-year-old Anton Rouget, the son of the Northern Elector—anything to show that the old Tomas still lurked within that depressed man.

As for Dally, I could well imagine the kind of crazy teen-aged thoughts that had made her set out to avenge her mother. She was at an age which knows no compromises and which relishes the thought of dying for a grand cause. Part of me was appalled and a small secret part of me was admiring. I could not imagine how an inexperienced girl with half-awakened magical powers could survive the terrors of

Fire Angels and the dog-faced beasts. Against my will, however, I nurtured a small hope. It was such an unexpected thing to do and such acts can turn out luckily.

Tomas did not go out harvesting with Shad. Tomas and Karac had had little food on their trek through the Red Mountains and Tomas was determined to rest properly and get himself back into good fighting condition. He spent his days training.

Negotiations between Julia Madraga and the embassy sent by the Duke continued. Every morning I would be in the room to greet the embassy with her, before slipping away to my other duties. Every evening she would tell me of how the day's talk went. To be honest, I did not know why they continued.

"It has reached a complete standoff," I told the others, "and has been so for many days now. The Duke is not prepared to be just a consort and Lady Julia has the constitution and the Church on her side. Why do they stay? If it must come to force of arms, surely the Duke would be wisest to move quickly while the Klementari are engaged elsewhere."

"Most commanders are unwilling to move during harvest time," said Shad. "He must hope that it can be solved somehow."

"Then he should have sent someone other than Garthan Redon," I said, for the tall Gallian mage who was acting as chief negotiator seemed astonishingly unyielding. I had the strong impression that Ren Garthan disliked me, for he had taken to staring at me with a very unpleasant look in his eyes.

The only good thing about the negotiating team was that Parrus was on it. Not that he acknowledged me but I was relieved to see that he was doing so well, even if it was in the ranks of the opposition.

Later that evening Tomas took me aside and said, "If it comes to force of arms, Dion, do not stay with Lady Julia to the bitter end. Leave yourself some escape. The Duke will not harm her, but you are not so precious to him. Even if he does not punish you, you will never have any kind of a life in his dominions again. Promise me you will escape. Make for Seagan. I have friends there who will look after you."

I was grateful for his advice, for indeed the future did look bleak should the Duke emerge victorious.

While Lady Julia negotiated with Garthan Redon, I found myself involved in negotiations of my own. Ren Daniel had approached me and revealed that he still had doubts about who to support for ruler. I did not tell anyone about our conversations on this topic, for I knew Ren Daniel was talking these things over with me because he trusted me.

He told me he did not think any woman, even Lady Julia, was strong enough to rule Moria, and he had all kinds of subsidiary objections to do with issues of marriage and succession. They were the objections I had made to Shad, the objections any reasonable person who did not know Julia well might have made. I did my best to convince him that Julia was no ordinary woman, that women could be just as capable of ruling as men, and that if she could put together an army as she had, relying on only charisma and a good reading of popular feeling, then she was capable of ruling Moria. When this did not work, I switched to blackening Duke Leon's name. I told Ren Daniel of his intrigues with Blanche Shomnee and of what I suspected of his collusion with Darmen Stalker and the defeat of the Patriarchal army.

"Can we seriously support one who is suspected of forming any kind of alliance with necromancy?" I told Ren Daniel. "Lady Julia may only be a woman but at least her hands are clean."

This seemed to work for Ren Daniel, so much so that one evening, eight days after Garthan Redon's mission had arrived, he came to me and said he was convinced now that Lady Julia was the best candidate for the throne.

"But as you may have guessed I am not the only mage here who has doubts about Julia's fitness," he said. "I have spoken with the others about Duke Leon's misbehavior, but they remain unconvinced. They would like to hear the evidence from your own mouth. Could you meet with us tomorrow morning before the negotiations begin and speak with them?''

I was delighted to agree and also to assure Ren Daniel that he could rely on my discretion in this matter. He had supported me in the council and kept quiet about any guilt he had seen during my mind search. I wanted to help him in return.

The servant who came to fetch me the following morning was either very stupid or very discreet. When I asked him where we were going he merely repeated that we were going to attend Ren Daniel. I couldn't imagine why he was being so secretive, for we saw no one except servants and Tomas coming back from riding.

It was a little disconcerting to discover that our meeting was to be the very same chapel where I had had my confrontation with the demon of Beenac and with Bedazzer. I hoped this was not a bad omen, but on the other hand it was out of the way and an excellent place for a clandestine meeting.

Ren Daniel met me at the door and, smiling a little nervously, drew me down into the room. The morning sun had only just begun to slide in through the high side windows, and the chapel was dim and smelled of dust. How cold and bare it looked without the statues behind its iron grills. What a lot of people there were. I had not realized that there were so many doubting mages. Almost all the Gallians were there, and many Morians as well. They stood very formally, as if drawn up on parade. Their faces were grim.

Ren Daniel had drawn off to the side and I was standing facing them alone, wondering if I should just start speaking, when I heard a door closing behind me. A group of hooded men came into the room.

Their leader came up to me, pulling back his hood. It was Garthan Redon. Fear started prickling down my spine. This had all the hallmarks of a trap. But why?

Garthan took out a paper.

"Enna Dion Holyhands, previously known as Dion Michaeline. By the powers of the White Colleges of Gallia and Moria, I have a warrant here for your arrest. You are charged that in Gallia three summers ago you did willfully and with knowledge have congress with Andre Gregorov, a necromancer, and with his familiar demon. The charge therefore is necromancy.''

"No! These charges are false," I gasped. "I never . . .''

"You deny you had knowledge of the demon before you fought with it," said Ren Garthan.

I was too startled to lie properly.

"No, I . . .'' What could I say to this? It was true, but how would it look if I agreed? ''I am not a necromancer,'' I said lamely. How could this be happening? Surely any moment now these grim faces would break into smiles. Many of these men had been my friends, or at least I had thought so.

"How can you believe this of me? Ren Daniel, surely you cannot believe this of me.''

"These are dangerous times, Enna Dion. How can we help but doubt you?'' he said. ''You have admitted yourself that you knew this demon before you fought with him. And I have seen guilty thoughts in your mind which would be better for examination.''

"Such insistence of innocence just makes you look more guilty. Save your breath for your trial,'' said Ren Garthan.

"Trial?''

"You must return to Gallia and be tried.''

Gallia. Dear God. Back into the Duke's power. I could not. I must not.

"But I can't leave Lady Julia now. You . . .'' Suddenly I saw things more clearly. ''You want to separate us, don't you? This is all to weaken her.''

"It will only weaken her even more to have a suspected necromancer in her train,'' said Ren Daniel. ''Enna Dion, be reasonable.''

"Reasonable! If you suspect me so, I offer myself for mind search. Here! Now! What need can you have to take me to Gallia? You know the Duke bears me no love at this time.''

"Nonetheless, now that the charges have been laid you must stand trial or stand forever as a suspected necromancer. Necromancers are cunning creatures, Enna Dion, and you are a powerful mage," said Ren Garthan. "How can anyone here feel sure that what we shall see in your mind is the truth? The White College will be far more able to deal with this."

There was a general muttering of agreement around the room. I looked at the mages surrounding me. They didn't actually believe any of this, did they? And yet there was not one friendly face among them. Only Ren Daniel looked slightly apologetic.

"Enna Dion, part of the charge against you is that by using necromancy you have been a malevolent influence on our dear Lady Julia. The Duke has leveled this charge against you and we agree that he has reason. How else can Lady Julia's unwomanly behavior be explained?"

"What? How can you believe such rubbish?"

"Well if it is rubbish," said Ren Garthan, "it will come out in the trial. It is the only way to clear your name."

"I will not go to Gallia. Anywhere else but there. Even Darmen Stalker was given such consideration."

"You will go to Gallia and you will stand trial as you should." Ren Garthan pulled something out from under his cloak. A black iron witch manacle!

"No!" I cried. "No! I won't put that thing on."

Panic gripped me. I wanted to thrust him away, but I held myself back. I didn't want to hurt these people who should be my friends.

"Enna Dion, submit yourself to the rule of the White College. If you are innocent no harm will come to you."

Escape. I must escape. There were windows above me. I gripped magic to me and threw myself up at them.

And suddenly the air was as thick as jelly. I strove and strove towards the window, but somehow I couldn't get to it. The air was buzzing all around me like a million bees. Vibrations shuddered through my bones. Magic strove in my veins and in my muscles and still I could get no further. My arms could not even flail. The force of the magic was slowly closing in on me, pushing me downward.

I looked down. All around me stood the mages with grim faces. With the curious detachment that comes from magic, I saw how evenly they were spread out. They had planned this. Garthan Redon had tested my powers, so he must have known how many they would need, and from the beginning they had been arrayed in formation. The cunning bastards! I thought bitterly.

I tensed my arms and sent out a blast of power—there— toward one of them I knew was not very strong. Incandescent light flew from my fingers towards him, seemed to hit something, shattered, exploded in a shower of falling sparks and was gone. I tried again and again. Each time the same thing happened. They had been trained in the capture of necromancers. We all had been. Slowly as men reel in a fish, they were tightening the force around me.

Garthan Redon called out instructions. The ground came up beneath me with sicking slowness and inevitability. I heaved and heaved against the force, felt it once or twice give slightly beneath my striving power, saw the sweat on the faces of the mages around me, but it was no good. The force held. Eventually I was pinned to the ground by a great smothering blanket of force pressing down on my chest, causing me to gasp for air like a landed fish.

Yet still I held them off. When Ren Daniel came across the floor to put the witch manacle around my neck, with only the power of my eyes I pushed at him and he slid slowly away over the marble floor.

"Enna, don't make this difficult," he said exasperatedly.

He came at me again. Exhaustion ate at the edges of me. Little stars were appearing before my eyes. But I could still push him away. Damn him. I did it, and did it again.

"Aye, that may make her see reason," said Garthan Redon behind me. I slid my head around and saw two soldiers holding a struggling and shouting Tomas. One had a knife at his throat.

"Give in, lady, or we'll hurt your brother," said the man.

It was the surly servant who had led me here. He pricked Tomas' throat with the point of his knife. Bright red blood welled out. I heaved power at him, but he was so far away.

"Don't give in, Dion," shouted Tomas. "The longer you hold out the sooner someone will discover us. You must hold out."

He yelped as the men punched him, and then suddenly he twisted and flung himself away from them, falling into the wall of mages around me. The force pinning me down loosened, I gave a great heave and . . .

Splat! I was flat on my back again. I could see Tomas at the edge of the circle, the two men kicking and kicking him with a sickening sound of boots on flesh.

"Stop! stop!" I screamed. "I give in."

I let Ren Daniel come up and put that horrible thing around my arms and neck.

"I'm sorry to have to do this," he said as he clicked the manacles shut.

He was sorry!

The suffocating sense of helplessness was hardly lighter than the mages' force hand been.

Then the mages were relaxing all around me. Garthan Redon was bent over me. He put his fingers to my temple. There was painful thud and then blackness.

Snap. Blinding sunlight filled my eyes. My temple stung. Sensing danger all around I tried to sit up, but my head spun around and someone pushed me, not ungently, back to the ground.

"Just stay there," said Parrus. "You can't get away, so for God's sake don't try. Nobody's going to hurt you."

He turned and walked away. I remembered bitterly how happy I'd been to see him among the negotiators. Betraying sod! I was lying on grass and all around were trees and fields and the singing of birds. I craned my aching head. There was a cart turning on the roadway and they were saddling horses.

There was a rustling of leaves behind me. I rolled over and saw Tomas wriggling on the ground nearby. He was wearing a witch manacle also. With a faint clanking of chain, he lifted his hand and put it in mine. He had a black eye and a split lip.

"I'm sorry, sister. I tried to help you and instead they used me to defeat you."

I was very frightened. I wanted to cast myself on his shoulder and cry and beg him to help, but I knew he could do nothing, so I bit my tongue and tried to calm the sobbing breath that seemed to be choking me.

"I followed you," he continued. "I had a feeling. When you started to scream I ran for help, but that fellow, that bastard servant who brought you there, he must have seen me following because he grabbed me before I got anywhere. Oh, sister. It broke my heart to see you so defeated. Like a bird with its wing cut off."

"Where are we, Tomas? What's happening?"

"They put me to sleep too," he said, "but I gather they brought us here hidden in a cart. Lady Julia would never have given you up so easily. She cannot know. But she will have her hands full. Most of those mages have stayed in the castle with her. I hope she knows how they have betrayed her. Now they will probably load us onto horses so that we can travel faster."

"I am afraid, Tomas," I said because I could no longer help it.

He put his arms around me. The chain on his manacles dragged across my chest.

"I know, Dion. But at least we are together. And I have faith in Lucien and in Shad. They will not give us up easily. And you still have friends in Lammerquais and Gallia."

Kitten Avignon. And the Dean of the College had always treated me justly. He was a good man and would stand against Duke Leon if need be.

If need be. Duke Leon was as guilty as I was, if associating with Andre Gregorov was a crime. Would he really want me to give evidence that would implicate him as well?

"Tomas! The Duke cannot want me to stand trial."

"What?"

Quickly I told Tomas of Duke Leon's close friendship with Andre Gregorov. Of how we both knew now that Gregorov had been the demon itself, masquerading as an ordinary mortal. The story that he was merely a necromancer had been put out to protect the Duke and Gallian aristocracy. To be close friends—and in some cases even to sleep with—a secret necromancer could be excused but to do these things with a demon would have tainted all of them forever.

"If I am tried, these things must come out. Surely he won't want this evidence revealed. Oh Tomas, he doesn't even have to try me; he could just keep me in prison at his pleasure for years. He's done it before. Or I may never reach Gallia at all."

"Hush," said Tomas. "Hush, don't think on it."

"This is a very affecting scene," said Garthan Redon. He appeared above us suddenly, his shadow blotting out the sun. "But it's time to mount your horses now, people."

Someone cut the ropes around my ankles and Redon pulled me roughly to my feet.

"Come on, Monster," he said.

He pushed me over to the horse. His hands were rough and his face sneering. I was glad it was Parrus who helped me mount for he at least was merely cold.

Now that I was safely manacled, they seemed to feel that ten men-at-arms and ten mages would be sufficient to control me. I counted them as I rode along to keep my mind off panicking. It was a lot to control one helpless woman. But then there was Tomas and the possibility of pursuers.

And Fire Angels. Oh God. I suddenly thought of the necromancer. I hoped the necromancer had no idea of what was going on, because with only ten mages to protect me I was a sitting target. Panic turned my breathing ragged again. I told myself he could not know and tried to believe it, but the Duke would know. Would he tell his beloved Blanche Shomnee? After all the care the Klementari had taken of me when traveling through open country, ten mages seemed woefully inadequate.

As we stopped for the evening, Tomas made a break for

it, simply knocking over his guards and running. As the thought entered my head to try the same thing, someone pushed me to the ground and held me there until Tomas was brought back, bleeding from a blow to the nose.

"You are just making it hard for yourself," hissed Ren Garthan at Tomas.

"Do you think I will let you just make away with my sister?" shouted Tomas. "The Duke will never give her a fair trial. She knows too much about his friendship with Andre Gregorov."

There was a thud and Tomas hit the ground unconscious. Garthan must have used magic to knock him out.

Two men-at-arms started dragging him away.

"No," I screamed, "No, don't. Heal him. Oh God, someone see to his hurts. He'll choke on his own blood."

Parrus went after my brother. Garthan seized my hair and pulled my head back.

"You're making things much worse for everybody, telling your brother these kinds of lies about His Grace. I should keep my mouth shut in future. Monster."

"Don't hurt him. He's done nothing," I cried, remembering how the men-at-arms had cheerfully kicked Tomas and terrified that some unlucky thing would happen to him now. We were horribly at their mercy.

Some of the mages had a great deal of mercy, however. As I sat shivering in an upstairs room of the empty house we were staying at, one of the mages came to tell me that Tomas was alive and well, but that they had decided to keep him drugged for the next few days. This mage was a middle-aged man with a mild, pleasant face, one of a handful of mages who were actively kindly to me. They were all much older than I and they were so used to treating young women with avuncular kindness that they could not stop themselves. The rest of the mages avoided my eyes as if I was unclean.

Whatever the reason, I was thankful for the mage's kindness and repaid it by trying to subvert him.

"I am afraid of the Duke. He has no love for me. This thing is political and you know it."

"It is the United White College who will try you," said the mage with an infuriating patient kindliness. "The Duke has no influence there. Be of good cheer, Enna. And don't go upsetting your brother with these horrible fears."

The following day we traveled speedily onward through the same countryside that I had traveled so triumphantly with Lady Julia, an irony not lost on me. We made faster time than she had. The countryside was still very sparsely populated, but there was usually an open inn in the villages we visited. The Ducal embassy had left horses at some of these inns, so that twice that day we had fresh horses. I wondered how long they had planned this arrest. How long had the other mages in the fortress known that I was charged with necromancy? I could not recall any of them acting suspiciously. I was such a fool. I vowed that if I survived this, I would never play the game of politics again.

Parrus sat with me the next evening. Not wanting to provoke anger, I contented myself with asking after Tomas and thanking Parrus for caring for him. Then we sat drinking our soup silently together.

A short time later there was a knock on the door. It was Garthan Redon.

"And how is the monster?" he asked Parrus. He grabbed my chain and pulled my face into the light. "Are you behaving yourself?"

"Redon! You'll hurt her!" said Parrus, pulling the chain out of his hand.

"Humph," said Garthan. "I'll take over now if you like. I'll watch the little monster."

I looked pleadingly at Parrus. There was an anger in Garthan's eyes that really frightened me.

"I think I'll stay here," said Parrus quickly.

Garthan smirked. "That's right, you used to poke her, didn't you? Well, I wish you well, though I can't admire your taste." He flicked my cheek with his finger. "Fare thee well, Monster."

"Why do you call her that?" said Parrus angrily. "She's not been tried yet."

"Because she is a monster. Nature must have been sick when she spewed up this creature. A woman has no business having such powers. What is she to do with them but make trouble? If there was some way of stripping you of your power, Monster, I'd have it done here and now."

He went out, slamming the door.

"Thank you for staying, Parrus. I don't like him."

"Aye, and he hates you. He is the Duke's man. The Duke has no reason to thank you for your meddling."

"Parrus, you can't possibly believe I led Lady Julia into invading the South."

"I have no idea what you have and haven't done," said Parrus. "But I'm certain it was ill-advised. How ridiculous to think that Lady Julia could be sole ruler. What possessed you to go up against the Duke like that? I knew you were getting too stuck up with your own importance. I told you that for all your power, you were only a woman. You should have listened to me."

I wanted to shout at him but he had shown himself to be a friend to me, so instead I bowed my head and bit my lip. The helpless can only bide their time.

"Oh, Dion," said Parrus. He sat down beside me and touched my shoulder gently. "I wish we had never left Cardun. We were happy there, weren't we?"

I was so surprised I looked up. The moment his eyes met mine, he looked away and sighed.

"Now you have made such an almighty mess of everything, you'll be lucky to ever return there."

I did not really want to be reminded of that. I told him I was tired and wanted to sleep.

"I will be outside in the hallway all night," he said as he left. "You will not be alone."

I had a sudden nostalgic memory of him waiting all night outside Shad's room in the hallway of the inn. It seemed so long ago.

·22·

Screaming. The room was full of orange light. Sulfur and rotting roses. Before I knew how, I was at the door struggling with the handle, which moved but would not open. Oh God, I couldn't get out. I hammered and shouted at the door. Just outside the window something screamed with cackling laughter.

"Help, help," I screamed in a voice that was drowned by more laughter and a cacophony of screaming. Something exploded and the whole room shook.

Suddenly the door was flung open.

Parrus seized me and dragged me through the door. We ran down the inn hallway. Orange light was streaming in the windows at both ends and yet we stumbled in suffocating darkness within. Yellow and orange flames were leaping through the door below us as we stumbled down the stairs. A figure loomed out of the darkness.

"Here, give her to me," said Garthan.

"Have you got the key? We've got to get her free. We need her. Where's Dommie? He went for the key."

"Go find him. He was heading for the stables."

"What?"

"Go, damn you. I'll take care of her."

435

In the flickering light I could see the doubt on Parrus' face. I clung to him.

"Don't leave me, Parrus."

There was more screaming from outside. Another explosion rocked the building, flinging grit and cinders everywhere. Garthan aimed a blow at Parrus' head.

I screamed and threw myself at Garthan, iron-weighted hands swinging, and he staggered under my heavy weight. I struggled with him, hitting at him with my manacled fists. Then Parrus was on him. Sudenly Garthan turned and was gone, running.

"What in Tanza's name . . . ?"

The air was suffocating with smoke and the smell of demons and fire roared searing through the open door. A figure lunged at us. Not Garthan.

"I've got it," shouted the mage. "Come on back here." Two pairs of hands seized me and began bundling me toward the back of the inn.

A door slammed shut behind us. The tiles were hot under my bare feet. The room was dark. "Down here," said the other one, pushing me under what seemed to be a bench. "Here, Oh Seven, I can't see. Make a light, Parrus."

They didn't have the experience to know the dangers of it and I never even thought to tell them not to.

Blue magelight sprung up in Parrus' hand. In it I could see the man shoving a key into the lock of my hand manacle. I ripped them off as he opened them.

There was an ear-shattering scream of laughter and suddenly the wall of the room burst open in an explosion of fire. Suddenly I was lying on the floor under the two mages in a small cocoon of crystal-pure air while all around us a hot orange inferno of fire streamed past.

Crushed against the floor, I saw that Dommie had dropped the key. I reached out for it and got it just as the fire went out, leaving us all in blinding blackness. The two mages crouched over me groaned and moved. They would have used up a lot of their power.

"The key," croaked Dommie hoarsely.

"I've got it," I said. I worked my fingers round the neck manacle until I found the keyhole.

"Oh shit," screamed Dommie.

I was crushed against the floor as another inferno swept over us.

Holding as much of the key as I could, I slid it into the hole. The flame moved in a huge jet around the room, setting the wall, the ceiling, and the benches alight. The heat was searing. There was another burst of cackling, as though a group of Fire Angels were standing outside. I felt the lock give, pulled off the manacles, and was free.

Just in time, too. As a feeling of power raced though me, Dommie slumped down exhausted beside me. The jet of flame was circling back toward us.

"I'll try to lead them off," I hissed at Parrus. "Please, find Tomas."

I leapt up, spreading a defensive spell over the three of us. There was a chorus of shrieking like a chorus of hawks swooping to kill and suddenly I was engulfed in flame.

I let it stream over me, waiting for it to stop so I could see again—see what to do, who to attack, where to go. But it didn't stop. It just went on and on. I could no longer see Parrus, though I had felt him dragging Dommie away and hoped they were safely out. Perhaps if I moved, it would help him.

I braced myself for impact. Fists of stone, I thought and shot straight up into the air as fast as I could.

Smash. I burst through the roof of the inn, scattering debris everywhere. Suddenly I was free of the fire, standing on the roof of the inn.

Whoomph! A Fire Angel came down beside me. It threw back its head and cackled, but instead of attacking me, it turned and spewed a blast of fire out onto the ground beneath us. Small black figures scattered to and fro in the fire, screaming. The Fire Angel laughed. I reached out with my power and engulfed it as I had the one in Annac. It was harder this time, for it was tougher, much tougher, and I had not yet fully recovered from my fight with the mages two days before. It was a strain to overcome it. The reek of sulfur and roses clogged my nostrils.

Then suddenly it went out like a snuffed candle.

At that moment the roof collapsed. I leaped off it, threw myself down, and came to land at the edge of the forest beyond the inn.

"Parrus!" I shouted, searching for him magically in the ruins. There was nothing left alive in the ruins of the inn, but the forest all around was full of running figures. I could only hope.

With a beating of wings and roaring of fire, two Fire Angels landed on either side of me.

One down. How many to go? I thought as I grappled with the next. It was even stronger than the last, or maybe I was weaker. It took long sweaty minutes to put out. All the while the other stood calmly behind us, blowing out bursts of flame. When I had smothered the first, I turned and engulfed the next one with power. Another slow struggle, but finally it was finished and at last I was alone in the cool dark night, the inn burning hot and brilliant behind me. With a sigh I turned. And saw it was not the inn that was burning behind me but a Fire Angel.

As I braced myself to lunge for it, it opened its mouth and blew out a blast of flame that hit the ground just beside me.

A great pillar of flame shot up, grew arms and legs, took on a human shape, a head, a mouth. A mouth that opened wide and filled the night with cackling laughter. A mouth that spewed out flame that hit the ground beside me and grew into the shape of another Fire Angel, and another, till I was surrounded by a circle of five of them making my ears ring with their mad cackling. Suddenly I saw why the Klementari had never let me fight them before. Tiredness filled my limbs.

I should have run earlier.

I leaped into the air, the cool black sky, and set off now, flying like an arrow.

In a moment they were there beside me, all around me, making the night boiling hot, reaching out like great fiery fists and engulfing me and then letting me slip free until they engulfed me again.

I tried to make for the east. Or if not the east, away from the great bulk of the Red Mountains that was on my right.

But as I plunged through one roaring red and yellow fireball after another I was unable to tell which way I was going or even if I was simply plummeting toward the earth.

My nostrils stank with the smell of hot sulfur and rose. Demons, demons all around. My eyes were dazzled with the flame. Doggedly, I pushed on and on while my mind ran round and round, desperately trying to think of a way to escape. I wasn't going to be captured? Me? Surely not. Surely this was not the end.

A sinister heavy tiredness was beginning to overwhelm me. My hands were shaking. My sight blurred.

I forced myself onward until I could no longer go forward, until the reserves I was calling upon were no longer there, until I could no longer hold myself in the air. I pulled a last shred of shielding magic around me and felt everything sliding away.

There was cold dirt under my cheek. I could not remember how I had hit the ground. I was so exhausted I could hardly move. The hand I put out in front of me felt unreal, as if it was made of wool. Everything swam. But my heart was filled with rejoicing. They were gone. There were no Fire Angels. Somehow I had lost them.

Then as the joy filled me, I heard footsteps on the earth before me. I saw bright light and felt warmth. Someone reached out and rolled me over. It was a hand made of fire and I looked up at five great pillars of flame.

I came to with the sound of fire roaring in my ears. My skin was burning hot. I was clasped flat against the chest of a Fire Angel like a baby in swaddling clothes. The sky over its shoulder was grey, blotted out and reappearing again as its wings beat steadily above us, the beating sound growing softer and louder against the roar of its flesh.

Exhausted calm filled me, but just as I was wondering at it, the Fire Angel turned me around in it arms and suddenly I was hanging in its hands, looking down. Far below, a dizzying, shattering drop away, was the earth. I felt a frisson of fear. The Fire Angel laughed its cackling laugh, and in a hideous parody of mother and child, it turned its head and fastened its lips to my temple. It sucked my skin for a moment. Though it felt hot, its touch did not burn. It smacked its lips.

"Fear," it said. "Sweet and sparkling."

Then it opened its arms and dropped me.

For one heart-tearing moment, I scrabbled for its flesh. My hands passed through and I fell screaming. Oh Aumaz! I tried to summon the strength to fly but there was nothing left.

Smack. Heat and the sound of wings. Another Fire Angel had caught me and held me. Tears were running down my face. I begged it not to drop me. It laughed and licked my face and its arms loosened.

"Stop that!" snarled a voice close by.

Something grabbed my arm, wrenching me away so that my bones cracked.

I was dangling in midair. Below was a dizzying drop to the barren rocks. Hysteria was rising in me. I began to cry and scream and beg the Fire Angel winging lazily in the air above not to drop me please, please. I couldn't take it again. Oh please!

It laughed. Suddenly I was surrounded by the great beasts, jostling each other in the air, a flurry of burning wings. Their lips and tongues were all over me, sucking me as if I were some kind of sweetmeat or a bunch of grapes dangling in the air. The air was filled with their laughter. Meanwhile I clung on to the angel for dear life, feeling its long tongue stroking my hand.

We plunged through the sky down toward something spiky, the carcass of a dead animal, its ribs sticking up through its moldering flesh like spikes. A great swirling horn spiked the sky. But it was not made of bone or skin. It was stone. A great stone cathedral, its roof still unfinished.

I was a mess, covered in the sweat and filth of fear, my clothing charred and torn, my skin blistered and throbbing with pain. The skin where they had licked me stung. My breath came in great dry gasps.

I had exhausted my powers and eaten into the life force that kept all men and women upright and alive. Part of me had thought my power was endless. Even the struggle with the mages had not really exhausted it. This time, however, it was all gone. I could not stand up. The Fire Angels carried me with them, cackling and sniggering. My feet dragged uselessly on the ground behind. I no longer felt any fear. I wished only for oblivion, to be left alone to be nothing.

At last we stopped moving. One of them pulled up my head with its crackling hand. I gazed blearily ahead. A throne and someone on it. I no longer cared.

The angels let go of my arms. I flopped onto smooth slippery stone. So cool and quiet. Fiery hands gripped me and pulled me up again. This time I was cast down with bone-shattering force. I felt a terrible pain as my hip struck the slippery floor and I slid scrabbling along it. The room was filled with cackling laughter.

Then, "Stop it!" shouted someone. "Wasteful creatures! You'll kill her."

A beautiful laughing face appeared above me. He had curling chestnut hair and angelic blue eyes. The eyes laughed at my pain, but the hands were tender enough.

"Welcome to my Kingdom of Demons," said a voice. "Tsch, tsch, Enna Dion, you are in a state. And these naughty beasts. Yes, you are naughty beasts. They are treating you so badly."

He sounded like some kind nursemaid consoling me for a cut finger.

"Perhaps you would like to rest now, Enna Dion."

I dared not answer for fear of his response.

He was gentleness itself. He put his cool hand on my face and drew my eyes closed.

"Sleep now. Sleep."

I had enough strength to feel a moment of pure terror before I went down into the darkness.

◆

The Politics
of Demons

◆

·23·

$\mathfrak{I}$ jerked awake and sat up quickly. It was silent—a deep heavy silence. I had been lying in a great bed under a rich red silk quilt and linen sheets the yellow color of old cream. The bed was richly hung in silken curtains and long silken cords with tassels. Beyond it the room was dim, but cozy with a warm light like firelight. Fire Angels? No. I was alone in this tall richly hung chamber.

What was this? I was clean and wearing soft linen. Shouldn't I be bloody and covered in scratches and filth? Had I dreamed that desperate battle with the Fire Angels and the horrible flight afterward? Had I been rescued as I slept? I rubbed my face hard, trying to awaken my addled wits. It was some moments before I noticed the chill of iron against my forearms. A pair of delicate iron bracelets hung lightly on my wrists. Witch manacles for all their fine design. At my neck was a smooth iron collar. It fitted tightly but not uncomfortably. Touching it, I had a vision of a fist tightening and squeezing the breath out of me. Quickly I pushed the thought away.

Where on earth was I?

I slid my feet over the side of the bed. Though there were rich carpets on the floor, the floor beside the bed was icy

445

cold marble that sent a chill up my legs. I was overwhelmed by a deep bone-shaking tiredness.

Suddenly the doors flew open and the room was filled with chilly silver light.

"Ah, my queen, you are awake!" said a voice.

It was Darmen Stalker, and behind him floated two trays which set themselves upon a nearby table. Darmen Stalker! I remembered that it was his face that had bent over me as I had lain exhausted on the floor, surrounded by mocking demons. I lacked the strength to do more than glower at him from under the heavy weight of my exhaustion.

He clapped his hands.

"Back into bed," he said. "You have dangerously exhausted yourself and you must rest, my dear queen." His voice had a kind of delighted sneering tone to it, especially when he said the words *my dear queen*.

I did as he said because I was fairly certain I'd fall over if I tried to get up. It seemed wise to marshal my strength for the moment.

As I lay back down, the quilts and pillows moved around me as if straightened by invisible hands. I was startled, though I tried not to gratify the closely watching Stalker by reacting. Meanwhile the trays unloaded themselves onto the table, covers lifted themselves off food, and tea poured itself into cups. It looked as if the room were full of invisible servants, but I was pretty sure Stalker was doing all these things himself. A white cloth trailed through the air like a solitary ghost and arranged itself on my lap. I watched apprehensively as a teacup glided toward me. A necromancer might well get a great deal of pleasure from seeing scalding tea spill "accidentally" over a person. I caught the teacup safely enough, however, and the food that followed tasted good and did not contain any unpleasant surprises.

Darmen Stalker leaned against the bedpost and watched me with a benign look on his face. As well he might. Was he already tapping me for my power? Was that why I felt so exhausted?

"You will have to rest and let us take care of you," he

said. "You almost killed yourself struggling against my angels. Very foolish."

I felt a kind of detachment born of my tiredness and the deep unreality of the situation. I knew I should be afraid, but instead I sipped my tea and said conversationally, "So they are your angels. You are not just a messenger."

He smiled pleasantly. "No indeed. I, and no other, am the one you so poetically call the Great Destroyer. Is it not appalling to think how you of the White Colleges have let me slip in and out of your net?"

It was. It was too horrible to think about. I could have been furious and anguished about it but I wasn't going to give him the satisfaction.

"Was the whole of the Revolution of Souls your doing then?" I asked calmly.

His eyes glittered with amusement.

"Alas, I wish, but I merely made the most of an opportunity. A country that is killing its mages is too good a chance to ignore. I came for the fodder for my demons and found it was so very easy to fool the Hierarchs with superstition and dreams, that for three years I have been feeding off this land without the White Colleges having even a whisper of my existence. I had not thought to escape their notice so long. I was fully prepared to have them chase me off much earlier. Nothing lasts long in a world of demons. It is a world of change and most marvelous chaos. But these three years have been delicious: Making the Hierarchs dance to my tune. The power I have had. The chance to bring the kingdom of demons into my own plane to enjoy the company of my equals. But even more delicious was finding you, my queen. With you at my side I begin to see infinite possibilities."

Company of equals? What was he talking about?

"So you have decided to come out of the background, have you," I said. "Don't you think the White College will be a problem if you openly make yourself King of Moria?"

He threw back his head and laughed and laughed as if I had said the stupidest thing in the world.

"A king of mortals," he cried. His derisiveness was infuriating, but I kept my temper. "Who would want to be king of a bunch of pallid worms crawling between heaven and hell? I am a king of demons."

This was such a crazy remark that for a moment I assumed it must be some kind of jest.

Then he leaned toward me and said, "They are magnificent creatures. Such power and freedom from petty fears. We mages are more kin to such creatures than we are to mere mortals. They are us released from these fleshy cages. Who would aspire to rule mortals when they have such mightiness at their command?"

His soft vehment words brought back the memory of the time I had felt the pull of Bedazzer's power, of the fascination I had always felt for demons, their soaring freedom, their might, the violent colorful wonder of them. A king of demons. The glory of it.

Reality came back with a sickening lurch. He was insane. How could anyone seriously hope for such a thing? We were nothing like demons and nothing to demons. They were so vastly cunning compared to us. More important, we mages were their favorite source of food. Who would put a leg of ham on a throne and call it ruler? How could he believe himself a king of demons?

He did not see the amazed disbelief in my face for he had turned away.

"Let the Duke of Gallia be King," he said. "Let him have his little prize. I prefer the role of puppet master, and I already have his strings in my fingers. Think how he would love my little Blanche if she showed him how to be king of the whole peninsula. Demons are cunning enough for such a ploy."

It was almost as if he saw himself as a demon. I stared wonderingly at him trying to comprehend this insanity, and as I did so he stopped and cocked his head as if he was listening to something. It must have been something inside his head, for I could hear nothing.

"Very well then," he said suddenly. "My greatest subject wishes to meet you."

He turned and motioned at one of the long dark wall-hangings and it began to draw itself sideways. Behind it was a huge mirror, taking up the whole wall of that high chamber. The mirror exactly reflected the world in my chamber except for one detail. Sitting on the chair beside the reflected bed was a neat personage whose snow-white skin glowed with a faint red glow.

I forgot the horrified amazement churning inside me. This was most definitely a demon, but not the great rough beast that Bedazzer had always been in demon form. Though this creature had the red eyes and sharp toothed demon's snout, its face was flatter and much more human-looking. His naked skin was smooth and hairless and fine like the skin of a child, and his shape was neat and slim. He sat with almost feminine grace, his feet tucked neatly to one side and his huge hands with their long talons delicately resting in his lap.

I glanced quickly at the chair beside my bed to see if it was empty, which of course it was. The demon in the mirror smiled at this. No doubt he had seen the suspicious fear in my mind as clearly as if I had spoken it. Demons read minds, though in my small experience their perceptions can be clouded by their own ruthlessness.

This was a demon who was used to humankind. The kind of demon I could imagine appearing in Stalker's mirror and offering to buy his soul in return for the kingdoms of the world. Was this what he had offered Darman Stalker? Had he tricked Stalker into believing himself a king of demons? In the same way Stalker had obviously tricked Hierarch Jarraz into thinking he could make the Kingdom of Heaven on Earth?

I had no doubt who was really in control here. Yet this demon was far more harmless-looking than Bedazzer. Which probably meant he was far more dangerous.

"Oh, do not be always comparing me with your pathetic friend," sighed the demon. "He is hardly worthy of your notice. A gross interloper in places that he has no right to. Shake him off your petticoat tails, my queen. He is a misfortune of your youth. Now you have me to serve you."

He rose and executed a courtly bow.

"You already know something of my power. For I am the one you call Smazor. The Destroyer of Moria."

Smazor! This was Smazor. Sweet Tanza. The demon of the Run, the maker of the Great Waste, the creature that had destroyed the Wanderers' homeland. All I had read about his killing frenzy came back to me. I fought down a sick fear. He could well claim to be a root cause of the Revolution of Souls, and now here he was feeding off the results of his actions. It had the kind of sinister inevitability that bred despair.

"Yes, there is marvelous symmetry to it all," he said.

He bowed again. "It's gratifying to impress someone of your power, my queen. For I must say, I admired how well you fought us. You are a great mage. And even though your last adversary was a pathetic worm of a creature, still, to defeat a demon—that is something special."

Flatterer. Such courtliness always made me suspicious.

"You wound me, my queen." The demon smiled urbanely.

"Then Bedazzer is not one of your number?" I asked. So the Klementari had been right. He had been trying to prevent other demons from gaining control over me. It was well known that demons hated each other. They were beings of chaos and jealousy. This made the fact that there were five of them serving Darmen Stalker truly remarkable.

"Oh, it is remarkable," said Smazor. "I am a remarkable demon. Few of us have the power to communicate with mortals at all. Most of us are so overwhelmed by gnawing hungers that we become nothing but great mindless blackness moving across the face of our world, pawing through the dirt for remnants of life. But I not only control my hunger, but I have power over four other demons as well. They cling to my coattails for the morsels that fall from my lips. I am a King of Hell."

"I would like to see these other demons sometime," I said.

The moment I spoke I was angry at myself. Here I was,

chatting over tea as if I was in the finest salon in Gallia. I should be trying to think of ways to subvert Smazor and his minions away from Darmen Stalker, not asking to make their acquaintance.

"She is wondering how to get control of me," said Smazor.

"It was only a matter of time," said Stalker. He smiled silkily. "You haven't a hope, my dear Queen. Smazor knows you are no demonmaster. You'd use him and then send him away foodless into the waste. He is happy serving me."

The demon smiled fawningly at Stalker.

"It is a pleasure to serve a clever and powerful master," he said. I remembered Bedazzer again and how he hated his slavery and being reminded of it. Was Smazor so different from him? I could not help admiring Bedazzer's sulky surliness, especially when compared to Smazor's fawning.

Smazor pulled himself up sharply.

"Very well," he said. "If that's how you're going to be, I shall take myself off." And suddenly the mirror was empty.

I almost smiled at the ridiculousness of it all; that the creature who had laid half of Moria waste could be so easily offended. *Almost* smiled. I did not really believe in his offense any more than I believed in his fawning. The only real feeling demons have is hunger, a gnawing bottomless hunger. Smazor was just pandering to Stalker's madness.

But why do that when he could have used it against him? Stalker's belief that he was powerful enough to be their king put him in a uniquely vulnerable position. He could easily be tricked into destroying himself for their pleasure. And yet he had survived, how long? Three years? Probably even longer than that.

"I have no illusions," said Stalker looking at the empty mirror. It was almost as if he too, like a demon, could read my mind. "I know the burdens of their hungers intimately. How could it be otherwise when we are one spirit?

"I know they do not serve me out of love. They are not naturally servile. They are too magnificent for that. They serve me because I feed them. How could it be otherwise with demons?''

Yes, that was why Smazor and his four demons served Darmen Stalker. He commanded them using their names and fed them his life force and the life force of others in return for their services. And they managed to keep their hungers enough in control not to upset this balance. Perhaps a bound demon who remained in his own world was less resentful of being a servant. At least he got to feed.

I was surprised, however, that they had not tried to persuade Stalker to bring them through into our world so that they could get free the way Smazor had before. Probably Stalker did not have the power to do so, or maybe he was still sane enough to refuse to do it.

Stalker went on, ''And I will continue to feed them though with you at my side, my queen, I shall not need to feed them as much of my own substance. I will give them yours instead. With your help I can continue this game indefinitely. Or at least until I have finished with this peninsula.''

''The White College will stop you. You can't continue to get away with this,'' I cried, more out of desperate hope than certainty. My attempts to remain calm were failing in the face of Stalker's horrible confidence.

''Ah, the White College. You think they'll be a problem, do you? I don't. I could fake my own destruction, move to another place, subtly master the Duke as I mastered the Hierarchs. When I tap you, my queen, I shall have three times as much power and no need to find human fodder to use it. Think what miracles of mastery I could then perform.''

I did not reply. I was searching desperately for some way out of this terrible maze. Perhaps I could get control over the demons by promising to bring them into this world. Play them off with politics. Try anyway.

''Ah,'' said Darmen Stalker. ''You are trying to think how to turn them against me again, aren't you? It is your logical path. I should save myself the trouble if I were you. Even if they wanted to go with you, you could not take them. I know their names, you see. All five of them. You will never be able to overcome that, my Queen."

Their true names. Then he had ultimate power of command over them and I had no hope in that direction. I was beginning to feel I had no hope at all.

"I should not even try to subvert Smazor if I were you. He is far too cunning. He will ask you for some of your substance to seal the bargain and then try to take all of it. And the others are even worse. Accept your plight. You are guarded by five demons loyal to me, who can read every thought you have. You are in the middle of a trackless waste patrolled by vicious beasts who will tear you apart. And my Soprian mercenaries are brutes who will use you savagely if they get the chance, though they will leave you alive. Their leader, my good friend Zorzar, is the man who tortured your sister for my demons' pleasure—a duty he always performs with keenness."

"Pig," I said. I could still feel Tasha's pain. I wanted to spit at him. I could barely lift my shaking hands from the bed. He had won. He had broken through my calm and he knew it.

"This is a place of pain," said Darmen Stalker. "The demons require the taste of strong emotions to feed properly. But if you are smart, it need not be the place of your pain."

He caught me by the throat. His hand lay on the iron manacle around my neck and the threat was clear. His thumb stroked my cheek.

"So many necromancers get a taste for inflicting pain, but I am not one of them. There is no reason why we should not deal politely together. I am about to do you the honor of making you my queen. When you have been cherished back to your full health, my dear, we shall be joined and reign together as one in my Kingdom of Demons."

I felt despair leeching away what was left of my strength. I leaned back against the pillows and looked at him.

"And now, if you have eaten your fill, it is time for you to rest," he said. He reached out and flicked my temple with a finger and everything went black.

* * *

I dreamed. I dreamed of a beach where a thousand tiny bones crunched underfoot. It was the old, old dream, the dream in which I had first seen Bedazzer, the dream that had begun it all. I should have been filled with horror, but the place was still so wondrous. I stood at the edge of the ocean, a jellied ocean of little faces which screamed as the waves smashed them on the shore. The little mouths sucked at my bare toes.

But it was no longer night. The sky was a flat yellowish grey like a dirty piece of parchment. I could see the rocks just offshore clearly. Once a demon had crouched there, but now the rocks were empty.

Running footsteps scrunched over bone. Hands gripped my shoulders.

"You are mine," shouted Bedazzer. His terrible demon's snout loomed in my face, filling my vision with glaring red eyes and sharp teeth. Black wings towered over me. "Smazor will not have you. You must get away from Sanctuary."

"How?" I cried.

"I will help you. I have been to the depths of Hell. I have sucked the dry bones of the dead. I have ground their dust between my fingers. And they told me."

He leaned closer. His acid drool stung my ear as he whispered softly, "His name is . . ." Then he said a word so strange and formless I could hardly understand it, let alone write it down now.

I formed it in my mouth, just to feel the strange syllables on my tongue.

"Ssh," he said, putting a talon softly against my lips.

"Who . . . ?"

Suddenly the sky turned black as a bruise.

"Slave," thundered a great voice above us, as if someone had opened the box we were in and was shouting down at us. "Worm. Leave her alone."

"No," shouted Bedazzer. "She is mine by right. I found her."

An enormous black claw reached out of the sky and snatched me screaming away from him.

I fell and woke with a start in the great red bed again.

"Quickly," shouted Smazor. His face filled the mirror. "Quickly. Stalker is busy and the blood beasts have been withdrawn to feed. Get up, get up! You can get away if you try. I know how."

"How?" I cried, throwing myself out of the bed. "Why?"

"If Stalker taps you he shall have twice as much power," hissed Smazor. "I have no wish to see that. It will be hard enough to break free as it is."

I looked about for shoes or clothes. How would I escape in a nightgown and bare feet? Panic gripped me. Could I trust Smazor?

"Come *on!*" he shouted. "I will see you outside. Now! There's no time."

I rushed over and flung open the door. The figure of Darmen Stalker loomed over me.

"You fool," he sneered. "Where are you going? I told you it was hopeless." He pushed me back into the room. He was quite strong enough to do that without magic.

"She decided to just run," said Smazor, curled in the mirror like a smug cat. "She thinks even death would be better than being tapped by you. She's quite the moral hero."

"No," I protested, torn between astonishment and horror. Was this all a trick then? To make me look bad in Stalker's eyes? Why?

"Now she is formulating a plan in her head. The minute she gets the chance, she will fornicate with any demon she meets, to prevent her power coming back so fast and win herself time. That way she will be able to delay the time when you start tapping her."

I gaped at him. This was a blatant lie. Though it was a good idea.

"You are a fool," said Stalker without heat. "What did I

warn you about letting them steal your substance? Well, it's easily fixed.''

He leaned over and flicked my temple and everything went dark again.

·24·

She awoke in a chamber hung with dark red silk. She could not remember anything—not who she was or why she lay there. She tried and tried to remember, but her thoughts kept whirling around and around like a whirlpool of stars— glittering, swirling, and ultimately futile. They were like ice which seems to have a hard shape and yet at the touch of a warm hand dissolves into a drop of formless moisture.

There was a strange metal band around her neck. She could not remember why it was there, but it bothered her and she tugged and tugged at it. Eventually she got out of bed to see if there was something to get it off with.

On one side was a huge mirror and on the tables before it were garments made of the softest, most beautiful fabrics in glowing reds and whites and blacks. Seeing them she forgot about the band. She touched them just for the pleasure of it.

"They are yours, my queen," said a voice. She looked up, and sitting in the mirror just a few inches from her was a cheerful middle-aged woman in simple clothes. She looked plump and friendly and she nodded at her and said again, "They are yours. Why not try them on?"

Delighted by the thought, she seized the most beautiful, a red silken gown, and tried to pull it on over her nightgown. But the narrow sleeves would not go over her nightgown's

457

sleeves so she pulled the nightgown off and put the red gown over her naked flesh. It smoothed over her skin in the most delicious way and it was firm around the waist, stiffened with something hard like whalebone. Since it fitted perfectly it felt delightful, but somehow the front was wrong, for try as she might, it would not come up over her breasts. The curve of the neckline which came under her breasts was stiffened like a little ledge. It seemed to be intended to push her breasts up and out. They were quite nice little breasts, round and even and pink-nippled. But it would not do. She felt uncomfortably vulnerable with such sensitive parts of herself exposed. She went to undo the gown and as she did a man's voice said, "Oh, do not. You look so delightful."

Startled, she looked up and saw that the apple-cheeked lady had disappeared and in her place stood a man.

She whirled around to look behind her. He was not in the room with her—only in the mirror. How strange. She was not sure if it mattered that she could see her reflected self standing half-naked in front of this interested-looking man.

Then that thought disappeared, for she was suddenly struck by the fact that her reflection's breasts seemed bigger.

"Like them?" said the man. He was slim and very handsome. And he was completely naked. She could not help noticing his well-made genitals.

He strolled forward and stood beside her reflection. There was something in his eyes that made her cross her arms over her chest.

"No! No!" he admonished. He reached out and pulled her reflection's arms away from her chest. This had no effect on her own arms at all. But when he began to run his hands across the reflection's breasts, he did so with such sensuousness she could almost feel his delightful touch.

Her reflection threw back its head with pleasure and sighed. She felt a little envious.

"You are a pretty woman," said the man. "But you could be a great beauty. Look!" As he stroked and smoothed them, the reflection's breasts grew even larger and firmer under his touch.

"And we could do this too!" He ran firm hands appreciatively down over the reflection's flanks and belly, stroking them again and again, and slowly the reflection became taller. Her waist became tighter and her body became more shapely.

"See how beautiful you are now." He gently rubbed the reflection's genitals through the silky dress. It responded with a moan and the man nibbled its cheek and neck.

The reflection turned to him. She saw the man's sex jutting out before him. The reflection caressed it with its hand and the man began to slide its gown up over its firm thighs with appreciative slowness.

She was growing damp. She wanted to be in the mirror feeling the satiny skin of the man's sex and feeling the caress of his hands on her thighs.

"Stop that, Smazor," said a voice behind her. "I said you were not to tempt her."

A man in a black and grey robe stood in the doorway behind them. She turned and saw that he was really there.

The man in the mirror turned and snarled like a beast and then disappeared, leaving only the reflection of a slim, scared woman clinging to a bedpost.

"I have forbidden them to have intercourse with you," said the man inexplicably. "We cannot have them leeching away your powers before you are well. It does not stop them from tempting you. The management of demons is very complex that way."

He turned and smiled at her. He had blue eyes, curly chestnut hair and a beautiful face. He was very handsome. She felt arousal return, creaming in her belly.

"You were tempted, weren't you," he said softly, and he reached out and stroked her nipples with a finger. She felt a momentary disquiet. Did she know this man? So intimately? But he seemed to know her and his touch felt so wonderful, so erotic. When he pushed her back on the bed and got on top of her she was more than willing.

But once he was inside her, it wasn't that great. He seemed to enjoy it, but he pinned her arms down so she could not touch him and whenever she tried to move her hips to follow her pleasure, he bit her or slapped her face—gently, but hard enough to be scary.

"Hold still, you slut," he would say.

The feeling that she was doing something wrong dried up her arousal. She lay there bored, looking at the canopy above, feeling his sweat dripping on her bare chest until at last he finished with a grunt and got off her.

"Yes, I remember now," he said, wiping himself and straightening his robe. "Pleasant, but uninteresting."

He seemed to be talking to himself. She had the curious feeling she no longer existed.

"You knew it would be so. You are not really one of them anymore," said a voice.

There was someone in the mirror again—a beautiful woman, more beautiful even than her own reflection had been. The woman lolled naked upon a daybed that wasn't in the real room, her hand lazily stroking her belly.

As she sat on the bed mopping up, she was conscious of a stab of envy at the woman's beautiful nakedness. . . . She bet men did not treat *her* so shabbily.

The horrible man certainly liked the woman well enough.

"Well at least she does not try to suck your soul out while you have her," he retorted, but his eyes were glittering under half-closed lids.

"You know how you love it," purred the woman. "Nothing exceeds the pleasure of us." She seemed to slide out of the mirror and the man left the room quickly without another word.

She had the feeling that they were going to meet someplace else.

She felt annoyed at being so used and quickly forgotten. She decided to keep away from the man if she could.

Try as she might she could not remember what she was doing in this place. She tried to remember, but her thoughts would begin chasing each other round like racing dogs, quickly intent upon other matters. Then she would feel a faint disquiet, as if she had forgotten something, and she would find herself striving to remember what it was she had forgotten and then occasionally she would find herself remembering that she had been trying to get herself to remember. On the whole it was easier just to let her thoughts go their own way.

Sometimes she would discover that she had an iron band around her neck. She did not like the horrible thing and tried to get it off but it would not come. It was to find some way of getting it off that probably made her open the door of the red-curtained room and peer out to see what was there. Soon, without knowing how, she found herself wandering, walking and walking and looking at everything. The iron band was forgotten and remembered and forgotten again in all this wandering.

How wondrous everything was. She was in a huge dark stone palace. Narrow, gloomy corridors opened out again and again into huge shadowy chambers hung with dark velvet curtains and black silk tapestries embroidered with gossamer red threads in strange swirling patterns.

Once, when she lifted a corner of a hanging, she found behind it the cool luminescence of a mirror, a mirror so huge it was like staring over a towering cliff. She felt dizzy and dropped the hanging quickly.

Herds of fat dark candles sat squat amid great pools and cascades of wax, lighting the rooms with a cold yellow light and giving off a greasy spicy scent. Their shadows leaped on the hangings, making the blood red patterns dance and twine.

The floors of the rooms were of grey stone, chill and gritty on her bare feet. Sometimes in her wandering she longed to sit down. But there was no furniture in the rooms. There were only the dozens and dozens of statues. Some were huge, as tall as the ceiling, and some were a little shorter than she was and often bore headdresses of greasy candles or candle wax. Some had the faces of beautiful serene people, saints perhaps, while others had the faces of snarling beasts with snouts and teeth and wings like bats. Many were actual beasts, fearsome dogs, slimy fanged toads with long delicate suckered fingers or lions with toothy mouths and glaring eyes. In some rooms even the pillars that splayed up to the shadowy roofs were statues—wondrous falls of stone beasts, writhing and twining down from the ceiling in a turmoil of arms and legs and paws and webbed feet; fur, feathers, fins, and scales. Sometimes she stood for hours by one or another of the astonishing pillars, with her fingers tracing the carved creatures that were tumbling down, trying to make out the individual creatures. They seemed to melt into each other in a chaos of forms and everywhere she found full human lips and gaping toothy mouths that seemed to belong to nothing so much as the pillar itself and which seemed to bite forward into the very air.

Once, as she traced the shapes, she felt the stone grow warm under her hand and suddenly the shapes began to move and writhe. Claws and fingers caught at her she leaped back and screamed and ran and ran until she was in her red bed-chamber again, hiding under the covers, unable to remember why she was so frightened. The reason for her fear had disappeared into the muddle of her thoughts, but a vague palpable unease stayed with her.

The statues were alive. She had always known that. Sometimes the lions or dogs turned their heads and growled as she passed. She did not think they could leave their pedestals, or at least, they never did. Sometimes when she was lost the beautiful stone women would move their heads and with stiff arms point the way back to the dark red chamber. They seemed harmless, and yet. . . . They whispered behind her as she passed. They were always watching her, stone heads turning to follow her, red eyes glowing into the shadows.

Once a big stone dog opened its mouth and a great grey tongue as long and sinuous as a snake came sliding out and ran along her arm. She was mesmerized by the wondrousness of the moving stone. The tongue was cold and gritty, but still it felt strangely delightful and she felt something else where it touched her, the feeling of something slipping away.

Then red eyes of a huge stone saint beside the dog jerked open with such violence the whole statue shuddered.

"Stop that!" it shouted in a thunderous voice, and brought its stone fist down on the dog's head with a mighty blow, smashing the head to bits and cracking the body in half so that the life, not unnaturally, went out of it.

"Now off you go," said the stone saint, sternly flapping its hands at her. "Do not be so foolish as to let that happen again."

As she scuttled away she saw that all the statues in the chamber were alive, watching her with their avid red eyes.

She began to be fearful when she wandered the chambers, even though the incident with the stone dog melted away like all her other memories. Yet at the same time her feet seemed driven to wander through the dark rooms. The statues, the writhing carvings, the huge dark tapestries that sometimes swayed for no apparent reason over the huge cold mirrors; all these things filled her with a disturbing sense of beauty, of wonder, of magic. The chambers seemed to go on forever and yet she had a confused suspicion that she was in some enclosed space.

In much the same way she could not remember why she did not like the horrible man, but whenever she saw him in those shadowy rooms she ran away quickly, making sure he did not see her. It was a pity, for sometimes she longed for flesh and blood company—someone who might tell her why she was here and what she was supposed to be doing.

She saw the man often. He seemed to be at one with the stone beasts who were always alive around him. Sometimes the tongues of those beasts flickered quickly out and licked him as he walked past or their hands rubbed his bare flesh. Often she saw him embracing one of them. The red glow of the stone beasts' eyes turned his pale skin ruby.

Once she came upon him having sex with one of them, huffing and puffing away with his hand upon its spread buttocks, while it squatted before him with a beatific look on its face. She slipped away quickly.

There was someone else among those endless chambers too. Sometimes she was sure she saw a flash of blue or a human face made of flesh not stone peering at her from behind a pillar. Once she saw a young girl in a blue dress standing in a doorway and she chased after her, calling for her to come and walk with her for she was tired of all these stones. The girl vanished without a trace, but in chasing this phantom she came to a place she had never seen before, a place where a wide stone staircase led up toward grey light.

Cautiously she climbed the stairs. At the top was an enormous space filled with great pillars and a cold greyish light. She looked up and gasped and clutched the stair rail, for the walls soared dizzyingly up and up until they ended in huge arches. Great arched windows filled the walls so that she could see the sky.

The chamber stretched away before her in a forest of pillars. She could not see the other end. She could not see any statues either and the pillars were free of carving. It was better up here, she decided, and for a long time she wandered among the pillars, looking up through the windows, to where the clouds dragged themselves across the sky like engorged grey slugs.

As she progressed down the chamber it became lighter and she saw that at this end, the chamber was open to the sky. The arches stuck up like broken ribs, like spikes trying to catch those slowly dragging clouds.

Then she heard a voice calling "Dion, Dion." She turned in wonder to see who was calling and saw that she was at the opposite end of the great chamber. Near that wall was a huge raised area and upon it a kind of long flat stone table. The stone table was carved round its sides, she saw with displeasure, but the voice seemed to be coming from there.

At one end of the table was a big, round stone like a roller and as she hurried toward it she saw that something else was lying on the long stone table, something moving. It was a man. She cried out when she realized it, for the poor creature's legs were crushed under the great roller. She could not see his legs on the other side of the roller, for they were covered with a cloth—a good thing too, for there were flies buzzing about. There was an unpleasant rotting smell.

"Dion. Help me," cried the man hoarsely, struggling on

the flat stone. He was clamped down to the stone table with great iron manacles.

"What must I do?" she cried, realizing that he was calling to her. She must try to help him.

"Release me! Quickly! Let's get away!"

Then as she stared at him in confusion he said, "Oh God. You poor cow. He's got you too, hasn't he?"

He flopped back against the table.

"Who are you? How can I help you?" she said.

He obviously knew her. Did she know him? He didn't look unfamiliar. He had blue-black hair, a beak of a nose, and a swarthy complexion, but under the olive of his skin, his fine-boned face was pale and puffy with bruises. His arms were bared and covered with blood-crusted cuts on which the flies crawled.

"There is water in that bowl," he croaked. "Please bring me a drink. I'm parched."

She filled a cup from the big stone trough by the wall and brought it to him, held it to his lips as he drank, wetted the corner of her nightgown and mopped his face with it.

"Do you know me?" he asked when he had drunk.

She had to admit she did not.

"But you know me," she said. "What is this place?"

"This is Sanctuary," he said. "Poor Dion. Still, I don't doubt he will keep you better than me." He leaned confidentially towards her. His skin smelled of salt and metal and fever.

"Keep an eye open for Dally," he whispered softly. "He has not caught her yet. There is a demon taking care of her, I think. Have you seen her? A young girl in a blue dress. She comes here sometimes when all is still. At first she laughed and said I was well served. Maybe she's right. But lately she cries. Perhaps she has forgiven her uncle after all. If you see her tell her I understand everything. Will you do that for me?"

All the time he whispered she worried at the manacles that held him down, but she could find no weak point in them.

"You want to help me?" he croaked at last. "Look, there

is a knife over there. Go get it. Good. Now place it on my throat. No, further round. . . . There, where that artery is. Now. Cut down hard! Quickly! Cut.

"Don't just look at me like that. Can't you see I'm done for? You can make it quick for me. Please, Dion. It's the only release. Damn you, do it."

She couldn't. . . . And as she wavered and he began to curse and scold, something bit her on the leg.

She squeaked and jumped back from the table. The knife fell from her hands with a clatter. The hem of her nightgown ripped and a face leered toothily up at her from among the carvings around the table's side. Red eyes glowed. The carvings. She should have known they would come alive. The whole side of the altar, yes that was what it was, an altar, was moving and writhing. The surface of the table undulated around the man as if it were soft. Stone hands were stroking and groping at him.

"No!" howled the man.

"Good try," said a voice, and she turned and saw the horrible man.

"Come away from there," he said, pulling her roughly off the raised dais. "How did you get up here?"

"You've mind-blasted her," gasped the man on the table.

"No indeed," said the horrible man. "She's a strong one. I could only put a part of her to sleep. Magnificent creature. She is almost one of us in power. Perhaps with time. . . ." He took her chin in his hand as if her face was some kind of precious object. "What things I shall be able to do when her power is added to my demons. I'll hardly need to use human fodder. She'll wake up when I start to tap her and then she'll know everything and remember everything and feel everything. Till then she has no more mind than a little child. She won't help you."

He pushed her away roughly then so that she almost fell.

"Go on, you, get out of here."

He turned and went over to the altar. The altar still writhed and stroked at the man lying wincing on it. The horrible man picked up the knife she had left lying there and began sharpening it with long smooth strokes from a whetstone he had taken out of his pocket.

"When I called up my demon army, this room was ankle deep in blood and I was so exhausted I slept for two days afterward. That will not be a problem soon."

Then he put the knife on the man's throat.

"Maybe you'd like me to kill you. Too proud to beg still?"

"Go to hell where you belong," croaked the man on the table. "As long as I live there is hope of vengeance."

The horrible man laughed.

"Some hope," he said. "Still, cling to that if it keeps you going, for this will last a long time. The demons will do more for the sake of one morsel of your life force then they will for fifty pallid ordinaries. And there's a lot of juice left in you."

With sudden violence he dug the point of the knife into the man's shoulder. Blood spurted and the man howled in pain. Shrieking with anger at such cruelty, she flew at the evil man, but some kind of force came up before she could even reach him, a kind of flash of red light that knocked her back hard on the ground. The evil man came and stood over her, his hands on his hips in a homey scolding style, for all the world as if the knife he was holding was not dripping human blood on the cold grey stone floor.

"Why are you being so stupid?" He pushed her with his foot. "Get out of here. You're being a nuisance."

"Why are you torturing that man?" she screamed at him. "Stop it. I won't let you."

"Zorzar!" shouted the man. He leaned down so his face came close to hers and said, "I do it because I can. And if you don't shut your silly face I'll do it to you too." He looked up. "Ah, Zorzar, will you take this silly bitch back to her room. And don't hurt her. She's still healing up."

Rough hands dragged her to her feet. It was a soldier clad in dark leather armor. He twisted her arm around her back and pushed her ahead of him along the chamber. Behind her she heard the man scream again and a strange greedy sucking noise, like thousands of mouths in a jelly sea, coming from the altar.

All the time he was forcing her along, this Zorzar muttered in her ear and the things he said were horrible. He described in graphic detail the torture that they would wreak upon the poor man on the altar and all the pain he would feel. He twisted her arm against her back till she thought it would break and when she struggled he just twisted harder. As they reached the dark rooms at the bottom of the stairs, Zorzar's words became darker too. He began to describe how he would torture her when he was given his "time" and then, in gloating detail, how he would rape and abuse her. His hand gripped her breast and he twisted her nipple. At this she threw herself back against him and when his grip loosened, she ripped herself away from him and raced away down the corridor to her bedchamber, where she bolted the door on his running footsteps and shouted obscenities.

She would have thrown herself under her bed but it had a solid base. So she huddled on the floor behind it and at last Zorzar went away, leaving her shivering in the darkness. Her thoughts were whirling and changing like flurries of sand in the wind so that she could not quite remember how Zorzar had come to be there in the first place.

As she sat there with the bedcover twisted over her head, she head a rustling behind her. One of the wall hangings was pulled aside. A young girl in a blue dress crawled out from behind it. Fascinated she watched her crawl.

"Who are you?" she asked.

"What do you mean? You know me. Now listen to me, Aunt Dion. We've not got much time. I'll tell you how to get out of here. I have a message for you from Bedazzer. He says Darmen Stalker does not know the names of the demons who serve him. He only thinks he does and the demons allow him to think so, so that he will feed them. They do not give out their true names to every foolish mortal who wants their help. Demons are not made for slaves. But you already know Smazor's true name. Bedazzer says he told it to you on the beach of bones. All you need to do is to speak a binding ritual using the name he told you and you will have complete control over Smazor. Think of it. Smazor, the great demon of the Run. Your own slave.''

Then a cunning look came over the girl's face. ''What is the name Bedazzer whispered to you on the beach of bones?''

She could only look back at girl. She had no memory of this person Bedazzer. She found herself laughing nervously under the girl's darkening gaze.

''I don't remember anything,'' she said.

''You're useless,'' shouted the little girl angrily and slapped her face. She fell backward and suddenly, it must have been the pain that reminded her, she remembered the poor man on the altar.

''No, no,'' she cried. ''Oh, the man. The poor man. He told me to look for a girl in a blue dress. He meant you. He gave me a message to tell you.''

''I don't care what he said, you useless woman.''

''He said he. . . . He understood everything. Is that right? Yes, that's what he said. Oh, can't we help him somehow? Set him free? He is in such pain. The evil man tortures him.''

The little girl sat very still. An odd stricken look had come on to her face.

''Are you sure you don't remember the name of Smazor,'' she said after a moment.

''Smazor?''

''Oh, forget it,'' said the little girl contemptuously. ''Mumma was right about you. You're weak and useless. She would have done better.''

The girl pushed her away hard. Then she took a pillow from the bed and crawled back under the wall hanging. She stared after the little girl in confusion until she had marshalled her thoughts sufficiently to look under the hanging and see where the girl had gone. She could find only a blank stone wall. She searched and searched the walls for an opening, until she forgot why she was searching.

·25·

The evil man came to her room. He grabbed her hand and wanted to take her somewhere. At first she refused to go. She remembered this time why she thought him evil. Then she saw Zorzar lurking at the door of the room and guessed that if she did not go with the evil man, he would make Zorzar force her to go. So she let him lead her out through the shadowy rooms. She kept the man between her and Zorzar in a way that made both of them laugh.

"What have you done to that poor man?" she snapped at them angrily. "Are you still torturing him?"

The evil man looked half amused and half curious at this.

"So you don't know what has happened to him?"

"You don't really think she killed him?" said Zorzar.

"I wondered if she had something to do with it. Smazor says there have been rogue demons about. I wondered if they have been courting her."

"Rogue demons," scoffed Zorzar. "If you ask me, you should be looking a bit closer to home. There's something very untrustworthy about these demons. They seem to do just as they please."

"Demons always seem that," said the evil man serenely. "We have the minds of lawyers. We are always finding some loophole to the rules. But I doubt my crew would help her.

Demons understand politics better than that. I feed them and so they will not offend me lest I banish them.''

"I wish I had your confidence, Stalker. Any demon's a dangerous tool, and five demons . . .''

"Stop complaining,'' said Stalker calmly. "You have your fun.''

They had come to a great carved door she had never seen before. A dark red glow came from within it.

The evil man, Stalker, turned and bowed mockingly to her.

"My queen,'' he said, "I now present your empire to you. May it give you joy.'' They passed through the door.

The reddish glow shone from out of a huge pit. Heat steamed out of it and the whole place smelled foully of rotting meat. There was a walkway along the nearer side of the pit and on the other side was a great stone wall. It was the wall of the great cathedral, she realized.

Her thoughts seemed less confused today.

The wall of the cathedral shone with a slime that was covered with oval whitish lumps like hairy ulcers on the stone. As she watched one of the lumps broke open with a ripping sound; she realized that they were some kind of enormous cocoon. A shiny brown lump slid out of the cocoon and as it did so a tremendous howling arose from beneath them. She could not resist peering over the edge of the walkway, though she was sorry almost immediately. For the pit below was filled with white bones and lumps of red meat through which broken bone showed. The smell was terrible, and down among those bones scrambled creatures. She could see them quite clearly a little way below. They were shaped like people, but they were bigger and were covered in rough greyish hair. Their faces were like the faces of savage dogs with snouts and enormous fanged mouths that drooled. Some of the creatures squatted on all fours, gnawing at the bones, but others had scrambled over the bones to the sticky brownish lump from the cocoon and were poking and ripping at its jellied covering. A small damp version of these creatures was quickly revealed. She had seen statues of these creatures, but in the flesh they were much more horrible.

"These are my watchdogs," said Stalker instructively. "Those who know enough would recognize them as blood beasts, although few on this innocent peninsula would recognize them. I make them. Is it not delightful? I make them out of dead bones ground with the entrails of a dog and a little magic. They have a tremendous hunger for rotting flesh. They are grave beasts, but they will still hunt you down and rip you apart if you try to flee. Just remember that." He took her hand in one of his smooth soft ones. "Now come, my dear, come with me and meet your subjects."

At the end of the walkway there was an earthen ramp and suddenly they were outside. It was night, but everywhere were torches and huge fires. Behind them the great bulk of the cathedral rose jagged against a cold starry sky. Occasionally fireballs shot across the sky and the sound of shouting came from the distance. She thought nothing of the shouting and the fireballs at the time. They simply seemed a natural part of the horrible scene.

Before them she could see an enormous earthworks. Women and children were dragging stones and men with great pulleys were hauling the stones up onto high walls which were being built around the earthworks.

Stalker gestured with mocking grandeur.

"Your palace, my queen," he said.

But she hardly heard him speak, for her eyes were drawn with a kind of creeping horror to the people toiling below them. They wore only rags and their bare flesh shone with sweaty filth in the torchlight. Their faces were thin and exhausted, their movements painfully slow. Sometimes they sagged into a heap on the dirt.

Men with cruel faces and black armor like Zorzar's stood all around, beating the people with whips and blows and lashing them to their feet when they fell.

"How can you make these people work like this? It is night. Time to sleep. These people need rest."

"You are so soft-hearted," he said. "How very promising."

"If I am queen as you call me, then I order that these people be allowed to rest," she said angrily.

Both Stalker and Zorzar found this very amusing. She felt a vicious streak of hatred pass through her, but before she could do anything about it, Stalker reached out and took her chin in his hand again and said, "You might be the queen, my pet, but I am the king. King of Sanctuary, king of the demons and king of you. What I say here goes. Come now, my queen. It is time for you, at least, to rest. Tomorrow will be our wedding day."

Her memory was improving. When she awoke the next morning to see Stalker standing at the end of her bed, she remembered all his talk about wedding days. She tried to run away. She didn't want to be in any kind of marriage with this hateful Stalker.

Invisible hands stopped her and arrayed her in a red dress which was cut low at the front, though it did cover her breasts. It was slit in several places in the skirt, however, so that her legs were displayed. As she struggled with the invisible hands, feeling desperate and trapped, five creatures like fanged humans, seated majestically on thrones, looked out from the mirror and laughed. It was the stone beasts in bodies of flesh. She longed for the calm of the days past.

Zorzar stood outside in the hallway with five of the cruel-faced men in black she had seen whipping the slaves. She tried to run back into the room when she saw them, but Stalker caught her and pushed her along before him and Zorzar and his men formed into a guard on either side.

She had a very bad feeling, which turned to terror when she saw that they had come to the hall of pillars. She threw herself against the nearest man and tried to break through the cordon, but they caught her. Zorzar took hold of her and twisted her arm painfully behind her back. She was not sure why she was so afraid, but she could see her fear gave them great pleasure and she promised herself that she would try not to show it.

They took her to a pair of thrones on a dais at the end of

the room of pillars and forced her to sit in one of them. A little way off through the pillars she could see the other dais, the one with the altar on it. She saw that it was empty and the sight gave her a certain obscure comfort.

Escape was still in her mind, but the black-clad guards had arrayed themselves all around the dais and it would not be easy. So she sat there for the moment. Stalker sat down beside her. Like her, he wore a red robe, though his covered more of his body. He took her hand. She snatched it away, giving him another chance for laughter.

He pinched her cheek.

"Why so cross? A woman should be happy on her wedding day."

He paused as if expecting the obvious retort, so she did not make it.

He went on, "You need not be so afraid. I will not hurt you today of all days."

He looked very sincere as he said this, but she could not bring herself to believe him. She tried to seem calm, though the fear settled like a blackness in her mind and would not let itself be forgotten.

Behind them, tall arched windows let in a hard grey light. A statue crouched beside her throne—a huge toad. Its grotesquely long, thin legs were almost level with its face and the long, splayed fingers on its skinny arms rested on the ground before it. Its mouth was set in a huge full-lipped grin. Its eyes glowed red. With a grinding sound its head turned and it leered at her. She looked away quickly.

"For your pleasure, my dear Queen, I have arranged some entertainment," said Stalker. "Bring them in," he shouted.

The stone beast gave a rumbling growl and the great iron doors at the other end of the room swung open.

A large group of people scuttled in like a swarm of fugitive beetles.

"Ah, more of your subjects, my Queen," said Stalker with such a revolting look of satisfaction that she felt like hitting him.

The newcomers wore bright peasant costumes of red and

blue, all embroidered with leaves and circles and flowers. That was all that was cheerful about them. They were walking skeletons. Their skins were grey and covered in sores, their hair shaved. She remembered the people laboring in that quarry the previous night. Were these the same ones? Had they been up all night only to be brought here? She felt certain something horrible was going to happen to them. It appeared that they thought so too.

Yet after they had scuttled nervously across the floor to stand before the dais, and after Stalker had nodded, one of them took out a little pipe. The others formed into circles and as the piper began to play, they danced to his tune.

The music was familiar to her, making a great heart-turning sadness well up in her breast. She suspected it reminded her of some great happiness in the past, but all she could remember was spicy scented sweet oil trees stretching tall toward a blue sky.

There was a thump. A faltering of the pipe music bought her back to herself and she saw that one of the dancers had fallen. She leaped up from her chair and ran over the floor to pick the poor woman up. None of the other dancers had stopped to do so. Their faces had looks of terrified effort which made a horrible parody of their light and cheerful movements. A hand caught her just as she reached the dancers and jerked her back. At that moment a man turned in the dance and tried to pick the woman up and a couple of the black-clad guards stepped up to him and punched him in the belly so that he sprawled backward.

The dance came to a confused stop. One of the men in black picked the fallen woman off the floor and, slinging her over his shoulder, took her away down the hall towards the altar.

"No," she screamed when she saw this, but hard hands dragged her back. The one who had hit the man reached out to pick him up too, but he had already scrambled to his feet and skipped unsteadily out of the guard's reach. He gripped his partner and began to dance again. The pipe took up his movement in music and the dancers began to circle and turn again. She was dumped back in her throne. Stalker shot her an amused look.

This time she watched the dance. It was horrible. The dancers were supposed to skip lightly about, but they were exhausted and starving and all they could do was hobble and hop like very badly made puppets. The guards leered with amusement and began to thrust feet and the ends of whips on the floor to trip the dancers. Several stumbled and eventually another one fell and was dragged away.

It was too much for her.

She turned and shouted at Stalker, "Stop it. Stop it. Let them rest. Can't you see how tired they are?"

"Doesn't this dance please you then, my queen?"

"No, let them rest," she cried.

He clapped his hands. "Enough! The dancers do not please my lady. Take them away!"

The dancers screamed and a couple of them tried to run. Their faces showed abject terror as the men in black closed around them and began to herd them down the hall toward the altar.

In that moment she realized she'd done the worst possible thing.

"No. Don't hurt them," she cried. "Let them rest."

"Oh, of course," said Stalker. "They are going to get plenty of rest soon."

The stone beast beside him sniggered.

"Please don't hurt them," she begged, taking his hand. "I liked the dance. It was just they were so tired."

"You soft-hearted creature. How amusing this will be. I have something very sweet for your soft heart now." He clapped his hands and the iron door open.

A little boy of about seven came hesitantly in.

"Come, child, come over here," said Stalker. "Sing for the lovely lady. Yes, that's right."

The boy halted before the dais. He was so thin and small that with his shaven head, he looked like a skull on legs. He had beautiful dark nervous eyes.

Her mind was still full of those unfortunate dancers, but

she did her best to pretend to listen. Her hands trembled in her lap.

The boy opened his mouth and began to sing in a wavering voice. Quickly, though, his voice steadied. The fear in his eyes disappeared in his concentration on his song. His voice was as thin and pure as spun glass and he sang a song that would have charmed birds off the trees.

When each silver note of that song was finished, he sang another one even more beautiful. They were songs praising some being called Tanza. She listened, and though the blackness of fear did not recede, her hands ceased trembling. She wanted to hold this little child, to keep him safe with her.

"You like this little child?" asked Stalker.

"Yes," she said.

"You could have him as a little page."

"She'd like that," said the stone beast. Its red eyes were avid. It was grinning. Both of them were grinning.

"Come closer, boy," said Stalker. "The queen likes you and wants to make a pet of you." The child came forward. She took his tiny fragile hand and squeezed it tight. He smiled trustfully at her.

In that moment the stone beast's great splayed hand darted forward, seized the tiny boy, lifted him to its mouth and with a great snap opened his jaws and bit off the child's head. Blood sprayed out, splattering all over her and . . .

I screamed and screamed and flung myself back over the chair. Terrible thoughts and images filled my head like an attack of carrion birds. Darmen Stalker and the stone demon were laughing with cruel hearty laughter. Blood still ran from the demon's lips. It was a joke to them. They had taken that child's life as a grotesque joke. A red killing hatred seized me.

I flung myself at Stalker, screaming and flailing with fists and claws, a ripping tearing hurting machine. I bit him and got in a few good blows before a stone hand gripped me round the waist and pulled me off.

"I'm going to kill you," I shouted, kicking at his laughing face as I dangled in the bloody hand of the demon. I was mad with rage and hatred and a big grin spread across his face.

"You are so amusing, my queen," he laughed.

The demon squeezed me hard against its body and rubbed its great stone toad's head against my cheek and shoulder, smearing me with gore. It purred.

"Let her go," said Stalker. Amusement had vanished from his face.

"Master," whined the toad, but its arms loosened and I leaped away from it quickly, only to be seized by the guards. Stalker peered into my face.

"So you've come back to yourself. I am impressed. How strong you are, Dion. You're just in time to enjoy your own tapping."

He ordered the guards to manacle my wrist to my throne.

"I must leave you to see to some things, my sweet Queen, but fear not. I'll be back before you have a chance to miss me."

The stone toad had reached out a hand and was running it dreamily up and down my arm.

"And you can come with me, Smazor," said Stalker sternly. "Unless you want to be punished by missing out."

The red light blinked out of the stone toad's eyes, leaving it just a particularly grotesque and bloody statue. Stalker, followed by his men, walked away down the great hall till they were lost among the pillars.

They left one, thankfully not Zorzar, to guard me.

I closed my eyes. The terrible images of the last hour were screaming in my head. The dancers, the little boy, the blood. How I wished I was still that forgetful being I had been but a few minutes ago. I could not control my breathing. It came out in sobs and I could not seem to stop shivering. Oh God, oh God. I must try and see past these terrible sights to find some way of escape. But past these events was only the tapping. A desolate sense of my own helplessness fell on me like a stone.

Faint cries were coming from the other dais. Were they killing the dancers?

"Once again I find you in despair, little mage," whispered a voice at my side.

I could never have imagined in a million years, how my heart would jerk alight at the sound of that endearment.

I opened my eyes and saw a faint red flickering in the stone toad's eyes.

"Bedazzer?"

"Careful," hissed the statue. The guard before me turned briefly to look at me, but his real attention was taken up by what was happening beyond the pillars and after a moment he turned back to watch.

"Why this useless despair, little mage?" said Bedazzer. "You can save everyone if you remember. Remember what I told you. Remember Dally. You know Smazor's name. Use . . ."

Suddenly there was a screech from deep within the statue and the red light went out. I was alone.

But my mind was working again. Bedazzer's words had cut through the dark cloud of confusion. I remembered Dally. Where was she now? I remembered Karac chained to that altar. Oh God! I had done nothing.

No. Must think. Think about Dally. What had she said to me? Darmen Stalker does not. . . .

Did Darmen Stalker really not know the names of his own demons? The whole thing was unbelievable. It was too strange and convoluted to be believed, and yet, how very cunning if it was true. How typical of the torturous convoluted minds of demons. They did not like being slaves, but they were ever hungry for life force. They might well be willing to give of their power in return for being fed like this. Darmen Stalker's five demons had done very well from their counterfeit of slavery.

How insidious. How clever. How demonlike. I wondered briefly how often they had pulled this trick on necromancers and demonmasters. They had fooled Darmen Stalker. He believed himself so in control he did not question their inconsistencies. He even seemed to believe himself one of them.

It was terrifying. I had been completely at the mercy of

those demons these last few days. Any one of them could have sucked me dry at any moment in an orgy of feeding. Fear crept icily over my skin just thinking of it.

But they rarely cooperated. They would not have been able to tolerate seeing one of their number have me. It was probably the politics of demons that had kept me alive. And now the politics of demons was going to free me.

Smazor's true name. The word that was going to free me. Oh God, I couldn't remember it. No. Calm. Calm. My mind was long trained in remembering words and spells. What was it? Remember back now. When did you last see Bedazzer? On the beach of bones. All of a sudden I remembered everything, the beach, Bedazzer, and that strange formless word he had whispered in my ear. I ran over its prickly alien syllables in my mind. I hoped this was not some convoluted plot of Bedazzer's. I knew full well that he was helping me because he was jealous of the others, not because he was trustworthy. I remembered how he had manipulated me into killing Norval.

I gripped on to my calmness tightly. I was going to summon a demon and bind him to me. If I had felt unclean before. . . .

With an eye on the back of the guard, I began to mutter the summoning ritual under my breath till I came to the words, "I summon you."

Then I spoke the name.

For a moment nothing happened. Had I spoken too softly? Then the statue beside me let out a hiss.

"Bitch," it said. "Who told you that name?"

"An enemy of yours," I said softly. I had done it! I had control of Smazor, the great destroyer.

"Here, what's going on?" said the guard, coming towards me.

"Kill him," I said to the statue.

"Feed me first," growled the demon.

I spoke the name again softly under my breath so no one else could hear. "Kill him," I said.

The guard was close enough by now for the statue to strike

him with its stone fist. In a smash of skull and stone, he fell at my feet. The red winked out of the statue's eyes.

Quickly I summoned Smazor back, whispering the name under my breath again.

"Shut up," he hissed at me. "You fool. Do not go shouting my name about for all to hear. Feed me. Them we will be bound together and I . . ." He made a hissing sound again as if the words were too bitter for him to speak, but I got the idea. Unless I fed him with my own substance I would have to use his name every time I ordered him, and his true name was dangerous in itself.

"Very well," I said. "First release me from all my manacles." As his hand shot out toward my neck I remembered just in time the legalistic nature of demons. "And do not harm me or kill me while doing it," I snapped. "And do not tell Darmen Stalker that I command you."

The demon let out another hiss.

"Do it now," I said. "Or shall I use your name again and louder so everybody hears and you will be like a toy ball tossed between mages."

"Mistress," said Smazor.

His stone hands pawed at me as he broke open the chain that bound me to the chair and the iron rings around my neck and wrists. It was revolting to be so touched.

"Don't paw me," I snapped at him. There was natural slave master in me after all.

I stood up. Free at last. A wonderful sense of power came charging through my veins. I felt ten feet tall. I felt like throwing my arms about and dancing for the sheer pleasure of movement.

The demon's stone tongue flickering out of its lips and sliding along my shoulder brought me back to horrible reality.

"Feed me, Mistress," it said. The hunger in its eyes killed all the pleasure within me and grim practicality took over.

I put my hand against its mouth, a mouth that was still stained with the child's blood and gore. There would be time for revenge soon now.

The stone toad's mouth opened and the creature began to suck my hand, rolling it around in its mouth with horrible slurping sounds. My skin felt hot and prickly. I began to feel that dragging of life out of me that I remembered from Tasha's dream. I was horribly frightened. I didn't want to do this. How would I know what was enough? When could I safely stop? It was not painful exactly, but it was as if my heart or some such thing deep inside me was slowly being drawn out along my arm. The pulling increased. It was like being pulled under by a wave. Sweat was standing out on my brow.

"No," cried someone beside me. Dally was there, pulling at my arm.

"Not like that, you stupid cow. It'll take too much. You didn't tell it how little to take. Stop, Auntie, stop."

At that moment the sucking increased tenfold. I struggled and ripped my hand out of the toad's mouth, breaking contact so suddenly I fell back against the throne. Dally landed on the floor. The stone toad bent toward her.

Fist of stone. Fist of diamond. I swung my magicked fist down on the statue's head, and with a crack it fell off and rolled on the ground.

"Dally, are you safe?"

"I'm fine, Auntie. I'm better off than you. Don't you know anything about demons?"

"No, and neither should you," I retorted. The enormity of the truth about what Dally had done with Bedazzer plucked at my mind, but there wasn't time to think about it now. "Get yourself out of here quickly before you get hurt."

"I wouldn't worry about me if I were you. Your new demon's probably gone off to tell Stalker everything."

"I told it not to," I said. Which was no guarantee of anything, I thought. I began running softly as I could through the pillars to the other dais. "Get back there."

"No chance. I'm going to help you. I'm going to avenge Mumma. I didn't come here for nothing."

"I'll do it," I said, turning to stop her. "You're just a child."

Someone screamed just ahead.

"Smart bitch. Did you tell your slave not to help Stalker anymore?"

"No, I . . ."

"You should be glad to have me along. Bedazzer told me everything. He told me that if the other demons find out Smazor is enslaved they will turn on him and try to destroy him. So we'd better tell them so that they're too busy to help Stalker. Then we can finish the bastard."

"Not we," I shouted, but it was too late. She had raced past me. People were screaming up ahead and something had crashed. There was no time now to tell her to get out, to leave the demons to me, to stay away from Bedazzer who was just as dangerous as the rest. In that moment the opportunity was lost.

There was a flash of power and a red ball of fiery magic smashed into a pillar above Dally's head. I flung a defensive spell around her just as a man appeared among the pillars and snatched at her. It was Zorzar and he saw me immediately.

His jaw dropped.

"Oh shit!" he cried. "Stalker, she's . . ."

Before he could say any more I threw out a bolt of power that slammed him to the floor.

She was a brave girl, that Dally. Though another blast of power exploded, this time over her, and was only stopped by my defenses, she kept on running out into the open space beyond the pillars, shouting at the top of her lungs.

"Dion Holyhands knows Smazor's real name. He is a slave and she controls him. Gnash your teeth, you demons, for soon she will own you too."

Anything else she shouted was lost in the sudden deafening wave of noise that shook the cathedral. It was a terrible yowling screeching sound, as if a hell full of cats had spilled open, and then just as suddenly it was gone, as if a door had slammed shut on them. I raced out of the pillars toward the dais into an unearthly quiet.

The dais was covered in altars and people chained to altars, squirming on them or huddled terrified around the sides. On the steps of the dais stood the red-clad figure of Darmen Stalker. Before him stood Dally with the purposeful guards closing in around her.

She was shouting defiance at Stalker and as the first guard lunged to grab her, she threw a bolt of power at him. She still hadn't gotten the hang of it, for the power of it threw her back out of the encircling guards. She landed on her feet and came staggering back toward me.

Stalker had staggered back under Dally's blow too. He looked terribly surprised. The guards looked surprised too, but that was because they saw me. Instantly, in a great wave of movement, some took to their heels and others drew their swords and came at me.

A shout leaped mightily out of my throat. I gathered myself, let out a surge of power, and threw it along the room, knocking them all over one by one and then knocking them over again till they lay still. I had seen them do terrible things to others. I felt no shame harming them now.

Meanwhile Darmen Stalker was muttering something. It was only when he shouted, "Come, I command you!" that I realized that he'd been speaking out the demons' names, or at least what he thought were the demons' names. Now we would see if Bedazzer was speaking the truth.

There was no response and he began muttering again, this time louder. I turned toward him. He must be stopped. Even though he obviously could not command those demons, they might still hear his cries for help and come to his aid.

But even as I turned Dally was racing toward him again, tensing herself to throw another bolt of power at him.

"This is for my mother, Tasha Holyhands," she shrieked as she flung it out of her fingers.

"Come, I command you," shouted Stalker as the red light of power obliterated him from my sight. This time he fell backward under the blast.

I was running toward the dais now. I saw Stalker stagger up beside one of the altars. He was changing, shriveling away. His beautiful face was beginning to look like a nasty brown sponge, his body becoming stooping and sticklike. His voice came out in a hoarse croak. My God. He must have been using demon magic to keep himself alive. How old was he really?

I readied a surge of power, but as I did so, Dally leaped on him. She had a huge knife in her hand and she was stabbing him, stabbing him and screaming in a frenzy. Blood spurted out of him. His arms scrabbled at her but she clung to him like a small, savage baby.

Stalker collapsed under her. The pair of them disappeared behind an altar. I reached the dais and sprang up the stairs, splashing through the blood on the floor. Dally was crouched over a heap behind one of the altars. She was still screaming and stabbing, though now the knife made only a dry rustling as it hit Stalker's body. His spirit had been released from its fleshy cage now, well after its time from the look of the wrinkled old man's body that lay at Dally's feet.

There was no blood anymore, though plenty was splattered all over the floor and Dally and the prisoners who were chained around the foot of the altar. They watched as she stabbed away, their teeth bared in animal triumph.

"Stop, stop," I cried, pulling Dally up and squeezing the knife from her hand. It fell to the ground but I did not hear it clatter. Suddenly I heard a sound that must have been going for some time—a distant yowling squealing sound, sharp as nails on stone. I heard a distant thudding too, or rather I felt it as a vibration through my bare feet. I thought suddenly of demons and a labyrinth of dark halls below us filled with statues and carved pillars. Pillars that held up the floor of this chamber.

The others must have heard it too, for now all the prisoners let out a terrified cry.

Dally had gone limp in my arms. I shook her and she stirred.

"Quickly," I shouted. "We have to get out of here."

She nodded and I let her go. She seemed to be able to stand. I pushed her toward the end of the dais.

"Quickly, Dally, just get out of here. I have to free these people. Please! Run!"

The prisoners chained to the altars behind me wailed. The yowling was becoming louder. I had to free them. I ran back along the dais using magic to pull chain out of stone, help people up and heal those who were bleeding or could not seem to walk.

Soon Dally, accursed child, was helping me with inexpert blasts of magic and a long crowbar she had found. I shouted at her to go but she just pulled a face at me.

Suddenly the yowling burst forth at ear-splitting volume. All five altars turned brilliant red. I scooped the last screaming sacrifice off the top of the last one, and as I did so fingers and teeth clawed and ripped at me. The prisoners chained around the sides screamed and kicked at the writhing stone teeming with mouths. I dragged them off, gathered them up by their chains and turned toward what I hoped was the door.

The yowling reached a deafening pitch. The altars were jiggling around on the dais. Two of them seemed to lunge at us. I flung them back so that they smashed against each other. At this the pillars began to fling themselves down and the floor began to cave in.

A few people who had been struggling across the floor disappeared screaming into the hole. I ran after the others, casting a defensive shielding around them for as far as I could reach.

It was a chaos of falling stone and demon screams. The Fire Angels could no longer appear without Stalker's magic, but they could still make themselves manifest in the stone.

I cast spells over great gaping holes in the floor and made huge falling pillars higher than trees bounce off my magic. By the time we reached the door, the blood was starting to sing in my ears. Smazor must have taken quite a bit of my power.

Beyond was a plain stone corridor with teetering walls and blocks collapsing from the roof. The door at the other end had broken open, showing the sky beyond. I shoved my back against a wall and hung on, pushing my power into those stones, stabilizing the corridor so the others could run down it.

As I did so, the yowling increased a hundredfold. I could feel it coming though the stone, vibrating in my bones. I could hear the individual voices in that cacophony. I could hear words. Though I could not understand them, they sounded like threats. I put my head down and hung on for my life.

"What is Smazor's true name?" said a still little voice in my head. "Tell me."

I looked up. Dally was standing there. The yowling was vibrating so much in me that she seemed to shudder before me. But I could hear her voice. She was using magic, speaking to me inside my head.

"Get out of here," I shouted at her, bespeaking her in the same way and doing it so loudly she staggered back against the wall, clutching her head.

"I won't go until you tell me Smazor's name. And if you let these stones fall you'll kill me."

There was a smug look on her face and it filled me with fury.

"Then you die," I screamed. "Better dead than a demon-master, Dally."

I began pushing myself down along the wall towards the door.

"Now get out of here. I'm going to let this go on the count of five. One! Two!"

"You bitch," screeched Dally. "Tell me, tell me."

She flung herself at me, kicking, screaming, and hitting me with magic and I must have been very close to my limit because something snapped inside me and walls fell down toward me and the ceiling after it. I clutched at Dally to try and protect her but she escaped my grasp and ran for the door.

"Stone, stone. I am stone," I thought and I pushed myself into the spell as the darkness smashed down. The cold calm form embraced me and held me, tight and silent as I fell into black.

Someone was calling my name. "Dion, Dion," he shouted with an edge of desperation.

It was dark. Everything hurt. I seemed to be lying between rocks. There were rocks everywhere and I couldn't see.

"Dion," called a voice. "Dion!"

Where was that voice coming from? Over there? I yearned toward it. I longed to answer it.

I turned and pushed toward the voice using all my strength, all my power. It was slow work getting through the stones, like swimming through thick mud. The voice got closer. Calling my name.

"Dion, Dion."

It was Shad. Oh, how I wanted to see him again. I swam faster.

Now I could hear the sound of sliding rocks. Light, there was light!

A pair of hands reached into the hole and pulled me out.

It was Shad, holding me tight against him, kissing my gritty face. "Oh my darling, my darling. Thank God. You're all right. I was afraid you were gone."

It was dark. There was distant torchlight.

"Is it night?" I said. I was dazed with magic and stone.

"You've been buried since midday," he said. "Why did you stay down there?"

"I was a stone," I said. "Stones don't. . . ."

I couldn't think of how to explain it. Maybe I had been unconscious. Maybe I had forgotten that I was anything else. I might have stayed there forever had I not heard him calling. Ever since I have wondered what beings lurk, forgetful, in the shape of stones.

"I heard your voice," I said. "I wanted to see you. What are you doing here?"

"I came to rescue you," he said. He smiled at me with shining eyes and I saw that he'd been weeping. "I couldn't believe you were dead, though it seemed certain you must be."

I let him hold me close and the warmth of his body drove the coldness of stone away.

·26·

Shad had not come alone to rescue me. The moment they had heard of my capture, the army of Klementari who had been so cautiously digging in in the Red Mountains burst out of their barricades and trenches and came storming across the Waste Land. Although they were harried by Fire Angels all the way, within two days they had arrived at the walls of Sanctuary. It was the fourth day of my captivity by then. They attacked the fortress of Sanctuary immediately with all the power, magical and physical, at their command. It was their fireballs I had seen shooting through the sky over the cathedral that night.

Darmen Stalker's conviction that he was really some kind of demon had made him supremely and foolishly confident. A lesser man might have tapped me immediately, but Stalker merely watched the Klementari's attacks with a calm and disdainful eye and waited until the morning of the sixth day, when I was at my full power.

After many futile assaults on the walls of Sanctuary, and after enduring the attacks of the Fire Angels, the Klementari were just gathering themselves for another attack when they heard the yowling of the furious demons and saw the implacable fortress cathedral of Sanctuary come crashing to the ground.

There was still much to do. The Klementari killed the escaping blood beasts and mercenaries, rescued the prisoners,
and searched the rubble for survivors, but these tasks were
nothing compared with the struggle that had seemed to face
them before. The Destroyer was gone and the gateways he
had made for his demons to enter our world—the mirrors
and the statues—were smashed.

Not bad work for someone who was only a burden though
I did not manage to get Symon the Raven to admit as much.

By the time I woke in Shad's tent the following morning,
they were hard at work cleaning the ruins of the cathedral
of its demon taint and destroying all statues. The majority of
the Klementari had already left the encampment, however,
and had gone storming home to Ernundra.

The first thing I asked about when I awoke was Dally.
Had she got out of the ruins? Was she safe?

Tomas and Lucien, who had searched long and hard for
us both, told me no sign of her had been found. To assume
that she was dead, crushed in the collapse of the cathedral,
seemed the only logical conclusion. Yet I had a sinking feeling that Bedazzer, having gained a foothold in our world,
would not allow that to happen and that she was somewhere
out there, still with him whispering in her ear. I remembered
our argument about Smazor in the collapsing corridor and
wondered what dark pathways Dally would be traveling if
she had indeed survived. I had thought she was a rude and
passionate little girl, but I could not bring myself to believe
she was evil or capable of murder and torture. I hoped she
would quickly be repelled by Bedazzer's ruthless greed and
leave him and perhaps return to us. She had been lonely as
I had once been lonely, desperate to avenge her mother, and
Bedazzer had taken advantage of that. When had the alliance
begun? I remembered she was even more ignorant of demons
and their cunning ways than I had been. And as for wanting
to know Smazor's real name, she was just the kind of young
person who might have thought to use demon power to do
good in this world, not realizing how such power could taint
and corrupt its goals and in the end its user. When I thought

of that, I almost hoped that she had been crushed in the destruction of Sanctuary.

I did not tell Tomas and Lucien about Dally's alliance with Bedazzer, but I did tell Shad. I told Shad everything.

For a day or so I remained quietly in Shad's tent. The stone that I had turned myself into seemed to have seeped into my bones and joints and for days afterward they ached. At first I could barely hobble around. Beg merely snorted at my complaints and said she had to put up with such pains all the time. She was more sympathetic about my loss of power to Smazor, though she did not think I had taken too much damage. Mages usually recovered from being drained by demons much better than other people, she said. Perhaps that was how Tasha had found the strength to escape from Sanctuary all that time ago.

Worst of all were the memories: of the little child killed by Smazor, of Karac lying in agony on that altar, of the pain and death among the slaves, and of Darmen Stalker with his insane confidence and his smug cruelty and the feeling of his body against my skin.

I could only be thankful that I had not known who I was during most of that experience. I would always remember these things. And I would remember the lightening of my heart when I had heard Bedazzer's voice. An evil friend— but somehow I was not as afraid of him as I had once been. I knew now that it was not my longing for him that kept him coming back to me, and it gave me a feeling of freedom. Life is too difficult to feel guilt over being saved twice by a demon.

Still, I was glad to have Shad there to act as a confessor and comforter.

It was he who healed me the most. He brought me hot baths, rubbed warm oil into my aches, and held me when bad dreams woke me at night. His cheerful, easygoing ways were the best medicine of all.

After three days I was able to walk rather than hobble, and it was then that Symon called a meeting of the Klementari remaining at Sanctuary.

He told us that a substantial portion of the Ducal army was now camped outside Beenac. The Duke of Gallia and Lady Julia were negotiating over the basis of their future relationship and the throne of Moria. It looked likely that the Duke would prevail in these negotiations. Though Lady Julia was popular and well-supplied with conventional troops, most of her mages had returned to the Ducal army. Her only magical troops were the few surviving phalanxes of the Patriarch's army.

"It is now time for us to decide if we will interfere in the affairs of the Morians," Symon told the clan leaders, "and if so, what form that interference will take."

Three days later, after a long hard ride over the Great Waste, over a thousand of us—Klementari mages, Shad, Tomas, Lucien, and myself—took flight as ravens and like a great black thundercloud crossed the Red Mountains to Beenac. We carried the Holy Regalia with us, though I am still not sure how the Klementari managed that.

This was the first time Klementari magic had actually been used on me and I was delighted by its lightness. Somehow I felt more like a raven and less like a mage in the shape of a raven. I enjoyed the flying, the wind passing over my wings. Along the way I found myself looking at Shad the raven to see if he too was enjoying his flight. It is difficult to read the faces of ravens, but I am certain he was. I couldn't actually recognize anyone in raven form except, strangely enough, Symon. "Stay behind me," he had said before we changed shape, "and follow my lead."

As we circled like a great black cloud around the central tower of the Beenac fortress, I could feel the mages in the Duke's army below scanning us, but the tentative probes of magic seemed to pass by us without touching. The flock began to separate into great banks of birds dropping away with masterly precision. I kept behind Symon, who, surrounded by a pack of ravens, swooped down beside the main tower, wheeled, banked, and suddenly dove right at the main windows.

Magic began to tingle all around me and suddenly *smash!* the window before us shattered and we were streaming through it. We were changing, changing, falling, the air full of glass and feathers and magic, defensive spells up, falling, bones and muscles straining into new shapes.

Smack! I landed in my own human body on my own two feet on the marble floor of Hierarch Jarraz's audience chamber.

The room was full of people. There were solders from the Patriarchal army, soldiers from the Ducal army, and soldiers from the South. There were aristocrats, both Gallian and Morian. In the center of the chamber several important people were seated along a long table covered with parchments. There was the Patriarch, a priest in the robes of a Hierarch, Lords Sercel and Rouget, Ren Daniel and, at either end of the table, the Duke of Gallia and Lady Julia Madraga. Lady Julia was the only one who had not risen from her seat at our glass-shattering entrance. She looked quite calm, as if she was expecting the whole thing. Perhaps she was the stuff of rulers, for I knew perfectly well she had not known we were coming.

Symon stepped forward, coolly flicking a little shattered glass from his black cloak. He bowed and said, "The Klementari have regained Ernundra and now we have come to witness the election of the new ruler of Moria. And we have brought the Elector of Magery with us."

I stepped forward, and as I did so someone put the holy iron crown of Moria in my hands.

"She cannot stand as Elector," shouted the Duke. "She stands accused as a necromancer."

I had been expecting this objection and, I have to admit, I had been rehearsing my reply.

"If it is necromancy to slay the demonmaster, cast down his Sanctuary, and destroy the demon Fire Angels which have been plaguing this land while you have sat by and done nothing, than I am pleased to be called a necromancer," I cried.

I must say I was gratified by the result. Although the Duke did not dissolve in a puff of frustrated smoke as I had pictured, the effect on the rest of the audience was most satisfactory. There were smiles and cheers all around.

"Quick. Name your candidate," muttered Shad in my ear, nudging me forward.

I gripped the iron crown firmly in my hand, walked up to the table, and said in a voice I hoped was not too tentative, "As Elector of Magery and bearer of the Holy Regalia, I name Lady Julia Madraga as my candidate for the throne of Moria."

The Patriarch turned and poked the Hierarch in the shoulder. After a moment of whispering the Hierarch stood and said loudly, "And I, Hierarch Bessez, Elector of the Church, also name Lady Julia Madraga as my chosen candidate."

"I, Lord Alceste Rouget, Elector of the North, also name Lady Julia Madraga as ruler of Moria," shouted Lord Rouget. "That is three Electors, My Lord Duke. I believe we have the majority."

"This a farce," shouted the Duke. "This election is unconstitutional. It is held under duress, under the threat of violence from these 'people.' "

He waved a disgusted hand at the group of Klementari. "I charge you gentlemen to help me eject them from the chamber so that we can have a fair and honest election."

He drew his sword and suddenly swords were being drawn all over the chamber. Shad was at my side with his sword drawn, and Tomas too. Lord Lucien and Lord Sandor, father and son, faced each other across the table with drawn swords.

So this is it, I thought, there is going to be civil war after all. Panic filled me and yet, in that moment, there came to me words I had once heard spoken in a dark cave in the forest outside Annac.

"No!" I shouted. "Shall brother fight brother now that the Electors have chosen? You are all Morians."

There was a moment of silence—a moment of gut-wrenching panic-stricken silence as fate decided which way to jump.

Then suddenly Lord Sercel said, "I will not kill my own son for a foreign ruler. She speaks the truth. The Electors have chosen. I see no duress. The election is constitutional."

And he threw down his sword. All over the room there came the clatter of swords hitting marble as the civil war ended before it had begun. A lump came to my throat when I heard it.

It was one of the best moments of my life.

✦ Epilogue ✦

Ernundra

Though the earth was the color of ash, at least the area around Sanctuary had been green, even if it was only with boneseed. Here in Ernundra only a few scraggly brown bushes grew in the grey soil.

The Klementari were hard at work, turning the earth, spreading seeds, and covering the ground with a mulch of leaves that they had brought all two days' journey from the Red Mountains in baskets on their backs. Alongside them labored those of the Burning Light who had survived Sanctuary. There were several hundred of them, for Stalker had been stockpiling fodder—probably against the time when he would have to escape a vengeful White College. The Klementari had cared for the surviving prisoners and as a result, though most ordinary Morians had decided to return to Moria, many of the Burning Light worshippers had decided to stay and help rebuild Ernundra. Despite the terrible experiences the Burning Light had undergone at the hands of Darmen Stalker, they were people who tended toward the spiritual life. In the years to come many of them would adopt the Klementari religion, and many others would settle in the renewed Waste Land near them, to become their loyal neighbors. Ironic, considering that they would once have burned the Klementari at the stake.

"I hear you are Lady of Ruinac now," said Causa.

"Yes," I said. "Lady Julia named me so at her coronation. Tomas arranged it. He arranged for the rest of our family to be awarded extensive lands too. Lady Julia has waived the rule against mages owning land, at least for our generation."

"Tomas even organized lands for me," grinned Shad. "I was amazed at his generosity."

"Humph!" I said. "He just didn't want his sister mated to someone who wasn't a lord."

"A lord. That's a pretty fine thing for a woodcutter's son, or would be if I was lord of more than wasteland. Where are the folk I can order hither and thither in a lordly manner? That is what I want to know."

Causa smiled and said, "It was a wise choice. You know our ways of caring for the land, Shad Forest."

"It will be a long task, but definitely one worth giving a lifetime to," said Shad.

"Aye," I said. "The land around Ruinac is already well on the way to recovery, what with the boneseed and all the dead who are buried there. I am pulling apart the great cathedral to make sure nothing ill continues there. Though I wonder. . . . So much death and pain. Will anything good ever come from such a place?"

"The land takes death and makes life from it," said Causa. "That is one of its powers. I am going to have a child," she said suddenly.

Even Shad looked a little surprised.

"An autumn baby?" he said politely.

She laughed.

"How diplomatic you are, Shad Forest. Dion is more honest. Look how she stares. I have borne children before and I am not yet fifty. And pregnant women are a great source of life force. The child in my womb will nourish Ernundra as Ernundra nourishes it. Come, I shall show you something." She moved away down the hill.

"Most of our women have conceived children," she said as we followed behind her. "That is how you feed a land, by living on it and caring for it, loving it, by bearing children to cherish it when you are gone."

"Is that why everybody is carrying those little bags of earth round on their backs?" asked Shad.

"Yes. In that bag is a little piece of Ernundra. We carry it with us always to remind us that we are part of it and hope that it may be nourished and awakened by our life force. We shall never let ourselves be separated from it again. Look at that hill over there. Beg has discovered remains of one of the old Spirit Chambers there."

"That's wonderful," said Shad. "Do you have any hope of reawakening the Istari?"

He had fallen behind. I turned and saw that he had taken off the kerchief he had round his neck and was filling it full of earth, letting it trickle slowly through his fingers. Sometimes I forgot he was a Klementari. I wondered if I should do the same, but I just could not bring myself to believe in the idea.

I saw Causa smiling at me as if she read my thoughts. I wondered who the father of her child was.

"Where is Symon?" I asked her.

"Symon is still in the Red Mountains undergoing his cleansing. He must do so before he lives in Ernundra so that he will not taint it with warlike thoughts. The Raven's cleansing is longer than that of the others. His mind has been dedicated to the planning of violence, and that is a hard thing to cast off."

It was times like these that I remembered just how alien the Klementari were. I would have thought the person responsible for the Homecoming would have been the most rewarded among them. Instead he seemed the most punished. Still, Symon had obviously accepted that it must be so.

"Do you think you are finished with your need for a Raven?" said Shad with a frown on his face.

"Oh, I think so. We cannot expect Symon to continue to

hold himself apart from us. That would be a death of the spirit. Why do you ask?''

"Lady Julia is to marry the Duke of Gallia. He has no love for you. And if the balance of power should change between them and he becomes ruler . . .''

"He will not," said Causa, with all the serenity of one who has already see the future, "and if he does, well, it is much quicker for a person to become one of violence than it is to become one of peace.''

I could not help sharing Shad's unease about Lady Julia's marriage. A wise political decision, but the Duke was a very cunning man and liked power. I was also certain he *had* made a pact with Darmen Stalker. By rights he should have been cast from his throne for such an act, but that is not the way politics works.

Lady Julia was at least as cunning as he, however, and would likely hold her own. Still, I did not feel comfortable in any place where he was. I could not forget how he and his mages had betrayed me, and I would not return willingly to Gallia again.

At least Lady Julia would not have to worry about Blanche Shomnee. Lady Blanche had entered the nunnery at Quainard. I, for one, was going to visit that nunnery regularly to make sure she was not indulging her dangerous taste for necromancy. I found myself surprisingly sympathetic to Lady Blanche, however. I could understand the temptations of necromancy. I had felt them myself. I had seen them in Dally.

Oh, Dally. Why had we not read the signs earlier? The secretiveness, the sudden knowledge of magic. It must have been she who had put the mirror in my room that terrible morning at Silva's house when I had seen Bedazzer leering at me. How easy it is to be wise in hindsight. Was she alive? I hoped she was all right. I hoped she wasn't being led into anything irreversible, soul-destroying, unforgivable. . . .

But how could she resist it? She had no one to warn or guide her. Whatever his other failings, Michael of Moria had been there to warn me against the consequences of demon contact, and there had been others like Kitten Avignon who had shown me better ways of overcoming loneliness. If Dally had survived, she was alone.

"Look," said Causa.

Down below us a little spring bubbled out of a hollow. The water running from it had carved a deep gully in the ashy soil. All along the stream were lush green plants, some in flower. There were even saplings.

"This is the spring your mother made when she dug up the regalia," said Causa. "She brought life to this place. I think it is significant that she already carried you in her womb when she did so."

I leaned forward to look at the place where the spring bubbled out of the earth, wondering if there were still any marks left by her fingers in the mud, but of course there was nothing. I knelt and let the water run over my hand and took a drink of it. It tasted more delicious that I would have thought possible in this place of ash and dirt. I thought of my mother lying here asleep twenty-two years ago. There had been a time not so long ago when I had avoided thinking about her, but now it gave me a slightly melancholy pleasure to do so. I realized that somewhere in the long, hard time since I had left Cardun I had come to believe that she had cared for me. It was a blessing—a secret source of happiness and faith.

AVON EOS PRESENTS
MASTERS OF FANTASY AND ADVENTURE

CHANGER
by Jane Lindskold   78849-7/$5.99 US/$7.99 CAN

BETRAYALS: BOOK FOUR OF THE BLENDING
by Sharon Green   78810-1/$6.50 US/$8.50 CAN

SHARDS OF A BROKEN CROWN:
VOLUME IV OF THE Serpentwar Saga
by Raymond E. Feist   78983-3/$6.99 US/$8.99 CAN

WARSTALKER'S TRACK
by Tom Deitz   78650-8/$6.50 US/$8.50 CAN

FIRE ANGELS
by Jane Routely   79427-6/$6.99 US/$8.99 CAN

THE WODAN'S CHILDREN TRILOGY

A retelling of the Siefried legend
with all the romance, magic, and myth richly
detailed and skillfully unveiled

By DIANA L. PAXSON

THE LORD OF THE HORSES
76528-4/$5.99 US/$7.99 Can

DRAGONS OF THE RHINE
76527-6/$5.99 US/$7.99 Can

THE WOLF AND THE RAVEN
76526-8/$5.99 US/$7.99 Can
